MAYA BANKS

"If you haven't read this series yet, you totally should."—Jaci Burton, *New York Times* bestselling author

DARKEST BEFORE DAWN

A KGI NOVEL

BERKLEY

$7.99 U.S.
$10.49 CAN

ISBN 978-0-425-27699-0

DARKEST
BEFORE DAWN

MAYA BANKS

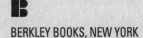

BERKLEY BOOKS, NEW YORK

BERKLEY

An imprint of Penguin Random House LLC
375 Hudson Street, New York, New York 10014

DARKEST BEFORE DAWN

A Berkley Book / published by arrangement with the author

ISBN: 978-0-425-27699-0

PUBLISHING HISTORY
Berkley mass-market edition / November 2015

PRINTED IN THE UNITED STATES OF AMERICA

10 9 8 7 6 5 4 3

Cover art by Craig White.
Cover design by Rita Frangie.
Interior text design by Laura K. Corless.

Penguin
Random
House

CHAPTER 1

HONOR Cambridge applied one of the colorful Band-Aids with yellow smiley faces over the tiny prick that had been made on the arm of the four-year-old boy and offered him a reassuring smile. In flawless Arabic, she told him how brave he'd been not to show fear or distress in front of his mother and upset her further.

He gave her a toothy grin that already showed signs of male arrogance even at such a young age, as if to tell her of *course* he'd been brave.

Though Honor held no medical degree, her training was advanced and she'd learned a lot through trial by fire. Technically her job was as a relief worker, offering aid in its many forms to the poor and oppressed in the small villages caught between warring factions and the never-ending struggle for supremacy.

Her family supported her absolutely, but she also knew they questioned her burning need to devote her life to the service of others. They were proud of her, but they also wished she had chosen other, *safer* places to offer help. Not the war-torn Middle East when the threat wasn't just from other nations but *within* their country as well from groups, divided by religious, political and cultural differences and unable to tolerate the differences of others. They all wanted to force others to bend to their way of life, and the lengths they went to impose their beliefs on those who didn't share the same ideology still managed to appall and bewilder Honor despite the fact that she should be hardened by now. Nothing should shock her. And yet . . . Every day she managed to be surprised, because there was always more. When she thought she'd seen it all, something always managed to catch her off guard.

But to become jaded and cynical was the kiss of death. The day she could no longer feel compassion for the innocent and the oppressed and anger at the senseless violence and despair that was so pervasive in the region she served was the day she needed to find a staid, mindless nine-to-five job, have a safe life where the most dangerous thing she encountered was rush-hour traffic.

Honor put her hand on the boy's arm to direct him to his waiting mother, who was already holding the large care package filled with things most people took for granted but were precious commodities in villages where running water was a luxury.

The entire building suddenly shook and the floor buckled beneath Honor's feet as though an earthquake were occurring.

No one screamed. But looks of terror, all too common on the faces of people who'd become dear to Honor, were shared by everyone. Eerie silence ensued, and then . . .

The world exploded around them, a terrible storm, a whirling vortex of heat, fire and the acrid smell of explosives.

And blood.

Death had a smell all of its own. And Honor had seen more blood and death, had smelled it, had witnessed the horrible sight of the very essence of life slowly seep from a once-vibrant human being. An innocent child. A mother seeking only to protect her young. A father slaughtered in front of his entire family.

Chaos reigned as people ran, no clear direction in mind, and yet Honor viewed the goings-on calmly, as if she were apart from her body and viewing dispassionately the attack on the relief center. One of her coworkers—her friend—

screamed at her to take cover and then went utterly still, death in her eyes as blood bloomed over her chest. She sagged like a puppet, her expression not one of pain but of great sorrow. And regret.

Tears burned the corners of Honor's eyes as she finally forced herself into motion. There were children to shield. Women to save. The vicious extremist cell would not take them all. It was an oath, a litany that repeated over and over in her mind as she shoved children and mothers alike out of the rear exit and into the desert heat.

One of the women grasped Honor's hand when Honor turned to go back in and pleaded with her in Arabic to come with them. To run. To save herself. The extremists would have no mercy. Especially for Westerners.

Honor gently extricated her hand from the woman's desperate hold. "May Allah be with you," she whispered, praying in her heart that God, any God, *every* God, would stop the hate and bloodshed. The senseless killing of the good and innocent.

Then she turned and ran back into the building, or what was left of it. Dimly she registered that the lightweight but cool western flip-flops she usually wore had somehow fallen off her feet in the chaos surrounding her, but the last thing on her mind was protecting her feet when her life was at stake.

She searched frantically for her fellow relief workers. The two doctors who worked tirelessly day and night, sometimes going many nights without sleep because the need for medical aid was so great. The nurses who did the work that many physicians in the United States did and with far less advanced technology or diagnostic tools.

Everywhere she turned, all she saw was blood, rivers of blood. And death. The stench made her stomach revolt and she clamped a hand over her mouth to prevent herself from being violently ill and to silence the scream that welled from the very depths of her soul.

There was no solace to be found anywhere she looked, but she could at least be grateful that she didn't see the bodies of many children, or their mothers. Most had fled, well trained and accustomed to such attacks. Honor's comrades, her friends, the people who had the same calling as she, hadn't fared as well.

The very earth exploded beneath her. Around her. Stone and debris pelted her, battering her in an endless wave of pain and terror. She took a single step, wincing when something sharp cut into her tender foot. And then the already sagging roof collapsed, sending her sprawling painfully across the ravaged floor. Debris rained down on her. No, that was the ceiling caving in on her, pinning her beneath rock, rubble, a shattered beam. The cloud of dust and smoke was so thick she couldn't suck air into her tortured lungs.

She wasn't sure if it was the thickness of the smoke and decimated plaster that made it impossible for her to breathe or if it was the mountain of rubble she was buried under, pressing mercilessly down on her until she was sure every bone in her body would be crushed, unable to withstand the unbearable strain.

Pain was present. It was there. She knew it. But it was distant. As if it were trying to penetrate the thickest fog surrounding her. Numbness crawled insidiously over and through her body, and she wasn't sure if it was a blessing to be unable to feel what had to be excruciating pain or if this was the curse of death.

Her death.

Her eyelids fluttered sluggishly as she struggled to remain conscious, too afraid that if she gave in to the encroaching darkness, death would win the ultimate battle.

She wasn't a stranger to death. She saw it on a daily basis. Nor was she in denial of the enormous risk she took by working in a country not only at constant war with neighboring countries, all with different agendas, beliefs and differing levels of fanaticism, but also divided within their own borders, each region determined to overtake the entire country and force their will on those with opposing viewpoints.

And then there were those who *needed* no reason to murder, terrorize and victimize their fellow countrymen. Those were the worst of all. Unpredictable. They reeked of fanaticism, and their only agenda was to strike fear in the hearts of all who crossed them. They wanted glory. They wanted to be feared by their enemy and revered by other factions too afraid to engage them in battle.

They wanted the world to know of them. Who they were. They wanted people to whisper their name as if afraid of conjuring them by speaking of the monsters too loudly. They'd fast learned that the quickest way to elevate their status, gain worldwide media attention and be able to recruit the elite, the best of the best, ones not only unafraid to give their lives for their "cause" but who embraced the glory of being a martyr was to target Westerners. Americans in particular.

The U.S. media gave the glory seekers precisely what they craved. Around-the-clock coverage every time they launched another attack. And with that attention came ambition for more. They'd grown bolder, rapidly expanding their network, their power giving pause to the very nations that would ordinarily condone such hatred of the West.

Such power made leaders of oil-rich countries nervous. So much so that an unprecedented summit had been called, bringing together sworn enemies to discuss the ever-growing problem of a fanatical group with power, wealth, military might and unprecedented numbers joining with each passing day.

Men and women from all corners of the earth. What could possibly inspire such hatred? Such a thirst for pain, violence, hurt and suffering?

Honor shuddered as the numb shell surrounding her showed signs of fragmenting, and for a moment pain assaulted her, taking her breath. Black crept into her vision, the light growing dimmer and dimmer. Tears burned like acid, but she refused to give in to them. She was alive. At least for now. None of the other relief workers had been as fortunate.

The building looked as though a meteor had hurtled through the earth's atmosphere and decimated the entire area. Half of the roof had collapsed, and judging by the creaking and groaning that echoed with the faintest whisper of wind, the rest wasn't far behind.

She'd never get out. And for that matter, perhaps her fellow relief workers *had* received mercy from a higher being. A quick death was surely better than what awaited any survivors discovered by the bloodthirsty savages who'd wrought such devastation.

Why had she been left to suffer? Why was she without mercy and grace? What sin had she committed to survive only to be condemned to hell, a fate worse than death? A cold chill dug deep into her battered body and clung tenaciously to her bones, her blood. She was freezing from the deepest recesses of her soul when around her the world was on fire, the flames of hell greedily consuming its victims.

"Get a grip, Honor," she muttered, her words slurring, evidence that she was in shock.

Here she was whining because she was alive. She'd survived the impossible and worse, her coworkers hadn't and she'd dared to *envy* them? She'd been spared when no one else had. It had to mean something. Her life had purpose. There was still much for her to do. God wasn't finished with her yet, and here she lay amid the rubble of destruction acting the ungrateful child for having lived. Never had she felt so ashamed. What would her family think? They certainly wouldn't be upset that she was still alive. Her death would cause them endless pain. She was the baby. The youngest of six siblings and she was dearly loved by all. They might not like that she put herself at such risk, but they understood her calling and supported her. They were proud of her. If for no one else, she would survive for them.

The sound of raised voices, barked orders and debris being shoved aside froze Honor where she lay trapped. Panic welled, her heart accelerating wildly. Her breaths, already ragged and painful, grew even more so. She closed her eyes and willed herself not to make a sound.

The soldiers were picking through the ruins looking specifically for the Westerners—the people who ran the relief center and offered aid to refugees. Their triumph over the success of their attack sickened Honor. There were gleeful shouts as one after another, a worker was found dead. Tears tightened her throat when it was suggested that the bodies be dragged from the clinic and lined up so photos could be taken and shown to the world, a warning to others that their presence was offensive.

Oh God, what would happen when they found her? They were systematic in their search, almost as if they knew who the relief workers were and how many there were. If they were happy over so many dead, how much more excited would they be to have a live hostage? Someone to make an example of.

The building creaked and groaned, the remaining walls protesting the weakness of the structure. More debris rained down, pelting the entire area. Honor barely managed to hold in a sound of pain when something hit the objects covering her, causing them to crush her even more.

The invaders were suddenly cautious and wary, their talk going to whether it was safe to continue their systematic body count. When one suggested they get out immediately—before what remained of the shell of the building fell down around their ears—an argument broke out, the voices loud and harsh and entirely too close for Honor's comfort.

They were near her and drawing closer all the time. She could all but hear their breaths, feel the urgent exhalation over her neck even though she knew that wasn't possible. But she felt hunted. Just as prey surely must feel when a predator was closing in for the kill.

She closed her eyes and prayed to live when just moments earlier she'd lamented the fact that she *hadn't* died. A fervent prayer became a litany in her mind not only to live, but to survive. To escape, unscathed, the terrible fate she'd endure were she discovered by the soldiers who thought nothing of raping, torturing and killing women. Or children, for that matter.

A shudder quaked through her body before she could call it back, and then she held her breath, hoping she hadn't betrayed herself. She forced calm she didn't feel to settle over her body, blocking out the pain and gut-wrenching fear. Never had she been more terrified than she was at this moment. No amount of preparing, no number of close calls with militants bent on destruction could possibly have given her a glimpse into the reality she'd spent too many months to count mentally bracing herself for.

In her heart she'd felt it inevitable that she would face

ultimate fear, pain, but she'd never truly allowed herself to think she could be killed doing what she felt was her calling in life. Her parents had tried to convince her. They'd pleaded with her in the beginning, even going so far as to say they didn't want to lose their "baby."

Her four older brothers and older sister had all gathered to attempt to persuade her not to go, pulling out the big guns, telling her they wanted her to be a part of her nieces' and nephews' lives. Her sister had tearfully held Honor's hand tightly in hers and chokingly said she wanted her sister to be at her wedding, at her side, even though her sister had no plans to marry anytime soon.

She'd almost given in to their emotional blackmail. Inwardly she winced. *Blackmail* was too harsh a word. All they'd done and said had been out of love. It had been her mother in the end, sensing Honor's battle between wanting to please her family, wanting their happiness, and answering her need to serve others in embattled, terrorized nations, who had gathered the family together and quietly but firmly told them to stand down.

There had been so much love and understanding—and pride—in her gaze as she'd looked at Honor, tears glittering brightly in her eyes. Honor had felt it like a tidal wave, consuming her. Love, her mother's love squeezed her insides and warmed her heart as nothing else ever had.

No, her mother hadn't wanted Honor to go, but she understood. And she had told her husband and her other children that it was time to let go and allow Honor to fly. To be whom she was meant to be. It was her time to shine, when throughout her young life she'd been the quiet one, reveling in the accomplishments and happiness of her siblings as each followed their chosen paths.

Her mother's speech had shamed her siblings and her father, though that was never what Honor wanted. Each had offered their unconditional support and her father had hugged her tightly, gruffly telling her that she would always be his baby and to promise him she would make it back home.

Her chest swelled and ached, tears burning her eyelids

once more as she considered the possibility that she would break her promise to her father.

Another rumble rolled through the battered building, and more debris and parts of the ceiling still intact came tumbling down on and around Honor. She heard coughing and muttered curses and then hope sprang to life when she'd thought she had none.

The militants came to the agreement—the conclusion— that they needed to evacuate the crumbling shell before they got trapped. Or killed.

The talk became lighter, relief seeping into some of the voices that had argued for their departure. They pointed out that dead bodies went nowhere and no one could have possibly have survived the explosions and deadly snipers who'd picked victims off as they attempted to flee.

Honor stifled a sob of grief. So many senseless deaths and for what? Because they were rendering aid to people desperately in need?

The next words she heard, growing fainter as the men began their retreat, froze Honor to the bone.

They would return once it was safe and locate each victim, ensuring that none of the aid workers had eluded death. God. They knew each worker. Had studied their targets. And provided Honor could even free herself before they returned to do their macabre accounting, they would know she hadn't died.

Which meant that they'd ruthlessly hunt her because above all else, this group was intolerant of failure. And if even one—Honor—escaped with her life, then their objective had not been achieved.

CHAPTER 2

HONOR came awake with dim awareness, her mind fogged. Disorientation had her in its firm grip and she struggled to make sense of her current situation. At once, pain slammed into her, as though it had simply been waiting for her awareness, annoyed that she'd slipped into unconsciousness and evaded its harsh, punishing pull.

She panted softly and peered through the piles of debris atop her and experimentally tried to wiggle her body, testing not only for more severe pain that would signal serious injury but also to see if she had any chance at getting herself out of the rubble pinning her to the floor.

It was pitch-black, signaling that night had fallen. She breathed a sigh of relief before quickly realizing that she wasn't out of the woods by a long shot. The night only helped her if she could somehow extricate herself from her prison and be mobile enough to flee into the protection of the dark.

Before despair could completely envelop her, she firmly pushed the negative emotion away. She was in enough danger without her convincing herself she had no chance. At this point, hope was all she had. And a very strong will to survive. To not be defeated by men who thrived on pain, fear and complete subjugation of everyone who didn't hold to their ideology.

She would get home. She would find a way. And by God,

when she did, she'd send the biggest "fuck you" to the terrorist cell that had murdered her coworkers—her friends—and let them know that a simple American woman took their best shot and survived it.

Imbued by a new sense of purpose and determination, she set her mind to figuring out what she could move and what the best course of action was to pull herself from the carnage under which she found herself imprisoned.

The minutes ticked by with agonizing slowness. Pain was her constant companion. Sweat bathed her body, but she was too damp for only sweat. She knew she was bleeding. Not horribly so and not fast or she wouldn't be conscious. But sticky warmth clung to her skin and she could smell it now that the acrid smell of mold, plaster, destroyed stone and wood and the chemical smell of explosives had diminished, carried away by the night wind.

She took her time, testing each part of her body, starting with her feet. She wiggled her toes and then flexed her feet and then rotated her legs as best she was able, wincing when her knee bumped into a jagged piece of stone. The walls of the clinic were completely stone, the ceiling made of wood with heavy beams supporting the structure. The floor was concrete and no amount of sweeping or cleaning prevented the sand from blowing in and accumulating on every surface. It made trying to keep a sterile environment one bitch of a job, and infection was always a worry among the doctors and nurses.

Her knee felt tight. Swollen. And very sore. She bent it slowly in small increments, not wanting to do further damage if it was badly injured, but she desperately needed to have the use of her legs. Her arms weren't as important. But she needed her legs and feet to get her the hell away from this place. As quickly as humanly possible.

She couldn't count on help coming in. No rescue. The State Department had issued a decree ordering all U.S. citizens from the region, and there would be no aid for those who ignored the warning. There were no U.S. troops in the area. No embassy. No American presence here at all.

And no other group or country's military dared to oppose the militant savages for fear of reprisal. They were too busy holding a summit where everyone talked the issue to death instead of taking action, a fact that infuriated Honor.

How could any government turn away from the pain and suffering of countless men, women and children in such a widespread area? Why wasn't there more public outrage? God only knew it was reported in the media around the clock. Was everyone so fatigued by the constant coverage that it had become tedious and they'd distanced themselves? Or were they just so smug and comfortable in their safe environment that they had no care for the plight of others?

She harnessed the helpless rage that clawed at her, and she held it to her. It served to heighten her determination and strength to free herself.

After her careful examination of her limbs and the areas of her body that protected her most vital organs, she was satisfied—or perhaps merely hopeful—that she could do this.

She started with her hands, scratching and shoving away all manner of clutter, swearing when her fingers caught on sharper objects, slicing the skin and causing her to bleed. Her fingernails tore raggedly, ripping into the quick, but it was minor compared to the pulsing pain in the rest of her body and only sharpened her drive. The more setbacks she incurred, the angrier she grew, and adrenaline took the place of pain and the self-defeating thought process her mind seemed to be caught up in.

It was hard to work, positioned as she was—on her stomach or rather awkwardly angled slightly to her side. It forced her to work mostly with one hand, the one not bent under her body and useless except to clear what it could reach.

She had no concept of the passing of time, only the urgency that she escape before dawn, when the killers would no doubt return to resume their body count. She bit into her lip to hold back her tears of grief, determined that they wouldn't beat her. Only she could tell the stories of the now-dead heroes and heroines who'd devoted their lives to helping others. Only she could bear witness to the atrocity committed here, and their bravery and selflessness would not go unheralded. Not if she had anything to say about it.

After what seemed to be hours, she had uncovered the

entire upper half of her body and for a moment she sank down, resting her cheek against the floor as she prepared for the next step. Somehow she had to turn over and sit as upright as possible so she could work on freeing the lower half of her body. Her legs. Her only hope for getting away from this place.

Gathering her strength—and courage—she began twisting her body, wincing as every muscle protested the awkward movement. She felt weak as a kitten. Sweat now soaked her tattered clothing. Between it and the blood coating portions of her body, her pants and shirt stuck to her like they'd been glued on.

Her injured knee would give her the greatest problem. She had to rotate her entire bottom half, regardless of the weight pressing down on it.

Gritting her teeth, she planted one palm down on the floor and twisted her upper body so that her other hand hovered inches above the floor on her other side. She pushed upward, straining, twisting and then gasping as pain splintered through her legs. Both of them.

God, would she be unable to walk after all? Had she broken them both, and was she in too much shock to feel the breaks? The only pain she could identify was in her knee.

Again, she wiggled her toes and feet, seeking reassurance that she hadn't imagined being able to do so moments earlier. She paid closer attention this time, leaning in an uncomfortable, awkward pose as she concentrated fiercely on whether she felt pain or weakness.

Then the thought occurred to her that the reason she wasn't feeling pain or weakness could be that she couldn't feel her legs at all. As soon as the panicked thought blazed through her mind, she shoved it impatiently aside. Irrational, hysterical thoughts had no place here. If she'd been paralyzed she wouldn't be able to move her feet or know that she was capable of moving them, and she wouldn't feel the throbbing pain in her knee.

Her fears at a more manageable level, Honor braced herself and stared determinedly at the mound covering her lower half. She was absurdly pleased, and excitement coursed through her veins when she felt the soft whisper of night air

over the toes of her left foot. She wiggled again, paying more
attention, realizing that they were poking out of the rubble.

A shudder overtook her. Thank God the militants hadn't
gotten close enough to her to see the end of her foot protrud-
ing. They would have uncovered her to see if she was dead
like the others. Upon finding her alive? She slammed her
mind shut, refusing to continue down that thought path.
They hadn't found her. They wouldn't find her. So there was
no need to torment herself with what could have been. She
was more focused on what would never be.

Her lips thinning, pressing together in a vow not to allow
a single sound past them, she turned her body with more
resolve this time instead of the experimental twisting she'd
done at first. A grimace shook the line of her lips and she
ground her teeth together, her jaw aching from the pressure.

Determination was alive inside her. It took over. Became
her. In that moment, failure to make her escape wasn't even
a remote possibility. A pained hiss exploded from her open
mouth, her breaths hard as she exerted more pressure, straining rigidly to rotate her hips and legs.

Fire blew down the back side of her legs as they scraped
at the jagged edges of rock, metal, wood and glass. Her
stomach jolted and squeezed inwardly as if seeking to rid
itself of any content when her injured knee banged into an
immovable object. She saw stars, and tears burned the edges
of her eyelids. It only made her angrier. Her fury grew until
she shook with it.

"Why won't you help me?" she raged, her gaze casting
upward before shame fell over her much as the building had.
"Sorry," she muttered, closing her eyes. "But I could really
use your help right now. An angel would be nice if you're
too busy to see to it personally."

She huffed in another breath, found the center of calm
that was nestled in the rage boiling through her veins. Yelling
at God wasn't going to get her anywhere. And as the old
saying went, God helped those who helped themselves, and
right now she wasn't doing anything remotely helpful. Whining, wishing she'd died and constantly battling tears weren't
the hallmark of someone worthy of the gift of life. And yet,

here she lay. So close to freedom while the others also lay close by, their souls already gone from this world.

She had a purpose. She thought it again. It bolstered her spirits and eased some of the fear eating away at her insides. Maybe everything up to now had merely been preparation for her true purpose instead of her having already found her purpose and serving it. She wasn't going to find out if she didn't get her ass out of here before the sun rose.

Turning off all the raging emotion building like a volcano about to erupt and refusing to acknowledge pain or the current limitations on her body, Honor attempted to turn again. This time she didn't stop when the hideous scrape seared her legs or when her knee, so tender and swollen, screamed its protest of her movements. She refused to stop until finally both heels were planted on the floor, her feet and toes directed upward.

Her knee throbbed angrily, stretched by the new position and her leg lying flat and unbent. Hastily, she pushed herself upward until she leaned forward, palms planted amid the debris surrounding her.

Though her eyes had grown accustomed to having no light, it was impossible to see anything with detail with the entire area blanketed in suffocating darkness. Tentatively she reached down, feeling her way along her legs, her fingers lightly brushing over the obstacles that lay between her and freedom.

She swore when she encountered the heavy beam that she now remembered falling on her in the explosion. It had been what banged her knee up before she'd wound up face-down on the floor, the weight of half the building bearing down on her back. When the world had come crashing down on her, she'd fallen to her back but had instinctively rolled over, trying to protect herself in any way she could.

For a moment, she paused and dug her fingers sharply into her temples, pressing and rubbing in tight circles, digging in and applying firm pressure in hopes that she could make at least the dull drum in her head go away and clear the residue of murky fog that had stubbornly clung to her ever since she'd regained consciousness.

It was sheer will that had kept her from simply acquiescing and fading and giving in to the threat of darkness in her mind, the thought that if she just let go, then the pain and fear, *everything* would simply go . . . away. But the reminder that when or even if she awakened, she would face a nightmare worse than death, that she would be thrust into the very bowels of hell and once again lament the fact that she'd survived, kept her sharply focused on her task.

It was one thing for the regret over having lived to have insidiously crept through her mind in a moment where she'd opened her eyes to pain, deep sorrow and confusion and to have briefly succumbed to the shameful thought in a moment of weakness before she'd collected her wits and regained her iron resolve—something she'd always possessed—and quite another to be in a situation where she gave the cowards responsible for this massacre the satisfaction of hearing her beg for death.

That angered her as much as the senseless deaths of so many good and generous people. People who'd never hurt another living soul. Whose only purpose was the driving desire to help those in need who couldn't help themselves.

The hell she'd ever show fear or be so cowardly as to beg those bastards for anything. She'd denounce and spit on their "beliefs," giving them the middle finger even if it wasn't the actual gesture but pronounced in her every look, her response, even her breath. Her dying breath.

Even better to flip them the bird alive. Back home, having thwarted their plan to annihilate every last one of the relief workers. Be smugly triumphant and say with more than words, *You didn't beat me. You couldn't beat me.*

It was a fantasy, a goal that kept her clawing at the remainder of her bonds. She worked with renewed energy. Faster. Angrier. Flinging rock, chunks of plaster, decimated pieces of chairs and exam tables. Everything but the beam that lay across her legs.

She felt around, noting that she'd cleared everything from atop the beam. Then her hands dipped lower and she leaned forward as far as she was able, her breath squeezing out in tortured breaths as she strained to discover a way out from underneath the heavy piece of wood.

A thoughtful frown curved her lips downward and her forehead wrinkled. She moved her hands lower to confirm the fact that the bottoms of her legs didn't in fact lie on the floor, but rather there was a layer of rubble and debris, and her legs were trapped between that layer and the beam.

She moved her hands outward, feeling to the sides to see if the beam had any support other than her legs. Sure it was heavy, but it didn't feel like she was bearing the brunt of its entire weight. She wouldn't have been able to turn over if she were.

Sure enough, the beam lay uneven across her legs but there were mounds of debris on either side of her that the beam was propped up on. She had maybe an inch of space between her leg with the injured knee and where the beam slanted across her, but on the other side, the beam pressed against her skin, but the weight wasn't unbearable.

Excited, she began to dig at the rubble underneath her legs, leaning up and this way and that in an effort to wiggle out every single obstacle between the backs of her legs and the floor. When her bleeding fingertips brushed along the rough concrete, hope flared, bursting into an inextinguishable flame. She *was* going to get out.

After shoving the rough and jagged pieces farther away from both legs, she reached behind her, leaning back as far as she could, planting her palms on the floor for leverage. Then she began the arduous task of inching backward, praying that enough space had been created between the beam and her legs to allow her to slide free from her final barrier to freedom.

It sapped every ounce of her strength. She was inhaling and exhaling noisily, trying to drag precious oxygen into her lungs as her entire body strained to pull her legs from beneath the heavy wood.

Each inch was agony. This time she didn't curse the tears that not only threatened, but slid down her cheeks. She was too focused on her goal to care. Besides, if she managed to pull off her escape, she could consider them tears of relief.

She felt a burst of exultation when the going got easier as the thicker part of her legs pulled loose. As her legs grew smaller toward her feet, she was able to move much quicker. Finally the tops of her feet bumped into the barrier and she was forced to stop, take a short break to catch her breath and then breathe away the pain and tension.

She flexed her feet forward as far as she could flatten them. She turned them to the side, gritting her teeth at the pain the twisting motion caused her battered knee. But it worked. Her feet slid under the beam, rubbing against the coarse wood. She could feel splinters embedding themselves into the soft skin of her arches, but she was too close to victory to even pause.

She welcomed the feel of the tiny wood shards piercing the tops of her feet, because it meant she was almost there. At the end, she didn't even feel the splinters cutting into her, though she felt the warmth of blood on her skin from where the beam had abraded the tender flesh.

Her hands slipped and she nearly fell back when her feet finally escaped the barrier. She scrambled upright, because if she let herself relax even for a moment, she might never muster the will to get up, get out. Flee.

Triumph surged, hot and wild in her veins. But as she lurched to her feet—or rather attempted to do so—her triumph left her sagging like a deflated balloon. Pain lanced down her spine, all the way down to her feet and then back up again, racing toward the base of her skull, where it seemed to ricochet. For several long seconds her head drew spasmodically from the pain shooting up her neck, almost as though she were having a seizure. She breathed through the pain until at last it subsided to a manageable level and the rigidity finally left her neck so she was able to move once more.

She shook like a leaf. The effort to stand, something so easy and taken for granted before, had sapped her strength and left her huddled on the floor as limp as a dishrag.

No. Not now. Damn it. She had not spent the entire night freeing herself from the wreckage of the clinic only to lie there and await her fate at the hands of men who were so evil that she couldn't comprehend such a capacity for hatred and violence. No. They would not get their hands on her. She'd take her own life before ever allowing her fate to be decided by monsters. And she wasn't ready to die yet. She had a lot of life left to live. This was only a minor—okay, a major—bump in the road.

Everyone had them. Maybe not everyone faced gun-wielding, rocket-launcher-carrying crazed maniacs who used explosives as naturally as others breathed and whose mode of transportation was tanks, but she'd survived relatively unscathed. Physically. She'd carry the mental scars from this day for the rest of her life. She had no doubt.

This time she tested her strength very carefully, pushing herself up with her hands, bending her uninjured knee down to the floor to give her lift, but she was careful to angle her hurt knee out so that it bore no weight and didn't press into the floor. Getting up with two hands and only one leg wasn't the fastest mode of travel, but it would get the job done. She was prepared this time and not acting like a hasty fool out to get herself killed by running madly from the destroyed structure that had been home to her for the last year.

She didn't allow herself to feel sorrow as she scanned the area, putting only as much pressure on the left foot bearing her swollen knee as was necessary to limp forward and make slow progress through the devastation. She had to have the necessary tools to survive on her own. In a foreign land with no American military presence, no American embassy, no refuge or sanctuary and no way to get back home unless she could somehow get word to her family.

She couldn't look at the broken, bloodied bodies she knew were there but thankfully were hard to make out in the dark. She had to be smart, a passive observer, and look for things that would help her escape. Not just from this building and the men who'd attacked without provocation. But the entire country.

Somehow she had to find her way down the long, winding, arduous path home.

CHAPTER 3

"YOU want me and my men to do what?" Hancock asked mildly, not betraying his feeling of *What the fuck*.

Guy Hancock, or Hancock as he was generally known, although not many knew his given name, faced Russell Bristow, his incredulity over Bristow's stupidity not showing, but there nonetheless.

Hancock's identity changed with the winds, and at times it was hard for him to keep up with who he currently was. It was a tired existence, one he grew wearier of all the time. But at least he had a purpose. Or at least he had at one time. Now he wasn't as sure as he'd been earlier on. Time had robbed him of that strict code of honor until he wondered just how close to the line he was and how close he'd come to becoming the very thing he worked so tirelessly to extinguish and protect the innocent from. He knew no other life except killing. Manipulating. Mastering the masters of evil and exacting justice in his own cold, methodical way that had nothing to do with any established legal code.

He'd long ago forgone any semblance of a conscience. He had an unwavering and deeply ingrained sense of honor, but not everyone would agree that with honor came a conscience. And his personal code was just that. Personal to him. He didn't see in black and white. His world was steeped in gray. Great looming shadows that threatened to consume him. At times he felt hunted—and he was—but it was as though he knew his time was limited. The urgency of taking down his target, one he'd waited a very long time to get close to, was like a ticking time bomb. Success had eluded him, and now time had run out. Hancock would never get this close again. He knew it. His men knew it. They felt, too, that they would all likely die carrying out their mission. And yet none turned their back on their duty. They embraced death as the result of victory. Nothing more.

Russell Bristow's lips curled in distaste, anger flaring in his eyes. The stupid bastard wasn't smart enough to mask his emotions or control his temper. It would get him killed, and Hancock mentally shrugged. It would mean one less asshole in the world and one less person he had to take out himself in the end. But until his ultimate goal was achieved, he needed to keep the stupid bastard alive, though he'd love nothing more than to break his neck and rid the world of his foul presence. Bristow was a means to an end, and so Hancock had to rein in his utter distaste of the man until he served his purpose. *Then* he would die, because Hancock would never let such depravity live.

"Don't you mean *my* men?" Bristow snapped.

Hancock lifted one eyebrow and simply stared the other man down, pinning him with a gaze he knew others feared and were intimidated by, until a mottled flush worked its way up Bristow's neck and he fidgeted like a bug under a microscope. He looked away and then back but didn't meet Hancock's eyes this time. His fear was a stench in the air that offended Hancock and disgusted his men. Courage came in many forms, shapes and colors. Courage wasn't always necessary to succeed. Determination was. But fear bred stupidity. Fear caused mistakes. Fear could lead men to betray themselves, their cause and anyone impeding one's goal of others.

Bristow was loyal to none save himself, and Hancock never made the mistake of thinking otherwise or of misjudging him—or anyone else, for that matter. Bristow would sacrifice Hancock and all his men if he felt at any time his life was in danger. And it was. It was Hancock's and his men's job to ensure that Bristow felt safe and invincible. To feed his natural arrogance and desire for power. If he knew just what he was up against, he'd crawl into a deep dark hole, terrified, and Hancock's last link to his objective would be forfeit. No, he needed Bristow in all his stupidity and vainness. Maksimov knew what he was dealing with as well. A puppet. A man who thought he was in control and yet was easily controlled by others. In a game of chess, the most important match of Hancock's life, he had to make it appear that Bristow was easily manipulated by Maksimov and yet move him in such a way that it positioned Maksimov as *Hancock* wanted. So that in fact, Hancock manipulated both men without either being aware.

"As you are all on my payroll and take orders from me, that makes all of you my men," Bristow said, his voice not as commanding as it had been a moment earlier. But then he was a coward, always employing others to do his dirty work for him. If his options were to stay and fight with his men or abandon them and run, he'd run. His kind always did. It was precisely why Hancock had his own team here under the guise of having vetted and employed them for Bristow. Bristow had no knowledge of the fact that Hancock's team had worked together for years and that their loyalty to one another ran deep. That they answered to Hancock and no other. Ever.

In a world where Hancock trusted none but a precious few, his trust was given to Titan, though it was no longer Titan. It wasn't . . . anything. The very government who'd created them, faking their deaths and then raising them from the ashes like the phoenix, had given them new identities and they were to have no ties to the outside world. The mission was all that mattered. Not people. Not politics or the delicate dance of diplomacy.

The government had created . . . monsters. Killing machines without mercy or conscience, trained to carry out orders at all cost. The good of the many always outweighed the good of the few. And when Titan grew too powerful, when they began to question their orders, their objective and how it aided the greater good, when the missions seemed to grow too personal, too inconsequential for a group of Titan's training and abilities, they'd been disbanded, branded traitors, loose cannons, murderers. Even *terrorists*. They'd been labeled the very thing they hunted and it still burned a hole in Hancock's gut. After living so many years with no feelings, no emotions, turning them off at will and doing his job with cool efficiency, he learned true rage. Not since his foster mother, a woman who'd made Hancock feel that he had worth and had given him the first and only sense of *family*, had been murdered in retaliation for her husband's mission, had Hancock felt anger and overwhelming rage. That mission had been personal. The only one. Big Eddie, the man who called him son, had come to him for help. Revenge. And even if Big Eddie hadn't asked, Hancock would have hunted Caroline Sinclair's murderer.

But things had changed since then. That was years ago, when Titan operated under the authority of the U.S. government, though only a select few even knew of Titan's existence. They had much freedom then to ferret out those who were a threat to national security, to take out any threat at will. And then, their own government turned on them, thinking them expendable and easily disposed of.

Even now the hunters had become the hunted, and any number of classified military groups had orders to kill on sight. Having gained access to a shadowy CIA operative's computer files, Hancock had learned a hell of a lot about the country he'd sworn his allegiance to.

No, not everyone charged with the defense of America and its people was evil and self-serving, betraying the citizens they were sworn to protect and defend. There were men and women who tirelessly took up the charge. But any one of those would kill Hancock on sight, thinking him a traitor to the principles they followed, lived, and would die for.

Titan had refused to die. They had evolved far beyond what their trainers in the beginning had taught them. And now, they not only fought to protect even those who'd betrayed them and countless innocent American lives but they had expanded their reach into a world filled with the same good and bad reflected in the U.S. government and military.

Innocence had no boundaries. No one nationality. One wasn't good or bad simply because one was a certain nationality or held a different belief system. Innocents died every day simply because there was no one to fight for them. Not even their own governments. Titan couldn't save the entire world, but they saved pieces of it. One piece at a time.

Taking out Maksimov—finally—would save a lot of lives. The sheer time it would take for someone else to pick up the remnants of his empire, to pick up the reins and take over operations, would enable other countries, other special ops groups to infiltrate and shut it down before it ever got back off the ground.

Because after Maksimov . . . Hancock shut his mind down, returning to the issue at hand, before Bristow truly understood the depth of Hancock's lack of respect and the fact that he in no way feared this man, that he was so confident of his superiority that he knew he could get to Bristow at any time and end his miserable existence. Despite his attempt to silence the many voices in his head, all replaying past events and ensuring his absolute focus on this mission above all else, a whisper slid insidiously through his mind, tracing each pathway so he had no choice but to hear it. It settled deep within him, taking root as it had done so many times before, and this time Hancock didn't even bother to uproot it, push it away, force it free so he could forget it was ever there.

After Maksimov you will be free of this life. It will be time for you to rest.

He nearly gritted his teeth. The whisper bothered him when so little else did. When so little else had the power to affect him. Rest could mean many different things to a man like him. But the one prevailing thought, the suspicion that took hold when nothing else would, was that in this case, rest meant eternal rest. And worse than the thought of it being final was the fact that he didn't fear it, didn't feel sadness or regret. All he felt was . . . anticipation. He didn't share his acceptance of this with his team or with the four people he considered family, the only people in the world who mattered to him. The only people he felt real emotion for. Love. Loyalty. Respect. And the knowledge that he'd die for any one of them. No, if they knew, they'd make it much harder for him. They'd never understand. They'd want him away from this life. They'd want him to live. For them. With them. They'd never understand that he could never adapt to civilian life—normal life. He didn't even know what normal was. He didn't fit into a world where everything was black and white, where gray wasn't accepted. He couldn't live or exist in a life where if something happened to someone he loved he couldn't go after the people responsible, couldn't make them pay. He would be expected to rely on and trust law enforcement and then the justice system to get justice for the person he loved. How fucked up was that?

He was a law unto himself, and that would never change. God help him, he didn't want it to change. Never would he sit back and allow someone else to do what was his duty alone.

Bristow was seething with impatience, taking Hancock's prolonged silence for disdain and insubordination. As much as Hancock wanted to tell him to get fucked, there was a higher purpose at hand, and Bristow mattered only as much as a pawn used to achieve that higher goal. Hancock wouldn't get rid of him yet. But he would allow the man to know who was really in control. Bristow would know not to cross Hancock, even as he wouldn't be certain why. It would be nothing Hancock said—directly. But Bristow would know absolutely.

"You pay me," Hancock said mildly. "I hired and pay *my* men. They follow *my* orders. Never think otherwise."

Though the statement seemed bland, a simple truth, there was a soft warning that Bristow didn't misunderstand. For a brief moment fear flashed in the career criminal's eyes before he visibly chased it away with a shake of his head, a scowl replacing any hint of intimidation. He hated the feeling of inferiority. That Hancock, so rough around the edges, hard and unyielding, not handsome or appealing by anyone's standards, could possibly make a man like Bristow feel so . . . subservient. And yet he was too aware of Hancock's power to challenge the man who worked for him. He was . . . afraid . . . of him. And that rankled most of all.

Hancock almost smiled, but he was too disciplined to do so. He wanted the little bastard afraid of him—of his men. And he damn sure wanted the power-hungry warlord to know just where his men's loyalties lay. It wasn't with Bristow, and he'd be a fool to ever believe so.

"Now, about this woman," Hancock said, deliberately bringing them back to the original subject. "What could be so important about a lone woman that you would risk pissing off one of the most powerful men in the world?"

Once again, anger flashed in Bristow's eyes. Impatience caused a twitch to his right eyelid, and he was barely maintaining a grasp on his temper. With anyone else, he would have already acted. He would have ordered the person who dared to question him and suggest *he* wasn't the most powerful man in the world to be killed. And it wouldn't be a quick merciful death either. Hancock had witnessed Bristow's depravities firsthand. He'd been forced to participate in order to prove himself. To enter Bristow's inner circle, gain his trust—and confidence—and position himself as Bristow's second in command.

The man was foul, and only the knowledge that when Hancock brought down his primary target he would then take out Bristow and dismantle his entire organization had kept him from killing Bristow on the spot. But he needed this man—or rather pawn, as loath as he was to admit it. Any idiot with Bristow's connections would do. It wasn't personal to Bristow or any greatness he perceived on his behalf. Maksimov, the primary target, the end goal, was a cagey bastard, and Hancock had come close too many times to count, only for the Russian to elude him.

He was determined that this was his final chase. It would all end here. He would bring down every kingpin in this macabre chain of evil. They preyed on the innocent, providing the necessary tools for anyone with the money and the means to wage war on the innocent. They were the cause of so much bloodshed. Rivers of it. Hundreds of thousands of deaths could be attributed to the links in the chain, but all pieces led to the same man. Maksimov. He had his fingers in every imaginable pie there was. If there was a way to profit from pain, suffering and terrorism, he found it.

Ironically, Maksimov provided equally to opposing factions, no doubt finding it amusing to see groups waging war against one another with weapons he'd provided, his pockets fat from the veritable monopoly he held on arms, explosives, every imaginable military weapon and even the necessary components to build nuclear weapons.

He was on every civilized country's most-wanted list. He was the most-wanted man in the world, and yet no one had succeeded in taking him down. Over the years, Hancock had tasted failure more times than he wished to remember as he relentlessly pursued Maksimov. Took advantage of avenues to him. Cultivated partnerships with those high up in the chain leading to Maksimov. Were it not for an attack of the very thing he swore he didn't possess—a *conscience*—he'd have nailed the bastard twice over.

He'd mentally berated himself a hundred times, and yet he couldn't find it within him to have true regret over the choices he'd made. The only thing he'd been able to summon was the iron will to never again put the good of the one over the good of the many. The price was too high. He'd sacrificed his objective for a single innocent. On not one, but two occasions. And when he imagined how many thousands of innocent people had died—were still dying—because he'd saved two innocents, two people who were nothing but good—everything he wasn't—it only hardened his resolve to never again forfeit his honor, his belief system. He understood that the loss of the two women he'd chosen to forfeit his mission in order to save would have been a travesty. The world needed people like Grace and Maren. But he had no choice but to once again embrace the emotionless existence he'd lived for so many years and wrap himself deep in the layers so he would feel nothing but the burning drive to complete his mission at all costs.

He would not feel guilt over sacrificing the few for the many. It was a choice no one should have to make, but it was what he'd been made into. His skills honed by fire. Taught by the best. The knowledge that completing the mission at all costs was necessary and that failure was not an option had been so solidly ingrained into him that it had become a part of him. No, not a part. It had become all-consuming, the whole of his existence. So deeply rooted in his soul that it became who he was. What he was. Until there was nothing left of the person he'd once been, and in his place a ruthless warrior had been born. Forged by fire. Resolve of steel. No hesitation to do his sworn duty and uphold the only honor and code he adhered to. His own.

"You think me a fool," Bristow hissed, some of his earlier fire once again flashing in his eyes, his temper quick and churlish. "I don't pay you to judge me. I pay you for absolute obedience. If you can't handle that, then show yourself—and your men," he added snidely, "to the door."

Hancock did smile then, but it was mocking, meant to demonstrate contempt for Bristow and his utter lack of respect or fear of a man used to inspiring both.

"No, you pay me to do your dirty work. You pay me to save your ass. And you pay me because you fear that the many enemies you've made over the years will get to you, so you sought to hire the best and you did. By all means, if you are so confident in your abilities to see to those matters yourself, then my men and I will go elsewhere. There is always someone looking for one with my capabilities and who would certainly be more appreciative of them. I'm sure you will sleep just fine at night, confident in your safety."

Fear didn't merely flicker in Bristow's eyes, like a shadow chased away nearly as soon as it appeared. His entire face whitened and he swallowed visibly. Hancock felt confident calling the coward's bluff because above all things, Bristow feared death. His own, that is. He had no regard for the death of others and enjoyed being the instrument of death. It made him feel godlike and powerful, that he could decide whether another lived or died. And he loved others to have that knowledge of who and what he was so they'd fear him, acknowledge him and placate him, even worship him.

And there was the reason he despised Hancock so much.

Because not only had Hancock proven himself invincible and impervious to death, but he held Bristow in no esteem whatsoever. He was confident in his own abilities and would never have to hire others to do his bidding. And he was a man others instinctively feared and deferred to. Bristow saw everything he craved—and lacked—in the man he'd hired, and he hated Hancock for it.

Not waiting, Hancock made a motion to his men as if to go, and he simply turned his back on Bristow, making sure at least two of his men had Bristow in their sight line so he didn't do something stupid like pull a gun and shoot Hancock in the back. Which would be completely in keeping with his character, because Bristow was both a coward and not one who could control his temper.

"Maksimov will want her," Bristow blurted out. "You have no idea how much. You don't know who she is, only that I told you I wanted her."

His tone was beseeching. He hoped to get Hancock and his men to stay without begging outright. He knew better than to command them to stay. And it tore at his already tattered pride to beg, to allow Hancock to know how much Bristow did need him and feared his world without Hancock there to be a barrier between him and his enemies.

It wasn't Bristow's desperation that stopped Hancock and his men. It was that one magic word. Maksimov.

Hancock slowly turned so he didn't tip his hand. He leveled a stare at Bristow.

"Maksimov wants a lot of things," he said matter-of-factly. "What makes the woman so special?"

"It's not her," Bristow said impatiently. "I mean it's not personal to her. You don't understand. She escaped from an attack on a relief center where she and many Westerners worked. She was the only survivor, and the militant group took no chances. They recovered all bodies and compared it to the list of people they knew worked there. They were the target. Once they discovered the woman wasn't among the dead and was nowhere to found, they launched a search for her. So far, she's evaded them and hasn't been discovered."

Hancock made a motion for his men to stand down and

take their places in the room once more. A protective formation so Bristow was watched from every angle, though Bristow wasn't smart enough to know that his every action was being monitored and that he'd be taken out immediately if he made one wrong move.

Hancock crossed his arms over his stomach in a deceptively relaxed and inquisitive mode.

"And why would this woman be of interest to Maksimov? So much so that you want me to track her and be the one to capture her before this group finds her? I doubt you have any interest in protecting her or saving her life, as surely when her pursuers find her—and they will—she'll be dead. Or wish she were dead."

Bristow seated himself behind the ornate desk he used for his business dealings. It reeked of wealth and opulence, but then Hancock would expect nothing less from a man who made certain everyone he came into contact with knew of his wealth and imagined power.

His eyes gleamed with . . . excitement. There was obviously something about the woman that gave Bristow an edge, imagined or not. His entire body bristled with impatience and anticipation.

"Because A New Era, the terrorist cell turning the country upside down hunting the woman, is well known and ruthless. They are feared by many. Entire nations fear them, and in fact even enemy nations have joined together in a summit to focus their combined efforts to stop them. They grow more powerful every day. They have unlimited resources and operate using fear and intimidation to achieve their agenda."

"And what is their agenda exactly?" Hancock asked.

"That's the question, isn't it? What does any fanatical terrorist cell truly want? They want power, reverence. They want people to not only fear them but to respect their capabilities. They want to rule the entire region, not just a single country or territory. They want nations to fear them and concede that they are superior to any military force. Their numbers grow steadily. They recruit far and wide. Men and women of any ethnicity, nationality. They are very persuasive and promise ultimate wealth, power and domination.

And so far, no one, no army, no country, no organized effort has been able to get close to them. They have few casualties and are unaffected by them. Everyone who joins feels it is a great honor to die for their cause, and that makes them even more dangerous because they have no fear of death. They are . . . unstoppable."

"What is Maksimov's connection to this group and why would the woman be of interest to him?" Hancock asked impatiently, tired of information he deemed useless.

There was no shortage of independent cells all seeking dominance in an already war-torn region. So what made this one any different than the others? But he'd detected a hint of fear—and respect—for this group he spoke of, and Maksimov neither feared nor respected anyone, though it made him a fool because he was weak, and without strong, ruthless people to do his bidding, he was nothing.

"They owe Maksimov money. He is their main supplier of arms and explosives. They believe themselves untouchable by anyone and have no fear of Maksimov, the fools. If Maksimov has something they want very badly, then that gives him an edge. And they do want this woman. Already word has spread through the region of a lone woman, a defenseless American woman who has evaded capture, and it makes them look weak. Like fools who can't manage to find a woman. They are furious, no doubt, and if they do find her and I have no doubt they eventually will—their reach is too far, their power too great—she will not die quickly. They will seek to make an example of her. They'll use her to demonstrate just how ruthless they are, and they'll use her to send a message to all who oppose them. I have no doubt Maksimov would not only pay much to have her in his possession but he would be indebted. To me."

He said the last with supreme satisfaction, arrogance and greed lighting his eyes. So this was his goal. To dangle something Maksimov wanted desperately in front of his nose and to be the one to deliver the woman to Maksimov. It would elevate Bristow's status with Maksimov, which would bring him more power and wealth. It would set him up for years to come, and when he was under Maksimov's protection as one known to be in his inner circle, Bristow's enemies would hesitate to strike at him, knowing that whatever was done to Bristow would be taken by Maksimov to be an insult—an attack—on Maksimov himself. And few dared to take on Maksimov, which allowed Maksimov to grow in power, expanding his already enormous reach and his empire into something truly frightening. If Hancock wasn't successful in taking him down this time, he knew his time had run out. He had firsthand experience with how ruthless Maksimov could be. He still bore the scars of his last run-in with the man, but thankfully, Hancock had been in deep cover and his appearance had been altered such that it was doubtful Maksimov would recognize the man he believed to be the minion of the man who'd gone against Maksimov. It was his only up close and personal contact with the man he'd hunted for years, and by the time Maksimov had gotten close to Hancock, his already disguised features were bloodied, bruised and swollen, so Hancock felt confident the man wouldn't recognize him. He planned to get very close to the man this time, and perhaps this woman Bristow spoke of would afford him just that chance.

He glanced at Bristow with interest, no longer viewing the task Bristow had ordered him to do as a delay he couldn't afford, a pointless endeavor that would only lessen his chances of striking at Maksimov at the first opportunity.

"So you want me to go after this woman, intercept her before the men hunting her find her and bring her to Maksimov?"

Bristow frowned and shook his head. "No. Not immediately. Bring her to me. I won't simply hand her over to Maksimov before gaining what I want from the exchange. And that will take time. Maksimov is reclusive and cagey. Not much brings him to the surface. If he really wants her, and I'm positive he will, I plan to make him wait and grow restless to the point he'll give me whatever I want. It will be a negotiation. If I don't get what I want from Maksimov, then I will bargain with the militants who want her so desperately. Either would give much to have the woman. Perhaps the militants would give me even more so they save face," he added with a shrug.

It was a stupid, dangerous game to toy with and attempt to manipulate Maksimov, but Hancock didn't warn Bristow of that fact. If the woman lured Maksimov into a personal meeting where he'd take possession of the woman, then that fit perfectly into Hancock's agenda, and he didn't particularly care what the consequences to Bristow were.

And it was equally stupid to bargain with a fanatical group because after giving Bristow what he wanted in exchange for the girl, they'd simply execute Bristow in very bloody fashion and take back not only what they'd given as payment for the woman but everything Bristow possessed, which would only add to their considerable wealth and power.

Anticipation licked through Hancock's veins and his pulse sped up, the taste of victory in his mouth. If all it took was capturing a single woman who was running and hiding from a terrorist group to enable him to achieve his objective, then he'd do it without hesitation. He'd have to ensure that Maksimov took the bait because it did him no good for Bristow to turn to the terrorist cell to get what he wanted. It had to be Maksimov.

He glanced up at his men and saw answering resolve in their eyes. They wanted to take down Maksimov every bit as much as he did. And like him, they grew weary of their existence or rather nonexistence. To the world, they were dead. To their government they were traitors and had been given a death sentence. To their prey, they were angels of death, without mercy or compassion. They were feared by all and they mattered to no one. To even the strongest, unfeeling soul, such a life eventually wore on them. They were all ready to step down from their cause and allow others to do the work they'd done without thanks or regard for over a decade. And make whatever kind of life was left to them, knowing that even after they stood down, they'd always be hunted.

"Give me what intel you have," Hancock said to Bristow, determination and resolve Bristow couldn't possibly miss in his tone. And Bristow had seen him in action long enough to know he didn't offer his assurances lightly. "I'll find the woman and bring her to you."

CHAPTER 4

HONOR clutched the heavy makeshift garment covering her entire body with one hand to keep the hem from swirling in the high wind. Not that it mattered, traveling at night as she was, with no one to see whether parts of her were exposed. But the habit was already deeply ingrained in the days she'd been running. Trying to avoid discovery.

The cloth she'd fashioned into a pack was lighter than it had been in the beginning as more and more of her supplies dwindled, so it gave her two hands to tamp down the unmanageable material instead of the one she was accustomed to having to use to wrest control of the wind-driven folds of fabric. Though her tangible burden might be lighter, the ones unseen were slowly eating away at her, pressing down on her with oppressive strength. Bone-deep weariness assailed her. And she had miles to go this night.

The sudden poetic quip that had slipped into her thoughts, *amusing* her, caused sudden alarm. There was nothing remotely humorous about her circumstances, and she was shocked that she could even conjure the trait. Maybe she was succumbing to the horror and stress of the last days. She thought "days" in general and purposely didn't cite the *number* of days because she'd lost track of time in the aftermath of the massacre and her frantic efforts to free herself.

She had no idea how many days had passed because she'd had no opportunity to stop, slow down, process and then compartmentalize her grief so it didn't incapacitate her. And it would. She would lock down, unable to get past the horrors she'd witnessed firsthand. She couldn't afford to allow herself to think. She had to act. To keep moving. Because if she stopped she would lose.

She refused to say *die* when referring to possible failure. Nor did she say *live* or *survive* when she fantasized about making it to safety. She'd made it a game. Hide-and-seek, Rambo style. The most epic game of hide-and-seek ever. She was hiding and they were seeking. Because to give in to the terrifying truth and acknowledge that grim reality was to breed the very thing she fought with everything she had and had been thinking in terms of life and death as being the ultimate prize. Which was exactly what it was. So she retreated into denial and formed an alternate reality where it was simply a game. Or a twisted version of those reality television shows when people were forced to fend for themselves against difficult odds and the person to overcome seemingly insurmountable obstacles and outlast the others was declared the winner.

She *was* in an impossible situation. She *had* to fend for herself. It was her only choice. And when she outlasted her pursuers and passed over the border where there was a U.S. presence, she won. She would defeat evil and she had to believe it. It was as simple as that. She was smart. She loved challenges—though this was *not* a challenge she'd ever purposely choose. And she wasn't afraid of adversity, though her perception of adversity had been irrevocably changed the day of the attack. There was adversity and then there was this. There was nothing that could describe what she was up against. And if she had any say in the matter, she'd never face this kind of adversity again. Nothing in her young life had prepared her for such a horrific ordeal, and it had made her rethink her calling a hundred times as she'd fled for her life, having to stay a step ahead of her pursuers or . . . die.

She shook her head, refusing to let reality creep back in. She hadn't come to this area without being prepared. She hadn't woken up one morning and decided to come here on a whim. She was fluent in several of the languages in the country, even the more obscure ones, and had extensively studied the culture, the many different dialects and subtle differences that signified a different region. She knew how to blend in and what the laws were for women. Never had she been so glad for all of that information as she was now.

Her mouth was dry, her lips parched and cracking. She was nearer to the village she'd been traveling toward for the last three days, but she had to find a place to rest, a place where she could survey the village and its inhabitants from a distance and study it closely before she ventured into it.

She'd traveled strictly at night, knowing she risked too much by spending prolonged periods of time in the daylight. One wrong move. One misstep. One lapse in her rigid disguise and she'd draw notice. And she knew her adversaries were close. Maybe even ahead of her and in the village already searching for her. She didn't *want* to go into the village, though she'd chosen one that was small and hadn't yet drawn the ire of the bloodthirsty savages who'd executed her fellow relief workers. She'd stuck to a strict regimen of sleeping by day and walking at night, keeping to the shadows, always on her toes and expecting the worst. It was a terrible way to endure and it was fast draining her reserves.

But she was running dangerously low on supplies, and she had to chance going into the village to restock the essentials. She'd traveled as long and as far as her injuries and exhaustion allowed, wanting to put as much distance as possible between herself and the site of the attack and the men who now hunted her. She would go without sleep today as she usually did and she would walk this next night, so it was imperative that she find the safest possible refuge before dawn so she could sleep as many hours as possible before nightfall.

She stopped a distance from the village and then surveyed the area for a place to rest and wait. She needed one that afforded her not only safety and protection, a place where she was undetectable, if such a place existed, but also a good vantage point where she could see the activity when the people awoke and began their daily routine.

If she hurried she could tend to her needs and get in an hour of sleep, two if she was lucky. The rising sun would wake her. The urgency of her mission today would wake her. And she desperately needed all the rest she could grab when it was imperative that she stay on the move at all times.

She was thirsty and hungry. But water was what she craved, what she needed. Her lips were dry and cracked, her tongue so devoid of moisture that it clung to the roof of her mouth and rubbed abrasively over the sensitive skin with there being no natural liquid to ease its way. She increased her pace, knowing there was little sense in maintaining the guise of her disguised form at night when no one would be out except . . .

Nope. She wasn't going there. She slammed her mind shut to block the fear that she was being stalked right this moment. That they'd caught up to her and if she alerted them to her position they'd have her. They'd win. Oh hell no. This game wasn't over. By her count, she was winning. All she had to do was maintain her lead. If she stayed just one step ahead of them, victory would be hers.

When she finally reached the outskirts of the village, she scouted the hillside overlooking the tiny rural populace and found a place where the rock formations were more prevalent. And they were large, jutting upward and spreading out, the configuration such that there was a protective ring around an opening in the middle. She would be shielded from plain sight. One would have to go beyond the perimeter of the structures in order to see her. But at the same time, it would enable her to take position in a place where she could have an unimpeded view of the village below while remaining undetected.

She sank behind the largest formation, one that faced the village, and winced when she had to reposition her knee so that it didn't bend beneath her. She stretched her leg outward and rested her back against the stone. It wasn't the most comfortable support, rough with jagged edges, but it kept her upright, so she wasn't complaining.

She needed food and water. Especially water. But her thirst wasn't as great as her need to have one moment to just sit in the quiet and breathe. Just a few steadying breaths and a moment to let go of the pain, the sorrow and the gut-wrenching fear that she could be captured at any time.

So for a moment she simply sat there and absorbed the night. This was a sparsely populated area and there were few lights emanating from the village, so the area was blanketed in dark, making the sky that much more visible. The stars were brighter, glowing like something alive, and she could see the heavy carpet of them for miles.

It was truly beautiful. She'd never been in a place where she could see so many stars twinkling in the black velvet sky. It looked like fairy dust. The beauty of the night gave her solace. Those few seconds before practicality had to take over had been needed. She was a little calmer now. She would overcome. She would win.

She dug into the bag carrying her waning supplies and pulled out the antibiotic pills she'd been taking since she escaped the ruins of the clinic. She'd walked through the rubble, hastily looking for anything that would help her stay alive. Water. She'd carried out as many of the bottles of water as she could, given her condition and the fact she had other items to carry as well.

She'd scored protein bars and MREs, grateful she'd seen the box containing them barely peeking from beneath the debris. And medication. Pain medication, antibiotics, sunblock and sunburn aid. It had a numbing agent she could rub on her knee to numb the pain from the lacerations and injuries to the skin.

After rounding up the things she could find that would aid her, she'd torn off her clothing and fashioned a hijab that fell well below her breasts and wore it over a hastily fashioned concealing robe from material the relief center gave out to women to make their clothing. Honor had cut a jagged hole through the middle of the swath and yanked it over her head.

It covered her completely. Not even her booted feet peeked from beneath the hem when she walked. And most importantly it gave her the ability to pull off the rest of her disguise.

She'd used rolls and rolls of medical tape to attach small

pillows to parts of her body to make her appear lumpy and shapeless. Indistinct. She padded her belly to make herself seem heavier, but she bound her breasts flat against her chest. Or as flat as she could make the generous mounds. Muslims weren't to wear revealing clothes of any kind, and for that Honor was grateful because her breasts drew attention, a fact she'd long cursed. With this manner of appearance, there was no difference between her breasts and the rest of her body. She looked like an older rounded woman whose back had stooped her with age.

It was automatic when thinking of her appearance that she pulled out the piece of bark that she used to apply and rub in the henna dye. She checked her arms, shoulders and neck even though they were shielded at all times. Still . . . She adhered to the motto that one could never be *too* careful. Especially when it came to self-preservation and the overwhelming instinct for survival.

She took out the mirror she'd taken from the clinic. Already the idea for how she'd hide had been formulating in Honor's mind as she'd collected up supplies in preparation to flee. And she knew a mirror was essential in order for her to ensure that the only visible part of herself stayed darker. Just as the penlight had been a source of light, no matter how small. Because she'd known if she had any chance, she would have to travel mostly at night and find a place to rest during the day and force herself to ignore the panicked demand in her head screaming at her to keep running, not to stop. Not for one minute. The logical part of her knew she did herself no good if she made demands of her body it wasn't capable of fulfilling. If she pushed herself too far, she'd only incapacitate herself, and then she'd be a sitting duck.

She pulled at the headdress until it pooled at her neck, and she breathed in, allowing the wind to blow through her hair. It was a heated wind, not a relief wind bearing cooler, sweeter air. But it helped to remove the sweat on Honor's neck and scalp and would dry it from her hair before she pulled the material back up into place. She picked up the mirror with one hand and the penlight with the other, turning it on.

Her eyes were always the first thing she looked into. It

gave her a measure of reassurance to know she was looking into her own eyes. Living eyes. It reminded her that she was a survivor.

She touched up places that likely didn't need it, but she did so to give herself the illusion that she was making herself safer from detection. Then she turned her attention to her hair. Her greatest liability.

Her eyes were brown and while she was usually fairer skinned, her time here had burnished her skin, making it a darker brown, though she was still noticeably lighter than the native women. But her hair was blond. A dead giveaway. In her time of panic as she realized the problem of her hair when she'd been hastily collecting supplies from the relief center, she'd considered simply shaving it all off. But a bald woman would get every bit as much notice as a blond one, perhaps even more.

Thankfully, her brain kicked in and kicked her in the ass and then took over, shoving panic and all the chaotic emotions out so that her only focus was on her escape.

Once she was far enough away from the attack site to feel that she could stop and take the necessary time to complete her disguise, she vigorously rubbed henna into any skin that could be potentially exposed, even with the mountain of material covering her body. She paid special attention to her hands, ensuring that they appeared worn. She'd smeared dirt and even made small scratches and cuts to her fingers and knuckles, praying the antibiotics would ward off infection, in an effort to make them look like those of the older woman she pretended to be. She'd torn off the remaining fingernails. Most of them had been ripped to the quick when she'd dug herself free of the rubble. The bruises and damage she'd sustained during her digging aided her because with the swelling and abrasions, her hands appeared gnarled and misshapen.

Once she was satisfied that she'd done as good a job as she could disguising her flesh, she turned her focus to her biggest danger. Her hair.

She'd meticulously coated every strand of her hair in the dark dye and then carefully applied the color to her eyebrows. And when she was finished, she waited precious minutes she couldn't afford for it to set in and then she repeated the process. And then a third time. It wasn't the best job, nor was it that convincing, but she was banking on the fact that no one would see her without her hair covered, and all but her eyes was hidden by the headdress. If a stray strand somehow blew free, it would appear dark, and for the few seconds it took for her to conceal it once more, someone wouldn't have time to truly study the color or judge its authenticity.

It was hard to see well with the tiny light source she used, and she didn't bother to even use the penlight. It was too risky. Instead she reapplied the dye to her hair, being as thorough as she had been the first time and ensuring that not a single strand was missed.

Finally finished with the repairs to her protection, she tiredly reached into the bag to pull out a protein bar, the bottle containing the last ounces of her water and the antibiotics and painkillers.

She drank first, sucking greedily at the liquid but tempering the urge to drink it down to nothing. Then she quickly ate the protein bar and chased it down with a small sip. She'd learned the hard way not to take the antibiotic or the pain reliever on an empty stomach. The first day had been hell with an upset stomach, her knee throbbing and her having to stop to dry-heave more times than she could count.

After downing both medicines, she reached for the binding around her knee, the last task before she could close her eyes for a short time. She'd taken special care to wrap it tightly before she fled from the clinic and to use some of the precious room in her pack for an extra Ace bandage and antibiotic cream to use along with the oral antibiotics she was taking.

The swelling had lessened some and the vivid black bruise had turned to a ghastly-looking mixture of green and yellow, which relieved her. It didn't appear to be anything serious like a fracture or dislocation. It was painful, definitely, but the tight wrap had enabled her to have mobility, something that wouldn't have been possible for a prolonged period of time if it were broken or dislocated. Not to mention she would have been screaming in pain and unable to continue after that first arduous day when she hadn't stopped for twenty-four hours.

She doctored the cuts, pressed around the kneecap to test for the degree of swelling and then deftly rebound it after using some of the sunburn aid, which contained the numbing agent lidocaine.

Although she needed her hands to appear beaten and weathered to keep up her appearance, she still applied topical antibiotic cream to the deepest lacerations because she couldn't afford for them to become so infected that she became ill and was unable to keep traveling. Knowing she would—hopefully—replenish her waning water supply in the morning, she used almost all of the remaining liquid to cleanse the dirt and pieces of debris still embedded in the skin. She hadn't dared pay attention to them, and until now, she'd been able to block out the discomfort of the embedded shards.

Now when she carefully pulled them free and poured the last of the antiseptic she carried with her over the wounds, she let out a hiss of pain and held her breath, simply breathing through it and compartmentalizing it just as she had everything else. After patting the areas clean, she rubbed the antibiotic ointment on each of the cuts and then wrapped them in gauze. Just for this little time of rest. Before she went into the village in the early morning, she would unwrap them and pack dirt over the wounds again, and she'd keep her fingers curled so her hands weren't readily visible by anyone. They spent much of the time beneath the enveloping folds of her garment, but when replenishing her supplies, she would need her hands and they would be exposed for a short time.

Up close, it would be more obvious that her hands were injured and not those of an older woman. But at a distance, with the rest of her costume giving the assumption of what she claimed to be, no one would look too hard at her hands. No one overly scrutinized any women here. It was forbidden. And while the Western culture ingrained in her chafed at the idea that women were commanded to only appear in public completely concealed, all but their eyes, and in some regions not even their eyes could be visible, she was grateful for the extreme laws women lived under at the moment because were it not for those laws, she would have never gotten as far as she'd come.

And since younger women weren't allowed outside their home without the escort of a male family member or an older woman, like a mother-in-law, posing as someone younger would also gain her unwanted notice. She didn't pat herself on the back for coming up with such a good disguise in the few minutes after she'd escaped the wreckage trapping her in the relief center. She'd been operating on raw instinct. Survival instinct. And she'd gathered every bit of her extensive knowledge of the languages and customs of the regions she worked in to help her not only escape her immediate prison but stay hidden in plain sight and pray that she was able to make it to a place beyond the seemingly all-encompassing reach of the militant group that terrorized such a widespread area.

After carefully replacing all items into her sack and ensuring that there would be no sign of her left behind, she once more leaned against the rough support the rock offered and closed her eyes, trying to push back the paralyzing fear of having to go into the village and show herself, even though only her eyes would be visible.

But eyes were the window to the soul, or so the saying went. Would her terror be there for the world to see? Would the villagers know of her pain, sorrow and abject fear just by looking into her eyes? Would she have the look of someone who was being hunted, who'd been handed a death sentence? For a second time? She'd been condemned to die in the attack, but somehow she survived. Could she survive being sentenced to death again?

It's a game, Honor. One you're winning. You can't let yourself think anything else.

Honor swallowed and slipped further toward the veil of sleep. She could pretend all she wanted. She could wear the armor of denial forever. But neither changed the fact that this was no game. This was a fight and nothing less. The most important fight of her life. *For* her life.

There was no room for second place. Second place got her unimaginable pain and degradation and eventually death. Her only choice was to fight as she'd never fought before.

And win.

CHAPTER 5

HONOR awoke with the first rays of sun that crept over the horizon, bathing the area in its pale light. She emitted a mental groan because all she wanted to do was sleep. For days. Even as uncomfortable as she was among the rock formations and the sand biting into her skin.

The wind had kicked up, showing promise of being as forceful as the night before when she'd fought to control the swirling hem of her robe.

She could have sneaked into the village in the dark of night and gone to the small river that was the life's blood of this village. It was where the people bathed, did their washing, got their drinking water and did any number of other daily chores. She could have washed her wounds and replenished her water supply, but she needed a small clay or metal pot—even a tin cup—to boil the water in now that she had run through the untainted water she'd gotten from the clinic.

But she wasn't fool enough to think she wouldn't have been discovered. Though the village was quiet and peaceful, not one that had yet been overtaken by outsiders, and they hadn't had to defend themselves from an outside attack, she knew they would have been trained, their men, young and old; even the boys and some of the women as well would have prepared themselves for the eventuality of occupation.

And they no doubt had nightly watch patrols, just to ensure that they weren't victim to a surprise attack in the dead of night.

There wasn't a village that took for granted that they were impervious to the plights of so many others. And as more refugees from other decimated villages fled to villages just like this, the danger to communities rose. Terrorist cells and fanatics saw them as easy targets and as nothing more than the expansion of their empire. They didn't see humans, good and decent people who hurt no one, who went about their daily life only wanting to be left in peace. People like those who'd struck at the relief center with such savagery had no humanity whatsoever. They saw themselves as superior to these simpletons, useless as anything but farmers and traders. Their women created beautiful accessories, clothing, decorative beading and fancier headdresses and long flowing gowns. People traveled far on their trade days to buy from the villagers. It was just another way they supported themselves and were able to sustain a livelihood.

As Honor slowly began moving, testing the limits and constraints of her body, pain shuddered through her, but she grimaced and continued on as if she hadn't felt the protests of a hundred muscles.

She focused mostly on her knee, as it was her most serious injury. She still wasn't sure exactly what was wrong with it, but the fact that she could walk on it without collapsing told her that it was bearable, and it would keep her moving toward her objective. She just had to move around and loosen up her muscles.

If only she'd been able to find other medications housed in the medical area of the relief center. Muscle relaxers would be a miracle. But all she had was antibiotics and what were considered over-the-counter pain relievers in the United States—ibuprofen and acetaminophen. Even if she'd been able to uncover the stronger narcotic pain relievers, she would have left them because she couldn't afford to take anything that would impair her. She had to be sharp and on her toes at all times, and the pain, as unwelcome as it was, certainly kept that edge for her. She couldn't relax when every movement hurt, and it reminded her to keep in character at all times, as if she were an actor in a movie—but this was no movie. This was the role of her *life*.

She slowly swallowed the last sips of water, licking her parched, cracked lips to alleviate the dryness, and allowed the soothing cool to trickle down her throat. She had no desire to eat again, and she had only a few MREs and one protein bar left. While she could replenish water in the village, she wasn't so sure about food. She had no money to buy it and only one possible item she could barter with. But she could go far longer without food than water, so water was her primary focus. And if she could find things she could fashion into bandages and possible clothing, then she could switch out the only garment she wore. It was dangerous to appear in the same manner of dress every day, especially in a different location every day. Eventually someone would notice. People would talk. The maniacs pursuing her would put two and two together and they'd know they were close to capturing her. Worse, they'd know exactly what she looked like and would identify her on sight.

Her fingers closed around the handle of the sharp dagger concealed in the folds of her clothing and secured to the tie around her waist keeping the material in check. She'd brought it primarily as a means of protection, but the true reason crept into her mind more and more on a daily basis.

In the aftermath of the attack and with her panic at epic levels, after she'd seen what those monsters had done to her friends and knowing that what they'd do to her would be ten times worse and in no way merciful, she'd taken the knife because she'd promised herself that while she would not go down without a fight and that she would fight to live—to survive—at all costs, if there came a time when she knew all was lost and capture was inevitable . . . She closed her eyes, shutting it out. Or trying to. But it was there. The promise she'd rashly made that horrible day. She'd kill herself before allowing them to overtake her and take her prisoner.

It went against every grain. This wasn't who she was. It never had been. Only in a weak moment of panic had she lamented the fact that she hadn't died with the others, and it shamed her even now. She was a fighter. She was strong. Taking her own life seemed the ultimate act of cowardice. And yet she wasn't an idiot. She knew she'd die anyway but only after days, possibly weeks of endless pain, degradation and torture. And she never wanted to get to a point where she begged someone else to kill her. Her pride was too great. She refused to give them that satisfaction. If it came to that, she'd do the deed herself and deprive them of their hollow victory.

Knowing she was wasting time and, if she was honest, spending way too much time avoiding the inevitable pausing to bolster her flagging courage, she pushed herself slowly and painfully to her feet and wrapped the ends of the sack carrying her now-meager supplies, tucking it within the folds of her garment. She secured it to her waist with the tie circling her midsection, leaving her hands free to defend herself if necessary.

She'd rigged the tie so that one firm yank would immediately loosen the robe so that it was easily pulled free of her body and she could better flee. But with the pillows still secured to parts of her body with miles of tape, being free of the robe wouldn't give her *that* much more speed.

But the dagger would come in handy. If she could get enough of a start, she could slash at the tape as she ran, eventually freeing herself of all encumbrances, and be able to pick up speed. She just had to pray that her knee held out.

When she peered around the tallest and widest rock she'd sought refuge behind, she was surprised to see that the road leading to the village was quite busy for this early in the morning. There were people walking in groups. Some alone. Some pulling small wooden wagons by hand, others urging a mule forward as the animal pulled a cart behind it.

She swept a glance over the village below and saw various booths set up, people already putting their wares on display and readying themselves for customers. It was obviously a market day in the village, one that drew many from outlying areas.

Allowing a small exhale of relief, she looked for an opportunity to slip from behind her secluded shelter and fall in to the mix of people making their way to the village below. Hiding in plain sight. Her pursuers wouldn't expect her to openly mingle with others in broad daylight. Not when she'd only traveled by night thus far and had hidden during the day to rest. Or so she told herself. If she dwelled on any other possibility, she'd stay in her current position, too afraid to move, and she'd lose her only opportunity to replenish her supplies before she once more took flight and forged ahead in her quest for freedom.

When there was a break in the parade of people, she hurriedly strode toward the road, taking her place like she was just one of the others on their way to market, but she was careful to assume the stooped-over shuffle of a much older woman. Her hand automatically went to her veil to ensure that it covered all but her eyes, and she kept them downcast so she chanced looking no one directly in the eye.

Then she glanced down at her hands before burying them in the layers of material flowing from her waist. There was still swelling, and dirt covered the cuts and lacerations, only giving the impression of a woman who'd worked a lifetime with her hands. She'd been careful to wash away any dried, crusted blood; her fingernails were broken to the quick and dirt covered them, embedded around the cuticles, coating the area where they'd been ripped away from her skin.

She was near the outskirts of the village and she could hear sounds bursting from the small populace. There was even music in the distance. Already haggling had begun and the booths were alive with people seeking to barter for items or buy them.

"Good day to you, sister."

Honor stiffened but forced herself not to overreact to the man who'd slipped up beside her undetected. She'd been too focused on the goings-on in the village and hadn't paid her fellow travelers the attention she should have. The man had spoken in one of the less common dialects. Had it been a test?

Before she could summon a response, he continued in a low voice, as if not wanting to be overheard by anyone. "There are outcasts here. They look for something. The villagers are wary. They surround the village and are searching the village thoroughly. A woman alone cannot be too careful. If you wish, you may travel with me. It would be an honor to aid an elder of our people."

Did he *know* who she was? How could he? Had she not been as careful as she'd thought? Was he warning her because he knew she was the one whom the militant faction searched for? And was he merely offering her reassurance that he wouldn't betray her by playing along with her disguise and calling her an elder of their people? Or was there something more sinister at play? Was he one of the very men she had to evade at all costs?

There was little she could do. If she suddenly fled, she'd certainly draw attention to herself. And again, she doubted the assholes hunting her thought she would have the balls to go into that village with them there, so close she could smell them. And if she traveled with this man who looked to be older, it would only add credibility to her disguise.

He was younger than she pretended to be, but he was not a young man and likely had a wife or wives and children. Perhaps in his forties, but it was hard to tell because hard work aged the people here far before their time.

"I thank you, my brother, and good day to you as well." Then injecting a note of fear in her voice, as would be expected, she turned but was careful not to meet his eyes, and she kept her head bowed in a gesture of subservience. "Why are they here? Is this not a peaceful village? What is it that they seek this day? And are we safe?"

She'd thought through every single word and purposely made her voice sound as aged as she appeared. She wanted no hint of an accent and she was very good at the languages of the Middle East, even the obscure ones that verged on extinction. She breathed a sigh of relief when she could detect no error in her effort. She only hoped a native hadn't picked up on something she herself couldn't hear in her voice.

"There is talk that the group that calls themselves A New Era seek an American woman who escaped a relief center bombing while all other workers perished. They won't stop until they capture her, so they are spreading themselves far and wide and splitting up so they can cover more ground. The villagers are uneasy. They fear this abomination will destroy the village and expand the area they have absolute control of. If this woman is found, she would be given up in hopes that the fanatics would spare them in exchange."

Honor was more sure than ever that this man knew *she* was the woman being hunted. Why he had offered to help her, she didn't know. But then perhaps he only wanted to lure her in, give her a false sense of security so he could be the one to hand her over to A New Era and reap the reward.

She didn't have time to ponder the choice or mull it over in her mind. It would be a dead giveaway, and no elderly woman would turn down the protection of another when apprised of the situation, so she did the only thing she could do. The only option available to her.

"I am grateful for your protection and gladly accept. I have need of only a few things. I have no desire to be caught in the slaughter of innocent lives."

"May Allah be with us both, my sister," he said formally. "Come, walk with me and we will acquire the things you need so you can be on your way. And may Allah walk with you wherever you go."

He knew. He had to know. And yet he acted as though he wanted to help her. She was both relieved and grateful but also terrified all at the same time. She hated feeling so exposed. She hated someone knowing that she was the one the intruders were here for. Guilt swamped her. She didn't want to be responsible for the deaths of innocent people. She didn't want to be responsible for an entire village being decimated. And she didn't want to cause the death of a man who knew who she was and was helping her regardless.

She fell into step beside him and he slowed his pace to match hers so he didn't leave her behind.

"Are you injured?"

He asked in a mild, concerned voice that put Honor on edge even more. She couldn't afford to trust anyone. What if he was leading her directly to the men hunting her?

She emitted a soft laugh, roughening her voice to sound hardened by work and age. "When you get to be my age, your bones hurt and you don't move as quickly as you did in your youth. But I am well. I still manage to get around just fine."

He nodded, seeming to accept her explanation. They continued on in silence until they reached the small dwellings of the village. From underneath lowered lashes, she surveyed the area with a keen eye. At the river, her prime objective, several women were doing their morning laundry. The mood seemed light, but perhaps they didn't know of the danger that had infiltrated their village.

She would make her way to the river first because it would give her an opportunity to view the booths and see if any had items she needed. She would be okay for food for a few more days, but it only seemed logical to restock if possible because she had no way of knowing when she'd get another opportunity.

The only thing she had of value that wouldn't draw immediate suspicion was an intricate, decorative bracelet that had been a gift from a grateful family whose son she'd tended to, and she had been warm and reassuring when the child was scared. She knew it was of value and that it was something the family couldn't afford to simply give away, but it would have been an insult to refuse the offering, and now she was glad she hadn't. It should be enough to buy food and another garment so she could change her appearance and alternate her manner of dress.

"Where do you seek to go, sister?" the man asked.

"The river," she said simply. "I have need of washing and to get enough water to travel back from where I came."

He studied her a brief moment, clearly weighing the truth of her words.

"I'll go retrieve the water for you. I have containers I can offer." He said so as if he knew that her containers were not those used here, that they were plastic bottles that looked decidedly out of place. "You go find what it is you seek in the village and I will return to you when I've gotten the water."

She nodded and inclined her head in a gesture of respect and of gratitude. Then she turned and shuffled slowly down the street lined with booths and all manner of things for sale. She needed to find someone who offered not only preserved food but also clothing or at least material she could fashion into a garment as she'd done with the large bolt of material she'd uncovered in the relief center, because she had only one thing to use as payment, which meant if she couldn't find a vendor who offered both, she would have to make a choice.

She stopped at several, pretending interest and even exchanging pleasantries in their language fluently, always mindful not to allow the natural youthfulness of her voice to slip in and to maintain the cracked, rough voice of a much older woman.

All the while she scanned the area, meticulously studying the crowd for anyone who looked out of place. The residents of the village didn't seem uneasy, which told Honor that her pursuers were being very discreet, just waiting for their prey to be seen.

Finally she found a vendor that offered not only a variety of flavorful, preserved food that would last her many weeks if she consumed only what was necessary to keep her going, but also bolts of material. Hijabs and long flowing robes in a variety of styles and colors were on display. It was all she needed apart from the water her anonymous protector was collecting for her. She needed to wrap this up and leave this place before she brought disaster on the innocent people who made their home here. She wouldn't trade their lives for hers. How could she ever live with herself afterward, knowing she'd sacrificed an entire community of good people just so she survived?

No, she would leave immediately and find a place to hunker down until nightfall so she could begin her journey again. Each day brought her closer and closer to safety, so much so that she could taste the sweetness of victory. But she wasn't arrogant enough to relax her guard no matter how close she was to safety, because such a grave error would get her killed.

An older woman tended the booth, and she was reserved but had an air of welcome and friendliness that put Honor at ease. Careful to not make a mistake in language, she concentrated hard on the words forming in her mind and was extremely conscious not only to ensure that she had the sound of an older woman with a harsher voice but also to hold the accent and render it as flawlessly as she was able.

To her advantage, the entire country had many spoken languages, despite its small size, and many of its people spoke multiple dialects, so as long as she got close to the correct accent and didn't betray her American roots, if the woman detected any subtle differences she would just attribute it to originating from a separate region.

With deference and respect, she told the woman what she required and then pulled out the intricately fashioned decorative piece of jewelry and asked if this would suffice as payment for the food and clothing she asked for.

The woman took the piece from Honor and inspected it closely, turning it over and over to catch all angles in the light. Then she looked back at Honor, honesty reflected in her gaze.

"It is too much for what you ask. Please, choose something else to your liking. This is a most valuable piece."

Honor's gaze flickered to the other offerings the woman had, weighing what she could logically carry with her. The load of an extra outfit would be heavy enough. The food would be inconsequential. But then she remembered she needed a bowl to boil the water from the river and a source of flame to start a fire in case the fluid ran out in the lighter she'd picked up from the clinic. Thank God for the addiction of one of the workers to cigarettes and the fact that he routinely sneaked them during slow periods.

"A bowl," Honor added. "And a flint for making fire. Do you have those things?"

The woman's shrewd gaze swept over Honor, her eyes probing deep as if uncovering every secret hidden within. Her scrutiny made Honor feel uncomfortable and vulnerable, neither a pleasant emotion to endure.

"You look as though you have pain," the woman said matter-of-factly. "With age comes pains and aches we have no control over. Come with me to my home and I'll collect the items you requested, and I will also give you a medicinal paste to apply over the muscles or joints that pain you the most. It will give you relief yet won't impair you in any way. My husband will watch over my display while we are gone."

Paranoia filled Honor. It was as if these people knew exactly who she was and for whatever reason sought to aid her. Okay, so two people didn't constitute everyone, but it was not a coincidence that the only two people she'd come into direct contact with seemed to know her plight—and had offered safe passage.

Though she appreciated the gesture and it brought tears to her eyes to know there was so much good in a world that seemed to be ruled by evil, the very last thing she wanted was for these people to suffer because they not only had not turned her in, but had offered her help and were in effect hiding her.

But to reject the woman's kindness would be an insult of the highest order, so Honor nodded and softly thanked her. The other woman smiled and then motioned to a man who was several yards away speaking to another villager.

They spoke in low tones and at some point her husband looked up at Honor, his eyebrows going up in surprise, and oddly, admiration—respect—flickered through his eyes before it was quickly swept away.

Did *everyone* know who she was? Her panic level was beginning to overwhelm her. She could barely breathe. Only the knowledge that they were out there. Close. Watching and waiting. Hunting. And that innocents could very well be killed were Honor to be discovered, because nothing mattered to these people except their objective. Only knowing that she could be responsible for senseless bloodshed caused her mounting hysteria to be pushed back, and she walked calmly with the woman to one of the small dwellings a short distance from where her booth had been set up.

Once inside, Honor allowed herself to relax just a little. She didn't feel as exposed in here, even though she knew she wasn't safe and that the walls of the small abode only gave the illusion of protection. It would take no strength at all to burst through the closed door in front, so if someone wanted in here, there was nothing to stop them.

The woman quickly and efficiently gathered the items

Honor had requested and then took a goodly amount of a thick paste from a bowl she kept on a shelf and carefully rolled it in layers of breathable cloth, forming a small, compact packet that Honor could easily secrete on her body or simply carry in her bag.

She had carried the items from the booth Honor had requested and helped Honor pack everything in the makeshift bag. After seeing that it was merely a blanket with the ends gathered into a haphazard knot to keep items from escaping, she made a tsking sound and left Honor alone for a moment, returning mere seconds later with a sack that was of sturdier material and had not only a drawstring to close the opening but a strap that could be worn over her shoulder, cross body, so her hands would be free at all times.

Honor looked directly into the woman's eyes, her gaze open and unflinching as her new protector secured the bag over Honor's clothing. She dropped any pretense because it was obvious the woman knew exactly who Honor was. And she had to know why.

"Why are you helping me?" Honor asked softly in the woman's native language. "You risk much to go against an army such as the one hunting me."

Anger blazed in the other woman's eyes and for a moment she was silent before she once more composed herself and the anger subsided after a few moments.

"They are an abomination," she hissed, betraying her outward look of calm. "They do not do Allah's work. They are not Allah's sons. They betray every true believer, those who know the truth. They kill their own kind. They kill those who oppose them. They kill the foreigners who only seek to give aid to our people. They do not do God's work. They do the devil's. They want power and glory and they want to be both revered and feared. And if they aren't stopped, not one single person, Muslim or those who follow any other religion or belief, who doesn't embrace their sinful ways will be spared. They will not stop at the countries and regions they currently occupy and terrorize. Even now, they expand, like a plague, bringing death and destruction to all they touch. They will send loyal servants into the world and we will see a time such as no one has ever seen before. Where no place is safe. No country is safe. The entire world will know what it is like to be here, to be one of us, and live every single day in fear of dying or losing a loved one to senseless, godless violence. And then what will we do? Where will we go? And who will stop them?"

The woman took a breath, her impassioned statement so honest and earnest that the words had spilled forth, that she barely took the time to breathe as she confided her fears—the unvarnished truth—to Honor.

"They have fooled many," the woman admitted. "They act godly. They are well versed in the Qur'an and they are masters at twisting the holy words, making them appear to mean what they do not. Many who follow them truly believe they are doing as Allah wills, that they are serving him and will be richly rewarded for their service.

"And this group operates on fear and hatred," she said in disgust. "Once initiated into the ranks of the group, disobedience or anything that could be construed as disloyalty is considered a crime against Allah and is punishable by death. And it is not quick or merciful."

She shuddered, sorrow touching her eyes as though she had firsthand knowledge of the things she related to Honor.

"They are used as examples in order to keep the others in line. They are praised and their egos stroked for not falling out of line and for proving their absolute dedication to their 'cause.' Those who don't are tortured horribly, and others, the faithful followers, are forced to inflict the torture as a way of hardening them. It's portrayed as an *honor* to be able to aid in taking the life and soul of one who has betrayed them. In the end, when the victim has reached the end of his endurance and death is imminent, he is beheaded at a group gathering and is cursed to hell, his every alleged sin related before everyone. Then and only then is his head cut off and then they *celebrate* . . ."

She broke off again and glanced one more at Honor, this time more than sorrow reflected in her eyes. They were awash with tears and grief. Honor understood such grief. The kind that choked you, threatened to shut you down. The kind that made you numb and almost unfeeling except for that keen sense of loss. And you embraced it because you didn't want to feel anymore. You didn't want to remember.

Unable to hold back, Honor reached across the short distance and laid her hand over the old woman's and squeezed in a gesture of comfort but also solidarity. To let her know she believed as this woman did. That Honor found the things she'd related as abhorrent as the woman had.

"You lost someone to this faction," Honor said quietly.

More tears glittered brightly in the woman's eyes, and for a moment she dropped her gaze as though collecting herself. She placed her other hand atop Honor's so that Honor's hand was now sandwiched between both of hers.

"Yes. A son. He *wasn't* evil. He was misguided. He thought what the group stood for, what they pretend to stand for, was right, and he had a strong sense of honor and he wanted to protect his homeland, his family. He wanted to provide for us so that his father and I would not have to work so hard any longer. By Allah, he did it for us," she said in a stricken, pained voice full of guilt that wasn't hers to bear, but she felt it nonetheless. And again, Honor understood that feeling. She still grappled with survivor's guilt, of being the only one to have lived through the murderous attack on the place where she'd volunteered.

The older woman paused, going quiet, and the silence stretched between the two women. The mother was lost in thought as if in a distant place, lamenting decisions of long ago and likely blaming herself for not being able to stop her son. Her heart went out to this woman. A mother grieving for her son, a woman who despite her strong religious beliefs and her devout spirit felt hatred that at times she felt ashamed of. Honor was sure of it.

"What happened to him?" Honor softly prompted.

The woman took a difficult swallow and then reached for a small cup containing water and sipped to ease the dryness of her mouth and enable her to speak further.

"At first he was devout. The perfect soldier. He climbed the ranks quickly, impressing his superiors with his intellect and the fact that he was an excellent strategist. But the longer he was there, the more he saw, the more he began to understand. He began to question. First himself, because he was still reasoning out in his mind what was wrong when it had felt so right in the beginning.

"But then they grew bolder, more aggressive. Targeting the innocent for no other reason than they *could*. They began to expand their grip on their territory, always greedy and wanting more. Complete domination. They felt invincible, that no nation could stop them. Not even the best military forces in the world. Their plans shifted and they began to think on a much larger scale, bolstered by their many successes. They were remorseless, godless monsters who thought nothing of killing women and children. Unarmed men. Of destroying peaceful villages that had never taken up arms against another and for that matter didn't even possess the weapons to do so. They were conquered effortlessly and every single man, woman and child was executed, the children being killed first, in front of their parents so that they felt the agony of their loss. They went down the line, killing all of the children first while their parents waited an eternity, grieving, hopeless, blaming themselves for not protecting their children. Only when the last child had been slaughtered did they start on the adults, and as with the children, they shot the women first so their husbands had to watch them die. Even worse, many were raped, right in front of their husbands, and there was nothing their husbands could do, no way for them to help. It drove them mad and when it finally came to them, they welcomed death, prayed for it and embraced it because they could no longer live with the horror of having their entire family violated and murdered right in front of their eyes."

"You don't have to continue," Honor whispered, the woman's sorrow so heavy in the room that Honor's chest was clenched and tears burned, threatening to fall. "This hurts you far too much. I don't want to make you relive it all over again."

The woman tried to smile, but all that came of it was a hint of a grimace.

"I relieve it every single night when I go to bed. I relive

it every single rising. I relive it every hour of every day. There *is* no banishing it from my mind."

Honor closed her eyes, long-held-back tears leaking down her cheeks. She would have to rub more henna on her face just in case before she left the woman's dwelling.

"My son was sickened. The truth was revealed to him in a vision from Allah himself. Allah revealed to him the group's true agenda. That they were instruments of evil and not good. Never good. And that my son should leave at once."

She sucked in an unsteady breath, her voice cracking, and she had to swallow back a keen of heartbreaking sorrow.

"He should have just left. Waited for the right opportunity. But he didn't do that. So convinced was he after receiving the word of Allah that what the group stood for was wrong and not in keeping with the teachings of the Qur'an that he confronted the leaders. He told them of his dream and that they must stop or face eternal damnation. They didn't kill him on the spot. Nor did they detain him. They toyed with him. They told him in absolute seriousness that they thanked him for sharing the word of Allah and that he must be a devout man indeed for Allah to have spoken to him and that they would take everything he'd told them into account and gather the members and discuss changes. And they let him go."

The woman glanced at Honor as if judging whether the younger woman believed such a fantastic story. But Honor stared back at her in earnest, absorbing every word. Still, the woman must have felt she needed to back up her wild claims.

"If you wonder how I could possibly know of such things in a group that is so secretive, my son kept a journal of every detail of his experience as a member of A New Era. He had it sent to me right after he confronted the leaders. Maybe he knew what was going to happen. Maybe he sensed they were lying and wanted someone to know what they truly are. And as for my knowing what happened after—the last journal entry was of his confrontation with the leaders—one of his friends in the organization, one who like my son, didn't like the actions of the group, came to me and told me what they did to my son."

This time, the mournful sound poured from the woman's mouth, soaring from the very depths of her soul. Tears ran freely down her face and her features were so stricken with grief that Honor couldn't even look at her without responding in kind, without remembering the horror of that day when every one of her friends and coworkers had been killed. She knew exactly how this woman felt. They were bound by a bond that no two people should ever have to share.

"They came in the middle of the night. My son had packed his belongings and had planned to leave at dawn to come home to me and his father. They pulled him from his bed and dragged him outside where all the others were already gathered. They gagged him so he couldn't speak, couldn't defend himself, couldn't denounce the organization and their agenda and possibly strike a chord with other followers.

"They told the others that he was a traitor to his brethren. That he'd committed an unpardonable sin by giving their location to an opposing military faction. He'd been bought off and had betrayed every single one of his brothers for money. He was an abomination not only to Allah but to their cause—Allah's cause. By the time they were finished denouncing him, the others were only too happy to participate in his torture. They were angry—furious—that he could do such a thing. They called him evil. Possessed by evil spirits.

"They tortured him endlessly for an entire week," the woman whispered, tears still spilling in endless trails down her cheeks. "And in this instance, they didn't behead him at the very end just before he'd die on his own as is their custom. They said that a traitor such as he didn't deserve the mercy of a quick and painless death. He was left there to slowly succumb to the torture they'd inflicted on him. He had no food or water in all that time. It took three more days!"

The woman put a fist to her mouth, biting down hard, her grief a terrible, tangible thing in the tiny dwelling. Honor couldn't help it. It was her nature to comfort others. To help them. No matter the cost to her. It was why even now she was fleeing for her life. Because she'd chosen a dangerous place to render aid. But it was also the area that was most in need because so many others didn't dare come here to help.

Honor wrapped her arms around the other woman and simply held on as they both shed tears for so many horrible, senseless deaths.

"I am sorry for your loss," Honor whispered next to the woman's ear. "He sounded like a good man and not at all like the mindless puppets these monsters command who embrace the promise of riches and power. He tried to right the wrongs. He is safe with Allah now. You must know that."

The woman pulled back a wan smile. She wiped at the tears with the back of her hand, and it shook as she lowered it to her lap once more.

"Thank you for saying that. I admit at times I've feared for his soul. I've prayed that he finds peace in the arms of Allah. But yes, he was a good man." Her chin notched upward, her gaze more determined. "When he learned of the true goals of A New Era, he fought back. And I admire him for that. But in my heart I wish he'd simply walked away."

Honor nodded her understanding. Knowing her time was limited and that the man collecting water for her was likely searching for her, she leaned forward to take the woman's hand again.

"Thank you for your aid. I can never hope to repay such kindness. But I must go now. A man who escorted me into the village and who is getting me water from the river said that the group is here, in the village. At least some of them. They surround it and even mingle at the market. Looking for me. I must find a way to leave undetected and without drawing suspicion. And then I must find a place to rest. I sleep by day and journey by night to lessen my chances of detection, but this morning I had to come into the village to get more supplies. I was nearly out, and was completely out of water."

The woman's eyes gleamed a moment and the first true semblance of a smile lit her face.

"You will stay here," she said triumphantly, as though she'd just solved an enormous dilemma.

Alarm took hold of Honor and she shook her head automatically. "No. Absolutely not. I won't endanger you and your husband—or the rest of the villagers—that way. It's best if I leave this place as quickly as possible so I draw attention away from you and the rest. You've been so kind and I will not repay such kindness by getting you killed for harboring someone they hunt for."

The woman's smile didn't falter. "They will not find you here. Even if they come inside to search."

Her expression was smug and more importantly confident. There was no hesitation, no fake confidence to falsely reassure Honor.

Honor looked at her in puzzlement. "How is that so?"

"Years ago when the fighting was so bad in this area, we feared we would be bombed on a daily basis. The attacks would only come at night. They were too cowardly to face their victims during the day. So my husband dug a shelter underneath the flooring of our home. It's deep and wide enough to fit two people. It's where we slept every night when we had the threat of bombing looming over us for months. You can go get your water and bring it here. I'll boil it to cleanse it while you sleep. When night falls I'll awaken you and you can be on your way once more with Allah's blessing."

"And what will your husband think?" Honor asked quietly.

"Any victory over this abomination calling themselves messengers of God and instruments of his will only pleases my husband. And he would never turn his back on a young woman in so much need. They will not find you. My husband made the opening in the floor undetectable. Those animals could be standing right on top of you and they'd never know. You need the rest and you need your wounds tended to. Allow me to do this small thing. I couldn't help my son, but I *can* help you."

"I don't know how to thank you," Honor said tearfully, relief falling over her like a cleansing rain.

This time the woman reached for Honor's hand and gripped it firmly in a clear gesture of solidarity. Determination passed from the woman into Honor. She could feel it.

Could feel the woman's resolve not only to help Honor but for Honor to escape and to live.

"You can thank me by living," the woman said simply. "Know this, Honor Cambridge. You have many who are praying for your safe passage and many who would aid you in any way, but you cannot afford to trust anyone, because just as there are many praying that you reach safety, there are also many who wouldn't hesitate to betray you for the riches that have been promised to the person who finds you."

Honor looked at her in utter shock. The woman knew her name. Her name had been distributed widely.

The woman smiled. "You have become somewhat of a legend in the span of a few days. Word of your escape from the militants has passed from village to village, all in awe not only that one lone American woman was able to escape the vicious attack on your relief center but also that you've managed to evade capture for over a week. You have become a beacon of hope to our people. Proof that A New Era isn't as invincible as they proclaim, as their reputation suggests. It is why you must pay heed to my caution and trust no one. You are a source of great embarrassment to the militants because while they wield much power and are feared widely, they have been unable to find you. Their rage is great and they grow angrier and more impatient by the day."

"I'm no one special," Honor managed to croak out around her astonishment. "I'm just an average, normal woman who wants very much to make it back home."

"You will," the woman said fiercely. "If anyone can accomplish this feat, it is you. You've made it this far, and you won't fail now."

CHAPTER 6

AN urgent voice intruded into the vast nothingness of Honor's mind, disturbing her deep, dreamless, restoring sleep. Despite desperately wanting to remain in the safe cocoon she'd rested in for the last hours, fear and readiness were too ingrained in her not to respond.

Her eyes flew open, seeking the source of the call, and she saw her protector standing anxiously on the bottom step leading down into the shelter her husband had constructed.

"I am sorry to wake you so early, but there is need of you to get ready and depart while the sun is still high in the sky."

The worry in her voice roused Honor, and she scrambled up, gathering her bag and straightening the new garment she'd purchased earlier. She'd put the headdress on once she was above ground level so she could touch up any areas needing more dye.

"What has happened?" Honor demanded even as she followed the woman up the stairs.

Waiting at the top was the woman's husband, who wore a grim expression.

"Sit," the woman urged. "I'll work more dye onto your face and in your hair. You can listen as I work. And I have an idea you may be opposed to, but I think given the circumstances it would be the perfect form of disguise to get you safely past the assassins."

Honor immediately complied, dread pitting deep in her stomach, causing a knot to form, but also intrigued by the idea the woman spoke of. So she settled down into one of the hand-carved chairs, curling her fingers together in her lap so as not to betray how badly she was shaking.

It was the husband who spoke first.

"The outcasts are here, and it was heard that they plan to stay in the area past sunset as it is known you travel exclusively by night. There is a group of people here for the market who came from the north, the direction in which you travel. You need to leave with them while it's still light. You'll blend in and the militants won't be looking for a woman traveling with others when she's strictly been solitary until now. It's your best—and only—chance. If you leave at night, they'll capture you for certain. And if you don't appear this night, they'll search the village and those harboring you will be killed instantly."

Honor looked to the couple in horror over the danger she'd put them in. She'd acknowledged that they risked much in helping her, and realistically she knew from the beginning just how much they risked, but hearing it said so matter-of-factly rattled her to the core. She didn't want these people to die because of their kindness to a complete stranger.

"And this is where my idea comes in," the woman interjected, as if sensing Honor's rising panic. "They won't be expecting to see you traveling during the day, accompanied by others, but they could possibly be tipped off to your disguise as an older lady hunched with age and a shuffling walk."

Nerves attacked Honor, instantly increasing the dread already present in the pit of her stomach. The taste of hopelessness and impending failure was bitter in her mouth. To have come so far, to have come so close, just a few days from the border into a safer zone with a U.S. presence, a place A New Era hadn't yet dared to encroach on, and be captured with freedom in sight. It was more than she could bear. She lifted a knotted fist to her mouth, determined not to show the depth of her despair to these courageous people. She felt it dishonored them when they'd shown so much of what she now lacked.

"Just listen to me," the woman said soothingly. "I think you'll agree this is a good idea. We will redarken your face and hair but smooth the lines in your face, making you appear younger. We will remove the padding that makes you appear larger, and though it may be painful given the injury to your knee, you must walk normally, as if you are unhurt. I'll apply the salve to your knee and other areas that pain you so you'll receive temporary relief.

"And there are men in the group, one who will act as your husband and walk just ahead of you as is customary. All of these factors—these changes—combined will throw those who wait for the old lady traveling under the veil of night off course. I believe you won't even draw their notice because they won't be looking for what you are. A young woman, in a more vibrant, younger woman's manner of dress, traveling with a group of people—family—in the daylight hours."

"I believe it is your only chance," the husband said in a resolute voice.

The absolute certainty in the husband's tone overrode any fear Honor had of venturing into the daylight. She pondered the woman's wisdom, and her idea had merit. She would, in fact, be the reverse of all intel A New Era had on her. They might not fall for it ever again, but if she didn't get past them this time, there wouldn't be a next time to worry over anyway. She had to take it one step at a time. Avoid one trap at a time. And as the husband had said, it *was* her only chance. Her only choice. She had to do this, because if she was discovered leaving under the shield of dark, the militants would know that someone in the village had given her sanctuary, and they would retaliate by murdering every single man, woman and child. The thought sickened her. These people had been kind to her, risking their lives to help her, and she'd be damned if they were repaid with violence.

She simply nodded her agreement as the woman first

thoroughly cleaned Honor's face, removing the embedded dirt and debris disguised by the dye to make her look older, with age-weathered skin. Then, with great care, she rubbed the dye into Honor's skin and then began reapplying it to her hair so that the natural blond was nearly black. She redarkened Honor's eyebrows, which were already brown, but a light brown color, in contrast to the honey blond of her hair. Honor, not wanting to take any chances, had dyed them the first time she'd used henna to cement her disguise.

Next she gently applied a thick layer of the odorless paste to Honor's swollen knee, whispering a prayer as she worked. Tears burned the edges of Honor's eyes because the woman prayed in the language of religion. Arabic. And she was asking for Allah's blessing and for his hand to guide her path to freedom.

When she'd meticulously applied the medicinal concoction to the many other scrapes and bruises, she instructed Honor to hold out her hands and then carefully went over each finger and rubbed the dye into the lines and cracks in her skin. Then she did the same to Honor's feet, but then she produced a pair of shoes, the kind the natives wore, soft and comfortable, but the woman assured her they were sturdy and would withstand the amount of walking Honor had to do.

"The shoes you wore are a giveaway," the woman patiently explained. "Not shoes a woman here would wear. Fortunately no one has seen them or they would have been noticed. But with you now wearing a different garment and shoes of a native, and the fact that you're departing well before the sun sets, you should have no difficulty in getting way beyond the village. There are no reports of anyone departing the market in any direction being stopped and searched or questioned. By all accounts, the snakes are just lying in the grass and waiting for you to magically appear in front of them. One would think they would have learned by now not to underestimate you, but their arrogance is too much for that. They think they have the advantage now because they know your habits and your patterns, and so they've set a trap and are waiting for you to fall neatly into it."

"I have you—both of you," she added to include the husband, "to thank for my not falling into their trap because that is precisely what I would have done had you not warned—and aided—me."

"Come, come now," the woman said, producing the garments for Honor to wear out of the village. "They wait at one of the booths, pretending interest until you arrive. You must hurry, though. We don't want to do anything that will arouse suspicion."

Honor put it into high gear and within minutes she was dressed appropriately, the strap of her bag secured cross body and a new hijab and robe folded carefully over her arm. She walked briskly to the door, testing the strength of her knee now that she was to walk normally. It protested the quicker movements and more weight being borne on the leg, but it was much more bearable than before, probably due to the woman's doctoring. But most importantly, she could maintain a normal pace without giving away her injury. It pained her, yes. But it had subsided to a dull ache and sheer determination would make it impossible for her to falter. At the door, she paused and turned back, needing to at least try to put into words her overwhelming gratitude.

"Thank you," she said. "You risked much for a stranger. I'll never be able to repay my debt to you."

"May Allah be with you on your journey," the husband said in a solemn voice. "We will pray daily for you."

"And I you," Honor vowed in return. "Allah be with your family always. I will never forget you. You will forever remain in my prayers."

"Good journey," the woman said as Honor opened the door and stepped into the sunlight.

The woman had directed her to which group to blend in with and she walked toward them, carrying her market purchases, but before she reached them, her way was suddenly blocked by a large, looming man. Her pulse leapt and her fight-or-flight reflexes screamed at her to be set free. It took every ounce of discipline she possessed to lower her head in subservience and murmur an apology in the local dialect.

"Very impressive, Honor. Doing the unexpected. Now I

understand why you've been able to evade capture for so long. And your accent is flawless. I wonder. How many of the languages in this region do you speak?"

The American accent, a hint of the south, a drawl so subtle it nearly wasn't audible. But she had an affinity for languages and accents, and her ears were sensitive to subtle nuances others would likely be unaware of. But he too obviously had a talent for languages or at least the one she'd spoken to him since he'd been aware that he could detect no accent, and he'd been looking for one.

Her pulse leapt again, this time thundering like a tornado through her veins but for a different reason altogether. He was American. He knew her name. Was he here to rescue her? Had news of her survival and of the militant group turning the earth over in search of her reached the public? Had he been sent to extract her? And if so, why hadn't he simply identified himself and stated his objective? Had he been concerned that her relief would give them away? That she'd become a hysterical, shrill twit and attract the focus of everyone in the entire village? Something about this— him—just didn't feel right.

Trust no one.

The woman's words filtered through her mind, dimming her excitement, and she forced herself to act indifferent, puzzled even, as though she didn't understand the language he spoke. Daringly, she turned her head up, meeting his gaze, forcing hers into one of confusion.

She cocked her head and shook it slightly, frowning even as she said in the local dialect, "I'm sorry. I don't understand. I don't spcak your language."

A glint of amusement briefly flickered in his eyes before his gaze hardened and his expression became equally hard—and gravely serious.

He wore the clothing of a native and yet there was no attempt on his part to hide what he was. Caucasian. Perhaps the reason he didn't show fear was that he was protected by his membership in a terrorist organization.

"I don't have time to play games. You don't have the time to waste. You were probably told that the men hunting you are waiting until dark, when you are normally on the move and that they will be looking for an older woman with a slow, shuffling gait and that they aren't checking those leaving the village. But that's untrue. They've set a perimeter well beyond the outskirts of the village so it doesn't appear that anyone is being investigated, but in fact, they've stopped every single person departing since the market opened and they are not simply waiting around for dark for you to fall into their hands. And despite the clever change in disguise and doing the unexpected, it will do you no good. They will stop your entire group and search each of you thoroughly and when it's discovered you are with this group preparing to depart, they'll slaughter every single one of them and they'll take you—alive—and into your worst nightmare."

The iron will that had kept Honor alive and moving since the day of the attack crumbled and lay in ruins around her, and she knew stark fear shone brightly in her eyes, giving herself completely away to a man whose agenda she was ignorant of. She didn't know if he was friend or foe. And it was obvious he knew a damn lot about *her*, which put her at a distinct disadvantage because she didn't have the first clue who *he* was. Only that he was American, which should have relieved her, but there was something in that rock-hard face, the ruthlessness she could see lurking in the shadows of his eyes. At this moment she didn't know whom she feared more, the American or the militants lying in wait for her.

"Why are you telling me this?" she asked bluntly in English as she stared directly into his gaze, trying to pick up on any tell, any indication of his intentions.

But he remained devoid of emotion, his expression utterly inscrutable. He gave nothing of himself away, which frustrated Honor. Everyone gave up something. It was always there for a trained eye to see. But this man was impossible to read, as though he'd had years to perfect a facade that no one could penetrate.

He could be military. She hoped with all she had that he was U.S. military and that his hard shell was a result of his training and experience in a region of the world where bloodshed was more common than running water.

"Because I'm going to take you with me so you aren't captured by the men who won't stop until they've captured their prey."

She studied him for another long moment. "So you've come to rescue me? Who are you? Who sent you?"

He arched one eyebrow, clearly surprised by her resistance. Perhaps he'd expected her to fall into his arms, sobbing hysterically, thinking him her savior. But she hadn't stayed alive as long as she had by blindly believing *anything*. Or taking anything at face value. And she couldn't afford to start now. Not when she was so close to her ultimate goal of finding her way home.

"Does it matter?" he asked mildly. "All you need to know is that my men and I will get you out of the country and out of A New Era's reach. Or would you prefer to take your chances with your group of protectors and lead them blindly to certain death?"

Honor bit into her lip, deeply conflicted. Why *wasn't* she happier to see him? Why *wasn't* she falling into his arms, relieved and grateful? Was that not why she was so desperate to cross the border into a country where there was an American presence? And that presence had just planted itself in her path, offering her safe passage. Perhaps it was because it had been too easy, too convenient, the timing either impeccable or coincidental. And she wasn't a believer in coincidences. Especially when it came to her life.

"If they're searching everyone leaving the village and if they have, as you say, a perimeter set up encompassing all routes leading out of the village, then how do you and your men possibly think *you* will be able to get past their roadblocks, impervious to the very thing you've sworn will happen if I leave the village with a group of people? Aren't you a group of people just the same?"

White teeth flashed and she was reminded of a predator's teeth set in a snarl as they closed in on their prey. A shiver of apprehension skated down her spine and she absently rubbed at one arm through the heavy material of her garment.

"I plan to drive right past them."

Honor went rigid with fear. The people who'd awaited

her were clearly uneasy and were inching away, clearly wanting to be out of this place. And to be rid of her. They well knew what they risked by allowing her to travel with them, and now, with the arrival of this ominous-looking stranger, they were even more nervous. She couldn't blame them. And neither could she consign them to certain death. She couldn't take the chance that this man wasn't telling her the absolute truth. She would not be responsible for these people's deaths.

She waved them off, making that sudden decision when it became clear that they knew she was a death trap. The American was right. She wouldn't simply lead her supposed saviors meekly to the slaughter when it gave her absolutely no chance of escape. He, on the other hand, was offering one, and his arrogance suggested he actually thought—knew—*he* would be successful.

It came down to the lesser of two evils. One known and one unknown. She knew what fate awaited her at the hands of the savages who hunted her. She didn't know what the American's intentions were, but given that her only other option was certain torture, endless agony and death, it made the decision to go with the unknown the only logical choice.

"You've made your decision. Now move it," he said, no gentleness to his voice.

Somehow she'd imagined her rescue a little different. Perhaps at the hands of American soldiers who would at least acknowledge her as a sister, inquire as to her health. Not taunt her into making a decision. For that matter, shouldn't he have identified himself as a member of the U.S. military? Shouldn't he have identified himself, period?

She frowned. The military didn't just order people around for their own good, did they? But then she supposed that was exactly what they did on a daily basis when rescuing captives or hostages. Time was critical, and following orders was essential to their survival.

"What branch of the military do you serve and where are your dog tags?" she blurted, even as she stumbled along beside him, attempting to match his much longer stride.

She bit into her lip to quell the sound of pain as her knee

protested the vigorous motion it was unused to. It was silly, but she didn't want to show weakness in front of this warrior. And he clearly was a warrior. She wanted to show only strength, give him no reason to fault her, and she'd be damned if she'd slow him down.

Again his teeth flashed, but in no way was it in a smile. Quite frankly, he scared her every time he did it. He reminded her too much of the big bad wolf about to devour Little Red Riding Hood, only in Honor's case, she'd been wandering through the desert, not the forest, and there were no wolves here. But there were plenty of demons. Spawns of Satan himself. Evil ran strong here, stained with the blood of the innocents.

"It's a little late to be asking me for ID now," he said mildly.

He arrived at a military-looking vehicle and for the first time her blood pulsed wildly with excitement. It looked American, and while that might sound like a stupid thought from a clueless civilian, she'd worked throughout this region for a good while and she'd come into contact with all manner of military equipment and vehicles. She'd quickly learned to recognize friend or foe by subtle things maybe others wouldn't notice. But when your life depended on *knowing*, and assuming would get you killed faster than a stray bullet in a fight zone, you tended to fast become an expert on learning the differences between those who would kill you and those who would save you.

He all but shoved her into the back and slid in beside her, slamming his door closed while she struggled to right herself from where her head had plunged toward the floorboard and the heavy material covered her and twisted around her, preventing her from gracefully extricating herself. Then the vehicle lurched into motion, flattening her once more. Frustrated and angry with the lack of care her "rescuer" had offered thus far, she planted her hands on the floorboard and attempted to push herself upward and out of the tangle of material effectively trapping her legs and obscuring her vision.

To her shock, he planted a firm hand in the middle of her

back and shoved her even farther down onto the floor. Another man already seated in the back of the utility vehicle pushed her head underneath his legs, but he used care that the first man forwent.

When she would have protested, a hand circled her nape and fingers tightened around the slim column of her neck in warning. And though she'd been acquainted with the man who'd intercepted her in the village for merely a few minutes, she knew it was his hand on her neck, not that of the second who'd helped pushed her to the floorboard.

He squeezed once more and then, in direct contradiction to the brute strength of his grasp and seeming disregard for whether he hurt or scared her, he rubbed his thumb up and down the line just below her ear in a soothing manner, even as his grip remained tight.

"Do *not* move," the man ordered.

Material similar to the aid blankets they stocked at the relief center fell over her, blocking the light and encasing her in darkness. But it was too heavy to be one of the simple blankets handed out in relief packets. This was more of a utility blanket, or canvas perhaps. It was hard to make out the feel and texture when she was already swathed in a pool of her own garment.

The heat was suffocating. Sweat moistened the roots of her hair and bathed her forehead. It felt as though she were slowly baking in an oven. Even the air she inhaled was scorching, made stuffy by the heavy blankets covering her, giving her little space to breathe.

Her mind was ablaze with confusion. Had she merely traded one form of hell for another? Made a bargain for her life when both outcomes would result in her death?

The vehicle moved far too fast over the bumpy terrain, and Honor felt every single one of those bumps. The hand still wrapped around her nape remained firm though the American's thumb continued its idle, soothing, up-and-down motion. So she focused on that one simple comfort when she'd been denied comfort for so long and blocked out the battering her already bruised and sore body was taking.

She sensed the decreased speed the moment the vehicle

slowed and she went rigid, holding her breath, knowing they hadn't gone far. Were they being stopped? He'd very arrogantly stated that he planned to drive right by the roadblocks, and something in his voice had given her faith that he'd be able to do just that.

Very real fear took hold, paralyzing her. She didn't realize that she had begun shaking and still hadn't drawn a breath until the grip around her neck loosened and his fingers stroked through her hair beneath the layers of material covering her.

"Hold it together, Honor," he said.

For the first time she heard gentleness in his voice, felt it in his touch. It made her want to break down and sob. So maybe she needed him to be a ruthless asshole. As long as she stayed pissed, she remained focused and didn't risk falling apart at the seams.

"I need you to calm yourself." This time his voice was more authoritative, all hints of gentleness gone. "You're shaking like a leaf and the blankets are jumping around like they cover a litter of squirming puppies."

Her chest burned and she latched on to his command, willing herself to obey.

"Breathe," he said harshly. "Goddamn it, breathe or pass out. But pull yourself together. You aren't out of the woods yet, and now is not the time to let yourself go."

Honor heard other muttered curses, and she could swear she heard someone say, "Bad mojo." Maybe she was finally losing her weakening grip on her sanity.

The American tightened his grip around her nape as he'd done before and shook her, though not hard enough to hurt. Just enough to get her attention. And it did the job.

"I'm okay," she whispered.

Sweet, healing air flowed into oxygen-starved lungs. Her body relaxed and the burn subsided as she went limp on the floorboard of the now-stopped vehicle.

"Thank fuck," the American muttered, loosening his grip and then withdrawing his hand from beneath the blankets entirely.

As absurd as the sensation was, she felt bereft and cold

the minute the warmth of his flesh left hers. She clamped her jaw shut and kept it so tight that pain rushed her, but she did so to prevent her teeth from chattering.

It humiliated her that she'd fallen apart and acted like a complete nitwit in front of these men. It didn't matter if they were ally or enemy. Just as she refused to ever be in a position of begging the assassins who hunted her to kill her and end her endless misery, pride also stiffened her spine when it came to these men. She was acting like a helpless heroine in a dramatic novel where the female's sole objective was to highlight the manly alpha male's heroic ability to save her useless ass time and time again.

She'd come this far—for so many days—on her own, relying on no one but herself and her determination to survive. She mentally chastised herself and firmed up her resolve to not show such weakness in front of these men, regardless of who they were, ever again.

A thousand questions burned her lips. She wanted to demand answers. It took all her discipline not to interrogate her "savior" and ask him what the hell his plan was and what he planned to do with her. Because she wasn't entirely certain that he was one of the good guys, despite *knowing* the bastards gunning for her weren't the good guys.

Quiet descended over the interior of the vehicle, and she heard the sound of a window sliding downward. She closed her eyes and remained limp, pushing her thoughts into a blank void of nothingness. Calm was the only thing that would save her, and so she simply did as she must and drew it around her like one of the soft quilts her mother created for her loved ones.

She allowed herself to drift into those happier memories, pulled images of her parents, her brothers and her sister into her mind and surrounded herself with their love. It allowed her to float free of her current circumstances, the danger cloaking her like a dense fog, and remain still and serene, blocking everything but the smiling faces of her loved ones.

So ensconced was she in her alternate reality that she didn't register the vehicle lurching into motion again. It wasn't until the American's hand delved beneath the blanket, lifting it, and then his fingers slid over her chin, turning it so she was angled to partially face him, that she realized they had resumed traveling.

"Honor?"

The one-word question conveyed it all. He was asking if she was all right. If she was still with them in the mental realm or if she'd lost the battle for her sanity and retreated deep into herself.

"Who are you?" she asked hoarsely.

CHAPTER 7

HANCOCK'S gaze flickered dispassionately at the stubborn, courageous woman with grudging admiration he didn't allow to show. He didn't want to feel anything with regard to a woman who was nothing more than a pawn. A means to an end. A tool he would use like any other intel or weapon in order to take down a man who'd caused more casualties than most wars, and he'd suffer no remorse whatsoever.

It wasn't in his nature to underestimate anyone or any situation, and yet he could admit that he'd underestimated Honor Cambridge and her resourcefulness. At first but not any longer.

When he'd left Bristow, the cowardly bastard was pissed because Hancock had left none of his men behind for his protection, leaving him to rely solely on the other lackeys he called his security. But Hancock had fully expected to apprehend his quarry and be back in a short amount of time. Instead, he'd spent days combing through villages, questioning the locals and keeping his ear to the ground as rumors had started to whisper on the winds of a lone woman who'd eluded a vicious terrorist organization for over a week.

Over time, the gossip had become less secretive and a legend had arisen, a beacon of hope and a symbol of courage. She had become iconic to the vulnerable and oppressed people who lived without hope, in fear of A New Era and their unpredictable savagery. There was no rhyme or reason to their vengeance. No one foolishly thought themselves safe or beyond the reach of the militant group that had ballooned into a monstrous, gluttonous leech, drinking more blood and craving more power. It was a hell of a way to live, knowing that each day could be the day they appeared in the crosshairs of the group and were dispassionately murdered with no regard whatsoever.

It was through the stories of her survival and escape retold, the reverence and respect already ingrained within their hearts—their pride in one fierce American warrior woman, as they'd labeled her—that Hancock felt as though he'd truly gotten to know the real Honor Cambridge. No longer was he guided by the sterile, peripheral intel he'd been provided giving him a rundown of her life, her training and how long she'd tirelessly and selflessly devoted herself to the needs of others in an area few would dare to venture into. The true heart of her and her motivation had been revealed to him by those who knew her, or knew of her. She was believed by many to be an angel sent from Allah. A courageous angel of vengeance who fearlessly ventured into places avoided by most sane people, who simply didn't care about the horrific suffering of those who lived their entire lives here and certainly wouldn't risk their lives to offer compassion and try to make their lives a little easier. To give them a single moment of peace when such a thing was alien and unknown to them.

Hell, even the U.S. military stayed out of the areas A New Era had a foothold in, not wanting to start a bloody war and sacrifice countless American soldiers in a battle that could never be won. If they weren't able to rid the world of the ever-growing army, they would fail. If they annihilated the lot of them, the terrorists would be held up as martyrs, inspiring others to revenge, which would give them victory even from the grave.

It was inevitable, of course. When the fanatical group felt they were powerful enough to turn their focus on U.S. holdings—and it was only a matter of time—then the United

States would have no choice but to retaliate. And it wouldn't be an easy or swift war. It would be fought over years with no clear victor ever being declared no matter what propaganda was circulated.

He'd expected Honor to be a terrified damsel in distress, throwing herself hysterically into his protection once she discovered he was American and that he was getting her out of the country. And she *had* been afraid. No sane person wouldn't be in her situation. But she'd kept it together and had refused to give in to the overwhelming panic and despair she had to be feeling.

She was hurt and exhausted. He'd seen the remains of the relief center and he was astounded that she'd survived, much less been able to flee and remain one step ahead of ruthless killers hunting her for days—a group that had endless resources and whose reach extended well beyond the borders of this country.

This was a tough woman. A fighter. He could feel regret that one such as she would have to be sacrificed for the greater good, but not so much that it would deter him from his ultimate goal of bringing Maksimov down. And now, seeing the horrific trail of death and terror that followed A New Era's every move, Hancock knew that he couldn't stop at just Maksimov, as he'd decided some time ago. This group had to be dismantled. Destroyed before their power became such that they were unstoppable.

He inwardly grimaced because he wasn't a liar, and he *hadn't* lied to her in so many words. Only because he hadn't offered her much in the way of words at all. He couldn't see her as human. An innocent. Someone who deserved saving because her life meant something and the world would lose one of the good. Because if he allowed himself those dangerous emotions, they'd interfere with vengeance for hundreds of thousands who had no other to carry out justice for them. Not to mention the ones who would follow. Who hadn't yet fallen victim to the brand of violence Maksimov sold—and inspired—on a daily basis. *Those* were the faceless people he allowed to infiltrate his conscience and take permanent root. Not a single woman—a martyr to his cause.

He wouldn't turn his back on the masses when so many others had—and would continue to do so.

He hadn't promised this woman ultimate salvation or even that he'd get her safely home. All he'd told her was one simple truth. That he wasn't going to allow her to be captured by A New Era. He'd said nothing further, leaving her to decipher what she would of the one promise he *had* made her. A promise he would absolutely keep. Or die trying.

And when the time came to . . . betray . . . her, he wouldn't lie to her then either. He had to prevent the scowl from forming on his face at the idea that he was betraying *anyone*. It wasn't betrayal to save the majority at the cost of one single person, woman or man. That kind of thinking was what had fucked up the last two opportunities he'd had to take Maksimov out for good, and he'd be damned if it would happen again. He wasn't a goddamn hero. He was the face and bringer of justice. Nothing more.

She would know that her fate meant something, though. That her life meant something—everything. Whether it gave her solace or not, he couldn't control, but he wouldn't allow her to think that her death was yet another senseless, meaningless statistic. And he would, as tribute to her bravery and sacrifice, send word to her family, letting them know their daughter, their sister, hadn't died for nothing. She would, if Hancock's plan was executed and carried out successfully, save too many innocent lives to count.

When Honor still looked expectantly at him, her eyes narrowing at his prolonged silence, he remembered that she'd asked, or rather demanded, to know *who* he was. He supposed she deserved that at least. And it would give credence to the idea that he and his men had been sent to extricate her, though he wouldn't actively cultivate that lie. What conclusions she drew were of her own making.

"I'm Hancock," he said simply. "And the men surrounding you are my team. They're highly skilled. The best. They won't let any harm come to you as we journey to a safer place."

Her eyes narrowed in suspicion as she studied him intently. She didn't like his vagueness, and furthermore she knew he was holding something back. In addition to being tenacious and extremely courageous, she had a sharp, intelligent mind and she was adept at reading people.

He sighed inwardly. It was never easy. He wanted to have no respect or admiration for this woman. He didn't want to feel anything at all. It would have been far better if she had been a hysterical, mindless, incompetent twit. He could summon disdain and annoyance for such a person. But he respected a fighting spirit. Bravery in the face of overwhelming terror. And the refusal to back down even when confronting insurmountable obstacles. These were traits he not only admired but had actively cultivated in all the men serving him. It had been ingrained in him, first by his foster parents, and later by the man who'd been Titan's first leader. Rio. The man who'd trained Hancock and taught him the necessary skills to be the ultimate fighting—and thinking—machine. Because battles were won not by brute force alone, but by strategy and the ability to correctly assess the enemy. By pushing detrimental emotion aside and feeling nothing at all. By becoming more machine than man.

"Just where is this 'safe place'?" she asked suspiciously.

"I'll let you know when we get there."

Again, a truth. Because they were winging it and with Honor once more slipping beyond A New Era's grasp, the terrorists would be more enraged than ever. They'd thought that victory was finally theirs after tracking her to the village and surrounding it, lying in wait to apprehend her.

As unpredictable as they were, and with the true extent of their reach and many of their allies secret and as of yet unknown, Hancock wasn't fool enough to think that because he'd gotten Honor safely from the village, it would be a simple matter of leaving the area. Her pursuers would know she had help, and they'd put two and two together and realize that Hancock and his men were the only logical source of that aid. It would take only minimal investigation to realize that Hancock and his men weren't who they'd appeared to be—members of A New Era contributing to the search for the American woman. They were now targets just as Honor was.

"How far is this journey to this place you'll let me know when we get to?"

She was sounding more pissed by the minute, and edgy sarcasm laced her every word.

He reached down and pulled her carefully onto the seat between him and Mojo. She likely hadn't gotten a good look at the member of his team on her other side or she would have been scared out of her mind.

Mojo was . . . He was the epitome of what Titan had sought and wanted to create at its inception. Already battle hardened and suffering what the shrinks all called post-traumatic stress disorder, he was an unfeeling, fighting machine. He rarely spoke. His moniker had been given to him because his trademark comment for everything was either "Good mojo" or "Bad mojo." Given their line of work, it was rare they'd ever heard "Good mojo."

He was big and scary-looking, mostly bald with a light layer of bristly short-cropped hair. It was only close up that you could even see he had hair. Scars lined his face and his nose had been broken numerous times. His eyes were flat and cold, the kind that made religious people cross themselves and utter a quick prayer.

But no, she'd obviously gotten a look at him already because she glared up at him, not a hint of fear or revulsion in her features as Mojo helped pull her up between him and Hancock.

"*Now* you want to help me," she muttered.

To Hancock's astonishment, Mojo almost smiled. Almost. It was the closest the man had ever come to anything remotely resembling a smile.

His teeth flashed. "Good mojo."

"Whatever," Honor said under her breath. "Hey!" she said, slapping at Hancock's hand when it delved underneath her robe. He slid his palm up her leg, pushing the material with it. "What are you doing?"

"I need to take a look at your injury," Hancock said, ignoring her indignation.

"You're just avoiding my question," she accused.

"What question would that be?" he asked in the same disinterested tone that suggested she was an inconvenience.

"All of them?" she snapped. "But we'll start with how long will it take to get to this mysterious place you're taking me?"

Her tone was frigid, but her eyes flashed and he realized that the few photos he'd been provided of her hadn't accurately portrayed her true character any more than the rundown of her personal data.

She looked sweet, innocent, benign and meek in the photos. Like a naïve do-gooder with the idea she was going to save the world but who had no idea of the reality of the situations she put herself in.

But in reality, she was anything but sweet or meek. There was a seething cauldron of fire simmering just below the naïve-looking features. And her will was strong, as evidenced by the fact that after surviving the attack, she'd run, and not recklessly with no plan or intelligence. She was cool under pressure, and she thought quick on her feet. It wouldn't do for Hancock to ever relax his guard around her. If he gave her too much of a reason to distrust him and his intentions—as she had every reason to—she wouldn't hesitate to bolt, and he didn't have time to spend another week running her to ground. This time he might not get to her before A New Era did.

"A few days. Maybe more. Maybe less."

He shrugged as if it didn't matter and he was confident he'd get her there regardless of the time it took. He needed her to believe him. In him. But he would never encourage her to *trust* him.

Honor's eyes widened in confusion. She even glanced at Mojo as if seeking confirmation, and then she made a sound of disgust as if realizing how ridiculous it was to try to read anything from the other man's expression.

"You don't have a helicopter? Like a badass helicopter? What kind of military unit sent to rescue a . . ." She rubbed a hand through her dye-caked hair in agitation. "What am I even? Not a hostage exactly. A missing person? But does anyone even know I'm still alive? That I survived the bombing?"

Pain flashed in her eyes. Not the physical kind, but emotional pain, as if thinking of her family and the grief they must be enduring not knowing if she was alive or dead, if she was hurting, scared, prisoner somewhere no one would ever find her.

She shook it off just as quickly, shoving the pain from

her eyes, and refocused them sharply on Hancock. She was unexpectedly . . . strong. He didn't often find himself surprised by anything. But Honor was just that. Something completely unexpected and yet refreshing.

"What kind of military unit doesn't even have a helicopter? How were *you* supposed to get out, much less get me out?" she demanded, incredulity evident in the question. "You think we're just going to drive out of here?"

And then her brow furrowed as if she'd realized something else. The woman asked too many damned questions, instead of showing some gratitude that he'd prevented the assholes tracking her from capturing her, and he was starting to get pissed. Were it not for him getting to her when he did, even now she'd be suffering horribly and would face days, even weeks of endless pain and agony. The conscience he'd severed from his mind whispered deep inside that he was going to subject her to the same fate. He was only delaying the inevitable, and worse, instilling false hope that her ordeal was over. And that just made him angrier. He didn't bother to hide it from her either.

Before he could voice his anger, she plunged ahead as if not understanding the danger of stroking his ire.

"And days? I would have been over the border in another day, two at the most, and I was *walking*. We're driving. It should only take hours!"

He curbed the harsh edge of his temper—barely—but he still sounded pissed when he spoke. "What I think is that you're spending far too much time asking pointless questions and looking a gift horse in the mouth."

He'd been unwinding the binding on her knee all the while she'd been raking him over the hot coals, and in his annoyance he pulled too forcibly at the last strip covering a layer of some kind of muddy goop that had pasted the bandage to the bare skin around her knee. The cloth yanked free, taking a thin layer of scab with it. Blood immediately welled and Hancock swore under his breath. He hadn't meant to hurt her, goddamn it. He had to gain her trust without divulging anything more than necessary, not act like the terrorists chasing her was a preferable option.

She flinched but then bit into her lip, the white edges of her teeth barely visible. Her face lost color, making the dye rubbed into her skin appear even darker and unnatural against such paleness.

Hancock cursed again under his breath and simply held out his hand for the swath of cloth Mojo was already extending. He dabbed at the fresh blood and then took the bottle of hydrogen peroxide Mojo handed over next and lifted his gaze to Honor's.

"This is going to hurt," he said, his voice an apology for already inadvertently hurting her.

"I'll get over it," she said, her gaze going stony.

Still, she closed her eyes and swayed precariously when Hancock dribbled the liquid over her entire knee, using the cloth to absorb the rinse. She looked like she was listing to the side and Mojo must have thought so too because he palmed her upper arm, his huge hand dwarfing her delicate bone structure, and steadied her, holding her up and in place.

"Thank you," Honor murmured, never opening her eyes.

"Bad mojo," Mojo said, shaking his head as he looked at the swollen knee Hancock was being a lot more careful with now.

"A New Era controls the airspace here," Hancock found himself explaining. As if she deserved answers. Fuck. It was as close to an actual apology as possible without actually telling her he was sorry. He continued, though his voice was still tight with anger. No longer at her, though. At himself for feeling the need to explain himself to anyone. And for taking out his anger and frustration on her. Hurting her unintentionally. "They have weapons capable of bringing down a fighter jet. A chopper would be child's play for them. We have to circumvent their area of control, and it's wide and growing wider with every day, before we can risk traveling by air. So until such time as it's safe, we'll be traveling on the ground."

"But why are we moving away from the border?" she asked, no accusation in her voice this time. Just genuine puzzlement.

Maybe he should just wash his hands of her and make Conrad take over the job as her babysitter. She clearly wasn't intimidated by Hancock, which pissed him off and bruised his male ego more than he'd like to admit. Conrad, however, hated everyone and didn't bother to pretend otherwise. He gave his loyalty and regard to his team. No one else. And Hancock was the only other person in the world Conrad took orders from and followed. He hadn't been any happier than Hancock about being sent like fucking errand boys to round up a woman who'd ended up taking up far too much time and effort on their part.

"Let's pretend for a moment that you got lucky and were able to get past the men surrounding the village waiting for you—which you wouldn't have. But suppose you did and made it to the border, where you assumed you'd be home free. You would have been nailed within a mile of crossing into the next country. A child could have predicted your destination. The shortest distance between two points, your attack and what you perceived as freedom, is a straight line. The nearest American presence. And once past the border you would have thought you were home free when in fact, apart from the fact that A New Era's minions are everywhere, a huge bounty was placed on your head, along with the fact that you were heading to the border being broadcasted far and wide. Any number of people would have been lined up, lying in wait, only too eager to hand you over to the enemy."

Anger simmered in her eyes and her features tightened. Her fingers curled into tight fists atop her thighs, and he had the passing thought that she was tempted to punch him. He almost laughed.

"You think I survived this long by being stupid?" she hissed. "That I'm a childish idiot who would think that crossing a mere border would somehow make me impervious to capture or harm? I'm a woman alone, traveling alone. Even were I not hunted by a group of assholes I would still be at risk from any number of other sources. I would never have let my guard down—and I still won't—until I'm on a plane back home."

Her chin came up, a defiant, challenging gesture as she issued the warning that she didn't trust him or his motives. No, she wasn't stupid. Never once had he thought that. Stupid would have been throwing herself in his arms and at his mercy and never questioning, just assuming that he had come to save her. Stupid would have gotten her captured within hours of her digging herself out of the rubble. Stupid did not survive over a week in a hot, barren, unfamiliar land with no one to help you but yourself.

"This is a pointless and childish argument," he said, purposely using her own words against her. "The border is being watched and heavily patrolled. The area between the border and anyone remotely friendly to your cause will be barricaded and sealed. And we'll get our asses shot down if we attempt to fly a helo out of here. Now, have I satisfied your ridiculous curiosity so we can stop wasting time?"

"Of course. What right do I have to know anything that affects my safety or that could get me killed? Yep, that's childish of me all right. By all means, oh lord and master. Lead on. I just hope to hell you know what you're doing because so far you've left a lot to be desired. I've heard a lot of talking, but no proof that anything you say is the truth."

CHAPTER 8

HONOR'S entire body hurt. Her head and knee ached vilely as they bumped their way over land without an established road, kicking up a dust cloud that could be seen for miles. They didn't seem overly concerned with their visibility, and she wondered why they hadn't opted to travel under the cover of dark as she had. It had certainly kept her alive this long.

She didn't remember the pain being this severe, but then she'd become very adept at pushing it away and denying its existence. There had been no other choice, because to stop or even hesitate would mean her capture. Now that she was somewhat removed from the immediate threat of discovery at all times, it was as though her mind could no longer block the screams of her body.

Several times, Honor would have sworn that Hancock and the fierce, uncommunicative man on the other side of her protected her from the worst of the bumps by steadying her body with their own. But it was likely her imagination. They were being thrown around just as she was. There was no softness in them. And they'd certainly given her no reason to believe she was anything more than a nuisance, a mission they'd likely objected to and had only carried out under strict orders.

But from whom? Had word spread of her survival? Did the U.S. government care enough about one lowly relief worker to risk some of their finest men, or worse, starting an unofficial war with A New Era? Or had her story reached the media and swept across the world in sensationalistic style, forcing the United States to act? And God, what must her family be enduring? She wanted to asked Hancock if there was a way they could be contacted. Just to let them know she was alive. But no, that would be cruel. She wasn't out of the woods yet, and to give them false hope only for her to end up dead after all would be terrible for them.

She wanted answers, but these men were as tightlipped as they came. Hancock didn't even answer her more innocuous questions without making it a federal issue. As if her fate wasn't something she had a right to know.

Anger blazed through her veins all over again at his domineering, asshole demeanor. But was she doing just as he'd insinuated? No, he hadn't insinuated anything. He'd very bluntly told her she was looking a gift horse in the mouth. A good bedside demeanor was purely optional. If they got her out of the country and on her way back home, they could all be flaming assholes for all she cared.

"How badly are you hurting?"

Hancock's soft question startled her, breaking the silence that had descended in the interior of the off-road vehicle. She couldn't help but swing her head toward him in surprise, wondering if she'd imagined the question. Or the actual . . . concern . . . in his voice. Surely she'd imagined that part at least.

Turning so fast made her promptly regret doing so. Pain speared through her head and suddenly black dots swam in her vision, her surroundings growing dim, fading almost to black.

Hancock swore and then suddenly she found herself eased downward, her head coming to rest gently on Hancock's lap. The other man lifted her legs and positioned them across his lap so that she lay between the two men.

"You didn't tell me you had a head injury. Just the knee injury," Hancock said grimly.

Already his fingers were delving into her hair and she

tensed, expecting him to be rough. But he was extremely gentle as he felt along her scalp.

"I didn't know," she managed to slur out. "How could I have known? I was in shock after the attack and then desperate to form a plan to escape—and survive. The only injury that registered was to my knee. It made walking . . . difficult."

"I can imagine," Hancock said dryly. "It's still very swollen, aggravated, no doubt, by all that walking."

His fingers glanced over a spot and she immediately cried out, blackness and nausea engulfing her.

"There it is," he said in his calm, unaffected tone. "You have quite a bump there. A concussion, likely."

"I haven't died yet," she said in a sour tone. "If it were that serious, I would have keeled over by now."

She heard a noise that sounded like a laugh, but Hancock neither smiled nor laughed, so it was obviously her delirium making its presence known.

"No, you aren't going to die, but you do need to rest so you can properly recover."

She started to snort but realized that would just hurt too much. "Kind of hard to rest and relax when you're running for your life."

The man holding her feet in his lap handed Hancock something that looked suspiciously like a syringe. *Three* of them. When had he gotten them and where? She hadn't detected movement, but then she wasn't all that coherent at the moment.

Fear gripped her and she reached up to stay the man's hand just as Hancock's hand closed around the syringes.

"What are those and what are you planning to do?" she asked fearfully.

"You need to calm yourself, Honor. You have enough stress without adding to it with unnecessary worry. I'm merely giving you an injection of antibiotics and pain medicine so it will take the edge off your pain and allow you to rest properly."

"I gave myself an injection of antibiotics before I escaped the clinic," she said. "And I took pills with me and I've been taking them three times a day ever since."

"Smart girl. You think well on your feet."

Was that a compliment? From Hancock the unfeeling, arrogant asshole? Maybe she was more screwed up than she initially thought, because now she was imagining things that simply weren't there.

"However, you have cuts and scrapes in dozens of places that are all susceptible to crippling infection—a complication we certainly don't need right now. And that knee is still pretty nasty-looking and is still swollen to twice its normal size. So in addition to the antibiotics and pain medicine, I'm also giving you a shot of steroids to help with the inflammation. I have a Medrol dose pack that you'll start taking tonight and continue for the next five days. You should start feeling relief as soon as tomorrow."

"We won't be to where we're going for five days?" she asked in alarm.

Panic skittered its way up her spine. Five days seemed an eternity. The days spent evading the murderers stalking her every move had been endless. She'd hoped . . . She'd assumed that now that she had help that they would be to safety in a short time. The idea of being exposed for so long scared her. They were a group of seven including herself, and she'd be of no help to Hancock and his men in a firefight. And they were up against an untold number of crazed militants who would never stand down until their objective was achieved. Capturing her.

She could practically see him shrug, though her eyes were closed. As if it weren't a source of concern to him at all. Was he really that confident in his abilities? In his men's abilities? She should take comfort in that kind of arrogance and self-assurance. But she couldn't quite quell the desperate fear that took over all else.

"I won't know until we get there," he said vaguely. "Now be still so I can administer the injections. It might burn, but it will go away quickly."

"It can't hurt more than it already does," she said through tight lips.

He obviously injected the pain medication first, a fact she was grateful for, because now acknowledged, pain was screaming through her body in unrelenting waves. She could feel the glimmer of relief as he pulled the layers of her garment up so her hip was exposed. She didn't protest with false modesty. At this point anything that gave her relief was more important than the fact he was exposing far more of her than she would have liked.

The man at her feet rotated her just enough so Hancock could access the back of her hip and then Hancock carefully swabbed the area, cleaning it with alcohol before efficiently administering both injections.

In a few seconds it was over and she sagged as Hancock readjusted her clothing. Already her surroundings were a warm, hazy glow and a wonderful leaden feeling had stolen over her body, chasing away the ever-present pain.

Still, she struggled against the heavy layers of unconsciousness and roused herself enough to open her eyes and direct her worried question up at Hancock.

"What if we run into trouble? I couldn't fight my way out of a paper bag right now," she admitted.

There was a hint of amusement in Hancock's tone. "Leave the fighting to us. I don't anticipate trouble—yet. So take this opportunity to rest up and heal."

Maybe he was human after all. Or perhaps she'd misjudged him. He was, after all, carrying out a mission. Just like any other soldier or special ops force or whatever the hell he was. Black ops maybe? He was certainly secretive enough, and he hadn't identified the branch of the military he served. Perhaps he was one of those who didn't officially exist and he gave her no information that she could inadvertently leak at a later date.

She didn't care. She would claim fairies rescued her just as long as she got back home. Safe. Alive.

"Thank you," she whispered, still holding on to the last bit of awareness she possessed.

This time there was genuine puzzlement in Hancock's voice.

"For what?"

"For saving me," she said, her words nearly unintelligible. "For helping me. And for promising you'd get me back home."

He stiffened beneath her. She could feel the muscles of his legs go rigid, and the hand that had been absently stroking her hand stilled and then withdrew.

"I made no such promise, Honor," he said in a tight voice.

Maybe he wasn't comfortable with people thanking him. If he was off the books and didn't exist, then he wasn't used to being thanked for anything. He and his men were ghosts. What a terrible way to live. Risking your lives for others and never being thanked.

"You trying is enough," she murmured. "You're my last and only hope. So thank you."

"Go to sleep, Honor," he said, his tone suggesting he had no liking for her words. "You need to rest while you can."

It was a command she had no difficulty obeying. She was more than halfway there already. All it took was letting her eyelids falls heavily so that her lashes rested on her cheeks and succumbing to the sweet call of oblivion.

CHAPTER 9

IT was many hours later when the group pulled to a stop at an underground compound where they would seek refuge for the night. Dark had long since descended, making the way slower going as they drove a path through the desert where no road existed.

It had taken Hancock longer than he would have liked, but he wasn't about to risk his men by stopping in the open in an area that wasn't defensible. At least here, they would be underground in a blastproof bunker, and they'd take turns at watch so they'd know if anyone ventured close.

His men were well used to operating on little to no sleep. They could stay up for days and still be alert and aware in a fight, so a few hours spent on watch would hardly impair them going forward.

He eased from the vehicle and then reached in and lifted Honor's small body into his arms, anchoring her against his chest as he strode toward the entrance Conrad had already hurried to open.

"Get the vehicle to cover," Hancock ordered, pausing at the entrance to issue orders to his men. "Mojo, you and Conrad take first watch. Two hours. Henderson and Viper, you take the next shift." He glanced at Copeland—or Cope as he was called for his cool-under-pressure way of being able to cope with anything. "Cope, you and I will take last watch. I'll get everyone up when it's time to get on the move again."

"Why we stopping now, boss?" Conrad asked, his gaze inquisitive.

Hancock could well understand why his men would wonder at his uncharacteristic stop. They usually pushed themselves, going days without sleep in order to achieve their objective as quickly as possible.

"The woman will be useless to us unless she has time to rest and recover."

"Bad mojo," Mojo muttered.

"I don't mind saying that this mission blows," Cope spoke up.

Hancock looked at his man in surprise. He couldn't ever remember any of his men taking issue with the many missions that were in that nebulous area between good and bad. Some of them soul sucking, taking a piece of them at a time until there was little humanity left in any of them. Hancock included. This mission was hardly one of their worst. They'd done far worse in the name of "good" and the protection of others. The innocent who couldn't stand for themselves. That was Titan's job. To stand for them. To protect them while they slept the sleep of the ignorant, never knowing how close they came to death.

"She doesn't deserve her fate," Cope said by way of explanation, his expression grim, actual anger brimming in his usually cold, emotionless gaze. "And I don't like the fact that we're deceiving her. She's . . . courageous," he said, as though struggling to come up with the right word to describe her. "She *deserves* to be spared. She held off those fuckers for over a week and evaded capture. I don't know of anyone, much less a woman, who can claim the same. She's already a fucking national hero, not only to the people here, but in the U.S. as well."

"Bad mojo," Mojo said again, making Hancock realize that Mojo's feelings mirrored Copeland's own, and that was why he'd uttered the first "Bad mojo."

Well, fuck. This wasn't *ever* a complication he'd encountered with his team. Not once. Not even when they'd forcibly taken Grace from KGI, shooting one of KGI's men in the process and damn near killing Rio later. And Grace as well. Not when they'd allowed Caldwell to abduct Maren when she was pregnant and vulnerable and keep her under lock and key until Hancock was forced—by his goddamn newly developed conscience—to intercede and blow his mission all to hell to get her out.

"One hero? Or the hundreds of thousands of innocent people who will fall victim to Maksimov if he isn't taken out for good?" Hancock asked in a challenging tone, reminding his men of their role in the world. Reminding them of their purpose. Their *only* purpose. Their mission wasn't to judge, to decide who was worthy or unworthy. Their only job was to rid the world of the predators who preyed on the innocent, which meant that sometimes *they* were the very ones preying on the innocent in order to achieve their goal.

The dissension in his ranks mirrored his own thoughts too closely—thoughts he'd firmly shoved away, not allowing himself to feel guilt. Or regret. He didn't like it one goddamn bit, and he had to nip this in the bud before it got out of control and he had mutiny on his hands—something he'd never considered in a million years. His men were too steady. Too solid. Too focused. Just as he was. They followed his lead, never questioning.

Until now.

"I get it," Cope muttered. "But I don't have to like it."

"We don't *have* to like it," Hancock said tightly. "But we do have to do our job. Even at the cost of one innocent. The good of the many—"

"Yeah, yeah, we know," Cope said, impatiently cutting his leader off, again something Hancock's men never dared to do. "The good of the many takes priority over the good of the one. Team motto. Whatever. But it gets pretty damn old and it's why, after Maksimov, I'm done."

"You know we have to go after A New Era," Hancock said quietly, still holding Honor firmly against his chest.

Looks were exchanged between his team members. Some of acknowledgment. Some of resignation and acceptance. Some indecisive.

"Bad mojo," Mojo said in a disgruntled voice that clearly reflected his stand. And it wasn't with the mission or the "greater good."

"And what then?" Conrad asked, speaking up for the first time. "I'm in. I'm with you. You know that. But when will it be time to stop fighting the good fight and allow others to fight in our stead? There's always another asshole who needs taking out. After Maksimov, after A New Era, there will be another. There's *always* another. When does it end?"

Frustration licked up Hancock's spine. And the source of the conflict that had arisen amid his men was curled protectively in his arms. One small woman. A very small part of him wished she'd died with the others. Because then he wouldn't be here, having chased over half the country after her. He wouldn't be having this ridiculous conversation with his men, whose priorities had never wavered in all the time they'd worked under him. And yet one small woman had done considerable damage to their unity, and that pissed him off.

If she hadn't survived, things would be a hell of a lot less complicated.

"That has to be your choice," Hancock said honestly. "You can walk away at any time. No one's making you stay. Do we need you? Hell, yeah. There's no one I'd rather have at my back than the five of you. But everyone here would understand if you walked away at any time. After Maksimov, if you—any of you—are ready to hang it up, no one is going to have a single word to say other than good journey. And you'll always have my gratitude for your service. If you ever have need of me, all it takes is a call. We will *always* have your back. Once one of us, always one of us. Your retiring doesn't change a goddamn thing."

When his men remained silent, Hancock gave them an impatient look they couldn't misunderstand. Get the vehicle to cover and bed down for the night. They'd wasted enough time already. Time they didn't have to spare.

Then he simply descended the makeshift steps into the shelter and traveled across the small enclosure to the far corner, where he placed Honor on one of the cots so he and his men would be between her and the entrance. It was the safest place in the small compound.

They were well protected here, surrounded by reinforced walls and ceilings that prevented their heat signatures from penetrating and being detected by someone on the outside using heat-seeking instruments. And unless someone dropped a nuclear bomb on them, it was safe from blasts. Unless they sustained a continuous and heavy attack.

It was a leftover facility from the days when Titan worked under the U.S. government with full permission to carry out their missions using whatever means necessary. They'd been equipped with the best that money could buy. It was risky to come back here, but Titan had long ago been disbanded and only KGI and one lone CIA operative and his black ops team, who reported only to Resnick, the CIA agent, knew with absolute certainty that Hancock and his men were still alive and a definite threat to anyone who crossed their path. There was suspicion, especially among the upper echelons, those who'd had a part in Titan's creation, that Titan was still operating. Or rather had gone rogue. But only very few knew that they were very much alive—and more dangerous than ever.

He had no worries over KGI, even though they weren't exactly allies. Were they enemies? Only KGI could answer that, but they owed Hancock. He'd done much to safeguard Grace—and Elizabeth, an innocent child whose only sin was being born to a father who was wholly evil. Even if KGI hadn't known that at the time. They still might not know.

And he'd sacrificed his mission for Maren Scofield—now Maren Steele—the closest he'd gotten to taking Maksimov down. Until now.

So he doubted KGI would ever sell him or his existence out, even if he had been responsible for injuries to two of their men. They were too damn . . . honorable. Veritable Captain Americas. Everything Hancock wasn't and had no desire to be.

The CIA operative was another matter, but his government had turned on him, just as they'd turned on Titan. And even though Titan had damn near killed Adam Resnick and accessed his classified files, Resnick no longer had the allies within his own ranks to ever retaliate. He'd be a fool to go after Hancock on his own, and the man was no fool. He was cagey and smart and had dirt on everyone from the highest-ranking military personnel to the White House itself and everywhere in between. He was feared and hated by many. His days were very likely numbered. He had enough on his hands staying alive and away from those who would celebrate his death without adding Hancock to the ranks wanting him dead.

Those who now hunted Titan were nothing more than mercenaries. Not organized black ops groups. Few in the government knew of Titan's existence to begin with. So it was highly improbable that anyone would search for them here. And certainly not when A New Era controlled so much of the area. Collecting a generous bounty for bringing Titan down wasn't worth the risk of getting themselves killed in the process, and mercenaries had no concept of selfless sacrifice. Their mission wasn't one of honor or for the greater good. Their only goal was to line their pockets and elevate their reputation.

"Everything's locked down and secure," Viper said as he stepped into the small room. "Conrad and Mojo have set up watch so they'll know if an ant farts within a mile of our location."

"Then you and the others bed down and catch some sleep until it's time for your watch," Hancock directed. "It may be the last night we get any sleep until we deliver the woman to Bristow."

He purposely didn't invoke Honor's name. His men were already looking at her not as a means to an end, simply a pawn, but as a heroic human being. An innocent female who didn't deserve to be given false hope such as they were indeed giving her, even if they didn't lie to her in so many words. Theirs was a sin of omission, but it paled in comparison to their many other sins. There was no salvation for men such as them. They were resigned to eternal damnation, their souls so stained that they'd never see the light again. As the old but apt saying went, the road to hell is paved with good intentions.

Viper doused the lights, shrouding the interior in darkness as the men took to the few cots and bedrolls they carried with them. They were trained to fall asleep on command, their bodies well accustomed to taking sleep when they got the chance and to rousing, awake and alert, ready for action.

And yet Hancock found himself unable to do just that. Long after his men were already asleep, Hancock lay there, his bedroll just inches from Honor's cot, his thoughts consumed by the sacrifice he was preparing to lay at Bristow's—and ultimately Maksimov's—feet.

He had no idea of the passage of time when he picked up on a sound that would go undetected by most others. But his ears were attuned to the slightest change. Turning toward the sound, he realized it came from where Honor lay sleeping. Or he assumed she was sleeping.

The sound was so faint that at first he thought he imagined it or that it had simply been a noise she'd made in sleep, but no, there it was again. It sounded like . . .

Weeping.

Soft, nearly soundless weeping.

Fuck.

His heart clenched despite his having already hardened it toward this woman. She didn't sob noisily or wail her distress. In fact he wasn't entirely certain she was cognizant of the fact that she was crying.

Before he could think better of it, he pushed himself upward so he was on eye level with her and peered even closer, trying to discern her level of consciousness in the dark. Softly he reached out to touch her cheek to see if his supposition was correct, and his chest tightened further when his fingers came away wet with her tears.

She was crying in her sleep. God only knew what nightmares tortured her sleep. She'd seen and been through hell over the last week. Grudging admiration for her resiliency rose within him. She was perhaps the strongest woman he'd ever encountered. No, she wasn't a woman warrior like those who worked for KGI who could easily kick a man's ass twice their size.

She was strong *despite* her lack of fighting skills, her lack of knowledge in defending herself. She was resourceful and determined in the face of impossible odds and she didn't know the meaning of *quit*. When many would have already given up and resigned themselves to their fate or even taken their own life to spare themselves certain torture and degradation, she'd stubbornly clung to and fought for her life.

Carefully, so as not to awaken her, he slid his arms beneath her slight body, hoping she was still out from the pain medication he'd given her. He'd purposely given her a large dose so she'd sleep like the dead and gain much-needed rest and strength.

He lowered her to the bedroll beside him, telling himself that he merely didn't want her to awaken his men. When he was certain she was still sleeping, he settled back down beside her and drew her into the warmth of his body, wrapping his arms around her to offer her the simple gift of being held and comforted. It was the least he could do when he planned to betray her in the worst possible way.

With tenderness he didn't think he possessed, he pushed away the tendrils of hair obscuring her face and smoothed away the lines marring her face from the dream she was having. Fear radiated from her in tangible waves, and something deep inside him twisted and turned uncomfortably as he took in the fact that her entire body shook with those silent sobs.

In a whisper, so his men couldn't hear, he brushed his lips over the shell of her ear.

"You're safe, Honor. I've got you. Nothing will hurt you tonight."

Tonight was all he could give her. He had no idea what tomorrow would bring, though if he was successful in his mission, he knew what the immediate future would bring. He closed his eyes to ward off the images of Honor hurting. Damaged.

Dead.

It was doubtful that she would escape Maksimov unscathed, but even if that unlikely event occurred, she would then be turned over to the very group Hancock was fighting so hard to protect her from now. The irony burned. And she'd certainly not be escaping them unscathed—or at all. Whatever Maksimov dished out to her, it would be a mere fraction of what A New Era would give her.

He risked his life, the lives of his men. All to wrest Honor from the grasp of A New Era simply so Maksimov could use her as a bargaining tool. And hand her over to . . . A New Era.

Her fate was inevitable. Because the *right* thing to do was to turn her over to Maksimov, giving Hancock unfettered access to the man he'd made his sole mission to take down. But doing the right thing didn't always feel right.

Sometimes, doing the right thing was ten different kinds of fucked up.

CHAPTER 10

HONOR woke and stretched, her body immediately protesting her forcing her muscles into action. She blinked, bringing her surroundings into focus, and then glanced over the room to see some of Hancock's men still sleeping. There were four present, minus Hancock and one other, but she imagined they'd taken turns on watch through the night.

For that matter, she had no idea where they were or where they'd sought refuge. It felt like a cave. Stifling and claustrophobic. No windows or light, the air stale without the renewal of a breeze.

She took the few stolen moments of quiet and solitude to ascertain her condition without Hancock's close scrutiny through eyes that saw too much. She flexed her knee, relieved to find that it wasn't *as* stiff or swollen, though it was still painful and resistant to movement. Her head didn't ache as vilely as it had the day before, but that could be due to the remnants of the pain medication that had made her oblivious to all else.

She took several long seconds to do a self-evaluation, time she hadn't had the luxury of before in her desperate need to keep moving. There was no doubt she was bruised and had suffered cuts and lacerations in dozens of places on her ravaged body, but the only two injuries that stood to hinder them in any way were her head injury and the injury to her knee. Everything else was manageable, and for that matter, she wasn't about to allow herself to be an obstacle to the thing she wanted most.

Her ultimate escape. Freedom.

For that she could endure anything. She *had* endured everything over the last several days, pushing her body beyond its limits in her desperate effort to survive.

But now she had help and despite Hancock's taunt about looking a gift horse in the mouth, she wasn't about to make things harder by not cooperating fully. She might not like the man, and he might make her teeth grind in irritation, but if he got her out of this mess she'd bite her tongue and not do anything to make him regret rescuing her. Liking him was purely optional, though if he did manage to get her out in one piece, it made her nothing more than a petty, sulky child for holding a grudge over his less-than-congenial personality.

She decided then to stop acting like a petulant twit and keep her mouth shut from here on out. He wouldn't hear a single argument or complaint from her if it killed her.

She started when she heard a noise and glanced rapidly in the direction of the sound to see Hancock and one of the other men descend the steps into the tiny room that housed the rest of the sleeping men.

For a moment their gazes locked and even in the dim lighting, there was something . . . She shook her head as a fleeting memory chased through her mind, continuing before she could grab on. She frowned because there was something she was missing. Something nagging at her.

"Time to move out."

He didn't speak loudly, but then he didn't have to. Evidently his men were trained to wake on command and be alert and ready to roll out. The room became a flurry of activity. She pushed herself upright on the cot, recoiling at the nausea that formed in the pit of her belly. She recovered quickly—or so she thought—not wanting to give them pause for concern. Over her dead body would she delay them when she wanted to get the hell out of here worse than they did.

Hancock, damn him for never missing a single detail, immediately crossed the room and hunkered down next to her cot.

"Are you ill?" he asked in a low enough voice that it didn't carry to his men.

She was absurdly grateful that he hadn't embarrassed her or made her appear weak in front of the others. Her pride was important to her. It was all she had left. That and hope. Those two things would be all that saw her through the coming days.

"No. I just moved too quickly. I'm all right. Really."

"When was the last time you ate anything?" he asked, that piercing gaze raking over her bones as if he could see all things.

"Day before yesterday," she said with a grimace, remembering the tasteless, bland MRE she'd eaten on autopilot, chasing it with the last of her water reserves.

Hancock turned and called out to one of his men, who instantly dug out a packet and tossed it Hancock's way. Another came forward with a vacuum-sealed packet and canteen. He tore open both packs and dumped them onto the bed next to her.

A variety of dried items, some fruit and some that looked like meat, lay next to her, and it was all she could do not to fall on them like a starving wolf.

He leaned the canister against her thigh and then rose to his full height once more.

"You scarf down what you can while we get the vehicle out and packed. One pack is vitamin based and the other is protein. Get as much of both down as you can without making yourself sick."

She nodded, already making a grab for the food. To her surprise, it was good. It wasn't remotely appetizing-looking and it had no smell whatsoever, but flavor burst onto her tongue the minute it made contact.

She savored the first bite, enjoying it and wanting it to last, but then it sank in that he'd told her to get down what she could and they were readying to go. Which meant if she didn't pick up the pace, she wasn't going to get much to eat at all.

While she stuffed her face and drank from the canteen like an automaton, she curiously surveyed the preparation going on around her, marveling at how fluidly graceful this team was. They worked in silent unison, not needing to communicate.

They simply knew what to do and the most adept way of doing it. It was like watching a well-oiled machine.

A few moments later, Hancock approached carrying what looked to be an entire bolt of black fabric over his arm. She grimaced, knowing instantly it was for her.

"We are fortunate in that we are entering regions where burkas are the most common manner of dress for women. If you had worn one before, you would have drawn unwanted attention to yourself. You did well by not trying to hide completely."

There was a hint of praise that brought heat crawling up her neck and into her cheeks.

"This will keep you completely covered, and no one will question a woman wearing such a garment where we will be traveling the next two days."

Though the burka would be stifling and the height of uncomfortable, Honor was extremely grateful that it would cover her from head to toe. Even her eyes wouldn't be visible and she'd blend seamlessly with any other women if they were forced into a public setting.

Now the rest of Hancock's group was another matter. It wasn't as though a lone woman went around escorted by six burly warrior Westerners. Male chaperones for unmarried—and married—family members were common enough, but this group didn't have a chance of blending in or of being considered native.

Wanting to remove as many layers of clothing underneath the burka as possible, Honor quickly stripped down to the bare minimum, careful to keep the garment shielding her body, though none of the men looked her way.

She stuffed the discarded clothing into her pack and then crammed the last of the rations into her mouth, washing it all down with several long swallows of water.

When all the men were once more assembled inside, prepared to depart, Hancock performed quick introductions of his men and she committed each name to memory. She mentally rolled her eyes when he got to Mojo. Appropriate since the only words that had passed the man's lips within her hearing had been either "Good mojo" or "Bad mojo."

Mere minutes later, she was hustled into the waiting

vehicle, Hancock hovering at her elbow but not interfering as she hauled herself into the elevated backseat. Perhaps he was testing her range of motion, but she'd already vowed to herself that no matter how much her body screamed at her, none of these men would think she was incapable of carrying her own weight. Literally.

The only tell was her tightly clenched jaw as she settled into position next to Conrad, easily the next scariest man in the group after Hancock. She'd prefer Mojo, as ridiculous as it sounded, because Mojo was one mean-looking son of a bitch, but he hadn't been anything but gentle and patient with her. Conrad's features were . . . cold. His eyes were empty and soulless, as though the life had long been sucked from him and he was more machine than man, acting on orders like a robot.

She shivered involuntarily, once again wondering if her salvation was scarier than the alternative. Being sandwiched between two men who looked as though they were well acquainted with death and destruction should comfort her frayed nerves and ease some of the paralyzing terror that seemed permanently injected into her veins. They certainly looked capable of taking on—and defeating—anyone or anything. These were precisely the kind of men she needed if she hoped to escape the desperate clutches of A New Era. And yet she was nervous. Fear, her constant companion over the last week, clung tenaciously to her, deeply entrenched and refusing to surrender its choke hold on her.

Maybe she'd never feel safe again. Maybe even after she got home—she refused to say *if* she got home because unless she believed it, truly believed in it and Hancock's ability to get her there, she was doomed before they ever forged on. She could well see the nightmare of the attack and her friends and coworkers so savagely murdered and dismembered hovering in her conscious and subconscious for all time.

One didn't simply "get over" something like this. She had a much better understanding now of the horrors that enlisted military endured. Over and over. And why so many suffered so horribly on their return home. Why so many were diagnosed with post-traumatic stress disorder. How could anyone possibly lead a normal life completely free of their demons when hell was ever-present in the back of their minds? In their memories?

She unconsciously shifted closer to Hancock, seeking the warmth of his body, some of the rapidly coiling tension in her stomach loosening as his heat bled into her skin.

Then she stiffened, blinking as a vague recollection taunted her, licking at the fringes of her memory. She frowned, straining to call it forward. She'd been in Hancock's arms, her cheeks wet, chest tight with grief and fear. He'd held her. When?

Last night.

She must have been crying in her sleep. Hancock had lifted her from the cot where she slept and lowered her to his bedroll beside him and he'd wrapped his arms around her, anchoring her, rocking and soothing her, murmuring gentle words the entire while.

It took all her discipline not to yank her gaze to the side and stare at him as if she could somehow decipher the puzzle by looking into his eyes.

She wasn't imagining it. She hadn't dreamed it. She'd lain in his arms until some point when she'd drifted into sleep solidly enough that he transferred her back to the cot without her ever remembering. Until now.

Struggling to keep the betraying frown of puzzlement from deepening, she bit into her bottom lip and pondered why she was even making a big deal out of it. He was human, after all, despite her doubts to the contrary. Last night just proved he wasn't a complete dick and that he did have compassion. He obviously kept it under wraps for reasons unknown, but then she supposed that if he did this all the time, unselfishly put his life on the line for others, it didn't pay to get emotionally involved in any capacity.

She could understand why he'd view her and the countless others he'd helped as . . . things. Not human beings with feelings or emotions. Because then if things went wrong he would feel that much more. Maybe it was the way he stayed sane. Whatever his methodology, she was grateful, because it was working. And whatever got her out of this hellhole and back on U.S. soil, she was one hundred ten percent behind.

Still she couldn't help but glance up at Hancock when he wasn't looking, studying the firm outline of his jaw and his chiseled features that seemed set in stone. She wondered what his story was. What he and his men officially did or if they even officially existed.

What a terrible half-life that must be, to live and yet be nothing to the world, nobody to anyone. To continually put their lives at risk for strangers they didn't know and would never see again. Did anyone ever thank them? Truly thank them? She made a mental vow that whenever they got to wherever they were going, she was going to thank each and every one of them by name. They would know that she wouldn't forget that they gave her a chance at life. That they saved her from certain torture and death.

And at the same time, as incongruous as it might sound, it only reaffirmed her commitment to her relief efforts. No one would blame her if she never took another assignment. If she stayed safely inside the confines of the United States and enjoyed the protection and freedoms of living within its borders. Living in the ignorant bliss that so many Americans enjoyed—embraced. Most people would think her insane to wade back into the fray after such a close brush with the unthinkable.

But there were people in need. People without others to fight for them. To help them do something her countrymen took for granted. Survive. Be free. Hancock and his men were people who took up that fight. She'd devoted her life to the cause of helping others. Just because she'd faced adversity—and overcome it—didn't give her justification to simply step aside and quit. Allow others to assume the risk in her stead.

If anything it only made her that much more determined not to allow these assholes to silence her efforts. Her family wouldn't like it. They wouldn't go down without one hell of a fight, as they had the first time she'd come to this war-torn, embattled region. They would need time with her—time she'd gladly grant them—so they could ensure that she was well and truly safe. Alive. Unhurt.

But then she'd pick up the banner again and nothing would deter her from her calling. It wasn't something she could ignore, opting for a safe nine-to-five job. It was who and what she was, and to walk away was not only a betrayal of the people so desperately in need but a betrayal of herself, her ideals and her beliefs.

"Whatever it is that has you so deep in thought, it better not be a plan I'm not privy to."

Hancock's drawl broke through her thought process, startling her into lifting her gaze to see him studying her intently. What, did he think she was planning to run from him and escape on her own? Not likely. He was her best and only hope of getting home alive and she knew it.

So deeply entrenched in her fierce thought process was she that she spoke before censoring her words.

"I was merely making a vow not to let these assholes make me quit," she blurted out.

Embarrassed by her impassioned outburst, she ducked her head, her voice more of a mumble now.

"Most people would run home and never leave again," she said quietly. "I'm not most people and I'm needed here. And other places. Places most people won't go. But those are the places where the need is the greatest. And just as you have all risked your lives to save me—one person—then so too will I risk my life to help countless others. Your risk won't be in vain. My life means something. It has purpose. I won't go quietly, nor will I let those bastards frighten me into sticking my head into the sand and staying at home with Mommy and Daddy like a coward."

Her tone had grown fiercer with every word until they blazed with heat to match the intensity of her emotions.

The others fell silent, the quiet stretching and blanketing the interior of the vehicle. Some looked down. Others looked away, blindly, out a window or at simply nothing at all. There was tangible discomfort and she frowned, not understanding why. Were they pissed that they were risking their lives for someone who would willingly put herself at risk all over again?

She supposed it did seem as though she were ungrateful and uncaring of the sacrifices they made. They were probably wondering why the hell they were out here in the middle of the desert risking their asses for a woman who didn't appreciate their efforts or why they didn't just dump her out and leave her to fend for herself.

"I don't expect you to understand," she said in a low voice. "But I can't turn my back on these people. They have no one to fight for them. No one to aid them. And if I let terrorists sway me from my objective, then they win, regardless of whether I escape or not, whether I live or die."

She plunged ahead before any could respond, not that a response appeared imminent. They weren't exactly talkative. They made Hancock seem like a regular conversationalist, and he was a bare-minimum kind of guy at best. But his men? Had even less to say. But perhaps as their leader, they let Hancock do the talking while they did the acting.

"I don't want to appear ungrateful for what you've done—what you're doing. Nor am I being cavalier about the fact that you risked your lives to rescue me and pull me out. It may appear to you that way, but I can't possibly explain how much it matters to me that I not be manipulated and coerced through fear or threats."

Conrad muttered an indecipherable curse beside her, turning so he faced the window and she couldn't see his eyes or expression. She could swear that her statement had made them all . . . uncomfortable . . . and not for the reasons she'd cited. Copeland, or Cope as his team called him, looked *guilty*.

She swung her puzzled stare in Hancock's direction and for once found comfort in the fact that his face was an impenetrable mask, no emotion, opinion or judgment. No agreement or condemnation echoed in his eyes. He just regarded her with that steady gaze, his expression inscrutable as always.

Obviously her imagination was getting away from her and she was seeing things that weren't there. And now that she'd put it out there like an apology . . . Who was she kidding? It had been an apology, a plea for understanding and maybe even approval. Now it just pissed her off because she didn't need their permission to do what she felt called to do. They certainly didn't need or require her approval, nor did they give two shits what she thought of them, so why should she feel beholden to them as if because they saved her life, she gave up her power over her life to them? Her choices. Her decisions.

They didn't own her or her mind. Definitely not her choices. She owed them gratitude, absolutely. She owed them respect and her full cooperation for as long as she was under their protection. But she didn't owe them anything more, and she damn sure didn't need their permission to do with her life what she wanted—needed. Just as they didn't need—or want—hers.

Hancock merely shrugged. "If you get home, what you do afterward is solely up to you. You're a grown woman and you don't owe anyone an explanation for the choices you make."

For some reason it bothered her that he'd said *if* she got home. Not *when*. It bothered her a *lot*. Because Hancock was nothing if not completely calm and confident. He exuded absolute faith and self-assurance in his ability and that of his team. It was the first time he'd even hinted that she wouldn't absolutely get out of this mess. As if it were even a remote possibility she wouldn't. It caused her pulse to ratchet up and pound at her temples, resurrecting the ache in her head that had subsided and hadn't returned. Until now.

She wanted to crawl back into his arms and huddle there as she'd done the night before, albeit unknowingly at the time. But even now memories of feeling utterly safe and comforted floated back to her, bringing the events of the last night even closer to the forefront of her mind. She wanted that feeling back. Even if for only a few moments. Just long enough to dispel the sudden and unsettling unease rioting through her veins.

She could only imagine his reaction were she to do such a thing. It was obvious he had no desire for her to know he'd held and comforted her last night. His actions certainly hadn't betrayed him in any way, nor had he referenced the event. He acted as though it had never happened, and she strongly suspected were she to bring it up that he'd deny it and tell her it was only a dream. Even though she knew damn well it was—had been—real. She'd never forget the sensation of being in his arms and the comfort and strength she'd drawn from those few hours, even if it had taken her a bit to get it all back.

He'd shown her kindness when she'd assumed the very worst about him. But then she was fast learning he was multifaceted with so many layers that she could probably dig and pull back forever and never learn everything there was to know about him. The least she could do was respect his obvious wish not to ever acknowledge his actions.

Perhaps he considered it a weakness, but to Honor it had been something she desperately needed. He'd anchored her at her weakest, when she was at the mercy of her nightmares and despair had welled from the deepest recesses of her soul.

What to him was weakness was to her a badly needed infusion of strength. His strength.

She didn't respond to his dubious statement, refusing to show how his one lapse in confidence had shaken her to the core. It could have merely been a slip of the tongue, an inadvertent figure of speech, but then he didn't strike her as someone who ever allowed anything to carelessly fall from his lips.

Silence once more reigned and Honor focused on the barren landscape that sped by. She was well on her way into a self-induced hypnotic state when Hancock jarred her from her trance.

"We have to refuel several miles from our current position. It's a rural village but a crossroads and the epicenter of fuel distribution in this area, so there will be traffic coming and going in all directions. But we don't have a choice. We won't make it to the next available fuel supply. When we arrive, I'll get out and fuel the vehicle. There will be a place for you to relieve yourself. Conrad will escort you, but keep your head lowered at all times, one step behind him, and make it fast."

"I'm well aware of the culture and customs here," she said.

"Yes, I suppose you are," Hancock mused after studying her a moment. "But I never assume when it comes to life or death, so expect to hear more information you already know."

He had a solid point.

"How many regional languages do you speak?" he asked, surprising her with his seeming curiosity.

"I'm fluent in Arabic and seventeen other lesser spoken languages in a three-country block and quite passable in at least a dozen more. I'm particularly good at mimicry. I hear an accent and can immediately pick up on it."

Hancock lifted one eyebrow. "How long have you studied Middle Eastern languages?"

"I was self-taught in high school," she admitted. "Well, before that in junior high, but I went hard-core in high school. There aren't many high schools in the entire country that even offer Arabic as a course, much less the less-spoken regional languages."

"You must be a very good student to pull that off in less than a decade."

She shrugged, uncomfortable with the compliment even though it wasn't stated as such. It was more a statement of fact.

"I have an affinity for languages. In addition to the Middle Eastern languages I speak, I'm also fluent in French and Spanish and can carry basic conversation in German and Italian. It was just something that always interested me and I pick them up quickly. Once I got to university, I spent an extra three semesters beyond the time it would have taken to earn my degree taking every Middle East language course they offered and taking another dozen online courses concurrently. I knew what I wanted to do after college. My degree was simply a training tool that enabled me to better understand the culture I would be immersing myself in."

"What's the going rate for an angel of mercy these days?" Viper drawled.

She felt a quick surge of anger and to her surprise, Hancock shot his man a look of clear reprimand that had Viper clearing his throat.

"No disrespect intended," he said before focusing his attention through the windshield once more.

"I receive a tax-free stipend," she said through stiff lips. Somehow for him to question the reason for what she did, to reduce it to a mercenary business, pricked her nerves. "A very small stipend. Certainly not enough to make a living wage back home. My housing is provided for here, but I share—I shared," she added quietly, "quarters with three other women relief workers. And food is more often than not provided by the villages, though they have little to spare. The certified medical staff certainly make more—they'd have to be paid well to take this kind of job—but the people like me, we're basically volunteers."

She fell silent, refusing to say anything further—to defend herself any further when she had no obligation to justify her life to these men. Even if they were saving it.

"Since it will be obvious that we aren't from this immediate area, if and only if you must speak, do so in the common language, Arabic," Hancock instructed needlessly.

But this time she didn't remind him of her extensive knowledge. As he said, when life or death was the ultimate consequence, it never paid to assume.

CHAPTER 11

THOUGH Hancock had warned her—them all—that the village was a crossroads in a rural area, she hadn't been prepared for just how much traffic flowed through the village seemingly dropped in the middle of nowhere. It was as if the outpost served as a central hub to the entire country. Everyone traveled through this place when traversing the region.

Before they pulled into the outskirts of the settlement, Hancock had quietly warned them to stay close and stick together and for Conrad to get Honor in and out in minutes. Not only was the village an epicenter for people traveling to the far reaches and to other lands, but it was a place where one could acquire just about . . . anything.

Not only was the local economy supported by its steady fuel reserves and an army that protected those reserves day and night, but there were also arms dealers in every other tent, openly displaying their wares. It wasn't legal, but the government looked the other way, turning a blind eye to the goings-on in the small population.

It was hard to imagine a bustling marketplace where for miles there was literally nothing in every direction. Interspersed among the tents selling guns and explosives and defensive apparatus were women preparing food and selling it. Clothing. Supplies. Fresh water. It could all be had for a price.

There was deceptiveness to the air of festivity. An innocuous feel that was quickly dispelled once someone looked beyond the surface and studied the faces and stances of the people buying and selling wares.

Honor studied every single person they passed as they weaved their way through the village to the opposite end where the fuel tanks were. There was grimness, an air of expectancy, watchfulness and wariness. On constant guard, guns—assault rifles—at the ready that no one tried to hide but kept in plain sight at all times.

She shuddered, imagining what the reality of living such a life was for these people. Yes, she'd lived and worked in an area of unrest, but apart from outsiders encroaching, the village was peaceful. Full of people who only wanted sanctuary from the senseless violence that was so predominant here and who had no wish to wake up each day facing a fight for their lives. And until A New Era's attack, the village had gone largely unnoticed, even with the Western presence in the relief center. She had no doubt that her—and others'—presence wasn't well received by most, but they were left alone. And they did provide shelter, food and essentials for survival that even those who despised everything Honor stood for didn't quibble over accepting.

The people in this far-flung, hole-in-the-wall crossroads dealt with death and battle on a daily basis. Living in paranoia. Reacting instantly to any threat, imagined or real.

A very real chill worked its way to her bones, despite the heavy burka enveloping her from head to toe.

"Get ready," Hancock warned, his tone low and utterly grave.

Already his gaze was up and sweeping the area, those cold eyes taking in the minutest detail. There was only a nearly imperceptible twitch to his jaw that betrayed his unease and how on guard he was.

"Are you sure she should get out here?" Conrad asked, turning his gaze on his team leader. "We can always find a place in the desert and let her squat where no one is around."

Hancock shook his head. "I need to know if we're met with suspicion. I and the others will be closely watching as you and Honor go in to see what attention you gain. I need to know if they've been tipped off and know who you are."

"And if they are?" Honor asked in a strangled tone. "Isn't this basically setting me up as bait? Like leading a blind-folded cow to slaughter?"

"Yes," Hancock said bluntly, no apology in his voice. "But you aren't being meekly led to your demise. My team and I will protect you. I need to know who is enemy and who is oblivious to who you are and most importantly *where* you are."

"I wish I had your confidence," she muttered. "It's easy for you to say when you aren't the sacrificial lamb."

"That's where you're wrong," he corrected. "You, they want alive. Me and my men? Not so much. Completely expendable. And we're all that stands in the way of them getting their hands on you. So yeah, we're definitely taking the bigger risk here."

She was instantly ashamed at the selfishness of her thoughts. It made perfect sense now that he'd laid it out as matter-of-factly as he had. She'd never approached it from his mind-set, and it made her feel like a spoiled diva whose needs took priority over all others, at all costs. Even as the sobering thoughts dug into her consciousness, she sent Han-cock a look of apology he couldn't possibly misconstrue. But there was no acknowledgment—or condemnation, for that matter—in his eyes. But then he hadn't pointed out the fact that he and his men were at greater risk than she was to take her down a few notches. He'd merely stated a fact in that unruffled manner he had perfected.

They pulled up to the tanker on the periphery of the vil-lage, the one that had the clearest escape route should the shit hit the fan. Conrad immediately herded Honor from the vehicle, and she was careful to keep her head bowed in a posture of submissiveness and remain a step behind and to the side of Conrad as he hurried her into a crude hut used as a washroom.

First he went in and checked to make sure no one was inside. Once satisfied it was empty, he gave Honor firm orders to get her business done as soon as possible and meet him at the entrance, where he was pulling guard duty to make sure no one intruded.

She wasted no time, fighting with the heavy burka and squatting carefully over the disgusting hole in the ground that was already filled with human waste. She breathed through her mouth so the foul odor didn't fill her nostrils, afraid her stomach would revolt and she'd waste precious seconds throwing up.

It was uncomfortable as hell, bent at an awkward angle, holding the folds of her garment up so they didn't get soiled in the process. Her knee protested holding herself as steady as possible while she went about the business of relieving herself.

By the time she'd peed about two gallons, both legs were shaking and her hurt knee was buckling incessantly, causing her to balance precariously on her good leg. She hastily washed up as best she could with the discolored water in the washbasin against the wall and didn't even speculate on its cleanliness. It would only freak her out more than she already was.

She returned to where Conrad stood, his stance impatient even as his wary gaze constantly scanned the entire area. When he completed a sweep, he began all over again, never taking his eyes from the goings-on around them.

He glanced her way when he caught sight of her and dipped his head in the direction of the military vehicle where Hancock was finishing up the refuel. She fell into step behind him, and as Conrad continually did, she too kept a watchful eye on everyone in her sight line.

When they turned around the outhouse, Honor nearly froze. Only her rigid control prevented her from reacting to the sight of an armed man in fatigues lifting his assault rifle and pointing it at . . . Conrad.

Shit!

She couldn't just act like she hadn't seen it, and she had to act fast. Completely disregarding Hancock's—and Conrad's—strict instructions to not draw undue attention to herself, she launched herself toward Conrad as though she had fallen.

She crashed into the unsuspecting man, and the adrenaline surge that had spiked through her veins gave her much more strength than she thought she possessed. Conrad went sprawling just as a volley of bullets peppered the area right where Conrad had been standing a fraction of a second earlier.

Tensing, expecting pain from one of the bullets that had surely struck her, she hunched in on herself even as she dropped like a rock. Which was stupid because she and Conrad both needed to be on their feet so they could make their escape. But self-preservation ruled and she acted instinctively to prevent herself from getting killed. Even though she hadn't been the intended target.

Vicious curses from more than one location blistered the air, and Honor suddenly found herself roughly dragged to her feet, thrown over a shoulder and flopping like a fish out of water as Hancock sprinted toward the waiting vehicle.

Conrad had already regained his footing and was two steps ahead of Hancock and Honor. Hancock forcibly threw Honor into the backseat before he and Conrad dove inside. Their doors weren't even shut yet when the vehicle lurched forward, tires spinning momentarily as the driver floored it.

"Goddamn it. *Goddamn it!*" Hancock bellowed.

But it was Conrad's expression that sent Honor's heart into her throat. He was coldly furious. Rage simmered over and through his body, his face and eyes so black that she shivered. His jaw bulged from clenching his teeth together so tightly.

Everyone was pissed. At *her.* And she was utterly baffled. Genuinely puzzled. She'd saved Conrad's life. Didn't that get her off the hook for "drawing undue attention"?

"What the fuck did you think you were doing?" Conrad roared. "What about 'do *not* draw attention to yourself' did you not understand? Women here would never do such a thing. Swear to God, you must have a death wish."

"Bullshit," Honor snapped, pissed that the man wasn't the least bit grateful that she'd prevented someone from making Swiss cheese out of him. "You forget I work in villages like this. I see mothers protecting their children. Their loved ones. Every bit as fiercely as the males."

Hancock huffed out a breath that suggested he was hanging on to his patience—and temper—by a thread.

"Not in this village," he said through clenched teeth. "Women here are rarely seen and never heard. They do not interfere. Worse, you brought dishonor to the assassin because you, a lowly woman, thwarted his objective and the entire village bore witness to it. This is an outlaw town and the only rules are the ones enforced by the people who have the power to back them up."

"Good," Honor snarled. "I hope he kills himself over the humiliation of it all. One less asshole in the world, though if I hadn't interfered, then there'd be *two* less assholes in the world."

She stared pointedly at Conrad, her expression frigid.

"More likely he'll kill you," Hancock said grimly. "It doesn't matter if he knows you're wanted or if he's your enemy's friend. He would seek your death for no other reason than the insult you handed him."

"It's customary to thank someone when they save your life," she snapped. "Not tell them they're a fucking idiot who can't follow simple instructions."

"If the shoe fits," Conrad muttered.

"If you want to die so bad, I'll *gladly* oblige you," she seethed. "I'll shoot you myself, but you can be sure I'll be creative with the shot placements."

"Bad mojo," Mojo muttered, glancing over his shoulder at Honor with something that looked suspiciously like a glimmer of respect.

"It's over and done with," Hancock said by way of halting the back-and-forth. "Just get us the hell out of here, Viper, and don't let up on the accelerator. And damn sure keep an eye out for a tail or an RPG attack."

Honor sank against the seat, pain and intense heat bathing her side. She must have fallen on something when she hit the ground so fast. But over her dead body would she ever let these assholes know that she'd sustained another injury while saving their ungrateful ass of a teammate. They could all fuck off as far as she was concerned. Just when she began to tell herself that she misunderstood Hancock and his men and that they weren't really flaming assholes, they just as quickly dissuaded her of that notion by proving yet again just what jackasses they were.

The demon inside her, the very pissed-off outraged demon, wouldn't simply let it go as Hancock had commanded. She turned her head so she faced Conrad and stared him down unflinchingly, not giving a shit that he could snap her like a twig with two fingers.

"So you would have preferred I just stand there like some hapless twit and let you get killed? Really? Does your life mean so little to you?"

She couldn't keep the derision or scorn from her voice.

Conrad's scowl deepened and his features grew even blacker, if such a thing were possible. He looked like an angry storm cloud in spring tornado season. His brow was so furrowed that his eyebrows bunched together to form one continuous line of hair over both eyes. And those eyes glittered with fury.

"Ungrateful ass," she muttered, before refusing to look at him a second longer.

Instead she leaned back, tilting her head against the seat even though the rough terrain made it impossible for her skull not to endure battering from all the holes and bumps in their path.

She closed her eyes, shutting them all out. If she was lucky, she could fall asleep and they could just wake her up when they got to wherever they were stopping and she could be a good little hapless maiden and go sit on her hands while the big bad alpha males got their balls shot off.

It couldn't happen to a nicer group of guys.

CHAPTER 12

HANCOCK—and the rest of his team, for that matter—had fallen silent after her scathing putdown of their ingratitude. She'd made no bones about the fact she thought they were all complete unfeeling bastards.

She wasn't wrong.

His men didn't give a shit what anyone thought of them when it came to doing their job at any cost. Like they were ultimately handing Honor back over to the very men they were currently saving her from. And that was all sorts of fucked up. Yeah, they tended not to give a rat's ass whether they were saints or Satan himself. But it was in every man's eyes, expressions, demeanor, that Honor . . . mattered.

They respected her when they respected no one but their team leader and each other. And if that didn't throw a serious kink in their plans, he didn't know what did. What if he ended up with a full scale rebellion on his hands? What if his men grew a conscience, as Hancock had in recent years—and he had vowed he'd never let that conscience interfere in another mission—and refused to hand Honor over to Bristow, then Maksimov and ultimately A New Era? There were too many ways for this to go wrong. What if Maksimov decided to say *fuck you* to A New Era? He was out of their reach and probably the only unofficial organization that would be an even match with A New Era. Maybe even far superior because Maksimov had no cause, no emotion. The members of A New Era were ruled by emotion, rage, a sense of righteousness and justice. They had no problem sacrificing themselves for the greater good. *Their* greater good.

None of Honor's choices were remotely pleasant. Bristow was an evil bastard who got off on hurting women. Maksimov was brutal with his women, sometimes killing them with his depraved fetishes. In his world women were a dime a dozen and completely expendable.

And, well, if Bristow and Maksimov actually did turn Honor over to A New Era, she would endure unspeakable torture and degradation. She would pray for death, no matter how strong and fierce she was. No woman or man could endure what A New Era would dole out to her day after day, week after week until finally they killed her, and again, it wouldn't be slow or merciful.

Many other militant terrorist cells, while brutal and inhuman, killed their hostages somewhat humanely. Usually a shot in the back of the head, execution style. Or they simply sliced the head off in a public venue so others would fear them and take them seriously.

He glanced sideways at Honor, at her closed eyes, her lashes resting delicately on her cheeks. So damn innocent. An innocent who would serve as the sacrificial virgin just so hundreds of thousands of people would live. It wasn't fair. None of it was. But Hancock had come to grips long ago with the fact that it was impossible to have it all. Sacrifices had to be made, no matter the cost. He didn't have to always like it, but he knew it for the truth it was, and it was the only way to bring down people like Bristow, Maksimov, and eventually ANE, A New Era.

He couldn't tell if she was sleeping or merely closing her eyes to shut them all out. He couldn't blame her. She'd been pissed—rightly so. And she was right. Not one had expressed their gratitude. Only anger at her for not following orders and the unspoken sentiment that she'd damn near gotten herself killed for a man she didn't even know—or like.

Why had she done it?

It was a puzzle that had racked his brain ever since it had happened. He couldn't come up with one good reason, when she'd fought so valiantly and intelligently to elude ANE that she would simply step in the path of a bullet and shove his teammate to safety.

He wasn't used to women of Honor's caliber. The only women he'd ever met who had spines of steel and resolve better than any man's and yet were infinitely fragile were the Kelly women and the wives of KGI members. They were much like Honor. Exactly like her. Maybe that was why he could allow grudging respect for Honor, because the KGI women were fucking fierce and she was every bit the warrior the KGI women were.

"Almost there," Henderson called from the front. "Better get the woman up and lucid so we don't waste any time hiding this vehicle and transferring to another. Unless you want to bunk down again tonight?"

Hancock shook his head. "No. We need to keep moving. We'll switch out driving so the others can get sleep. I'll need at least one awake with the driver to keep a close watch and make sure we aren't being followed or driving into a trap."

Having issued the commands, Hancock turned his attention to Honor, whose eyes were still closed. As he studied her closer, he saw the lines of strain on her forehead, and her jaw was clenched, even in sleep. Almost as if she were in pain.

But given all she'd gone through, she was more likely having a nightmare.

He gently touched her shoulder, giving it a nudge.

"Honor. Honor, you need to wake up. We're on a short time line and we need to ditch our vehicle."

Her eyelids fluttered sluggishly as if she were swimming her way from unconsciousness. He frowned because she had always been ready without complaint, even when she was in a great deal of pain. But she never complained and she kept pace with him and his men. Again, how could he not admire this woman?

She licked her lips and frowned, almost as if she were

confused by the difficulty she was having becoming fully awake. He saw the moment resolve settled over her shoulders, shaking away whatever fog had been present. Her eyes gleamed with determination and she quickly scanned their surroundings.

"How long?" she asked.

"Three minutes," Copeland called from the front seat.

Honor nodded her understanding, squaring her shoulders.

Minutes later the vehicle came to an abrupt stop, causing Honor to lurch forward, the seatbelt ramming into her belly. To her surprise Conrad was there before Hancock to catch her, and then he carefully eased her back against the seat.

Conrad got out first and then the others piled out. Only Viper stayed behind the wheel. Hancock reached over to unlatch Honor's harness. His arm pressed into her side in order to reach the latch buried under the folds of her burka.

She winced and her face went pale. What the fuck?

He quickly unsnapped the buckle and prepared to help her out of the vehicle. But when he drew his arm back, the one that had pressed hard into Honor's side, he was stunned to see fresh blood smeared on his skin.

Dread took hold of his spine.

He lifted a hand to Honor's cheek, staring her intently in the eyes.

"Are you hurt?" he asked in a soft tone.

Her eyes were wide and frightened. She'd seen the blood on Hancock's arm. She was pale and shaken as her lips worked to answer his question.

"I don't know. I didn't think so. I felt a twinge of pain in my side, but I fell and just thought it was sore. But it hurts *now*," she said, gritting her teeth.

Hancock swore viciously and guilt, not an emotion he was well acquainted with at all, gripped his chest like a vise.

"Let me get you in the other vehicle. We can't afford to stop. But I'll take a look and see what's going on. If it's serious, we'll have to risk taking you to the hospital."

Fear immediately filled her eyes even as she shook her head.

"I'm alive. I'm not dying. I just hurt. And I've dealt with pain for over a week. I'll deal with it now," she said quietly.

Once again a surge of pride overtook him. She simply didn't know the meaning of the word *quit*. If only he weren't destined to betray her. To sacrifice her for the greater good. The world needed people like her, and it fucking sucked that the good ones were usually the sacrificial lambs.

"Let me help you. We don't know what's going on and I don't want you making it worse," he said in a low voice.

She nodded her agreement.

Hancock leaned in and slid one arm beneath her knees and the other between her back and the seat, gently lifting, watching for any sign of pain or discomfort in her eyes. He should have known he wouldn't find any no matter how much pain she was in. She had too much pride and determination to give in and appear weak in front of him and his men.

He retreated from the interior and turned Honor's face into his neck to protect her eyes from the scorching, blowing sand.

"Open the back," Hancock said as he strode toward the waiting vehicle. "Honor and I will ride in back for a few miles. I need a flat surface so I can see about her injury."

"Injury?" Conrad demanded. "What injury?"

"I don't know yet," Hancock said calmly.

Conrad let loose with a string of obscenities and continued to mutter and curse under his breath as he opened the vehicle and hastily arranged a comfortable place for Honor to lie. Then he stood back as Hancock positioned her carefully on the blankets Conrad had spread out. But Conrad didn't budge. In fact he pressed in close, touching elbows with Hancock, a grim expression on his face.

Hancock didn't reprimand his man. Beneath the fury, Hancock could see . . . worry. And guilt. Conrad assumed she'd taken a bullet meant for him, and it would eat him alive. Hancock and his men, every single last one of them, were protectors. Yes, they didn't always protect the good and innocent. Sometimes it took becoming the very thing they hunted so relentlessly in order to take out evil in the world. So that the innocent would prevail.

Only this innocent he couldn't save. Her fate had already been decided and written. Unchangeable. It would have been far more merciful for her if she had died in the clinic bombing. Because the short future she faced wouldn't go by quickly. It wouldn't be merciful. In fact, it would tear her down to her soul, and in the end, that would fade too, leaving only a hollow shell of the fierce woman she used to be. She would welcome death. Pray for it. And it would only make her captors all the more determined to prolong her hour-to-hour agony.

And he was responsible. *He* would have done that to her. Make it possible for her to be treated with less regard than an animal. And for what? The greater good? It was the philosophy Titan had always held as their creed, even when Rio led Titan. The man who'd taught Hancock everything he knew.

Hancock had always believed in that motto. He understood it. He lived it, breathed it, risked his life to uphold it. But for the first time, the idea of Honor's sacrifice being responsible for Maksimov, Bristow and ANE going down and saving hundreds of thousands of innocent people in the process made him . . . sick. It disgusted him.

Maybe it *was* time to hang it up. Disappear somewhere and start a new life where he would be known to no one and not relentlessly hunted. Somewhere he could be alone, never having to deal with the oblivious people he'd lost his soul for in order for them to continue their ignorant, happy existence.

But no. He had family. By love, not blood. They were the only people in the world he felt . . . anything . . . for. Affection. Love. Unwavering loyalty. There was nothing he wouldn't do for any of them.

He couldn't simply walk out of their lives and never return. They deserved better of him after all they'd done for him. They'd saved him. They'd given him purpose and a place in the world, even if it was a place so steeped in shadows and sins that he doubted he'd ever see the light again.

He'd long ago made peace with the fact that he wasn't a good man. He'd never be a good man. But for his family, he could and would be that man even if it was all a lie. Big Eddie, his foster father. And his brothers—Raid, a policeman, and Ryker, a former military man who went into personal security after his discharge. He'd heard from Eden that KGI was considering taking Ryker on. But he'd last spoken to her months before and only then to let her know he'd be out of touch for an indefinite period of time.

Eden. His baby sister who meant the world to him. She was everything good. Everything he wasn't. He wasn't a man who scared easily, or at all for that matter. He was calm in the face of adversity, his mind always calculating like a computer his options and possibilities. And he kept all his missions impersonal. Never forming any attachment or bond with anyone.

But nearly losing Eden—losing her for several hours when she endured horrific torture—had unhinged him. He'd been terrified. Out of control. Shaking. Emotional. All the things he considered weaknesses in his work.

Even as he considered that if he had no family he'd never face those very uncomfortable emotions and reactions, he knew that he loved the Sinclairs when he loved no one else. They were his only anchor in the dark world he was being absorbed into more and more with every passing day.

Shaking himself back to the task at hand, he glanced up at Honor to see if she was still conscious. She was, but her eyes were glazed with pain, though not a single sound passed her tightly closed lips. No betraying quiver in her body. The only evidence of her strain was her tightly curled fists on either side of her.

"I'll be careful," he said in an attempt to reassure her.

And then he didn't understand why he felt the need to say anything at all. If she hadn't put herself in the line of fire, she wouldn't be hurt and bleeding. He ought to still be pissed, but lying to himself did no good. He hadn't been pissed because she hadn't followed orders. He'd been pissed because when he'd witnessed what she did, his heart had plummeted into his stomach and unholy . . . fear . . . assailed him that she would be killed. And it had nothing to do with the fact that if she died his mission would be FUBAR.

Shut it off. All of it. His stupid thoughts and feelings. He began to roll the heavy material of her burka up her legs. When he got to her thighs he gave silent thanks that she'd worn athletic shorts and a sports bra underneath. The last thing he needed was to start fantasizing about what had to be a gorgeous naked body. He had enough issues to deal with without adding completely inappropriate lustful thoughts. He already had too many recently discovered weaknesses, and he had no wish to add to that list. Hell, he couldn't remember the last time he'd felt lust or experienced sexual urges. His missions were his mistress, the only thing he gave unwavering fidelity to. Getting off was something he had neither the time nor the desire for when so many lives depended on him.

There was blood smeared down her right side even past her hip, but he hadn't yet gotten to the source of the blood.

Finally he simply tugged the burka all the way over her head and tossed it aside. When he looked back, he sucked in his breath. Beside him, Conrad swore viciously again.

Right between her bottom rib and her hip was a still-bleeding crease at least six inches long.

"At least it's just a graze," Conrad muttered, but anger was still vibrating in his voice.

Hancock carefully palpated the area, forcing himself not to jerk away when she flinched.

"No sign of a bullet lodged in the muscle or tissue. It bled a lot, but it's not serious."

He glanced up at Honor to gauge her reaction to his assessment and saw relief simmering in her deep brown eyes.

"It needs stitches," Conrad said with a frown.

Hancock stifled a smile at how concerned he was for Honor's well-being despite the image he projected of being an angry, ungrateful asshole.

"Yeah, she does. I can get it done, but I'm not as good at it as you are, and you have far more medic training."

"I'll do it," Conrad said, pushing past Hancock, a med kit in his hand.

Alarm instantly registered in Honor's eyes, the first sign of fear in this entire fucked-up situation that she'd allowed anyone to see. Then she glanced at Conrad, who was crawling into the back with her, and unease billowed off her in tangible waves.

"I'll be right here," Hancock said in a soothing tone.

She didn't look at all relieved. Her eyes never once left Conrad, and every time he pulled something from the med kit and placed it beside her, her panic intensified.

Fuck. She was scared shitless of his man and was even more wary after Conrad had yelled at her and given her a scorching dressing-down.

"Can't you or Mojo do it?" Honor asked with quivering lips.

CHAPTER 13

TO Honor's astonishment, Conrad grimaced and actual regret flickered in his eyes. She was even more shocked when he curled his rough hand around her much smaller one and gave it a gentle squeeze.

"You aren't wrong about me," Conrad said. "I'm an unfeeling asshole. But you deserved more than what you got from us all when you saved my life. I was pissed, yes. But not for the reason you likely believe. I was pissed because it was my job to protect *you*. Not the other way around. And if I'd done my job right, you would have never taken a bullet for me."

Honor opened her mouth to argue, but Conrad silenced her with a black look.

"I also understand why you don't want me to stitch you. You don't trust me as much as you do Hancock and Mojo. You shouldn't. I'm not a good man. But I can make you at least one promise. I will do this and it will be done right and I'll do my best to keep the pain at a minimum."

"O-okay," she said shakily. "Let's just get it over with so we can get out of here."

Hancock sent her a look of regret. "We're leaving *now*. Conrad is going to stitch you on the road. It's our only chance. We can't stay out in the open for a prolonged time."

"I'll numb it," Conrad said in as soft a voice she'd ever come out of his mouth. "And I'll give you an injection for pain before I set the first stitch. You won't feel it. I promise."

"Thank you," she whispered, finally relaxing and accepting Conrad's honesty and also the fact he wouldn't hurt her any more than possible.

Conrad's features became a storm cloud once more and she shrank back against the covers, quickly rethinking her decision to allow him to stitch her wound.

"You have *nothing* to thank me for," Conrad said fiercely. "It is I who owe you a debt of gratitude I can't possibly ever hope to repay. And Hancock and his men are equally grateful to you no matter that they posture and act like angry assholes. You scared us all."

Her eyes widened in surprise.

"You're a courageous woman, Honor. I've worked and fought with allies and against foes. And no one has ever put their body in front of mine so I didn't get shot and killed. So yeah, if you want the truth, we're definitely pissed. But we were pissed because *you* could have been gunned down and we would have failed and not honored our promise to get you far beyond ANE's reach."

Heat suffused her cheeks and she forced herself to look away, not wanting the betraying tears blurring her vision.

"I won't hurt you, Honor," Conrad said in a gentle tone she would have never imagined coming from his mouth. It was all she could do to go back to an earlier assessment that they weren't unfeeling bastards with no conscience.

She lifted her gaze to Conrad's for the first time, seeking and searching for all this man had endured. He met her stare, unflinching, but the remnants of regret and guilt still lingered in his.

She lifted her hand weakly and slid her fingers over Conrad's. He reacted as if he'd been shot and started to yank his hand away, but then he halted his retreat, allowing her fingers to lace through his.

"You think you're a bad man. Why? The things you do are extraordinary. I only see a group of men who will die before they let A New Era find and kidnap me. I only see the good, Conrad," she said in a gentle voice. "Whether you want people to see it or not. But I see it and I see you, so you can drop the belligerent attitude and stop being a dick around me. You save people at great risk to your lives. Who *does* that?"

"It's what we do," Hancock said. "This is our calling, if you choose to look at it that way. But it's always been who I am—who *we* are. To rid the world of evil so no innocents suffer as they have in the past. And that's worldwide. I owe the American government absolutely nothing."

His tone had suddenly gone so icy that she shivered.

"They turned their backs on us and then attempted to hunt us to ground and eliminate every member of my team. My efforts aren't just constrained to U.S. interests or threats. Evil exists all over the world, and that is what we want to stop."

"And yet you consider yourselves bad men. That's a bunch of bullshit. Saving innocent lives is the epitome of good and courageous. Not many would devote their lives to ridding the world of evil."

A hint of a smile flirted with his lips, which made her mouth drop open. None of his men ever smiled. She wasn't even sure they had any emotions, bad or good. Their lives were decided for them, and in their job they couldn't afford emotions.

"Hancock, get a syringe with predrawn pain medication. I want her to have that first so she'll be relaxed and not in pain while I stitch her wound."

The pain medication took the edge off, but the pain was still there, though she braced herself, determined not to let anyone see her wimp out. She locked herself in a deep void where she floated free of her immediate surroundings.

But she was unable to hold back the flinch when Conrad got to the middle where the skin was more tender.

Conrad cursed and muttered an apology.

"It's okay," she said. "Don't stop. Just get it done with. I can take it."

Conrad shook his head, respect flashing in his eyes. But he did as she said and meticulously set the stitches but not before instructing Hancock to administer another injection of pain medication.

After the second dose, she no longer had to force herself

into a deep, dark hole. Her surroundings fuzzed and she drifted with the wind, feeling no pain or anxiety. Before she knew it, Conrad had finished and efficiently bandaged the wound after thoroughly cleaning it.

"We have a long drive. You should sleep," Conrad said gruffly. "The pain meds will help and you won't be aware of the bumpy terrain, nor will it cause you undue pain."

She nodded slowly, her reflexes dulled. And then fear took hold and her eyes flew open when she had just about drifted into oblivion.

"I'm helpless like this," she said in a panicked voice. "What if we run into trouble? I'll be completely useless. I'll get us *all* killed."

It was the same argument she'd used before when she'd been heavily medicated, only this time no amusement glimmered in Hancock's eyes as it had the first time she'd said nearly those exact words. In fact, utter seriousness was etched into his expression. Gravity and promise glittered brightly in his eyes and she drew comfort from the wordless exchange between them. Sometimes a single look said a thousand words.

Hancock put his hand to her forehead and wiped her hair back from her brow.

"You don't worry about that. You'll be of no use to us if you don't rest and recover. We *will* protect you. Now go to sleep, Honor. I'll wake you when it's time."

She frowned, but the pull of the medication was making her swimmy and she could no longer fight its effects.

Summoning her last moments of coherency, she gripped Conrad's hand, thinking he would be more willing to listen to her demand than Hancock.

"Promise me," she said, shocked at how difficult it was to get the words past her lips. "Promise me that if I hinder you in any way, you'll leave me and save yourselves. I've cheated death multiple times already. It's only a matter of time before death wins, and I refuse to allow you to die trying to prevent the inevitable."

Conrad's response was explosive. "Are you out of your goddamn mind?"

But she had already slipped under, fading away under the spell of the medication.

Conrad turned his furious gaze on his team leader, who didn't look any happier over Honor's demand.

"Jesus Christ," Conrad muttered. "Is she for real?"

"Yes, she is," Hancock said quietly. "Which makes our betrayal of her all the more reprehensible."

Conrad's lips formed a tight white line, anger and helpless rage flashing in his eyes.

"There has to be another way, Hancock. One that doesn't involve fucking over an innocent woman."

"Don't you think I've weighed all the options?" Hancock snapped, his carefully constructed control fraying precariously. He was displaying uncharacteristic emotion. But then so too were his men. "Don't you think if I had any other way to take Maksimov down, I'd do it? Honor is our *only* means of getting close enough to Maksimov to take him out for good. If there was a way, *any* other way, I'd jump all over it and send Honor home in a heartbeat, but goddamn it, she *is* the only way. We don't have to like it. We don't fucking like it. But it doesn't change what *has* to be."

His words were laced with bitterness. Anger, self-loathing. Regret. Guilt. Things he *never* allowed himself to feel—things he hadn't though himself *capable* of feeling—because to do so was asking for failure. And he would not fail a third time. Too many lives depended on this, his final—and only—remaining shot at taking Maksimov out for good.

"She doesn't deserve this from any of us," Conrad said bitterly.

Hancock sighed because damn it, this was precisely what he didn't want to happen. His men respected Honor, admired her courage and resiliency, and where before they'd never suffered a fit of conscience over doing the job, now they were adamantly opposed to handing Honor over to unspeakable torture and eventual death. Hell, it would be kinder if they just shot her and got it over with. But then Maksimov would elude them again. It always came back to that. Maksimov and their relentless pursuit of a monster the likes of which the world had never known. At any cost. Goddamn it. Any cost. Honor. She was the cost of succeeding in their mission and he hated himself for not having any other way. No other choice. He'd have to live with his goddamn conscience for the rest of his life.

"No, she doesn't deserve this," Hancock admitted. "But we have no choice, Conrad. You know that and it's why you're so pissed. Maksimov is responsible for countless deaths and endless misery and suffering. He has to be taken down, no matter what it takes. I don't like it any more than you do, but the mission comes first. As does the greater good."

"If I never hear 'for the greater good' again it'll be too soon," Conrad spat.

Hancock was just as sick of carrying that flag and adhering to that motto, but he didn't say as much to his man. If he showed any weakness, any reluctance to carry out the mission they were charged with, his men would revolt. And he couldn't afford that. They were too close. He could taste victory. Smell it. Could envision Maksimov's death and the end of a reign of terror unlike any other in the world.

Conrad's face was contorted in a scowl, and he packed the supplies back into the med kit and then crawled over the backseat, leaving Hancock with the unconscious Honor.

Hancock didn't move for a long time. He merely remained on his knees staring down at a brave woman. The bravest woman he'd ever encountered. The most selfless woman he'd ever met. And he hated himself for what he must do.

Finally he eased himself down and lay beside her, so his body was flush against hers. Paying heed to her injured side, he tucked one arm beneath her head so it was pillowed and didn't absorb the hard bumps as they raced across the terrain.

Then he slid his other arm over her abdomen, holding her gently against him, and then lay his head next to hers, offering comfort even while she slept.

CHAPTER 14

"GIVE her a tranquilizer," Hancock said grimly to Conrad. "I don't want her to see us getting on the plane. It will give her false hope and I'm not going to lie to her. It's better if she isn't aware of what's going on until we get to Bristow."

"Bad mojo," Mojo muttered, a deep scowl on his battered features.

Viper, Henderson and Copeland didn't look any less pissed.

"Nothing like turning a lamb loose among a pack of wolves," Copeland said in disgust.

"Look," Hancock said, simmering with impatience. "I don't like it any more than you all do. I'm not a *complete* heartless bastard." Even if until recent times he would have argued to the death that he was anything but just that. An unfeeling asshole whose soul was black and his heart long ago gone. He didn't regret saving Elizabeth, an innocent twelve-year-old girl. He didn't regret saving Grace, Rio's wife. And he damn sure didn't regret letting Maksimov slip through his fingers again to save Maren, a woman who was good to her toes and had a heart as big as China. But this time, he couldn't allow guilt, conscience or anything else to deter him from his mission. "But Maksimov has to be taken down. I let emotion cloud my judgment, not once, but twice when I was this close to taking Maksimov out. We won't get another opportunity. This is our last and only chance. Do I like what we have to do? Hell no. But can you live with your conscience if we save one woman at the expense of hundreds of thousands? Because Maksimov grows bolder and more powerful by the day. If he isn't stopped, many will suffer. If we stop him, only *one* suffers. Honor."

"And that's supposed to make us feel better?" Henderson muttered, shocking Hancock by expressing that he felt anything at all. For that matter, all of his men had turned into men Hancock no longer recognized. They were all unfeeling bastards. It was what made them efficient killers.

"There has to be another way," Conrad said stubbornly. "Can't we fake it? Send pictures of Honor and arrange a meet-up for the exchange and then take his ass out without Honor ever being at risk?"

"You know we can't do that," Hancock said in a low voice. "You're forgetting Bristow. We're bringing her to Bristow because Honor is a way for Bristow to get in tight with Maksimov, and for Maksimov, Honor is the ultimate bargaining chip with ANE. He won't take anything at face value. He's too smart to fall for a trick. He will know if we even try to fuck him over."

A round of vicious curses rent the air. Hancock echoed every one of them in his mind, but damn it, they didn't have a choice. Sometimes the greater good sucked balls. He was tired of deciding what the greater good even was. He wasn't judge and executioner, even if that was precisely what he'd been for the last decade. But years of being judge and jury and being an instrument of justice was weighing heavily on him, and he was tired. Tired of the deception. Tired of aligning his loyalty with the enemy so he could become the very thing he despised above all else. He just wanted . . . peace. To be able to sleep at night without the nightmares of his past replaying over and over in his tortured mind. He was a damned fool for ever thinking that was even a possibility. He knew that now, when before he'd been able to lie to himself and think it would all be okay once he stepped down. Because Honor would torture not only his dreams, but every waking moment. He'd never have peace. He didn't deserve it.

Without a word, Conrad hoisted himself over the back-seat, to where Hancock still lay with Honor nestled in his arms. At any other time, he'd cut off his arm before ever allowing his men to see him displaying tenderness. Any-thing but the robotic, inhuman persona that had become second nature to him. But now? He didn't give a shit. All his men had a soft spot for Honor. They wouldn't think anything of him offering her comfort. Especially since it was the least he could do when he planned to turn her over to a monster.

Conrad dug into the med kit and prepared a sedative. Then he glanced over at Hancock.

"How long you want her to be out?"

"Until we take her to Bristow. I'd rather she awaken in a bed and not immediately know her . . . fate."

It was delaying the inevitable, but he wanted to give her these last moments. As long as he could grant her. It was cruel, he supposed, to give her that much more hope. But if she could have just a few hours more devoid of fear and the horrific sense of betrayal she would feel the moment she learned the truth, then he'd give those hours to her.

Conrad scowled again but drew more of the medication into the syringe.

"She'll be out for a while," he said as he gently inserted the needle into her hip.

When he was done, he put away the supplies and then hauled himself over into the backseat without another word.

The atmosphere was tense in the vehicle. No one spoke, but then that wasn't unusual. They weren't a chatty group by any stretch of the imagination. Most of their communication wasn't verbal anyway. They'd worked together too many years. They could anticipate each other's moves without need-ing to be told. And they had their own set of hand signals.

But this silence was different. It wasn't the silence embraced by the men who lived and breathed the team. It was a pissed-off, surly, *helpless* silence, and none of them were happy about it at all. They were pissed that they cared.

And they were pissed that they'd considered, even for a moment, aborting their mission to save one courageous woman.

HONOR had slept, as Hancock intended, for the remainder of their hazardous trek over the desert to the airfield where the plane waited that would take them to Bristow. He never moved from her side, and in her sleep, she'd sought out his body heat, snuggling into his hard frame, her softness melding seamlessly. Like they fit. It was an absurd, stupid thought, but he couldn't prevent it from flickering through his mind. Just as he couldn't deny the comfort her closeness gave him. Comfort he didn't deserve.

Instinctively he knew she needed this. Human touch. Comfort. Contact. She'd been through a horrific ordeal and he was delivering her to worse. There was nothing he could do about her fate, but he could at least offer her a little peace, respite from the inevitable storm. And it wasn't nearly as distasteful as he would have thought. The idea that he could offer anyone, especially a woman, any measure of comfort was something he would have thought not only impossible but not in the least bit . . . enjoyable. That he would *like* it.

There was something about this small, fierce woman that got to him. And that pissed him off. Nothing got to him. Not when it came to the mission. To the greater good. He couldn't afford to be human, to feel emotion. Emotion could get him killed. It could get his men killed. And he owed them more than that. They were fiercely loyal to him and to one another. They'd put their lives on the line for him, just as he had for them, many times. Allowing a distraction such as the woman lying nestled in his arms would be a . . . disaster.

As he lay there, definitely not resting as she did against him, he realized he was even more pissed that she trusted him. Maybe she hadn't even acknowledged it to herself, but her actions defied whatever thoughts she had concerning his trustworthiness. She relaxed with him when she was vulnerable. Hurting, afraid, alone. She instinctively sought out his comfort and strength, clinging to it when she had nothing else in the world to hold on to. He'd become her anchor. In her mind, he was her savior, when he was the very worst sort of bastard.

He was worse than the animals hunting her. Worse than Bristow and Maksimov. Because none of those men would even attempt to lie to her. To gain her trust. To make her believe they were something they weren't. Only he did—was doing—that. And it burned like acid in his veins.

He owed her truth, that he wasn't her savior. That he was the instrument of her unspeakable torment and eventual death. *Then* she could hate him. Could never harbor illusions about who and what he was. And he'd never have to look into eyes filled with betrayal when she realized how wrong she'd been about him. But she'd proved that she was a fighter, and he couldn't afford any resistance. Any chance she would escape—and she would try. Over and over. It would slow them down and risk not getting her out at all. Even if her return was inevitable.

And so he lied. Not by words. But by actions. By omission. He didn't correct her assumption that he was here to bring her home. He let her draw her own conclusions, rationalizing to himself that it wasn't his fault if she came to the wrong ones. It was the worst sort of deception. Worse than outright lying.

Yes, he owed her the truth, but it was the one thing he couldn't give her.

When the vehicle came to an abrupt halt, Hancock automatically anchored her more firmly so he absorbed the jolt instead of her. Only when the doors opened did his hold loosen on her, and he lifted his head to see Conrad's grim face staring at him in resignation.

"Jet's already running. We need to load and go. We aren't completely out of the no-fly zone and these assholes have heat-seeking missiles that could take us out."

Hancock nodded his acknowledgment and then began gently extricating himself from around Honor, moving slowly so he didn't wake her from her drug-induced slumber.

"Prep another syringe," Hancock directed his second. "Just in case she rouses midflight. I want her out until she's in a bedroom and doesn't waken thinking she's in immediate danger."

It had already been said. It was unnecessary for Hancock to explain himself again. It wasn't something he ever did. Or had. Until now. It felt too much like he was justifying his actions, his decisions. Defending them. And that really pissed him off.

Conrad's eyes flickered, the only outward sign of the man's dislike for the mission, but he didn't argue. He merely nodded and dragged the med kit from the back as Hancock crawled over Honor to get out.

He waved off Copeland's offer to help get Honor from the vehicle. Honor was Hancock's responsibility. His alone. His men were already unsettled, their usually unquestionable resolve faltering. He wouldn't place them in the position of feeling they contributed more to Honor's fate. That sin was for him and him alone to bear for all time.

There would be no atonement. No grace for one such as he. He'd been unsalvageable long before this—Honor—but even if he'd had any shot at redemption, this would have sealed his eternal damnation. Hell was too good for someone who'd lived his life shedding the blood of others and sacrificing innocents for the fucking greater good.

How could he even face his family after this? How could he look the man he considered a father in the eyes? Face his brothers. And Eden. An angel with more compassion and goodness in her soul than any other person he'd ever known. Except . . . Honor. Somehow his betrayal of Honor seemed to be as unforgivable as if he'd sacrificed Eden. He'd dropped the guise of justice and his pursuit of Maksimov, not once but twice, to save other innocents. So why not Honor?

If he were truly honest, he would admit to himself, to his men, that this being their last chance was bullshit. There was always another opportunity given time and patience. But patience was what he was fast running out of. His resolve to end it now had less to do with it being his only shot and a lot more to do with the fact that Hancock was weary and he wanted out.

His selfishness would cost Honor . . . everything. Because

he was consumed with guilt, an emotion he'd thought he'd become immune to long ago, and he could no longer continue this empty, soulless existence. It was a choice, not between bringing Maksimov to swift justice or not, but between himself and Honor. Her life so Hancock could complete his final mission and walk away to live a half-life with no meaning, color or purpose.

He would exist. Nothing more. Nothing less.

He could end it all and simply kill himself, but that was too easy and he didn't deserve final peace. He deserved to wake each morning and look in the mirror at the man who'd fucked over a beautiful, selfless woman just so he could stand down and not allow the ever-encroaching blackness that spread like an evil stain over his soul to erase the last vestiges of humanity he possessed.

Reverently, as though he carried a precious treasure, he cradled Honor in his arms and boarded the small jet. He continued past the three rows of seats at the front of the plane to the back, where there was a sitting lounge that held a small sofa and two leather armchairs.

Using his shoulder, he brushed open the door at the rear of the plane and entered the tiny bedroom that housed a double bed with barely enough room on either side of it to squeeze between it and the walls.

Hefting her slight weight so that he could free one of his hands, he pulled the covers back and positioned one of the pillows so he could lay Honor down in comfort.

He eased her onto the mattress and gently lowered her head until it met the pillow. He tensed when she stirred briefly and then let out his breath when she merely emitted a sigh and snuggled deeper into the pillow.

He started to pull the covers up over her body but hesitated, knowing he needed to check her wound while she was still sedated and make sure the stitches had held and she wasn't bleeding. He would do all of that once they were in the air. For now, he eased his large body onto the edge. He cursed when he bumped his head into the wall as he took his boots off. It took careful maneuvering to accomplish the task in the very narrow parameters of the bedroom.

Hancock's head immediately came up, his eyes sharp. There had been no knock on the door, but he knew immediately when it opened, even as soundlessly as it had been done.

Conrad didn't say anything. He never even looked Honor's way. In fact, it appeared he made a very concerted effort not to let her into his line of sight, his face cold and unreadable, his eyes black, those of the killer they all were as he simply held out the syringe Hancock had requested.

Hancock took it from his man's hand and Conrad simply turned and walked out, his gaze never once moving in Honor's direction.

Hancock curled his fingers around the syringe, hating himself a little more with every breath. He'd never liked himself, but he would have never thought he *hated* himself until . . . now. He knew his job was brutal. That to others he was a heartless monster. Machine, not human. He had never hated himself because he knew that what he did was necessary. And righteous.

But now?

Self-loathing permeated every heartbeat. Because there was *nothing* righteous about sending an innocent woman to hell, no matter how many lives it saved in the process.

CHAPTER 15

HANCOCK only lightly dozed, not allowing himself to fall fully into sleep. Somehow, Honor had once more sought out his body and was curled into him like a kitten. His shirt was tightly fisted in her hands even in sleep, as if she were holding on to the only solid thing in her life.

Even her legs were entwined with his, and she rested on her uninjured side and her head was nestled not on the pillow he'd settled her on, but on his shoulder. He could feel the light puffs of her breath blow warmly over his neck, and he marveled at how something so innocent and benign could feel so . . . good.

Just holding her felt good. Right. As if she belonged there. Under his protection.

He slammed the door on that thought so swiftly that he nearly flinched. He wasn't her protector. But the fleeting thought had given him savage, albeit brief, satisfaction. He couldn't remember feeling something so *good*. He didn't have a lot of experience with good. Bad he could handle. Could process and compartmentalize it. Good? Not so much. That brief flash had been nearly intoxicating as for a moment he'd contemplated being the good guy. The knight in shining armor Honor seemed to consider him. And that was dangerous. No, not dangerous. Deadly. Because he could easily become addicted to an emotion denied to him until those few seconds ago.

He didn't have many more hours to endure and remain focused until . . .

He closed his eyes, shocked by the pain that splintered through his heart at what was to come. Something that felt suspiciously like . . . sorrow . . . filtered sluggishly through his veins, creeping into his heart, filling it with an unfamiliar pain.

He was blessedly distracted from the direction of his thoughts, and the danger they posed, when Honor stirred restlessly against him. He could feel her every movement, knew that she was gradually climbing through the fog of the sedative, feeling her way to awareness.

Not yet. Not now, damn it. He reached blindly behind him to where the prepared syringe lay behind his back. He'd put it within easy reach so he could hold her as he was holding her now but inject her if she woke before he wanted her to.

But mostly because he was a coward and he wanted to delay the moment when she no longer looked at him like he was some kind of goddamn hero and instead looked at him with all the despair of betrayal. He didn't *have* to see the accusing look in her eyes. His imagination conjured the image well enough on its own and it was enough to make him . . . *hurt*.

"Hancock?" she whispered against his neck.

He froze in the process of uncapping the syringe one-handed, but then carefully, so as not to startle or frighten her, he slid his arm back over his body and placed his palm on her hip, the syringe extended between his fingertips so she only felt the warmth of his palm. Even with her senses dulled by medication and having lived every hour of the last many days in constant fear of discovery, she'd known immediately whom she was with. No panic. No fear that she'd been captured by the people hunting her. She was completely relaxed and confident she was safe.

"Am I dreaming?" she said in a sleepy, confused tone.

It was a compulsion, nothing more. He couldn't have controlled it if his life depended on it. He brushed his lips over her forehead, right at her hairline.

"Yes, honey. It's just a dream. Stay asleep and keep dreaming of the good."

Her brow wrinkled as if she were sorting out his statement and pondering the truth of it. But then she shocked the ever-loving hell out of him, and he wasn't a man who was shocked by *anything*.

"Then if this is a dream, will you kiss me?" she asked softly. "If it's a dream, it's not real, so it won't hurt anything. And you'll never know you kissed me because this is my dream, not yours."

The thought rushed through his mind before he was even aware that it was there. *No. Not just your dream. Mine as well.* Fuck it all but this one mission with *FUBAR* written all over it.

He held his breath, unable to do anything more than lie there rigidly, her body molded to his like a glove. A perfect fit. What the hell was he supposed to do?

Another completely alien emotion gripped him by the throat.

Panic.

If he kissed her, it made his betrayal even worse. If he didn't kiss her, he'd deny her the comfort she so obviously wanted—needed. And he'd vowed to give her nothing but good until the time came for him to hand her over to the enemy.

Goddamn it.

Fuck! He was already damned to hell. An eternity of torment and endless pain and torture. What was one more sin on top of the mountain he'd already committed? Somehow kissing a beautiful woman paled in comparison to all the blood he'd shed.

"And is me kissing you what you want to happen in your dream?" he asked in a hushed murmur, not wanting to pull her even closer to full consciousness.

He had the syringe so close to her flesh, and he didn't want her to wake more fully. Hell, he didn't even want her to remember this. It would only make it worse when . . .

He shook the thought off again just as she whispered and nuzzled against his neck.

"Yeah. You aren't the badass you want everyone to think. I *see* you, Hancock. Maybe others don't, but I do."

His breath escaped in a hiss of shock and surprise, and guilt gutted him, consumed him until he was literally shaking with it. Before he could venture further into territory best left alone, he quickly inserted the needle and pushed the medication into her body.

She gave a flinch, her mouth parting against his throat, but he flung the syringe off the bed and quickly lifted his free hand to her chin, tilting it upward so his mouth could capture hers, swallowing any protest or question she might have voiced.

His entire body jolted as though he'd been struck by lightning. Every corny description ever penned about chemistry, compatibility, a first kiss was suddenly only too real. Even in an airplane, he felt as though the entire earth shifted beneath him. An earthquake in mid air.

He deepened the kiss because he was powerless to do anything else. Her mouth was like the strongest magnet. He couldn't have pulled away. An entire army couldn't have separated their lips.

It was like drinking liquid sunshine. As soon as his lips had met hers, she opened her mouth in a breathy sigh and he inhaled her. Consumed her. She tasted sweeter than anything he'd ever known.

He'd intended it to be a soft peck, nothing more. Just enough to satisfy her desire for a brief moment of intimacy. Human contact. Tenderness instead of the pain and violence she'd experienced for so many days. But as soon as he tasted her, felt the electric shock all the way to his toes, all thoughts of a chaste kiss and holding her until she fell back under fled.

She made a throaty hum that vibrated over his tongue. He licked at the inside of her mouth. Tasted every inch of the luscious haven. Satin and silk, velvety soft. The heat between them rivaled the scorching desert they'd traveled. Her fingers curled more tightly into his chest, her nails, the few that hadn't been broken to the quick, digging into his skin.

He'd wear the marks from those nails, and for a brief time he'd have a reminder of her brand on him. Her mark.

He wished to hell he could have them permanently tattooed
on his skin. It would mark one of the best memories—and
serve as a reminder of what he'd callously destroyed.

His grip on her chin tightened and then loosened as he
fanned his fingers out to grasp her jaw, holding her in place
as he devoured the sweet innocence she offered him. He
was already going to hell and this . . . this would be a memory that could sustain him through the upcoming darkness.
One single moment captured in time that he could pause
and replay over and over so it was this he remembered and
saw instead of other horrific images of Honor.

"I've never had a better dream," she slurred, her eyes
already half lidded as the draw of the medication pulled her
deeper into its web. "So many nightmares. They never stop.
First time I've dreamed . . . good. Thank you . . ."

Her voice drifted off even as he kissed her again, and he
kept kissing her even when she went utterly limp and her
lips went slack. And when he swept his lips higher, feather-
ing them over her cheek, his gut clenched when he tasted
her tears.

He closed his eyes and wrapped his arm around her,
dragging her more firmly against his body while being
mindful of her injured side.

She'd thanked him. God help them all. And she'd wept
because for once her sleep wasn't filled with terror and
death. He wanted to ram his fist into the walls until his hands
bled. He wanted to kill someone. Bristow, Maksimov, ANE.
The whole sorry lot of them. Every single person who would
put hands to Honor, hurt her, terrorize her, he wanted their
blood. But most of all he wanted his *own*. He was the biggest
monster of all. Because if not for him, the bastards would
never get their hands on her.

CHAPTER 16

HONOR fought through heavy veils of dense fog surrounding her. Her reflexes were dull and her tongue felt thick in her mouth. She was semiawake and yet couldn't summon the strength to open her eyelids.

A dull throb in her head made its presence known. Her mouth felt like cotton and even with her eyes closed, they felt dry and scratchy, like sandpaper covered them instead of her eyelids.

As she continued her slow swim to lucidity, she became aware that she was . . . comfortable. Softness surrounded her, conforming to her body so that every part of her was cushioned. Even the ache in her head abated somewhat as she registered the plushness cushioning her head.

She let out a soft sigh. This had to be another really good dream. Not as good as the one where Hancock had kissed her, but still good.

Her lips turned down into a frown as she processed that last information her sluggish brain fed her. Nothing *that* realistic could possibly be a dream. If she ignored the dryness of her mouth, she could still *taste* him. The lingering effects of that scorching hot, sexy-as-sin kiss. And it was delicious. She nearly moaned as the memory became clearer and she recalled just how thoroughly he'd kissed her.

What was it he'd asked her? *And is me kissing you what you want to happen in your dream?*

That was no dream. He'd been speaking to her as though she were dreaming, ensuring that she really wanted him to kiss her. Doubt nagged at her. Why had he done it then? Had he wanted to kiss her or was he merely giving her what she asked for?

Hancock didn't strike her as a man who'd ever do anything he didn't want. And certainly no one was going to force him to do anything.

And as more of that decadent dream—reality—floated back to her, she realized that his kiss had not been the kiss of an unwilling man. Nor had it been a simple kiss, one designed to satisfy her need. He'd devoured her mouth and then things had gone fuzzy again.

She frowned again and reached sluggishly down to rub her hand over her hip. He'd injected her with something. A sedative. Just before kissing her. So obviously he didn't want her conscious very long after he kissed her.

And maybe he hadn't wanted her to remember . . .

That was the more likely scenario. And it was just as well that was what he wanted because now she could pretend ignorance of the entire episode so she wouldn't be mortified every time he looked at her or she looked at him. She'd simply act as though she had no memory of the event.

But that didn't mean she wouldn't hold that memory dear to her, savor it, lock it away to be pulled out at will so she could relive that moment over and over.

For now, putting away the pleasure of that one stolen moment, she forced herself to the task at hand. She had to open her damn eyes and figure out where she was. And if she was safe.

It took far more effort than she would have liked to pry her eyes open. Her entire face was set into a grimace as she worked to lift what felt like lead eyelids. A sliver of low light registered and she took heart in the fact that she was making progress. After several more steadying breaths, and ensuring that she wasn't going to be sick, she forced them open all the way.

It was disorienting at first. Too much to take in all at once.

Nothing about her surroundings was familiar. The first thing she registered was that she was in a very comfortable bed. Not a cot, a bedroll or a makeshift place to sleep. It was an honest-to-goodness real bed with a mattress and linens to die for. Five-star-hotel quality, not that she had much experience with five-star accommodations. But this was *heaven*.

As she shrugged the last vestiges of fuzz from her mind, she swiftly examined her surroundings, looking for any hint that she was in danger.

The walls were painted in soft lavender, several floral paintings strategically placed to give the room an open and airy feel. The furnishings were expensive, custom-looking and hand carved. The wood was a deep brown, the contrast between the darker pieces and the more feminine-looking walls pleasing to her eye.

She felt . . . safe. No fear pricked her nape or caused the hairs on her arms to rise. But where was she?

She shifted in the plush bed, her intention to sit up, to get out of the bed and . . . do what?

The question was settled for her when her body shrieked its protest to her movement. She could feel the blood drain from her cheeks and pain lanced through her side, leaving her breathless. Her lungs were frozen, unable to suck air in or expel it back out. Panicked, she didn't know whether to lower herself back to the bed or continue her ascent. Either one was going to hurt like hell.

A noise at the door startled her. Her body jerked involuntarily, which caused another blast of pain scorching her side.

Hancock filled the doorway. He took one look at her and issued a vicious curse under his breath even as he strode quickly to the bed. He gathered her in his arms, his hold tight but not painful. He carefully eased her back down into the mattress, but even with the obvious care he took in moving her, pain washed through her, robbing her of breath just when she'd thought she'd gotten it back.

Tears swam in her vision, causing Hancock's grim, worried face to swim above her.

"Damn it, Honor. You shouldn't have tried to get up."

She said nothing for a moment, her nostrils distending

as she tried desperately to suck in oxygen and breathe through the remnants of the crippling pain.

"Where am I?" she asked weakly. "Are we safe?"

His expression became even more grim, a distant flicker in his eyes just before he looked away, neatly avoiding her gaze.

"Yes," he said after a moment. "We're safe here."

She closed her eyes. "Thank God. But where is here? Are we back home? Can I call my family?" A tear trickled hotly down her cheek. "They probably think I'm dead."

Hancock cursed again, the words blistering even though he uttered them in barely above a whisper. He knelt beside the bed and put his hand on her forehead in what could only be construed as tenderness. Her eyes flew to his in confusion, because he'd never made any outward show of softness to her except the times when he didn't think she would be aware.

"Right now, you have to focus on getting well," he said in that grim voice. And yet she heard something else in his tone. Something she couldn't quite put her finger on, and it bothered her. He seemed . . . uneasy. And Hancock was confident and unreadable if nothing else.

"How long?" she asked, and then regretted exerting herself by speaking so much. Who knew the task of talking would be so exhausting?

Pain had taken steady hold of her. It was raw and pulsing, rising up once more after the initial relief of being sucked back into the heavenly cloud of the bed she rested in.

"As long as it takes," he said vaguely.

His gaze searched hers, making her uncomfortable with his scrutiny. It was as if he could see every single thing inside her. As if he felt the pain radiating from her body. His eyes grew cold and his lips thinned. He seemed angry.

"You're hurt, or do you not remember getting yourself shot when you protected one of my men?"

Yeah, he was pissed and he was letting her know it. He didn't raise his voice. He didn't have to. In fact, if he had shouted at her, she wouldn't be as nervous. The low whip of authority in his voice was like a tangible lash of reprimand that she felt.

She licked her lips before parting them to defend herself and promptly found herself hushed when he placed two fingers over her mouth and his gaze dared her to defy his silent dictate for her not to speak.

"We can't move you until you're out of the woods," he said. "You lost a lot of blood and I'm giving you IV fluids and antibiotics. I was just coming in to see if you were awake and in pain, and you are both. So I'm giving you pain medicine so you can rest and heal."

She stirred, the protest strong on her lips. She didn't care how hurt she was. She was so close to freedom and home that she could taste it, and she didn't want to waste another single day. Every hour that she was away from her family was an hour they believed the absolute worst.

"There will be no argument, Honor," Hancock said in that cold voice of his. The one that made her shiver and become a weak coward. It disgusted her, and it made no sense that she could stand up to an entire terrorist organization and remain defiant in their attempts to hunt her down like an animal, and yet a single man had the capacity to freeze her and automatically make her back down with nothing more than words.

She was no fool, though. This man didn't need to back up his words. Anyone with sense could see into this man's eyes. He was a ruthless, cold-blooded killer. It would take someone awfully stupid to defy him, and she was not a stupid woman.

He pulled out a capped syringe and swabbed the end of her IV port. Though he had said he had her on IV fluids and medication, she hadn't even noticed the restraint of the IV line leading to her right wrist. Fat lot of good it would have done her to accomplish the feat of getting up when she would have had to lug an IV pole behind her.

"This will only take a second. Relax and let it take hold," he said, a soothing quality replacing his earlier bite.

She frowned when the burn of the medication first hit her veins, and she flinched. Hancock automatically rubbed his palm over her lower arm where the burn was the worst, but she wasn't even sure he was doing it consciously. This was a man who seemed incapable of tenderness, and yet she knew it for the lie it was. He'd held her when nightmares had plagued her fractured sleep. He'd kissed her and comforted her when she'd awakened, afraid and confused.

She couldn't figure this man out, but on some deep, instinctual level, she knew he wasn't a bad man. He wasn't who he even thought he was. And he'd deny to his death that he had one ounce of gentleness in him.

She wasn't sure the exact moment she'd decided to trust him. Maybe on some level it had been there from the start, even though she'd been wary of his intentions. His motive. But he'd kept his promise to get her far from A New Era's reach, and, judging by the furnishings of this bedroom, they didn't appear to be anywhere near the war-torn regions he'd extricated her from.

Already the medicine was making her fuzzy and she was only half conscious. Hancock started to rise, but with the last of her flagging strength, she lifted the arm with the IV attached and grasped his hand firmly so he couldn't slip from her hold.

He looked down at her in surprise but made no effort to extricate his hand from hers. He said nothing. He merely waited for what she wanted to say.

"Thank you," she whispered.

He scowled, and she realized he had no liking for her thanking him. His reaction had been the same the first time she'd thanked him.

"For keeping your promise to me," she managed to get out around the thickness of her tongue.

The last thing she registered as she finally succumbed to the medication was the dark, savage look of fury in his eyes. And something even more surprising.

Guilt.

CHAPTER 17

"YOUR wound is getting better," Hancock said matter-of-factly.

His brisk and impersonal examination of Honor's stitches told her that indeed he had no desire for her to remember those tender, unguarded moments that he thought she had no knowledge of.

"The swelling is almost gone from your knee. You should be able to walk on it in another day without pain."

"Does that mean we can go home soon? Tomorrow?" she asked, grabbing on to those last words and holding them to her with unconcealed excitement.

His eyes flickered. She almost missed it before he turned away, pretending interest in one of her other more minor injuries. There was something there. Something he didn't want her to see. It should have alarmed her, but she wasn't afraid of him. She trusted him. He'd told her he'd get her safely from the reach of A New Era, and he'd done exactly that.

Then he shrugged. "It isn't as easy as you seem to think it is. There are . . . things—plans—that must be put into place. It wouldn't do to make any hasty moves. We aren't out of danger yet."

It was vague and yet it was a reminder to her that, regardless of the fact that she felt safe with him, they weren't safe and they weren't immune to an attack. She frowned, wishing she knew where the hell they were.

She hadn't even seen one of Hancock's men in the days she'd lain in this bed, in this isolated bedroom resting and healing. Hancock had brought her meals. Hancock had dressed and tended her wounds. He'd even helped her bathe, much to her mortification. But he'd helped her in the shower with brisk efficiency that made it appear as though it were the most mundane task in the world. He'd patiently washed her hair, shampooing it several times with each shower to rid the strands of the dye. And then there was the body scrubbing that had her face so scarlet that she likely resembled someone with a bad sunburn. But again, he'd merely been exacting and thorough as he cleaned the henna from her skin, returning it to its original sun-kissed state. If he was trying to make her solely dependent on him, he was doing a damn good job, because even the thought of someone else in her—this—room made her uneasy.

This wasn't her room. Even if it had become hers over the last few days. Her room was at home. In her parents' house. She didn't maintain a separate residence in the States. It made no sense to do so. She was gone more often than she was home, and so when she visited between assignments, or simply needed a break when the pain and despair she faced on a daily basis became too much for her to bear without losing sight of her mission, she sought refuge at her parents' home. She slept in her childhood bedroom, a room they kept for her. One that was purposely unchanged from when she was a teenager still in high school.

It had all the things she'd grown up with. Her favorite stuffed animals. Her beloved books. Her language textbooks and all the research books on the Middle East, its culture, the differences and nuances of each individual dialect that changed from region to region.

Even her sports trophies, though she'd laughed at the idea that her parents would keep what amounted to nothing more than a participation trophy. She'd certainly won no championships, nor had she stood out as an athlete like all her siblings had. She was the odd duck of the family.

Honor swore to her parents they must have adopted her or found her in a cabbage patch because she was nothing like her siblings. She was so much softer. More empathetic. She lacked the ruthless drive to succeed, to be successful at everything she did like her siblings did. They called her a softy. Too kindhearted and tender to survive in the "real world," as they called it. And yet the world she lived in was the epitome of survival. Nothing at all like her family's safe jobs, safe homes, safe lives.

Her father was a former all-star athlete. He'd played multiple sports but had gone to college on a football scholarship and had even been drafted to the pros. But by then he'd met and fallen in love with her mother, and he'd told his children often that he wanted nothing more than to be at home with her and for her to have his children. A house full.

Most doubted his sincerity, and Honor's mother said that even she'd been skeptical at first. She hadn't thought her husband would be happy just walking away from such a lucrative career in the spotlight. But he'd never displayed one ounce of regret, and only a year after they married, they had their first child.

Playing pro ball would have kept him from home for the majority of the year. There was spring training camp. There was the entire football season and the playoffs if the team made it to postseason play. There was no doubt her father could have been one of the greats, but instead, he'd taken a high school coaching job in Kentucky, where he and her mother had chosen to live and raise their family.

It was a small town in Kentucky, not so northern that it came too close to the line between north and south. It had the hallmark of every southern town. Open, friendly and welcoming. Small enough that everyone knew everyone else and as a result, everyone's business was also known.

Honor and her siblings had grown up and thrived under the love and affection their parents had bestowed on them. Her brothers, every single one of them, excelled in one sport or another. As had her older sister. Her oldest brother had also played football in college and showed promise of being recruited by a pro team. He, like their father, hadn't entered the draft and no one had questioned that decision. But then their father knew well that some decisions were simply too personal to be discussed. They just were.

But where his father had gone into coaching, an adequate substitute for not playing the sport he loved, her older brother had chosen law enforcement and was the sheriff of their county.

Her second oldest brother *had* chosen a professional career in sports. Unlike his father and older brother, he wasn't a football fanatic. His entire childhood had been devoted to baseball and he was a natural. Even now he was playing with a pro team and had just signed another long-term lucrative contract before Honor had departed that last time.

The two younger brothers were both businessmen and partnered in several ventures. But that didn't mean they didn't carry the same abiding love—and gift—for sports.

Even her sister, the second to youngest and only other daughter in a sea of sons, was athletic and as graceful and fast as a gazelle. She too had gone into coaching after a brief stint playing professional softball in Italy after attending Kentucky State on a softball scholarship. Honor was very proud of her sister, who was the youngest head coach of the softball team in the history of the small university where she worked.

In the two years since her sister, Miranda, or Mandie as she'd been affectionately nicknamed, had taken over the program, the team had made postseason for the first time in the program's history. Her job was definitely secure. The university had seen to that. And she was very happy there because she was already being heavily recruited by other larger, more prestigious universities with much larger programs and that had long-heralded legacies in college sports.

But Mandie was a homebody at heart, while Honor was the complete opposite. Mandie liked her job. Liked getting her hands dirty and rebuilding a program from the ground up. She had no desire to walk into a program that was already well established and be a veritable figurehead. She wanted to make a difference in every aspect of the game.

Honor briefly closed her eyes, going back to the fact that her brother had signed another contract with his team right before she'd left. Her going-away party had been mixed with joy and celebration but also with heartbreak and worry. None of them liked what she did. They didn't understand it. They didn't try to understand it. Each of them had gone their own way and no one ever questioned them for it. No one questioned Brad, who had simply walked away from pro football with no explanation. Or why his burning desire to become a police officer had never been known to his family.

They only questioned her. And she knew it wasn't that they didn't believe in her—they did. They loved her. She never doubted that for a moment. They just didn't understand her. Didn't understand why her calling took her so far from the people who loved her when all her other siblings' paths had kept them close to home.

How could she explain the restless drive to make a difference in places that seldom received anything at all except death and violence? Brad should understand her better than anyone. He was a protector. The sheriff. He was responsible for a lot of lives. He was perhaps the only sibling she believed she had a kinship with. A shared burden. Surely their need to protect and save others had to come from somewhere.

"Honor, are you in pain?"

Hancock's low voice, laced with concern, drifted through her melancholy and brought her gaze to his; she saw him intently studying her face as though he were privy to her every thought.

She sucked in her breath and impulsively slid her fingers through his where they rested on the edge of the bed at her side and linked them together with a gentle tug. He flinched as though he'd received an electric shock, but he didn't remove his hand or pry hers away, a fact she was grateful for.

For this one brief moment, she needed the touch of another. Comfort. The promise of soon being held and surrounded by the love and support of her family. Every minute she was away was the worst sort of hell for them all. They likely thought she was dead, and if they were not certain of her death, then worse, they feared what her fate was. What she was enduring even now.

She prayed they thought she was dead until she could prove to them she wasn't. It was kinder than them torturing themselves with the endless possibilities of what could be happening to her. Besides, that wasn't going to happen. Hancock had her. He wouldn't let anyone hurt her.

It was foolish to think of anyone being invincible, impervious to the reach of A New Era, but she absolutely believed that Hancock could and would destroy anything in his path and would never let harm come to her. She knew it as surely as the sun rose in the east and slid into sleep in the west.

"What's wrong, Honor?" Hancock demanded bluntly, his eyes narrowing further as he searched her face for any sign of what was causing her distress.

She wasn't distressed.

She needed.

Heat crept up her neck and into her cheeks and she could only pray that the remnants of the dye as well as being in the sun for so long prevented him from seeing the evidence of the guilty blush.

She licked her dry, cracked lips and hesitantly, shyly, looked up at him from beneath lowered lashes.

"Kiss me, Hancock," she said in a quivery voice that could be construed as fearful. But she knew better. And judging by the look on Hancock's face, he also knew she wasn't afraid of him. Or of what she was asking.

His eyes flashed with uncertainty, a rarity for him. She knew that without questioning how. She just knew. But there was also a spark of something else altogether.

Answering need. Want. Desire.

It was gone almost before she registered it happening, but the eyes never lied. They were the door to a person's soul, or so the poets always said.

And just as she knew that Hancock was rarely if ever uncertain about anything, she also knew that it was even more rare for him to allow anyone to see what she'd just witnessed in his eyes.

She'd gotten to him and she knew it. Was stunned by it.

Good God, was she happy about it? What the hell was wrong with her? She didn't know this man and it was presumptuous on her part, not to mention arrogant, to think that she could discern anything about him when others certainly couldn't.

But she was already headed down a hazardous path that gave her a euphoric rush. Alive. She felt alive. Gloriously alive when death had been a suffocating fog surrounding her at every turn.

She'd made it free. Hancock had delivered what he'd promised. Her freedom from the horrible men hunting her like ruthless predators.

"Kiss me," she said again, her voice dropping to a husky whisper laced with need. "Just one time when we're both perfectly aware of it happening and neither of us can claim it never happened."

His eyes widened in quick alarm and then surprise. Both reactions were chased from his eyes as they hardened with the realization that she knew. She remembered. Perhaps she'd never forgotten at all but needed time for all the pieces to drift back together. Now that she had them all in place, she would lock that memory into her soul for all time. Savor it. One pure, sweet moment amid so much fear and chaos and torment.

He swore softly, but even as he did so he slid one knee onto the mattress and leaned his big, tightly muscled body toward hers until he hovered mere inches above her. Heat licked from his skin, warming her to the bone. She suddenly took in the huge disparity in their sizes. He was a mountain of solid steel, not a spare ounce of flesh anywhere on his body that she could discern. And she had a very vivid imagination.

But he made her feel small and fragile. Vulnerable. But not afraid. She licked her lips, suddenly realizing that perhaps she *should* be afraid, provoking the beast when she was completely aware and had all her senses about her. Or maybe not *enough* sense to resist poking the wild animal.

With a harsh groan when her tongue darted over her bottom lip, he leaned down and swept her mouth into his, hot and hungry. There was none of the almost delicate tenderness he'd maintained when he'd kissed her so reverently when he thought she was unaware of her actions or that he was kissing her.

He devoured her mouth, consumed her, tasted every part of her hungry tongue, showing her the staggering difference between a male trying to offer a woman comfort and a starving man demonstrating his ruthless dominance over her.

If it wouldn't hurt so bad, she'd rip every bit of his clothing off and strip herself naked and throw herself at him, or rather on him. All she managed was a low moan that ended in a hum and then a breathy sigh of pleasure and sheer contentment that was quickly swallowed up and inhaled by him.

With considerable effort, he dragged his lips from hers but didn't immediately distance himself from her. She wondered why she considered that a huge victory. He leaned his forehead into hers in a surprisingly tender gesture, his breaths blowing raggedly over her throbbing mouth.

"That was not a good idea," he said through tightly clenched teeth. "Goddamn it, that was stupid."

Okay, that hurt. She could admit it, and even if she couldn't, the very real physical reaction—her flinch—would have betrayed her.

She scrambled for something—anything—to say to break the awkward silent tension that surrounded them, stretching her nerves to their breaking point.

"How soon will I be well enough to go home?" she asked anxiously.

It had the effect of a fierce blizzard. His face became shuttered, locked down as fury so cold blistered through his eyes and then blasted her, sending wave after wave of goose bumps racing across her flesh.

He abruptly rose, turning his back as if he didn't want her to see any part of him or his reaction.

"You still have some healing to do before we can move you," he said flatly.

And then he strode to the door, yanking it open and then slamming it behind him with enough force to knock one of the paintings on the wall askew.

CHAPTER 18

HANCOCK knew he was walking a razor's edge in a true battle for his sanity. Worse, he was battling against what he knew must be done. The mission. The cost of completing his mission. All tied to one innocent woman with more courage and fire than he'd ever witnessed in one small female warrior.

He'd bullied her for days, ensuring that he and only he had access to the room where she was kept . . . prisoner. No way to leave the room, though as prisons went, he'd made sure it had all the comforts she could possibly need or want.

He avoided her questions. Natural questions. Questions she had the right to know the answers to. But the minute he answered them, all was lost. Because he wouldn't lie to her. And he'd have to face her, those large trusting eyes, and watch the light shrivel to nothing but haunting resignation. And worse, betrayal. She would know that he was the very thing she'd run from and fought against, the thing she now believed she was safe from. She didn't know—yet—that he was delivering her to the worst sort of evil, who would then hand her right back to the devil she knew.

And he couldn't bear it. Even knowing his time was running out and that every day that passed that he didn't tell her the truth about his intentions was simply a delaying tactic.

Because he wanted those few days for her. Hell, he wanted
them for himself. Just a few more hours, days, whatever he
could buy when she still looked at him with trust in those
warm brown eyes. With no fear or hesitancy to follow his lead.

With trust.

She trusted him when she should trust no one. He'd told
her as much. But Honor being Honor, the very thing she was
named for. God, the irony of just how well that name fit her.
How could her parents have known that she would live up
to the legacy and prophesy of that name?

No one had ever trusted him. His men respected him. They
obeyed him without question. They'd die for him without hesitation, just as he would do for them. They had loyalty that ran
deep in their blood. But they didn't trust him any more than
they trusted their other teammates or even themselves. They
were all too aware of what they were. Ruthless killers, willing
to sacrifice an innocent woman to achieve their means.

"When?" Conrad asked bluntly as he and his men gathered outside the huge mansion belonging to Bristow.

The irony of them already being stateside wasn't lost on
Hancock. Honor thought she was still somewhere in the bowels of the Middle East, and that their every movement could
be watched, that they were in danger of discovery. If she
discovered just how close she was to her family, he'd have to
tie her to the bed to prevent her from bolting out on her own.

He glanced at his men, at their tight expressions as they
stood expectantly, waiting for go time.

It was one of the few times Hancock had left Honor's
side, but he'd ensured she'd sleep in his absence, and Bristow's men knew the consequences of trespassing. Hancock
had made it very clear that no one was to be granted access
to Honor's private quarters, using her injuries as an excuse.

Bristow was impatient. Excited and edgy, like someone
who'd found a treasure worth more than all the gold and
jewels in the world. His anticipation was thick in the air when
he was in the room and it was why Hancock avoided him for
the most part. Bristow's sickness of the soul—the foul stench
that always emanated from him—was difficult for Hancock
to handle without it overwhelming his senses. He felt ill,

smothered by so much evil that he could barely breathe. It was suffocating him, like someone who was severely claustrophobic, and Hancock was anything but that. He could remain motionless in a cramped space a man of his size should never be able to fit into for days, weeks when necessary, waiting for that one opportunity. A rare window in which only one with ultimate patience would ever get to take down an elusive mark.

Bristow wanted to send word to Maksimov immediately, but Hancock warned him that if Maksimov knew of the woman before they were ready, he wouldn't sit back and wait as Bristow was currently doing. He'd come after Honor and he'd lay waste to anyone in the path of his quarry.

Hancock had made it very clear that Honor must heal before they arranged to deliver her to Maksimov and that it had to be on their—Hancock's—terms or they would lose any bargaining power they currently possessed. The only thing keeping Bristow alive was the fact that Maksimov didn't know where Honor was, and he made certain that Bristow realized just how dangerous and powerful a man like Maksimov was.

Bristow was dangerous and held much power in his own right, but Hancock made certain that Bristow feared Maksimov and rightly so. He spoke of Maksimov in a tone that Bristow couldn't possibly mistake, and Bristow had gone pale listening to Hancock's matter-of-fact recitation of just what Maksimov would do to achieve his means. Life and death meant nothing to a man such as Maksimov, who didn't just consider himself invincible. He truly thought he was immortal. A god among mere men, able to come and go as he pleased. A bringer of death and destruction, and he was unstoppable.

That kind of thinking nearly made it so in Maksimov's case. He was a cagey bastard, unlike others who'd come before him wearing that same shield of invincibility, convinced that no one could get to him, who had fucked up. They all did at some point. But so far Maksimov displayed no sign of carelessness. No sign that he took for granted what he thought himself to be. Indestructible.

Though he thought it, was utterly convinced of it, he still was careful to keep a tightly woven net of security around him, removing anyone he considered a threat to his cause. He was judge and executioner, and no one received a fair trial with Maksimov. If Maksimov even *thought* one was disloyal, had betrayed him or simply didn't have the will to do what Maksimov demanded, then he was discarded with all the care Maksimov reserved for disposing trash.

That kind of fear bought him a lot of loyalty. It bought him men who'd rather take certain death than face Maksimov after failing to carry out a mission. He bred relentless, desperate soldiers who'd die carrying out Maksimov's orders, sometimes by their own hand if they failed. It was a preferable fate to facing Maksimov and having to tell the dictator they had failed. Maksimov had no tolerance for failure. He didn't accept it in himself and he sure as hell didn't accept it from those who worked for him.

In all the years Hancock had hunted him, he'd found no weakness in Maksimov he could exploit. Not a single chink in his armor. The man cared for nothing other than himself. It was damn hard to get close to a man in order to be able to exploit his weaknesses when it appeared he had none.

But Hancock knew better. There was something. There was always something. He himself would have sworn he had no weaknesses. Nothing that could be used against him. But he also knew he was wrong. He had Big Eddie. Raid and Ryker. And Eden. Precious, innocent and good Eden.

He'd been careful never to expose them, never to allow anyone to know of their existence because they would most certainly be in danger every day of their lives. He even kept his distance from the fucking Kellys because anyone with eyes could tell that he respected them. He might not like them, their methods or their ethics. The things he considered their weaknesses. But over the years he'd grown to realize that they weren't so different from him. They just controlled their impulses better than Hancock did.

When someone hurt one of their own, they retaliated and carried out swift justice. And it wasn't the justice most people considered. They hadn't used the legal system. No, they'd carried out their own brand of justice, crossing lines Hancock had long ago crossed. From them he hadn't expected it, though. They were too rigidly set in good. Captain Americas, he'd always sneered at them and about them.

But some of the things they'd done in the name of justice were no better than Hancock had done himself on many occasions. He felt a stirring of admiration for P.J. Coletrane. The woman had been brutalized. The details still set his teeth on edge because he was furious at her team for leaving her vulnerable. For not covering her better. She deserved better than what they'd given her, and she'd paid the ultimate price.

And then she'd walked away from her team, not wanting to drag them into the muck of revenge. No justice. Cold-blooded revenge. She'd hunted down every single man responsible for the vicious attack on her, and she'd killed them all. And in the end, her team had caught up to her and they'd stood side by side with her, not allowing her to bear the brunt of the repercussions.

The Kellys were a different breed of people. The kind of people that Hancock once could have been more like had he chosen a different path. The right path. They were fierce protectors. The good guys. The ones you called on when you needed help. They were good, maybe as good as Hancock was himself, but where he stood out, having the distinct advantage, was that he was far more willing to delve into those twisted gray—no, not even gray . . . black areas. A line none of the Kellys would ever cross unless it concerned someone they loved. One of their wives. Their teammates. Any other mission would be run by the book.

None of them. Not a single member of the KGI group would ever stoop to Hancock's level. They'd never rescue a beaten-down woman who then took a bullet meant for one of their men and then repay her with treachery. All in the name of the greater good.

P.J. Coletrane's face came into his vision, her snarling features giving him an inward smile. He could hear her words as if she'd said them herself.

Fuck the greater good.

Yes, it was absolutely something she—and the rest of her team—would say. Especially Steele. The team leader reputed to be much like Hancock himself. Ice running in his veins. A machine incapable of feeling anything. Able to do a mission without emotion clouding his judgment and weighing him down.

But now? The ice man had been taken down by one small blond woman and a baby girl who looked just like her mama. Hancock was no longer sure Steele was the same man he'd been before. Except . . . except if his wife or daughter was in danger. Then there would be no controlling the man. He would become a ruthless killing machine unlike any the world had ever seen before. Hancock wasn't even sure that he could take on an enraged Steele if his wife's and child's lives were at stake.

Realizing his men were still silent and edgy, waiting for him to answer Conrad's question, Hancock jerked his thoughts to the present, swearing violently under his breath. He was off his game and his team knew it. Just like they were growing edgier by the day as they drew closer to . . . betrayal. The day when they'd hand Honor over to Maksimov, hopefully enabling them to take out the man once and for all. But it would likely be too late for Honor. They'd already resigned themselves to her death and there wasn't a damn thing they could do about it. But it didn't mean that every time he looked in his team's eyes he didn't see helpless rage burning in their depths. He was sure it was mirrored in his own, despite his best attempt to keep them from seeing just how tormented he was over what they must do.

"Soon," Hancock said in a low voice. "She's recovering more every day. I've been able to keep Bristow off her. He's afraid of me. But he's terrified of Maksimov and I've told him that Maksimov would not be pleased to be presented with a hurt and damaged Honor because it would lessen her value to ANE. He doesn't like it, but he fears us both too much to disobey me on this. And I've had one of you stationed outside her door at all times, even when I'm inside with her bullying her to eat and giving her pain medication when she overexerts herself."

"Except now," Copeland said mildly.

"Bad mojo," Mojo growled.

A prickle of unease chased up Hancock's spine. His men were right. He'd summoned them outside where he could speak freely to them. The walls had ears in Bristow's home. Nothing went unobserved. It was why he and his men were so careful not to be oversolicitous when it came to Honor. They treated her as a prisoner they didn't want damaged. Damaged goods didn't make for good trades.

But they had left her alone. For an hour now. What if Bristow had seized the opportunity to look in on his "guest"? He wasn't a patient man and he clearly hadn't liked being kept apart from her. All the work Hancock had done could be unraveled in just a few minutes' time in Bristow's presence.

He'd been too arrogant, too certain of his hold on Bristow, when he should have known better. Bristow believed himself invincible, and though he was afraid of and intimidated by Hancock, he wasn't afraid that Hancock would kill him. And that was where he was wrong. Hancock would take Bristow apart with his bare hands if he hurt Honor.

"Get back," Hancock said hoarsely. "Get back now. Find Bristow's men and make sure they are under control. Kill anyone who resists. I'll take care of Bristow."

"Hancock."

Conrad's cold voice penetrated the red-hot haze surrounding Hancock's mind, turning him once more into a ruthless killing machine.

"You can't compromise the mission over what he's done. If he's done anything at all."

"The hell I can't," Hancock spat. "I don't need Bristow to make the exchange with Maksimov. I did at first. But that contact has been made. All I have to do is complete the drop and then take the bastard and his entire network down."

"But not in time to save Honor," Viper said tightly.

Hancock swung his haunted gaze to his man. "Don't you think I would if I could?"

"Would you?" Henderson pressed, his face drawn into grim lines. "You've never wavered in a mission before. Why now?"

"You forget I sacrificed two opportunities to take down Maksimov to save innocent lives," Hancock snapped. "I won't do so a third time. Now move out. If he's touched Honor, if he's made her afraid, I'll kill him."

None of his men commented on the hypocrisy of Hancock's killing a man who would at least be more honest with Honor than Hancock had been. None dared.

CHAPTER 19

HONOR was so tired of being in the bed, she was ready to scream. If one more day passed and she heard, just as she heard every time she asked Hancock the question of when she could go home, "Not yet," she was going to hurt someone. And she was only fantasizing about one face to smash. When she wasn't fantasizing about the mouth attached to that face.

She was out of her freaking mind. Barking mad, crazy as a loon. It could only be explained by the insanity she'd endured over the last two weeks. Surely no one could come out of something like this with their mind intact. She wasn't an exception. She'd lost as much brain mass as she had blood, so she couldn't hold her fixation with the brooding badass huge question mark that was Hancock against herself. Or so she tried to convince herself. But she was failing miserably.

What kind of a freak was attracted to a man she didn't even know? A man shrouded with so many layers of secrets that even each individual layer had multiple layers. It would take eternity to discern the man beneath the cloak of mystery, and even then she wasn't certain there was anything but those secrets he wore like skin.

She was crazy. It was the only reasonable explanation.

And then she wanted to laugh at herself for using the word *reasonable* when explaining crazy.

The door opened and her pulse immediately leapt, anticipating the only man who'd come into her room in the past days. Yesterday, she'd been feeling restless and cagey and decided to test the extent of the damage done to her; she'd forced herself out of bed, determined to walk out of this room and figure out where the hell she was. At this point she was just desperate for a change in scenery. The lavender walls and cheery floral artwork were just taunting her, since the very last thing she was feeling was happy and carefree.

It had exhausted her, but elation had lent her a surge of strength when she'd finally shuffled to the door, only for that illusion of strength to evaporate when the knob wouldn't turn. She was locked in, and it only locked from the outside.

She wasn't a prisoner. Was she?

Not knowing what else to do, with her knees perilously close to giving out on her, she shuffled back to the bed and crawled onto it, her body protesting her every movement. And then a sound had her freezing and just as quickly turning to settle into place on the bed, angry at the guilt she felt, as though she were an errant teenager trying to sneak out.

She wasn't a prisoner!

Her pulse, already elevated, spiked, and it was like pressing the accelerator to the floor on a sports car. A man she'd never seen slid like an oily snake through the barely opened door. He didn't fit in this world. This place. But then where was here?

It was she who didn't belong here.

An uneasy sensation circled and swelled as fear boiled in her stomach and acid traced its way up her throat. Worse, the moment the intruder picked up on her fear, she *saw* him go hard with arousal. There was an unmistakable bulge in his expensive slacks that clearly outlined his erection, and low laughter escaped him. It—he—was vile and repulsive.

"Who are you?" she demanded with far more bravado than she felt.

She gathered the sheets in a tight bundle, shielding her body from his view even though she was fully dressed beneath the covers.

Just like that his eyes went flat and cold and a shiver went up her spine. Malice glittered brightly in the black orbs as he advanced on the bed. She opened her mouth to scream and he was on her in an instant, stifling any cry she would have made with a sharp slap to her mouth.

The blow stunned her into silence and only a small whimper of pain escaped.

"I'm the man who owns you. Temporarily," he added, the sound of his voice coming as a hiss, cold on her skin as though he weren't a living thing at all. A monster. Like so many of the monsters that haunted her dreams.

Where was Hancock?

Inside she was screaming for him. His name. Over and over. A litany, begging him to save her. Again. Who was this man? How did he get into her room? Hancock had told her she was safe.

Hadn't he?

She frantically searched her memory for the words. For what exactly he'd said to her. They hadn't had very many actual conversations. She would be certain of what he'd promised her. She was sure. She'd held the few assurances he'd given her close to her heart. A talisman.

Her scrambled mind could only come up with *one* promise.

He'd get her past, through, away from the terrorist cell hunting her, stalking her every movement. But surely . . .

No, she wouldn't think it. Wouldn't allow herself the loss of the only thing she had to keep her strong. That kept hope and faith alive in her heart. This asshole wouldn't take that from her.

"That's better," he said in a silky purr. "You're naturally submissive. I can sense it. You will be easily taught discipline and obedience, though, regretfully, my time with you will be short."

Her eyes shot darts, her lips drawn in a mutinous line. Submissive? Obedient? She wanted to tear his eyes out and then go for his balls.

If he thought her some helpless nitwit, boy did he have a surprise in store.

She batted her eyelashes with clueless innocence, giving this asshole her best "Honor eyes," as her family had dubbed them. The look that assured her that no one could ever remain angry at her long. The one that instantly got her out of trouble when she'd been stirring up mischief.

"I think you must have me mistaken for someone else," she said in a calm voice. "I don't know who you are or where I am for that matter, but I don't have a submissive bone in my body, and if you so much as try to force my obedience, I'll cut your heart out."

Yes, she'd spoken calmly, but there was blistering violence and absolute conviction in her tone, her expression. She hadn't survived as long as she had by being weak or being controlled by fear.

He threw back his head and laughed. "You seem awfully sure of yourself, Honor Cambridge."

"And if I fail, Hancock will finish the job," she said coldly.

At that, glee entered his eyes. Glee. A supremely satisfied expression gripped him even as he wound his hand tightly in her hair and yanked her protesting body close to his. He kissed her brutally, forcing her mouth open by using his teeth, slicing at her lips until her gasp of pain allowed his tongue to shove inside.

She struggled wildly, but he was far stronger, and she was weakened by her injuries. Tears burned her eyelids and she refused to cry, refused to allow this man the satisfaction of seeing her tears of pain, rage and worse, fear.

Where was Hancock?

"Hancock is renowned for his conquests," the man said, his breath stroking over her damaged, trembling lips. "It is said he can make anyone do his bidding. He can make anyone believe whatever it is they want to believe. Tell me, Honor, did he promise to see you safely home to your family? Think carefully. I also know Hancock not to be a liar. Interesting code, don't you think? A cold-blooded killer. A mercenary. With a code. He doesn't lie. And yet he can make you believe something he never promised. How easily you must have fallen under his spell."

"You won't make me believe he's what you say he is," she said in a frigid tone.

His hand wound even tighter in her hair and he yanked back, exposing her vulnerable neck much as a vampire would with its prey. God, she really was to the point of hysteria if she was calmly contemplating how like the fictitious monster this abomination was.

"I won't have to," he said with smug satisfaction. "He works for me. I paid him to bring you to me. You are a bargaining tool who serves a higher purpose. You'll get me what I want and then you'll get Maksimov what he wants. And then A New Era will get what they want."

He studied her a brief moment, purposely drawing out her terror.

"You," he finished triumphantly. "The very thing you thought you escaped will be your ultimate destiny. All you've done has been for nothing. But your escaping them greatly benefits me. Greatly," he murmured, dropping his voice as he raked his gaze over her shaking body.

"Come in, Hancock," the man called, evidently having heard something Honor hadn't. "I should have known you'd be back to look in on your little pet."

Bile rose in her throat. No. This wasn't happening. He was messing with her head. She closed her eyes, refusing to be drawn into his sick game.

Her head was yanked brutally back until she feared her neck would snap.

"Open your eyes," the man said, his voice snapping over her with the force of a whip.

Not because she wanted to, but because she had to, did she obey. She had to know what was truth and what were lies. When her vision cleared, she saw Hancock standing silently at the foot of the bed, his eyes intent and watchful, but it was the air of disinterest and the blankness in his gaze that terrified her.

"No," she whispered. *"No!"*

This time she screamed it, and then she kept screaming even when she reeled from the fist connecting with her jaw to silence her.

"You know Maksimov will not be pleased," Hancock said in a cool, unruffled voice. "You're a fool, Bristow. She was healing nicely. Now you've bruised the one part of her that wasn't already damaged. Her face. You know Maksimov likes a pretty face. He won't be happy that the merchandise incurred further damage at your hands."

Merchandise? She stared at Hancock in horror, knowing she couldn't control the shock of his betrayal from her eyes, and he didn't so much as flinch. There was no guilt, just steady resolve radiating from him in waves.

Oh God. No.

Honor rolled, the man suddenly allowing her to do so as if he saw exactly what was about to happen.

She barely was able to get her head over the side of the bed in time to vomit all over the floor. She registered the distant sound of a scuffle, angry words being exchanged, but her head was splintering apart with pain as she continued to heave when there was nothing more to expel from her stomach. And the pain from the stress on her injured side, the stitches no doubt torn, robbed her of breath. Her hair hung down in disarray as her head went limp. She simply no longer had the strength to hold it up.

Blood mixed with her tears dripped onto the floor, a macabre sight along with the contents of her stomach. Mostly bile. She felt sick to her very soul.

And then surprisingly gentle hands slid over her shoulders, one palming the back of her head, the other lifting the part of her that hung lifelessly over the edge of the bed. She shuddered, going into a frenzied attack. She knew those hands. Knew that touch. What was once her greatest source of comfort was now vile. Evil. She'd never felt so devastated in her life.

"Damn it, Honor, stop fighting me. You'll only hurt yourself more."

She reared her head back, hating that her vision swam with tears. She barely registered that the man Hancock had called Bristow was now gone, and in his place were all of Hancock's men. The whole traitorous lot of them.

"There is no way for me to hurt more," she said dully.

Someone, more than one man, swore, in more than one language, but her gaze never left Hancock's. He regarded her somberly, no hint of guilt. No regret for so callously betraying her trust. She'd been foolish to give it. That was on her. But then she'd had no *real* choice. No real chance. She'd fooled herself into thinking that she had one. She'd been doomed from the moment the clinic had fallen down around her and on her, the screams of her coworkers still echoing in her ears, the stench of blood ever present in her nostrils.

Shock and a keen sense of betrayal paralyzed her. She'd trusted him. Not at first, but she'd grown to trust him over the past days as he'd fought to get her out of the country and out of the hands of A New Era.

Someone, she never lifted her gaze to acknowledge who-ever it was, gently pressed a cup containing cold water into her hand and then provided her a basin, holding it a few inches below her mouth.

"Rinse your mouth and spit in the bowl," came the gruff order, the roar in her head, her ears, her heart too over-whelmed to register whose voice it was.

She did as instructed mechanically, like a thing pro-grammed. A machine with no feelings, no thought processes or choice. And when she finished spitting the foul taste from her mouth, she gulped down several sips of the chilled liquid to soothe her raw throat, made so when she'd screamed her denial of Hancock's betrayal.

Her gaze settled back on Hancock accusingly, certain that her pain and confusion shone brightly in her eyes. He regarded her quietly, dispassionately. But then, of course, he wouldn't have the grace to look ashamed. He wasn't her white knight, her savior. He was the instrument of her demise.

"You *promised*," she whispered brokenly, flinging the cup in his direction.

He shook his head in denial. "I never promised you any-thing, Honor," he said in a quiet tone that reflected no more remorse than was displayed in his expression.

"No, but you allowed me to *think* that I was safe . . . And that's *worse*," she said in a savage tone. "You could have told me. You could have corrected my assumption at any time. At least then I would have had time to prepare. Instead of thinking all the while that I was one step closer to freedom. You're a monster. Just like them. But at least they're honest about their intentions. That makes you worse than those murdering savages."

Hancock lifted one eyebrow, ignoring the pointed barbs she threw at him. "And have you escape me at the first opportunity? Yes, that's what I do with all my prisoners. I tell them precisely what their fate is so they can run."

Her face contorted into a helpless snarl. Much like a wounded, trapped animal awaiting execution from a hunter. "Like I would have been able to escape you and your . . . people?"

She swept them all with her scathing glare, growing more pissed by the minute when not one of them looked remotely regretful. They were all heartless bastards. Traitors to their countrymen. She couldn't look another moment at them. They sickened her to her soul.

"You escaped an organized terrorist group that far outnumbers me and my men and managed to elude them for over a week. So yes. I have no doubt you would have found a way to escape me as well."

She went silent, fixing her stony gaze forward and refusing to acknowledge any of them again. Nor would she allow the overwhelming despair threatening to engulf her to show. She wouldn't give them that satisfaction.

"Tell me," she said in a ravaged voice. Her rage was a terrible thing. Her sense of betrayal was far greater. Worst of all, she couldn't keep it from him. Couldn't keep how much he had hurt her from him or anyone else in the room. She'd been stripped of her dignity, her pride, her very soul. She had nothing left.

"What is to be my fate, Hancock? You owe me that much at least."

In the blink of an eye, the life had gone out of her. She was dangerously calm. Disembodied, no longer a living, breathing person with hopes and dreams.

She saw something savage in his gaze for one brief moment before he slid onto the bed next to her, ignoring her scooting as far away from him as she could. She couldn't touch him, couldn't allow him to touch her. She'd only throw up again.

"Why do you need to know?" he asked in a surprisingly gentle voice.

God, she needed him to be the asshole she'd thought him to be from the start. The opinion once formed that should have never wavered. She always relied on her gut when it came to people, so what did it say about her that she'd been so terribly wrong about him?

She met his eyes coldly, feeling layers upon layers of ice forming on her heart, her mind, her soul, encapsulating her in a freezing, bone-deep chill.

"So that I have enough time to carve a hole in my brain so I can crawl into it and die."

He instantly recoiled with a flinch. She heard a blistering curse from across the room and then someone stomped away, slamming the door so hard it finished the job of knocking the painting from the wall that Hancock had already set teetering the time he'd left after she'd asked him to kiss her.

What a stupid, hopeless, naïve fool she'd been.

"What an honorable soldier you are," she said in a mocking voice.

But her pain betrayed her. Like so much else had of late. She tried to sound bitter, angry, furious even. But she could barely choke the words out because she was still screaming on the inside, her pain so great that she could feel herself shattering into a million pieces.

"Whoring yourself out to get the job done. What exactly is the going rate for stud services these days?"

Anger glittered hotly in Hancock's eyes, but she was too far gone to care. Already she was retreating within herself.

His silence damned him. She knew he'd done just those things for previous missions. No, his jobs. *Missions* somehow invoked something with meaning. Value. Honor. Loyalty. Good. She was a job, just as other women had likely been jobs as well.

"Get out," she said, holding desperately to the last of her crumbling composure. "All of you. Get out!"

And as she lay there, broken, weeping silently for all she'd lost, she realized that the very thing she'd vowed Bristow wouldn't take from her—Hancock, her talisman and protector—had never been hers to begin with.

She had nothing further for anyone to take from her.

She had nothing, *was* nothing at all. Just a tool. A bargaining chip. A plaything for ruthless, evil men. And for just a little while, she'd slept with the enemy, figuratively speaking.

She'd made the mistake of trusting when she knew better. But at least she wouldn't have to live long with such heartbreaking regret. Her time was very short indeed. She closed her eyes, anguished by what was to come: the suffering and agony that would be inflicted upon her before she finally escaped into death's protection. She regretted that her death couldn't come sooner.

CHAPTER 20

RAGE ate at Hancock, though he was careful to keep his emotions in check—an art he'd perfected until it came as second nature to him as breathing. But he'd never felt this close to losing his tightly leashed control.

He held out his hand in the direction of his team, and one of them scrambled to hand over a med kit.

"Get Conrad back in here," Hancock snapped. "I need him to take a look at her stitches."

Cope, Viper and Henderson immediately exchanged grim, silent glances. At Hancock's barked order, Honor went utterly still and then rolled away so she faced the wall and curled in on herself, forming a protective barrier.

With grim resignation, he slid onto the bed next to Honor, one knee bent, so he was sitting facing the headboard and so he could take in the mass of honey-colored hair—she'd managed to get the original color back with repeated washings—and move the strands covering her face. And the evidence of her tears.

He pushed the strands away, ignoring her recoil and the fact that she was pulling herself further and further away from him, not only physically but mentally. His temper, raw and savage, spiked as he took in her torn lips, the thin trickle of blood that still seeped not only from her mouth but from her nose as well. A wicked-looking bruise was already forming where that bastard had touched her. Hurt her. Put his fucking hands on what didn't belong to him.

Hancock had known he was living on borrowed time. It was only a matter of when—not if—she discovered his intentions and that they were not those of the man she thought she saw when she'd looked at him before.

But now, the knowledge and understanding were there, staring back at him with dark accusation but worst of all, hurt and devastation that was beyond repair. He'd done that to her. And she'd been right when she'd said that what he had done—was doing—*was* far worse than what A New Era had planned.

The men hunting her hadn't lulled her into a sense of false security. They hadn't given her hope. Or tenderness or caring, all the while intending to sacrifice her. Trade her life for thousands of others.

Hancock had done all those things, and he'd known she would hate him. What he hadn't known was how much he would hate himself, nor had he known that her deep anguish would twist his gut into knots he had no hope of ever unraveling.

He rolled her over, mindful of not hurting her more than necessary, but he had to be commanding and firm. The very asshole she was now convinced he was. And he didn't deny he was just that.

"You're bleeding," he said grimly.

She shuddered beneath his seeking fingers, and he saw what the movement cost her.

"Where the hell is Conrad?" he bellowed.

He didn't want her in any more pain than necessary. Her mental anguish he could do nothing about, but he could at least alleviate her physical discomfort. He'd never regain her trust again. Not that he deserved it. But this, too, was unexpected. The pain he felt over the loss of something so precious.

Conrad entered, his fury a living, breathing thing. He wouldn't even meet Honor's eyes, not that they were available for him to meet, but he didn't know that because he didn't spare so much as a glance in Honor's direction. He only looked at Hancock, simmering with barely controlled impatience, awaiting his team leader's instruction.

"Give her something for pain. And to calm her," Hancock added quietly. "She's torn some of the sutures. I'm sure of it. Make sure and give her another injection of antibiotics."

"No."

It was said so softly that everyone froze, uncertain of whether it actually had come from her.

She turned her head over her trembling shoulder, her eyes downcast so they wouldn't see the grief and sorrow swamping them, making them giant pools that swallowed Hancock whole. But he saw. Only he was close enough to see what she tried so valiantly to keep from his team.

"No to everything," she said in a firmer tone, one that held an edge of the fury swirling in her eyes. "And definitely nothing that sedates me. I've had enough of having someone else's will being imposed on me. I get it. I'm going to die. But goddamn it, I'm not dying without a chance to fight. I won't go down without a fight."

Hancock sighed, unable to keep his respect for her and her indomitable spirit in check. And then he once more became the asshole he was and the asshole she thought him to be.

"I don't care much what you want, Honor. And you aren't going anywhere. Yet," he amended, remembering his vow that he wouldn't lie to her. Not that it would bring her any comfort or solace. But he would not lie to her. "I'll hold you down if need be, but Conrad will tend to your injuries and you'll endure it as pain free as we can possibly make it. And then you will sleep and heal."

"In a hurry to get your captive all better and *good* enough for the next monster you pawn me off on?" she asked, tears thick in her voice.

Goddamn it. She was killing him. Inch by slow inch. Eating a hole in his gut, his heart. Whatever was left of his damned soul.

He didn't answer her question. How could he when that was precisely what he intended to do? But his not wanting to see her hurt had nothing to do with Maksimov. The Russian wouldn't care what condition she was received in because he'd most certainly inflict his own brand of damage before tossing her like leftovers to ANE.

But he wanted Bristow to believe that Maksimov would be deadly pissed if Honor was damaged. It bought her more . . . time. Which was cruel. He admitted that. But goddamn it, he wasn't ready to let her go to her doom so quickly. He needed that additional time. Even if she didn't want it.

If Bristow believing Maksimov would kill him if Honor bore the visible signs of Bristow's attack kept her safe, then so be it. And yet it hadn't deterred the son of a bitch from jumping at the first opportunity to demonstrate his control over Honor and her fate. Or taking great satisfaction from scaring the living hell out of her. He fed off the fear of others. It was a heady aphrodisiac that fed Bristow's sadistic fantasies. Only he made them reality.

The only reason Hancock hadn't taken Bristow apart with his bare hands—what he'd vowed to his men he would do if he had harmed Honor—was that he'd seen one of Bristow's men making a discreet call when he'd seen the flurry of activity around Honor's room, and then he'd known.

He knew Maksimov would have a mole inside Bristow's organization. Maksimov had eyes and ears everywhere. Hancock would have expected no less. But he hadn't identified the mole. Until now. And his hearing, tuned to hear what most others weren't able to hear, made him realize he couldn't kill Bristow. Not yet.

Because Maksimov had only just realized that Honor was in Bristow's possession. Bristow hadn't contacted the Russian yet to arrange the transfer. Why, Hancock didn't know, but he had a good idea.

Bristow wanted Honor first. Before he gave her up so readily. He might want money, power and elevated status with Maksimov, but he was a twisted son of a bitch, and every one of Hancock's instincts told him that Bristow planned to live out every one of those sick fantasies with Honor before making the exchange.

And so Hancock had been forced to come in at Bristow's

request. Make it appear he was exactly what he was. A cold-blooded hired killer, without any feelings, remorse or guilt, and convince Honor that he was exactly as Bristow had described him.

He'd felt every flinch, could hear the screams of denial deep inside her when he'd called her *merchandise*.

Because he couldn't kill Bristow no matter that the urge had been overwhelming the moment he saw the damage he'd done to Honor. That not only had he destroyed her but he'd hurt her. Had purposely imposed his dominance in an attempt to break her, not realizing that she was already broken and that it had been Hancock who'd done it. Not Bristow.

Only after Bristow staged the exchange. Nailed down all the details and named a time and location. Only then could Hancock vent his terrible rage and take him apart. His death would not be slow or merciful. He fully intended to make Bristow pay for every word he'd hurled at Honor. Every blow he'd inflicted. Every tear, every rip, every drop of blood she'd shed.

Because it was the only way to vent the terrible rage swelling inside him, because he knew, just as Bristow would suffer, so too would Honor suffer horribly. And there wasn't one goddamn thing he could do about it.

His men picked up on the terrible internal war Hancock was currently waging, and their own stances relaxed some-what, sorrow and regret rolling into their eyes. They'd hated him. For the first time, they'd hated the order he'd given them. They'd even considered rebellion. He couldn't blame them. He couldn't blame their hatred because he hated him-self far more than they ever could.

But now they understood that he didn't like it any more than they did. He hated it even more because somewhere along the way, this mission—Honor—had become deeply personal. Much more so than it had been with Elizabeth, Grace and Maren. And yet he'd spared those women and he wouldn't allow Honor the same salvation.

He was a bastard who didn't deserve to die with honor or dignity. He deserved to be hunted down like the animal he was and to die a long, painful death with every sin he'd ever committed rolling through his soul like a never-ending litany.

He slid his hand up to Honor's shoulder, hating the revolting shudder that rolled through her body the moment he made contact. Her skin was so cold and she trembled with . . . fear. She, who'd never been afraid of him. Hell, she feared nothing, though she'd dispute it and say she was a coward. He'd put that fear in her eyes, and he hated himself more with every passing second.

He turned her, his grip firm and unyielding. She resisted and he didn't relent, but he swore in a silent vicious storm when he saw pain momentarily rob her of breath, but also of her strength. She sagged, falling onto her back with more force than he intended.

"Damn it, Honor," he hissed. "Hate me. Despise me. Whatever makes you feel better. But do not cause yourself unnecessary pain by defying me. I will do whatever it takes to force your compliance. In all matters and especially when it comes to you refusing to lessen your pain."

"Lessen my pain?" she asked hoarsely. "Are you even human? *You* hurt me, Hancock. You. Not the damn bombing. Not the bullet I took for a man I believed was risking his life to save mine, *not* to ensure that I was hastening toward my death. *You* hurt me and there isn't a damn medication or treatment on earth that will ever help that kind of pain."

She lay on her back, her chest rising and falling in quick succession, and around her flat lips were lines of strain. She was hurting like hell.

He motioned to Conrad, and Honor shoved herself upward in the bed, balancing on her elbows, tears he knew she didn't realize were there streaming down her cheeks at the pain her sudden movement had caused.

"No sedative," she yelled, choking off before her voice rose into hysteria.

She turned those accusing eyes on Hancock. "You owe me *something* and I want answers. That's why you wanted him to knock me out. It's why I've stayed locked up in this room all this time, because you didn't want me to find out the truth. Why? Why does it matter? And when I did find out, you didn't want to have to answer my questions. It's why you've told your minion over there to sedate me. Because you're too much of a heartless bastard to give me the one thing I'm owed. I saved your man's life. My repayment is the truth."

Hancock's jaw twitched, because despite Honor's rage, her outward show of strength, he saw something else just as realization hit him as to why she was so determined to be aware when Conrad repaired her torn sutures.

She was bracing herself for pain. Preparing herself for what was to come. Because simple stitches, while painful, were mere annoyances compared to torture designed to cause as much agony possible without killing the victim. To make them endure so long until the pain took over like a madness and they begged for death. Ultimate freedom. Peace and freedom from the misery of their existence.

So to imagine what would happen to her, knowing she was painting equally painful images in her head at the same time, made the fingers barely clinging to his own sanity threaten to finally slip.

And all he had left at the moment was his sanity. The intelligent, calculating part of his brain that carried him through every mission, no matter how much of his soul it sucked away. God knew the rest of him had already given in to the overshadowing guilt and despair.

"No sedative," Hancock said after studying her a moment longer. And his gaze never once left her face as he gave the next order. "But she gets antibiotics and she gets pain medication. Before anything else. Before you numb her for the stitches. And you wait until it starts taking effect before you so much as touch her."

CHAPTER 21

"THE pain medication does the same thing as a sedative," Honor accused, shrinking from Conrad's sudden presence at her bed. "It makes me loopy, and I *won't* be put off. I want the damn answers to my questions answered."

If a prisoner, mere *merchandise*, gave imperious orders to men who thought nothing of callously discarding her and sending her through the very gates of hell to greet Satan himself and then expected obedience, it was obvious the captive had indeed lost her mind.

What's the worst they could do? Kill her? Torture her? It wasn't like that wasn't her eventual fate. Delaying made it all the worse because it gave her too much time to imagine how she could survive even one day in the hands of a brutal inhumane animal whose only goal was to make her suffer.

"You'll be aware enough to ask your questions," came Hancock's dry, emotionless response. "However, you will *not* be aware of your pain if I have anything to say about it."

Since she well knew that implacable expression, she knew she wouldn't have a choice regardless of what he decided to do to her.

Bitter defeat brought acid tears, stinging her eyelids like angry bees. Beside her, Hancock stiffened, and for a moment his hand hovered over her arm before settling there, his fingertips resting on her skin. She jerked back as if he'd burned her and huddled further inside herself, making herself as small as possible in a room filled with impossibly large men.

Hancock reached down to lift the hem of her pajama top even as he easily slid the band of her bottoms down just enough to bare her hip. Furious at how helpless she was— she felt—she lay there stoic, refusing to show them anything else. No more weaknesses to exploit.

She felt the first needle slide in, controlling her pained reaction as the medicine burned. She barely managed to prevent wincing in accordance with the involuntary flinch when Conrad's hand pushed over the injection site and gently massaged the area to spread the medicine more quickly so the discomfort would abate sooner.

Then as if he hadn't just touched her with tenderness she knew none of them possessed, he deftly inserted the second needle and administered what she assumed—hoped—was merely the antibiotic Hancock had insisted she be given.

She waited for betrayal. Waited for the dim awareness that a sedative would bring. The numbing of all her emotions until she drifted off into nothing more than a manageable vegetable, unable to resist whatever they chose to do.

But other than the fog of the pain medication, which was already doing its job of tamping down the pain—her physical pain—she felt no other indication that she was impaired.

Apparently Hancock was capable of keeping promises when it suited him.

He waited long moments, watching her with eyes that missed nothing before turning and dismissing the others. The only instructions he gave his men were, "Keep an eye on that bastard and make sure this doesn't happen again."

She was too tired and sick at heart to even attempt to consider what he meant by his cryptic demand.

As soon as his men left, leaving her alone with her betrayer, she gave him no chance to take over the situation. No chance to have the advantage, though she knew she in no way had any advantage in this situation.

"Why?" she asked in a deceptively soft voice.

She knew that her terrible rage simmered just below the

surface, that it wouldn't take much for it to erupt into something horrible.

Hancock sighed and put more distance between them, a small thing for her to be grateful for, but she could admit that his closeness only made her feel more trapped, more vulnerable, and if she was going to get through this, she needed any advantage she could gain.

"I've been working undercover a long time, Honor," he said quietly, as if the walls themselves had ears and eyes.

Even as he spoke, he swiftly closed the distance between them once more, sliding onto the bed beside her, only this time settling himself to sit next to her, so both their backs rested against the pillows against the headboards.

"You weren't my intended target. You merely became . . . collateral damage. An unavoidable sacrifice for the greater good."

She made a low sound in her throat because he was subtly dancing around the issue when she wanted the straight, cold truth.

"I work for Bristow." A cold smile twisted those ruthless lips. "Or so he'd like to believe. That I'm no threat to him. And that suits my purpose just fine. He'll never know the truth until it's too late."

"He said you were adept at making people believe what you wanted them to," she said in a detached tone. "Perhaps he knows more than you think."

"Yes, he's aware of my talent. He simply believes himself impervious. He's wrong. I've been manipulating him since I came to work for him. I needed him only for the connection he has to a Russian named Maksimov. A man who has killed thousands upon thousands of innocent people. Women. Children. None of it matters to Maksimov. He's unstoppable. I've twice been close to bringing him down and he slipped through my fingers. I won't allow it a third time."

She knew that she had everything to do with the confidence with which he spoke of taking him down this time. And it scared the living hell out of her.

"What could I possibly have that any of you want?" she asked scornfully, attempting to hide the paralyzing fear and sense of fatalism as she realized she was a much bigger piece of the overall picture. Perhaps the only piece that mattered now. She was completely bewildered as to how or why. She was insignificant. A nobody. How could she be so important to not one but three very powerful men—and organizations? She knew why A New Era wanted her. To save face. By why Bristow? And why this Maksimov?

She was trapped. She'd never go home. Never see her family again. Tears glittered in her vision, but she didn't attempt to hold them back. She grieved for what could never be. For the loss of the one thing that had gotten her through so many long, painful days. Kept her going despite insurmountable odds. Hope. Hope that had been extinguished the minute Hancock revealed his cutting, impersonal betrayal. Without hope, there was only defeat. And . . . death.

Sorrowfully, she remembered that brief moment of weakness, when she had the knife in her hands and had contemplated ending it right then. And later, when she had obtained freedom from the rubble she'd been trapped in, her promise to kill herself before ever allowing A New Era the satisfaction of making her beg them for death. God, how she wished she'd given in to the impulse now. At least then she'd have the one thing that was now forever denied her. Peace.

"You escaped ANE," Hancock said simply. "You became a beacon of hope to an oppressed people. You gave them hope when they thought none available to them. ANE fucked Maksimov over on a deal. And Maksimov isn't a man to be trifled with. ANE owes him a *lot* of money. Bristow is trying to make a play at Maksimov. He's not stupid enough to think he can take the Russian out and take over his operations. He just wants a piece of the pie. He wants a place of importance within Maksimov's organization. So he sent me to find you before ANE eventually caught you. And they would have had I not gotten to you when I did."

She opened her mouth to let loose her rage and denial, but Hancock simply squeezed her hand, their fingers threaded together, and she didn't remember them getting that way. But when she tried to tug her hand free, his grip only tightened even as his thumb smoothed over the sensitive skin on her wrist.

"Bristow is setting up a meeting with Maksimov and plans to give you to the Russian, who will then dangle you in front of ANE's nose like the proverbial carrot in front of the donkey's nose. ANE has lost a lot of face and they will do anything to have you back in their possession so that one slip of a woman does not forever taint their honor and pride by permanently escaping them. Once Maksimov has you, he will then make an exchange with ANE, one that will cost them way more than what they owe Maksimov. But their pride is greater than their common sense, and Maksimov knows this. He will take advantage of it. He'll get what he wants, and ANE will get what they want."

"Me," she whispered.

And then she crumbled, yanking her hand from Hancock's grip as both her hands flew to her face in an effort to stifle the sob that somehow made its way out anyway.

"Oh God, why didn't I die that day? Why was I the only one to survive? I believed at first that I had a purpose. That my living stood for something. That I would make it home if for no other reason than so the world would know what these animals had done. That my escaping would be the ultimate act of defiance and refusal to allow them absolute rule and control over such a vast region. But it was all for nothing. All that running, the pain, the fear, all those nights of not being able to sleep for the nightmares and fear of discovery at every turn. I never had a chance, did I?" she asked, her voice small and achingly vulnerable.

Hancock's voice was rough. It sounded mean and pissed off. And all he said was one word and yet it conveyed a wealth of emotion.

"No."

She dug her palms into her eyes and rocked back and forth, her distress so great that she wasn't even aware of what she did or how very fragile she appeared.

"The medication has had time to take effect," Hancock said in the same even tone, betraying no hint of anything, as if he hadn't just sounded enraged seconds before.

It took a moment for her to realize who he was even addressing until she saw Conrad step from the shadows on the other side of her bed. She'd forgotten his presence. Had assumed he'd left when Hancock had commanded the others to do the same. But he was going to reset the torn stitches. And she'd bared herself painfully, not to only Hancock, but now also to Conrad. A man whose life she'd saved.

She went silent, not saying a single word, not issuing a single sound as Conrad quickly pulled the pieces of broken sutures from her skin and then reset them, making inarticulate sounds deep in his throat. Almost like the growl of an angry predator.

She retreated inside herself, already preparing her barriers, seeing how strong they could be and how adept she was at becoming someone, something, altogether different.

It took a long moment, the room cloaked in silence, for her to realize Conrad had retreated and only Hancock remained.

"You can go now," she said, no life in her voice.

"Honor, listen to me," Hancock said, an urgency she'd never before detected in his voice brushing over her like an electric shock.

She stared mutinously ahead, her gaze fixed on a distant object as she continued to retreat more and more into the silent void she'd built around her.

"Damn it, Honor. For once just listen to me. I know you hate me. Despise me. You have every right. But I need you to listen to me. Your sacrifice will *not* be in vain," he said fiercely. "Your bravery will not go untold. Your courage will not be forgotten. *You* will not ever be forgotten. I swear that to you on my life."

"What does it matter?" she asked dully. "I will die a coward, begging for death, wishing with all my heart and soul to die. How is that bravery or courage? I never want my parents to know the truth of my death. It's kinder to tell them I died in the bombing. Can you promise me that at least, Hancock? Can you do them this one small kindness since I know you won't do it for me?"

"No," he said in a pissed-off voice. "No, I will never let them believe you simply died. I will tell them the truth. That your life and death meant something. That your death saved hundreds of thousands of other people. So they never think your death was senseless and random. They deserve *that* truth."

"So it doesn't matter what I want, but then that should be obvious to me by now," she said, self-loathing filling her for even considering for a moment that it would.

She turned up her face to him and saw him recoil from whatever terrible look was in her eyes. Or perhaps it was the lack of what he saw in her eyes. Life. Meaning. That she no longer cared and had given up. Finally defeated.

"Why did you kiss me?" she whispered fiercely, hating herself all the more for this display of utter weakness. "Why bother making me care? Making me think you cared at least on the level of one human caring about another? Do you despise me so much then? I can't conceive of the kind of hatred that drives you."

She shivered and ran her hands up and down both arms, folding inward, becoming smaller and more inconsequential with every passing minute. Preparing herself, her defenses, strengthening them for the terrible future that awaited her.

"I care," he denied harshly. "I care too goddamn much, and that's why I'm so fucking pissed off, Honor. Because I'm not supposed to care. I'm not supposed to be human. I'm a killer. A mercenary. Call me what you will, but it's all true. Every possible terrible thing you can conjure. It's true. But you can never say I don't care, goddamn it. Because I care too much."

In that moment, Honor knew. She knew that Hancock wasn't quite as incapable of emotion as she'd thought. That he likely hated what he knew had to be done. But that wouldn't stop him because he believed in whatever his mission—job—was. And in order to, as he'd put it, save thousands of other lives, hers must be forfeit.

And he hated that.

But he hated that he cared even more.

How lonely and stark must his existence be? Devoid of all the things she took for granted being raised in a huge, loving family, surrounded by unconditional love and support. Things he'd obviously never had—never would have—because he'd never allow himself to have those things.

He didn't think he was worthy or that he deserved them.

She hated him for betraying her, but she understood in a twisted way. In his own way, he was honorable. Doing what most couldn't do but had to be done to rid the world of monsters. Even become the very thing he hunted. A monster of the worst kind.

Maybe if he hadn't made her care about him, the man, she wouldn't be as hurt or feel so betrayed. Perhaps she'd even understand better that her sacrifice, as he'd deemed it, was necessary.

But she couldn't simply put it aside like he did and turn off what made her human. It still hurt. It hurt more than the thought of torture and death. It hurt her that she'd trusted him, that she'd cared about him on a deeper level. That they had shared the intimacy—a bond—that she'd shared with no one else and it had all been thrown back in her face.

It hadn't meant to him what it had meant to her, and for that she felt foolish and humiliated.

Was her hurt pride truly worth the loss of so many lives? Did it even matter how she died or how she was sacrificed if so many others could be saved by one woman? Her?

And why now was she preparing to try to absolve him of the terrible guilt and suffering she'd seen so briefly in his eyes? What kind of naïve fool did it make her to even believe she could give him absolution or peace?

"I understand, Hancock," she said, allowing some of the cold aloofness in her voice to fade away, sincerity taking its place. "And I forgive you, for what it's worth. You're right. What is the good of the one compared to the good of the many?"

Hancock swore savagely, getting up so swiftly that it rocked the bed, and she braced herself, fuzzy from the pain medication. He paced the floor like a caged animal, rage radiating from him in wave after wave.

"Don't you *ever* forgive me," he hissed. "And you sure as fuck do not offer me an apology that disguises itself as understanding."

She gazed at him, allowing sorrow to fill her eyes. And resignation.

"You can't control my feelings, Hancock. You control my fate, yes. My ultimate destiny. My life even. But you can't control *me*. You don't get that choice over whether I grant forgiveness or understanding or even apologize that I'm not stronger, that I can't just stop fighting and accept that my death will save the lives of so many other innocent people."

Hancock stood still, stopping his pacing as he faced her,

his hands in tight, clenched balls at his sides as he shook with uncontrolled rage. She sucked in her breath at the raw agony swamping unguardedly in his eyes, something he'd never allow—or want—anyone to see. But she saw it where perhaps no one else would. Where someone else would merely think he was dangerously angry.

"I don't make many promises, Honor. And you shouldn't even trust me to keep them if given. But one thing I vow before all else is that you *will* be remembered. Your sacrifice will *not* go unheralded. Your family will be told the truth. Every ugly part of it. Because you and they deserve that much. Your life will not be forgotten. And goddamn it, you matter. You *matter*."

His gaze dropped and his fingers uncurled and curled in rhythmic motion she wasn't sure he was even aware of. And when he looked back up at her, she inhaled sharply at all that she saw in that one unguarded moment.

"You matter to *me*," he said hoarsely.

And then he stalked toward her bed, the predator that he was, but when he once more settled onto the bed, there was something fierce in his eyes that had nothing to do with the predator and everything to do with him, the man.

He framed her face in his hands and kissed her, pouring all of the tightly held emotion into that kiss. He devoured her mouth like a man starving. His tongue swept hotly over hers, leaving her breathless and aching.

He kissed her as if there were no tomorrow, as if this single moment were all they had, were all that mattered.

The kiss went on and on until she surrendered, relaxing against the strength and warmth of his muscled body. Then, surprising her, he pressed tiny kisses over the entire line of her lips, pausing at the corners, licking at them delicately with his tongue, and then he simply pressed his mouth to hers and left it there until they both had to gasp for air.

"You matter, Honor," he whispered against her lips. "Never think you don't. You matter to me," he said, echoing the same words he'd uttered just moments earlier. "You matter too goddamn much."

The anguish in his voice was nearly her undoing.

CHAPTER 22

HONOR awakened and the first person she saw hovering at her bedside was Hancock. She glanced accusingly at him, still shaken from the last moments before she'd succumbed to the effects of the medication.

Hancock sighed. "It was only pain medication, Honor. After we spoke, you were exhausted, not just physically but emotionally drained as well. Nothing would have kept you from drifting off. I gave you what you wanted. Answers."

He'd given her a hell of a lot more than the answers to the questions she'd asked. Much more. And she hadn't had time to sort through the tangle of emotions swamping her. She was confused, heart and mind completely at odds.

"Not all of them," she murmured.

"The ones that mattered," he said simply.

She pushed herself upward, testing the restraints that her injuries had placed on her body, satisfied she could do so without giving away the pain that swamped her.

"It was a very abbreviated version. One you might give in a debriefing. Not lying, but not giving the full truth either."

He nodded, unsurprised by her perceptiveness. Not many people saw past the facade he always, always had in place, and yet she saw so much deeper, to the man behind the iron mask, and he didn't like it one bit.

"I want it all," she said in a low voice. "If this is to be my fate, what must be done, then I at least deserve . . . everything. And this time no one is coming near me with a needle."

"And after?" Hancock challenged. "When you're drooping with fatigue and have gone pale with the obvious pain you're feeling even now, will you fight me then or will you allow me to give you this small thing—a few hours where you aren't hurting and you aren't remembering betrayal?"

She'd have to be blind not to see the flash of pain he couldn't control. Not in front of her. He might as well be an open book where she was concerned. For fuck's sake, she'd apologized to him. For being selfish. For not being strong. Didn't she realize she had courage that most men couldn't muster? Could never possess? Courage wasn't something learned. It was born in fire, by hell itself. It was bravery in the absence of fear, or perhaps masking fear.

She was the most fucking fierce woman he'd ever met in his life, and he knew there'd never be another like her. He could search the world over and never meet any woman—or man to equal her.

"After," she agreed, and he realized her steely resolve disguised just how much mental and physical pain she was even now enduring. "But first I want the whole truth. Not just the watered-down bare-bones truth you choose to give me. I want to know who this Maksimov is and why he's such a threat. Why a man as ruthless as Bristow is afraid of him and why you're so certain that he would just hand me over to ANE."

Hancock rubbed a hand over his hair and to his nape, gripping it in obvious agitation. It was obvious he had no liking for her question. He didn't even attempt to hide his revulsion, and that frightened the hell out of her, that he would react so violently. Yet, she also knew he would give her the answers she demanded. Was she prepared, truly prepared, for the unvarnished, ugly truth?

"Maksimov is a monster beyond your wildest imagination. He's cunning and ruthless and has no conscience." He visibly winced, shame entering his gaze as he stared at Honor. "Just like me."

She shook her head before she even realized she was doing so, adamant, her eyes going flat, angry.

"Don't you *ever* compare yourself to him," she said fiercely. "You don't fool me, Hancock. Don't even try lying or attempt to make me see what you want me to see. I see you. And you are *not* Maksimov."

He looked . . . bewildered, as if he had no idea how to respond to her impassioned statement. For a long moment silence reigned.

"Back to Maksimov?" she prompted.

"Killing is second nature to him. To him killing is as normal as breathing. As eating or drinking. If it gets him what he wants, he does it. He thrives on pain, torment." He winced again. "Torture. Rape. You can't imagine the twisted, sadistic things he does to the women he rapes. He's into every imaginable crime. He has no loyalty except to himself. He deals drugs, guns, bombs. Human trafficking. He's a fucking *pedophile* and he indulges himself even as he sells children to people who are as perverted and twisted as he is."

Hancock vibrated with rage. He simmered, like a volcano about to erupt. His eyes were icier than she'd ever seen them, and she'd been witness to that flat, emotionless coldness before, but never this degree of utter frigidity. These were the eyes of a killer. Eyes that evoked terror in whoever was his target.

"Money, making money, is a game to him. And no matter how much he has, he craves more. Because to him, money is power, and power, ultimate power, is what he wants most. He sees himself as a god. He'll never stop, and so someone has to take him down."

"You," she whispered.

He gave a clipped nod. "I'm the best chance anyone has of taking him out because unlike others, I don't have a heart, a conscience. I'm more machine than man. A programmed killing machine, willing to do whatever it takes to take him down. Even become the very thing he is. I *am* what he is. I'm no better than what he is."

"You are *not* a heartless killing machine," she snapped, angry all over again. "Tell me something, Hancock. Do you go out and find some innocent woman to rape and torture, prolonging her agony until she can finally take no more and then dispose her like trash? Do you prey on children? Are you a depraved pedophile who enjoys inflicting pain and terror on innocent children?"

His eyes were shocked, and he shuddered, revulsion swamping his eyes. "No! *Never! God*, no."

She smiled her satisfaction, and he didn't look pleased that she'd pushed his button and had gotten the reaction she obviously wanted from him.

"There is a difference between becoming *like* someone in order infiltrate his ranks in order to kill him and save thousands of lives and *becoming* that monster when you aren't on the hunt for one," she said in a soft voice. "You can tell yourself all manner of lies, Hancock. You can try to convince yourself that you're no better than Maksimov, but you and I *both* know the truth. Even though you'll never admit it to yourself. You do what you have to do in order to save countless innocents, but you hate it and you hate yourself. But that's not who you are. It's not who you will ever be. The world is a better place for having you in it," she said, even quieter than before. "Don't let evil win and let it convince you that *you* are evil. That you're some unfeeling bastard who craves killing, torturing and shedding blood. Because when you truly start believing that of yourself, *then* you will become the very thing you hate the most."

"Fuck me. Swear to God I don't know what I'm going to do with you, Honor," he said, his agitation obvious.

Her face immediately fell, and she turned, trying to hide it from him. Because they both knew exactly what he was going to do with her, and she didn't want to make him feel even worse.

How fucked up was that? That she wanted to shield him from her pain. That she didn't want to cause *him* pain. To add yet one more burden—sin—to stain his already tarnished soul. He had betrayed her. He'd deceived her at every turn. She should hate him. She shouldn't care how much pain she caused him or he caused himself. But she couldn't do it. She didn't understand this . . . connection . . . whatever the hell it was between them, only that it was there. A living, breathing entity that she was powerless against. She simply couldn't turn it off and make herself cold and unfeeling as Hancock could when he wished it. It wasn't her nature. It wasn't who she was, any more than Hancock was what he purported to be.

"That was a sorry thing to say," Hancock said in a low growl. "Goddamn it, Honor, I'm sorry. That was shitty and unforgivable."

"I thought I had already established that only I get to decide what is shitty or unforgivable," she said lightly.

And then she gave him a somber look and beckoned him with her hand.

Grudgingly, he came, settling onto the bed next to her. This time it was she who took his hand, when before she'd tried to avoid any personal contact with him. She curled her fingers around his and at first he was rigid, stiff and unyielding, but she simply waited, refusing to allow him to slip from her grasp.

Then with a sigh he relaxed and stroked his thumb over her knuckles.

"Look at me, Hancock," she asked softly.

At first he refused, but then finally he lifted his gaze to hers, and he looked . . . tormented. Something deep inside her twisted painfully and robbed her of breath. There was grief in his eyes and it *hurt* her. And it made her want to take it from him. To somehow ease the horrible pain inside *him*.

"I know you don't believe me. You don't have to. But you *are* going to listen to what I have to say and you aren't going to block me out because you don't *want* to hear what I have to say. Do you understand?"

He went utterly still and his eyes became even more haunted, as if he dreaded her next words. But he nodded slowly, his gaze holding hers. Those beautiful green eyes full of so much agony that it hurt to hold on to that connection. But she didn't look away. She didn't want him to perceive it as a rejection of who and what he thought himself to be.

"I don't hate you," she said, gauging his reaction. "I did, at first," she admitted. "I felt betrayed. I trusted you. I felt safe with you when I hadn't felt safe in a long time."

Every word was as though she'd thrust a dagger into him and twisted, the evidence there in the fathomless depths of those green pools.

"I'm not saying this to hurt you," she said, allowing the ache she felt into her voice. "I'm saying this to get to my point."

"I deserve far worse," he bit out.

She ignored him.

"But I understand, Hancock. You don't think I do because you don't *want* to think I do. But I understand why this must happen. I've already given you my forgiveness. What you do with that is up to you, but it's given nonetheless. You can't make me take it back. I won't take it back. It's mine to give. You don't get to decide what I give or don't give. You either accept it or don't, but it's given and when I give something, I don't take it back. Ever.

"Do I want to die? Of course not. I have so much to live for. So many dreams . . ." She drifted off, knowing this was pointless and would only make him feel worse. She shook her head to rid herself of the direction her words had drifted.

"But I know that my death is a necessary thing. And if my death means that Maksimov can no longer cause so much hurt to so many others, then I can die in peace. I'll know that my life *did* mean something. That my surviving the attack did in fact have a purpose. A much higher purpose. And that's enough for me. I can face death and not be afraid because I'll picture all those women, those young girls and know they are safe because you took Maksimov down."

He made an inarticulate sound of rage but didn't interrupt her.

"You showed me kindness and gentleness," she said quietly. "You didn't hurt me, and we both know someone else would have. They wouldn't have cared what condition I was delivered to Maksimov in. But you protected me and we both know that. And for that I thank you. But what I thank you the most for is giving me the truth. So that I don't go to my death terrified, alone. That I'll know as I take my last breath that my death wasn't senseless and without purpose."

Tears glittered in Hancock's eyes, shocking her with uncharacteristic emotion. He looked gutted. He had the look of a man tortured with demons that would haunt him for eternity. She wished with everything she had that she could take them for him. So that he could be free. Most of all she hated that her dying would haunt him for the rest of his life.

"I have two things to ask of you, Hancock. Just two. And they're simple. I'll never ask for another thing and I won't fight you. I won't try to escape. I do have some dignity and I've resigned myself to what must be. But I want you to promise me two things."

"Anything," he said hoarsely.

"Promise me that my death won't be in vain. Swear to me that you'll take Maksimov out."

"He's going down," Hancock said, menace in his voice. "I swear it, Honor. I will not let your sacrifice be for nothing. Never."

She briefly closed her eyes, steeling herself for the second request.

"Please spare my parents the details. You can tell them that my death brought an end to a maniac and his entire empire. But swear to me that you'll tell them my death was quick and merciful. Promise me you won't tell them *how* I died. They'd never survive it. I don't want them to know that I prayed for death or that I died screaming and begging for death. I don't want them to know all that was done to me. Please, Hancock. Please, I'm begging. Do this for me. For *them*."

Hancock gathered her hand in his, squeezing so hard it took all her control not to wince because she knew he wasn't trying to hurt her. It was the strength of his emotions, emotions he was trying not to allow to show but she did. She saw him. The heart of him. Past the outward facade he'd perfected over a lifetime.

"All your family will know is what a fierce, brave and loving woman you were. They will know of all the lives you saved and the courage you showed the entire time. When I said that you mattered, that you would never be forgotten, I never meant for you to think that what would be remembered is the way you . . . died."

The last came out strangled, as if just saying the word

wounded him deeply. He looked away from her, no longer able to keep their gazes locked and so she wouldn't see what he so desperately tried to hide.

"Thank you," she whispered, her own voice thick with tears.

"How can you thank me for being the instrument of your death?" he raged, anger and sorrow reflected in every word. "How can you offer *forgiveness* and *understanding* to your executioner? You should hate me, Honor. You should despise me. You should be plotting to kill me, to escape, to do whatever necessary to take me down, and all you ask is that I make sure Maksimov dies and that your family is shielded from the details of your torture and agony?"

Her face went soft, and she lifted her hand to gently stroke his cheek.

"You aren't my executioner."

"The *fuck* I'm not," he said, fire in his voice. "I'm not a goddamn hero. I'm a merciless killer who is willing to sacrifice everything that is good in this world so I can complete my mission. That makes me no better than Maksimov, no matter what you say or think."

He abruptly stood and she felt the loss of their closeness, suddenly chilled and shivering.

"You need to rest," he clipped out. "You're in pain. And don't deny it. Conrad is going to give you another injection, and I want you to sleep."

But she knew his order was only partly born of his belief that she needed rest and relief from the relentless pain that nagged her. He could no longer bear to look at her. Could no longer bear the guilt and horrible anger and helpless rage without losing all control.

Because they both knew her fate was inevitable, and he hated himself because there was no other way. No alternative. And they both knew it. He hated that she could so calmly accept what he could not and that worse, she'd given him forgiveness and understanding, two things he felt he didn't deserve.

CHAPTER 23

"THE exchange has been set up." Bristow said what Hancock already knew, his eyes gleaming with satisfaction. "Maksimov was very pleased when I told him I had the woman in my possession."

Hancock stood in silence, waiting. Behind him his men were just as silent, though he could feel the undercurrents, the tension radiating from them all. Because they knew that once Honor was delivered to Maksimov, she had no protection. And none of them were fool enough to think Maksimov wouldn't avail himself of Honor and enjoy her for a time before he made the delivery to ANE.

"You leave in two days' time. I have the coordinates and all the information you need. Maksimov has explicit instructions as to how he wants the woman delivered. I expect you to heed them all."

Hancock merely nodded and took the folder from Bristow's outstretched hand.

"Consider it done," Hancock said coolly.

Bristow tossed a thick envelope toward Hancock. "Half your payment now. The other when you make the delivery."

It took every ounce of his willpower not to kill the man right here and now. The envelope burned his skin. Blood money. He would give it to his men. They deserved it. But he wasn't taking one goddamn cent for sending Honor to her death.

"You can leave now," Bristow said arrogantly. "I'll see to the travel arrangements. Discretion will be necessary, of course."

"I will make the plans," Hancock said in a cold tone. "You hired me to do a job, but it will be done my way. My men. My mission."

"Very well. As long as you accomplish what I'm paying you to do, I don't care how it's done."

Without another word, Hancock turned and stalked from the room before he completely lost it and slit the man's throat.

His men followed, and the only thing that broke the silence was, "Bad mojo."

Very bad mojo indeed.

He couldn't even look his men in the eyes. He merely told them to rest and prepare for the journey ahead. No one argued. No one said anything at all. They merely melted away to their separate quarters, no one attempting to meet his gaze just as he had avoided theirs.

He doubted any of them would sleep the next two nights.

CHAPTER 24

HONOR was roused from a medication-induced sleep to a strong hand over her mouth and another cupping and squeezing one breast roughly, painfully. Her heart leapt as she struggled through the fog and haze from the medication.

"He won't save you this time, you little bitch. He's too busy planning your delivery to Maksimov, and I intend to make use of the little time I have left before I hand you over to the Russian. A man like Maksimov won't mind used goods. He certainly won't turn you back over to ANE before having his fill of you."

Bristow.

Oh God. Where was Hancock? Had Bristow drugged him to make sure he wasn't a threat? Or was he truly planning the exchange as Bristow had said?

When he tore her shirt, rending it in two and exposing both her breasts, she began struggling, the effects of the medication quickly disappearing as adrenaline kicked in and she fought with every ounce of strength she had.

He didn't slap her as he had before. He balled his fist and punched her in the mouth, leaving her breathless and panting at the pain. Then he punished her with his mouth, kissing her brutally, licking at the blood that seeped from her torn lip.

He stuffed a foul-tasting rag into her mouth, and to her horror she realized it was dipped in some kind of drug. Then he taped her mouth shut, trapping the material in her mouth.

But she wasn't going down like this. Yes, she'd resigned herself to her fate but not to being raped by this asshole. She'd die before allowing that to happen.

His hands mauled her, roving possessively over her body, delving below the band of her pants, pulling impatiently and swearing when she still resisted. Maybe he thought the drug would have rendered her senseless by now, but she'd had enough medication and drugs to have built a slight resistance and could hold out longer now.

She fought soundlessly, panicked by the fact that she could make no sound. No scream for help. For Hancock.

His fingers jabbed brutally between her legs and she went wild, bucking, kicking, fighting with every bit of strength and willpower she could muster. She could feel the effects of the drug, knew she was sluggish, but she drew on reserves she didn't even realize she possessed.

He cursed and hit her, again and again, but she didn't stop. Couldn't stop.

He bit at her breasts savagely, leaving marks and bruises. Tears of rage and helplessness burned her eyelids. She'd had enough of being helpless and powerless.

She managed to free one of her hands, and she ripped at the heavy tape, gasping as skin came away. She shoved the rag with her tongue, recoiling at the taste, but she managed to spit it out and then let out a scream.

He hit her on the side of the head and she nearly lost consciousness. And then he was on her again, tearing at his pants to free his huge erection. She was naked, her clothing in shreds. Something dug into her hip and she realized he had a knife attached to his belt. He wasn't even bothering to remove his pants. He planned to shove them down just enough to free his cock and shove it into her resisting body.

Knowing this was her only chance, she grabbed the handle, thumbing the snap that held it secure, and yanked as hard as she could. She rolled away, opening the knife, and stumbled from the bed, falling to her knees as she crawled toward the corner of the room.

"You think you can kill me with that?" he sneered.

"N-no," she said shakily. "But I can kill myself and fuck

up your arrangement with Maksimov, and from what I hear
he's not a man to fuck with. He'll be very pissed that you
didn't deliver the goods."

His eyes narrowed. "You're a horrible bluffer."

She brought the blade to her wrist and cut a thin line, just
enough that he could see the blood trickle down her arm
and drip onto the floor.

Panic entered his eyes and he backed off.

Her adrenaline was fast wearing off and she knew he'd
simply wait, outlast her. Sorrow filled her because killing
herself meant that thousands of others would also die. All
because she wasn't strong enough to allow this man to rape
her. Something that would no doubt happen over and over
when she was handed off to Maksimov and then to ANE.
Like a used piece of garbage. Worthless. Trash.

A sob escaped and the burn of the blade deepened as she
realized that she'd cut deeper, not even realizing it. She was
deep inside the shell of her shattered mind. She'd withdrawn
from the horror of it all.

Useless. A sacrificial lamb. Something to be used, raped,
beaten, tortured. Worthless. Nothing. Nameless and faceless. Just another statistic.

There was sound. It dimly registered. Oddly, it sounded
like a lion's roar, but she blocked it out as she did everything
but the knife, slowly draining her life's blood. But wait. One
wrist wouldn't be enough, and if she didn't cut the other
now, she'd lack the strength and the use of it that she needed
in order to cut her other wrist.

Clumsily, she transferred the blade to her other hand,
frowning at how slippery it was. And how weak she felt.

Slowly, blocking the pain, she made the cut as if she were
outside her body watching with disinterest as she drew blood
a second time. She watched in odd fascination as blood
welled and slid over her skin, staining the floor and smearing
her leg.

Another sound roused her and her grip tightened on the
knife. This was taking too long. So she lifted it, again surprised by how weak she felt, and she put the blade to her
neck. An arterial bleed would have her dead much faster.

CHAPTER 25

HANCOCK kept his meeting with his team brief, giving them the rundown on the intel Bristow had provided and what their plan of action would be. It was a grim, mostly silent exchange with Hancock doing all the talking except for the occasional "Bad mojo" from Mojo.

He didn't like being away from Honor, even for the half hour he took after he'd ensured she was asleep after being given a lighter dose of pain medication. She didn't like the fog, as she described it. It made her feel vulnerable and impaired. So he compromised, because he couldn't bear the thought of her hurting when so much pain awaited her.

He dismissed his men and immediately started across the house to the wing where Honor's room was. He was halfway there when his blood froze in his veins.

A scream shattered the eerie silence of the house. Honor's scream.

He ran, fear lodged in his throat, nearly paralyzing him. Only the desperate need to get to her, to protect her, shoved away the paralysis as adrenaline kicked in and the formidable killer swiftly rose to the surface, overriding all else.

He expected the worst, but when he burst into her room, his heart nearly stopped, because it was *far* worse than he could have ever imagined.

Bristow was standing across the room from where Honor was huddled in the far corner, clutching a lethal knife to her throat. A thin trickle of blood slithered down her neck, but then he saw that both wrists were slashed and blood ran freely from the wounds.

There was blood on her face, her mouth and jaw swollen and already bruised.

Murderous rage consumed him. He wanted to take the bastard apart with his bare hands, but he didn't have time. Honor didn't have time.

Her eyes were vacant and haunted. She'd retreated deep inside herself and he doubted she was even aware that he'd come. Too late. He'd failed to protect her. Again.

"I've got Bristow," Conrad said coldly, rage equaling Hancock's own savage in his voice. "You see to her. You're going to have to talk her down. She's not there anymore."

"Not in front of her," Hancock snapped. "She's already traumatized enough."

"Wait just a goddamn minute," Bristow demanded. "You forget you work for me. She's mine until I give her to Maksimov, and I'll do what I damn well please with her."

Conrad merely executed a crippling maneuver that had Bristow on his knees, wheezing for breath. Then he twisted the man's arm behind his back, pushing upward until the snap of a breaking bone could be heard. And just as quickly, Conrad herded him out of the room. Bristow was a dead man.

As much as Hancock wanted to be the one to kill the bastard and not quickly or mercifully, his focus had to be on Honor or she would die by her own hand. Fear seized him because Honor was completely naked and covered with bruises, bite marks, scratches. Had the son of a bitch raped her? Had he driven her to this? Was she was so traumatized that her only escape was to take her own life?

"Honor?"

His voice was pitched low, seeking to know just how far gone she was and whether she had any awareness of her surroundings at all.

She didn't so much as blink, and he panicked when the blade pressed a centimeter farther over her carotid artery.

He didn't dare approach her. She could very well perceive it as another attack. He cursed himself for not taking Bristow out the first time, and he cursed himself for leaving her unprotected for thirty goddamn minutes because Bristow was going out. He'd seen the man leave, and that was the only reason he'd held the brief meeting with his men.

The son of a bitch had obviously staged the entire thing, wanting to use Honor before he passed the leftovers to Maksimov. He hoped to hell that Conrad took his damn time killing the asshole. Judging by the rage in his man's voice, he felt confident that Conrad would derive great pleasure in making Bristow's death drawn out and very painful.

"Honor, sweetheart, it's me, Hancock. Bristow is gone. He's a dead man. He will never hurt you again."

His words were fierce, despite his attempt to keep his pitch even and soothing.

She did blink then, and she cautiously lifted her gaze to Hancock. Something deep inside him settled, and he allowed himself to breathe for the first time since he'd taken in her appearance. Recognition flickered but then vanished as anguish swamped her beautiful eyes.

What worried him now was the fact that her grip on the knife hadn't loosened at all. Her wrists were bleeding freely, more so than the shallow cut at her neck. He had to act fast and stop the blood loss before he lost her.

"Is he really dead?" she whispered.

"He's dead," Hancock said savagely.

She crumbled before his very eyes, the knife shaking, inflicting more damage, and it was imperative that he get it away from her now.

He took a chance and slowly moved toward her, his steps measured and nonthreatening.

He knelt in front of her, swearing violently under his breath as he took in the extent of the attack on her. She'd been brutalized. Mauled like an animal.

"Honey, give me the knife," he coaxed. "You're bleeding and I need to get it stopped before it's too late."

There was so much sorrow in her eyes that his heart seized.

"I'm sorry I wasn't stronger," she whispered. "I know you need me to get to Maksimov. But I couldn't . . . Oh God, Hancock, I couldn't let him . . ."

"Shhh, baby. It's okay."

He wanted to weep that once again she was apologizing for not being strong when she was the strongest person he'd ever known.

Her hands shaking, she extended the knife, and he took it, folding it back so it no longer posed a threat.

"I'm going to pick you up and take you to the bed so I can treat your wounds," he said gently.

At that, she went crazy, backing even farther into the corner, drawing her knees up and wrapping her arms protectively around her legs, hugging herself, rocking back and forth, her eyes wild.

She shuddered violently, shaking her head adamantly. "No. Never. Not in that bed. No. I won't stay there."

"Then I'll take you to my room," he said soothingly. "But baby, you're losing a lot of blood. I have to stop the bleeding now."

"You promise?" she asked hoarsely.

He knew what she asked. That he promised he wouldn't put her back in the bed where Bristow had attacked her. Where he might have raped her and had damn sure tried if he hadn't succeeded.

He curled his arms underneath her slight body and lifted, cradling her tenderly against his chest.

"I promise. You'll stay with me. I'm not leaving you even for a minute. I swear it."

She nodded and then turned her face into his neck and burst into tears.

He bristled with rage, every muscle in his body going rigid as the need for Bristow's blood filled his soul. He held her tightly, hurrying down the corridor to the wing where he and his men were housed.

Conrad was waiting, his expression grim.

"What did that son of a bitch do to her?" Conrad snarled.

"Not now," Hancock snapped. "Get me a med kit and a suture kit. We've got to get her wrists stitched and the bleeding stopped. She's lost too much blood as it is. The cut on her throat isn't as bad and won't require sutures. And get her pain medication and a sedative. She's never going to sleep after this."

Conrad swore but hurried away to get the necessary supplies.

Hancock carefully laid her on the bed, and she immediately curled into a protective ball.

"I'm just going to get you one of my shirts," he said so as not to alarm her.

She glanced down, horror reflected in her gaze as if only just remembering that she was completely exposed. Mortification swept over her delicate features and she began silently weeping all over again.

He took a T-shirt, one that would allow Conrad easy access to the areas that needed attention, and dressed her like a child unable to do the task herself. He brought damp washcloths and several large bandages so he could apply pressure to her wrists until Conrad could control the bleeding and stitch the cuts.

"Can you tell me what happened?" he asked quietly. "What did that son of a bitch do to you?"

"He touched me," she said, shuddering in revulsion.

"Did he rape you?" he asked bluntly.

She flinched and looked away. His heart was in his throat because she had the look of a woman who'd been brutalized, who had been driven to the very edge of hell. He was perilously close to losing his shit and that was the last thing she needed right now.

She needed tenderness. Gentleness. Things he had never thought he possessed until he met her.

"No," she finally said in barely above a whisper. "But he wanted to. He tried. I fought him and it made him angry. He hit me. He touched me. I grabbed his knife and told him I'd kill myself and his deal with Maksimov would go straight to hell and he'd be a dead man for promising Maksimov something he could no longer deliver."

Amid his terrible rage, pride rose at her ferocity. And her quick thinking.

"He didn't believe me so I cut my wrist. And then I realized that if I waited too long, I wouldn't have the strength to cut the other one. And then I went for my carotid artery because I knew I'd bleed out in seconds. Only then did he back off."

For a moment Hancock couldn't breathe. It was the height of hypocrisy that he was gutted over the fact that Honor had been terrified enough to kill herself when it would be the kinder of her two possible fates.

But he was a coward. He would witness Honor's death here. He wouldn't see what happened to her after she left his protection. And he'd promised that as long as she was under his protection, he wouldn't allow her to come to any harm. Twice he'd broken his promise. Twice Bristow had gotten to her when she was at her most vulnerable.

Conrad strode in without a word—he was tight-lipped—and fury emanated from him in tangible waves.

He began to cleanse the wounds at her wrists with brisk efficiency, and Honor looked anxiously up at Conrad, her nervousness and unease broadcasting through the entire room.

"I'm sorry," she murmured, including both men in her apology. "I could have ruined your mission. I could have messed everything up. I wasn't thinking rationally. He . . . hurt me."

She broke off as though she were embarrassed to admit that he'd hurt her and that she'd been terrified, and now she sought what, their forgiveness?

Conrad paused and visibly sucked in a steadying breath. Then he looked her directly in the eye, pinning her with his steely gaze.

"You do not apologize to me, to anyone. Ever. It is we who owe you an apology for leaving you in a vulnerable position even for the small amount of time we did. You're an incredible woman, Honor Cambridge, and I can honestly say I am privileged to have known you. You will never be forgotten by me."

Tears sparkled like diamonds on her lashes as she stared at the terse man in bewilderment.

"I was a coward," she said in disgust.

"Now you're just pissing me off," Conrad said in a surly voice. "Shut up and let me do my job."

She went silent, and Hancock smiled to himself. Conrad had no idea what to make of Honor. She baffled him. She was a puzzle he had yet to solve, and it ate at him. In the world Titan lived in, there weren't people like Honor. Selfless. Courageous. Brave. Putting others before herself.

"He's giving you pain medication and a sedative," Hancock said in a tone that brooked no argument. "You need to rest."

It was a testament to just how exhausted and beaten down she was that she didn't so much as utter a single protest.

She was silent while he stitched the cuts to her wrists. Though they'd bled quite a bit, they weren't nearly as deep as Hancock had feared, and the cut at her neck was so shallow that all it required was a butterfly bandage.

When it was done, Conrad gathered his stuff and he and Hancock walked toward the door.

"Hancock?"

There was fear in her voice that stopped him in his tracks. He turned and Conrad continued out as Hancock made his way back to where Honor lay in his bed.

"I don't want to be alone," she whispered. "Will you stay with me, please? I won't be a bother. I'll try not to be a nuisance," she hastily amended. "I promise."

He leaned down and brushed his lips feather light over hers. Then he laced his fingers through hers and gave them a reassuring squeeze.

His tone was infinitely gentle as if he feared breaking her. She was as fragile as he'd ever seen her, when before all he'd ever witnessed was her unwavering strength and stubbornness.

"I wasn't leaving you, Honor. I'm not going anywhere. I was just giving Conrad team leadership for the time being so I can stay with you. He's going to be my eyes and ears temporarily while I'm here. With you," he added for emphasis.

The relief in her eyes was nearly his undoing. She sagged

against the pillows, looking small and defeated. Tears shone brightly, catching on her long lashes.

"If you thank me, so help me God, I'm going to shake you," he warned.

A ghost of a smile hovered on her lips.

"Promise you'll stay even when the sedative takes effect?" she asked in a small voice.

He could tell it was already working. Her responses were slower and her speech slightly off balance, and it wasn't entirely due to the trauma she'd undergone.

"I'll be right here, next to you, the entire night," he said solemnly. "And if you have a bad dream, I'll hold you and kick its ass for you."

She smiled again, and he went weak to his knees. He realized a man would do a hell of lot to make a woman like Honor smile for him.

She opened her mouth and he shot her a warning glare.

"Don't you say a single word unless it's *not* an apology or a thank-you."

She laughed softly but closed her lips, but the gratitude was there in her eyes for him to see even if it went unspoken.

"And by the way, you're very welcome," he whispered, leaning in to brush his lips over her brow.

CHAPTER 26

EVEN under the effects of the sedative, Honor was restless and agitated in sleep. Hancock never left her side. He lay on his side next to her, cradling her small body with his much larger frame. When she trembled and made small guttural sounds in her throat that reminded him of those made by a trapped animal, he seethed in silence and rubbed his hand up and down her back, stroking and massaging.

His touch seemed to quiet her. When she became upset, she would relax and rest easy once more when he stroked her skin.

To his surprise, she fully awakened just a few hours after Conrad had given her pain medication and a sedative, but then he and Conrad had discovered the drug-laden cloth that Bristow had forced into Honor's mouth to force her compliance, and so Conrad had only administered a light dose, more to calm than to render her unconscious. Neither man wanted to be accused of doing the same to her as Bristow had done.

"Hancock?" she whispered, stirring against him.

His hold automatically tightened as he gathered her more fully into his arms.

"Yes, Honor, it's me."

She relaxed, seeming to wilt with relief. For a long

moment, her hand rested over his heart, her bandaged wrist reminding him of just how close to death she'd come. How desperately she must have fallen in those dark moments when Hancock hadn't been there as he'd promised to be.

Just one more sin to add to his endless list.

She seemed to be pondering something. He sensed her hesitancy and . . . fear. As though she wanted to ask him something but wouldn't. Or simply couldn't.

He slid his hand between them to cup his palm over the top of her hand.

"What is it, Honor? Is there something you need? Are you hurting?"

She inhaled sharply. "I know I said I wouldn't ask for anything more . . ."

"But," Hancock prompted gently. He knew damn well he'd give her the moon if she asked. The only thing he couldn't give her was what they *both* wanted most. Her freedom. Pain slashed in relentless waves through his heart for what he knew must be done. She was more accepting of her fate than he was, and that pissed him off all the more. She should hate him. She should be railing against him, calling him every vile name she could muster. He deserved them all.

She turned imploring eyes on him and he was lost. It was dangerous because if she asked it of him right now, he *would* let her walk away and fuck the mission and he'd never get another opportunity to take Maksimov down.

She lifted her free hand to her temple and massaged, but he didn't sense she was in pain. Just grappling with something difficult for her to talk about. So he simply waited, giving her the time she needed, and he didn't rush her.

His gaze brushed over her wrapped wrist, and helpless rage filled him all over again. For a woman like Honor, so valiant and courageous, never the coward she called herself, to have been so desperate as to attempt to kill herself, he knew it had been bad. God, what had that bastard done to her?

"He would have raped me," she whispered. "He wanted to. He t-touched me. And it hurt."

Hancock's chest tightened and his teeth ground together as he fought to keep his composure. He stroked his hand through her silky hair, gently massaging her scalp with soothing touches.

She glanced away, obviously embarrassed. Why? Because Bristow had attacked her? Because he would have raped her? Was she ashamed?

"I'm a virgin," she blurted. "I've never had sex with anyone."

Hancock went still, unsure of what to say. What to do. He was frozen to the bone, glad that she wasn't looking at him at the moment. Because God help him, he was turning over a virgin to Maksimov, who would delight in the discovery and make her initiation that much worse. He'd thrive on just how much pain he could cause an innocent.

But then she turned those pained eyes on him, eyes that pleaded with him.

"I know what will happen to me," she choked out. "I do. But I want to know if there is something you would do for me. It would mean . . ." She sucked in a deep breath. "It would mean *everything* to me."

He cupped her chin and rubbed his thumb over the bruise Bristow had inflicted.

"Ask me, Honor," he said quietly. "What is it you're having such a hard time asking me?"

"Would you . . . Would you make love to me? Now? Before you have to give me to Maksimov? Will you show me just once what it *should* be like so that I'll know? So that I'll have that one memory of something beautiful, something that no one else can ever touch. That can never be tainted no matter what else is done to me. So that when another man . . . hurts me, I can retreat to this moment and hold on. Shut out everything but this one perfect night. Will you do this for me?"

Hancock's heart threatened to burst out of his chest. He couldn't breathe. His torment was a tangible ache that no amount of wishing could make go away. She was begging him. Every inflection of her tone was pleading.

"I'm sorry," she said in a low, embarrassed voice. "I shouldn't have asked. Please forgive me. I'll never mention it again. I swear. You can go now. I'm okay."

There must have been something of the terrible anguish

in his expression because her eyes became shadowed and ashamed, her gaze dropping away after her embarrassed apology. She pulled the covers up to her chin and then buried her face against her drawn-up knees, wrapping her arms around them as she rocked slightly in agitation. She drew away, huddling as far away from him as she could at his perceived rejection of such a precious gift.

A gift he in no way deserved.

But what about what she deserved?

He had no experience with virgins. Innocents. He didn't partake in sex much. It was a distraction he couldn't afford. He took care of his needs when necessary but sex, like so much else in his life, was mechanical. No feeling, no heart. Just physical release.

And he knew, he *knew*, that with Honor there would be no hiding behind his iron facade. She had a way of stripping away the layers until he was raw and vulnerable and completely bare, with none of the protection he always surrounded himself with.

"Honor."

It was a whisper of a sound. He could barely form her name much less voice it aloud.

"Look at me," he pleaded.

At first she refused, staring stoically ahead into nothingness. He recognized it immediately. She was becoming more adept at retreating deep into herself, steeling herself for what lay in store for her. Pain. Humiliation. Degradation and finally death.

But goddamn it, she didn't need to retreat into herself with him. Never him.

"Honor, *please* look at me."

Reluctantly, she swung her gaze to meet his, and the hurt in her eyes knotted his throat. He couldn't breathe. Couldn't massage away the pain in his chest. The kind so deep that nothing could take it away. It would be permanently etched into his heart for all time.

"I was not rejecting you, baby. *Never* you. I was stunned. Humbled. And I was afraid," he admitted.

Her eyes widened in surprise. "Afraid? Why?" She was

clearly confused. She didn't think he feared anything at all. That he was invincible. And for the most part she was right. But she had no idea that his one weakness lay before him asking him to do what every part of his heart, mind and body screamed to do. Touch her with tenderness. Make love to her when he'd never made love to another woman in his life. Sex was sex. But sex with Honor? It would be the first time he ever offered more than simply his dick and his mouth to pleasure a woman. With Honor, he'd share everything that he was and everything he wasn't. And it scared the hell out of him.

"Because you deserve so much better than me," he said honestly. "I don't know if I can be what you need. You deserve to be treated gently, like the treasure you are. You deserve for that gift to be cherished and respected, and I'm not a good man. I'm selfish. I have no experience with virgins. And I would *hate* myself if I hurt you. I would despise myself. It would kill me if I hurt you, Honor."

He closed his eyes at the absurdity of such a statement. He *had* hurt her. And he would hurt her again. He would give her to a man who would hurt her endlessly. Who would then give her to men who would degrade and torture her until she prayed with every painful breath for mercy and for death. Never had he hated himself more than he did in this moment. He despised who and what he was, when before he'd merely accepted it as a necessary evil in order to do his job. To try and make the world a better place. Sacrificing Honor in no way made anything goddamn better.

"You're wrong," she said, lifting her chin, daring him to defy her. "You wouldn't hurt me. You would be gentle and sweet. And you're also wrong about this being a gift from me. It would be a gift from you to me. This time, I'll not ask for another thing from you. I swear it. I won't make you feel even worse for what you must do when we both know you have no choice. But tonight . . . Tonight is ours to do what we want. No rules. No mission. No saving the world. That's for another day. But tonight I want to feel something other than fear and hate and pain."

Her eyes became haunted, as his surely must be.

"I don't want to be alone tonight, Hancock," she said, in

a low, embarrassed voice as though she hated revealing a weakness. That she needed someone to comfort her and touch her even for just one night.

"You will *not* beg me for anything," he said harshly. "I would give you the world if I could, Honor. I swear I would. If only . . ."

He closed his eyes, slamming shut the wishes and *if onlys*, knowing that path led only to unfathomable pain.

"Don't," she said, her voice filled with sorrow.

To emphasize her statement, she pushed a gentle finger to his lips. Unable to resist such temptation, he flicked his tongue out and sucked the tip of her finger into his mouth.

"No one is ever guaranteed a tomorrow," she continued softly, tamping down the emotion, knowing it hurt him. And tonight she was determined they both forget their pain. Just for a few stolen hours.

"But we have tonight. Bristow is no threat. Your men will guard you well. Please, grant me this last request, Hancock. I would like to know how it's *supposed* to be. I don't want to die without ever knowing pleasure."

"You're so sure I'm capable of being this fantasy lover," he said in a near growl.

She shook her head, her eyes flashing. "Fantasies are for people who can't see or touch what it is they want. I don't want a fantasy, Hancock. I only want *you*. And as I've never done this before, I'll hardly know if you do it wrong," she added ruefully.

"I won't do it wrong," he said gruffly. "I'd never touch you with anything but tenderness, as much as I'm capable of anyway. I'm not a gentle man. I'm rough and demanding. I don't trust that I can be what you need right now. What I want would probably send you screaming and crawling under the bed."

Her eyes widened, but not in fear or even shock. There was definite curiosity. And interest. Her face became flushed and her eyes took on a hazy glow that told him she was aroused by what he'd said, how he'd said it.

He hadn't intended it to be arousing. He'd wanted to scare the holy hell out of her so she'd rethink this insanity. But the selfish part derived great satisfaction that she'd responded as she had, her lips parted in silent invitation.

God, the things he'd like to do to her mouth.

He put a tight clamp on the coarse, base ideas running circles in his brain and making his dick so hard it felt as though the skin would simply split under the pressure.

She deserved a gentle initiation. Not down-and-dirty fucking. He closed his eyes, swearing at his choice of thoughts. The idea of other men holding her down, raping her like mindless animals made him sick. His erection lost its rigidity and bleakness entered his soul.

"Tonight," she reminded him, as though she had reached right into his mind and plucked out his thoughts.

She rotated and rose up over him, leaning into his chest, bumping her nose into his in a charmingly clumsy manner. But damn it, she had no business putting any strain on her stitches or further aggravating her injuries.

As carefully as he could and making sure she didn't take his gesture as rejection, he eased her over onto her back and arranged her to his liking, inspecting every angle to ensure that he would cause no hurt to her wounds.

"You will lie back just as I have you," he said in a husky voice he didn't recognize. "You will not hurt yourself, tear your stitches or otherwise worsen your injuries."

She swallowed visibly, her eyes glowing brightly with excitement, her lips full, cheeks flushed with desire. She was the most beautiful thing he'd ever seen in his dull, colorless existence.

"I will be as gentle, tender and patient as a man ever was in making love to a woman," he vowed just as he lowered his body over hers, fitting his mouth to hers.

He was careful to keep his weight from her slender body, not wanting to hurt her in any way. He couldn't offer her anything. He couldn't grant what they both desired most. But he could give her this one gift she asked for. He would make love to her and show her what it was like between people who . . . cared. The word whispered insidiously inside his mind, forcing him to acknowledge that on some level he did care deeply for Honor Cambridge.

He admired the hell out of her. Respected her. Thought her a woman without equal. He couldn't conceive of what he could have done right in his life to have this one night with her. Right before he delivered her into the hands of evil.

He took his time, studying and learning her body inch by delicious inch. He kissed every mark, every bruise or wound and then lapped gently at it to soothe any sting he might have caused.

Her hands cradled his head when she could reach it as he continued his thorough exploration of her body. When she was quivering, not in pain, but nearly shuddering with desire, he became more aggressive and demanding, but still mindful of her fragility.

He sucked and nipped at her neck, quickly figuring out that it, like her breasts, was one of the most sensitive regions on her body. Or at least that he'd discovered so far. Her ultimate female nectar, he was waiting to taste, drawing out the anticipation—and hers.

Several times he got close, skimming his tongue and lips and then grazing his teeth along her belly and just above her soft mound. She moaned low in her throat and then made the sound of a frustrated woman nearing the end of her limits.

He smiled and lifted his fierce gaze, savage satisfaction gripping him when she returned every ounce of his ferocity in her own gaze.

And then finally, he gave in to what they both wanted so badly.

Using a feather-light touch, he brushed the tips of his fingers over the plush lips of her sex and then carefully parted them, inhaling as he scented her need and saw her delicate pink flesh glistening with the evidence of her intense arousal.

Still, he cautioned himself to go slowly. Not to overwhelm her. She was small. A fighter, yes, a scrapper who didn't know how to quit. But she was delicately built. His hands easily spanned her narrow rib cage, easily trapped her hips in his firm grasp, holding her bottom captive against the bed.

He lowered his head and she whimpered low in her throat

and then gasped sharply when he tongued her from her small opening to her taut clitoris that puckered and strained upward to receive the tiny flicks of his tongue.

He rolled the bud around with his tongue, teasing and tormenting, deriving every bit as much pleasure from the act as she was.

She was wetter, much more damp, but he still wanted to make sure she was ready—able—to take him. He was a large man in all areas. Strong, muscled. Lean. An ultimate weapon for destruction. And seduction.

Yes, he'd seduced women to get information. He'd never hurt even one of them, and he'd made damn sure he made the sex good for them. But for him? He had simply turned it off and performed by rote, never allowing himself to feel this kind of need—*obsession*.

He drank of her sweetness. So much innocence. He'd never had such innocence. He tongued and sipped until he had to hold her down to keep her from hurting herself.

When he was certain she was hot and wet enough to take him, he shifted his powerful body over hers and gazed down into her half-lidded eyes.

"Are you sure, Honor?" he asked even as his dick rimmed her slick entrance.

"I've never been more sure of anything in my life. Please, Hancock. Do this for me."

He wanted to thrust in her so deep and hard that there was no separation between them. That for these precious few seconds, they were one person. One heart and soul.

But he mustered every ounce of control he possessed and eased carefully forward, watching her eyes widen as she stretched around him. And then a grimace touched those eyes and he halted.

"No," she protested. "Either pull back or just push in. Quickly, please. I can feel something stretched, like it's about to tear, and it hurts this way. Please make it go away."

If he retreated, then she'd have to repeat it all over again, and he'd spare her what hurt he could. Closing his eyes, gritting his teeth tightly as though he were experiencing the sweetest agony, he thrust all the way home.

She bucked upward, crying out, even as his hands had solidly anchored her hips. He immediately peppered her face, eyes, forehead, nose, lips, with kisses, "sorry" a litany between each kiss.

"I'm so sorry I hurt you, Honor," he said, allowing the torture in his voice to tear free.

Her smile slid into the deepest recesses of his very being.

"Move with me," she invited huskily. "It doesn't hurt so much anymore. And if you . . ."

She dropped off shyly, averting her gaze.

His heart turned over in his chest.

"What do you need for me to do, baby?" he asked tenderly.

"Touch me," she whispered. "Put your mouth on my breasts."

He slid his hand between their joined bodies and stroked one finger over her slick nub and was rewarded with an instant surge of heated moisture coating his dick. He groaned even as he lowered his head to suck one straining nipple into his mouth, coaxing it to rigidity. He took his time, tonguing in and lapping, circling a damp trail around the puckered crest. Then he turned his focus to her other breast, giving it equal attention until she was breathless and moving restlessly beneath him.

"Now?" he asked, the words straining past his clenched jaw.

"Now," she agreed, her eyes glowing with desire she didn't try to hide from him.

He gripped her hips, not to hurt her, but to hold her in place, carefully anchored between him and the bed so she didn't hurt herself. Then he surged forward. He withdrew, dragging his dick through engorged, highly sensitized flesh, each stroke of her velvety plush pussy sending electric shocks down his spine. His balls gathered tightly to the point of pain, but this wasn't for him. He wasn't taking. He was giving. His final gift to her.

He had to push that thought away as heavy, aching sorrow filled his heart, his lungs, his very soul. And instead he concentrated on making this as pleasurable as he hoped she would think it to be.

He pushed deep, holding himself there, closing his eyes and simply giving himself over to the rush of pleasure enveloping him. Sweetness that he'd never before known in his life surrounding him and pulling him further into its web of ecstasy.

"Please," she begged, her voice hoarse with strain. "I need you now, Hancock. I'm so close . . . but I don't know what to do."

She sounded panicked and unsure of herself. He gathered her close, wrapping his arms around her fragile body, and held her as she deserved to be held the first time someone made love to her. Only his hips moved, undulating up and over hers, pushing deep and then withdrawing.

But when her mouth nuzzled against his neck and nipped before kissing a line to his ear and sucking the lobe into her mouth, he saw stars and his body was no longer his to control. It was hers. Only hers.

He powered forward again and again.

"Yes," she moaned. "That, Hancock. That. Please don't stop. I'm so close but I don't know what I'm close to!"

The frustration and innocence in her voice drove him those last precious inches over the brink. He slid one arm down underneath her sweet ass and lifted her, angling so he could drive even deeper, and then he set a pace that left them both gasping, moaning, writhing.

Her legs slid around his, anchoring her to him.

"That's it, baby," he whispered. "Lock them around me and hold me tight. Trust me to get you where you want to go. Don't be afraid. I'll be there to catch you. Just let yourself go."

After his second thrust, with her legs locked around his, she shattered in his arms, shivering, quaking, her cries splitting the night. The surge of wetness around his dick stole the last of his wavering control and he followed close behind her, making sure she went first, that she found her pleasure and release before him. Only when she was in the throes of her orgasm did he plunge deep and hold himself there, emptying himself deep within her body.

He'd never felt a sense of homecoming that rivaled the touching of two hearts, body and soul. He knew he never would again.

CHAPTER 27

HANCOCK held Honor tightly in his arms as they lay side by side, ensuring that her injured side wasn't the one she lay on or put any pressure on. Quiet had descended and neither made effort to disturb the peace that enveloped them.

She snuggled deeper into his embrace, as if she could burrow inside him and stay for all time. Didn't she know she'd already done that? That no matter where he went in this life, he'd carry a part of her with him. And all the regret for what could never be.

He hated himself. His hatred was a living, fire-breathing entity that had taken on a life of its own, slowly consuming him until nothing would remain except the hollow shell of a man-machine. Because no man would ever allow the woman lying in his arms to come to harm.

She was silent, but as he gazed at her, he could see that her brow was furrowed and her eyes shadowed. He frowned. Had he hurt her after all? Did she regret what she'd asked him to do? Because there was not a single part of him that regretted making her his. Taking something that would never belong to anyone else. Her innocence. Her virginity. The honor of being the first man to have ever made love to Honor.

If that made him a primitive, chest-beating beast of a caveman, so be it. He'd certainly been called worse.

"What are you thinking?" he asked softly. "Did I hurt you? Do you regret what we did?"

Her eyes immediately became fierce. "No. Never! I will never regret this. It's just that . . ."

Her eyes lowered and shame burned red on her cheeks.

He tilted her chin up with a gentle finger. "What is it, Honor? You must know you can tell me anything."

"Even if what I say breaks a promise I made to you?"

This time his brow furrowed. She hadn't made many promises. Only not to ask for another thing. Ah. That must be what she was grappling with. She had another request, but she felt honor bound not to ask because she'd promised she wouldn't ask for more and she was a woman who kept her word.

"Tell me what you want," he said, stroking his fingertip along her jaw until she leaned into his touch, closing her eyes with contentment.

"I know I said I would ask for nothing more than for you to make love to me, but . . ."

"But?" he prompted.

"But I would very much like to touch you. To make love to you," she said earnestly. "I want to taste you. I want to give you as much pleasure as you gave me."

He groaned. "Baby, if you don't think you gave me pleasure, then we need to have a *serious* come-to-Jesus meeting right now. I have never felt more pleasure in my life than when we made love. Never."

Her eyes widened with surprise. "But, Hancock, I was a virgin. I had no clue what I was doing! How could it possibly have been enjoyable to you?"

"Trust me, baby. If it had been any better, I'd be a dead man."

Her eyes laughed at him, but then she sobered. "Would you mind so terribly much if I touched you and tasted you like you did me?"

"Men would kill for an opportunity for what you're offering, Honor. I'm no exception. But I want a promise from you in exchange."

She sent him a puzzled look.

"You will do nothing that hurts you. If I even think you're in pain, it ends. I won't budge on this, Honor," he said, his tone grave so she'd know he was utterly serious. He didn't want to piss her off, but neither did he want her in pain while trying to pleasure him, for fuck's sake. He who didn't deserve anything but hatred and cold disdain from this beautiful woman, inside and out. Who shone like a radiant ray of sunshine, warming places in him that had only ever felt cold and darkness.

But she only smiled, her eyes lighting, her expression so giving and generous that it humbled him.

"I promise," she said solemnly. "But Hancock, just so you know? Getting to touch you and give you even a tenth of the pleasure you gave me will never hurt me. I want it too badly for pain to even register. Give me this. Give yourself this," she added gently, almost as if she knew he felt he didn't deserve it but that he also wanted it like he wanted to breathe.

Then her eyelashes fluttered and cast downward, her cheeks a dusty pink as though she were embarrassed.

Once more he slid his fingers underneath her chin, coaxing it upward so he could see into her eyes and see what bothered her.

"Tell me what is frightening you, Honor," he said, injecting every ounce of patience and tenderness he was capable of into his voice.

She swallowed and then took a deep breath. "I'm not sure how to please you, and I want that very much, Hancock. You gave me so much. I never imagined it could be like that. I don't deceive myself into believing I can give you even a fraction of what you gave me, but I want you to feel good. I want what I do to you to feel good. But I don't know how."

The last came out in frustration, almost anger. Self-directed anger.

"Can you show me how to please you?" she whispered. "Can you show me what to do and how to do it?"

Already moisture beaded the tip of his dick, and her gaze was drawn to the pearls, seemingly fascinated. Almost as if she couldn't help it, drawn to the sight, she leaned down and delicately licked one of the drops away.

His entire cock jerked and his hips bucked, curses tearing from his lips. His fingers formed tight fists, gathering the sheets in his hands as he held on for dear life.

She immediately pulled away, her eyes stricken, tears welling in her eyes.

"I'm sorry," she rushed to say, as if fearing she'd made him angry. Then she pounded her fist against her leg, causing him to instantly catch her hand to ensure she didn't reopen the stitches at her wrists. He rubbed his thumb caressingly over her skin and then brought her hand to his mouth and kissed each knuckle. Every fingertip, drawing each into his mouth and suckling them.

Then he allowed each finger deeper entrance, licking at the tip and then the underneath of her smooth fingers, taking it to the back of his throat and then swallowing around it.

Her eyes widened in sudden understanding. He was showing her how to please him. How to take his cock in her mouth and please him.

"Honor, you did *nothing* wrong," he said, not recognizing the tender caress that suddenly became his voice. He sounded throaty and seductive, like he was wooing the most important female in the world. One he must make his or die.

"God, if you did anything righter I'd shatter. Look at me, baby. See me. Really *see* me."

Reluctantly, she lifted her eyes to meet his.

"Do I look like I'm not pleased with anything you're doing? See me, Honor. See what you do to me. I'm as naked and as vulnerable as a newborn babe, and believe me, I do not like feeling that way. Except," he said, drawing it out, "for you. With you. Only with you."

She smiled then, relief lighting her deep brown eyes until they warmed him to his very soul.

"There is nothing you can do that I won't love and be begging—yes, that's right, Honor, I said begging—for more. You'll have me on my knees and at your mercy for just a touch from you. Your mouth. Your nipples. Your body. I want it all."

"You don't mind my inexperience then," she said in a pleased tone.

He gathered her face in his hands, tangling his fingers in her hair as he took her mouth in a breathless motion. Then he pulled back, still running his fingers through the silken strands of her hair as if he simply couldn't get enough of touching her.

"I love that I'm the only man who's ever touched you this intimately. I'm glad that I'm the only man you've ever touched so intimately. The only man who's had his dick in your sweet mouth and felt the touch of that velvety soft tongue. God, what you do to me, Honor. Damn me to hell for taking such a precious gift when I have nothing to give you in return except heartbreak and betrayal."

Tears burned his eyes and he did nothing to shield his emotions from her, something he would have never done in the past with anyone. No one saw into him. Not even his family. They caught glimpses, but only what he wanted them to see. Just enough so they'd know he did love them.

But Honor got all of him. Every single thing he'd spent a lifetime suppressing. Building impenetrable fortresses around the things that mattered to him until they simply no longer existed. He became what he set out to become. The ultimate assassin. No feelings to muck things up. No emotions to interfere in a mission.

But he'd known for a while now that his heart was no longer in it. That he no longer had a heart or a soul. Honor had been the final nail in his coffin and after this—her—he'd walk away and never look back. He'd live the kind of life Honor would have wanted him to have—or try. How could a man ever live with peace knowing he'd destroyed the very essence of good? Even if it was to take out the very face of evil and save thousands of innocent women, children and men?

Was it really worth it?

Was it?

Honor's eyes narrowed as she stared back at Hancock. "You do not have the look of a pleased man right now."

He smiled. Really smiled, allowing the demons and shadows that haunted him and would haunt him the rest of his life to slip away, because nothing would interfere in this one brief shining moment in the sun. He'd wrap himself in Honor's light and goodness and keep it always.

"That's because your mouth isn't where it should be," he murmured, thumbing at her bottom lip before slipping it inside, rubbing softly over the top of her tongue.

"Then show me," she said, breathless, her respirations speeding up, her nipples puckering into taut, rigid points.

Unable to resist, he slid his hand between her thighs and slipped one long finger inside her, enjoying the hiss of pleasure and surprise that escaped her lips.

Oh yes, she was wet and excited. Over the idea of pleasuring *him*.

He tossed a pillow onto the floor beside the bed, and then he reverently and ever so carefully lifted her in his arms and then lowered her onto her knees on the pillow so it would cushion her from the hard floor.

He sat on the edge of the bed, thighs spread, his dick straining upward, flat against his abdomen, pre-cum still beading the tip. Honor looked at it again and unconsciously licked her lips, eliciting a groan from him.

"Baby, you have to stop that," he said hoarsely. "I'll come before I ever get inside that sweet mouth, and right now I'm dying to get in there."

"Then do it," she said sweetly, her innocence flowing over him like cleansing rain. "You do it, Hancock. I want you to have control. Show me what you like. How to please you. I won't fail you."

Jesus H. Christ. How could she possibly fail to please him? Just her touching him pleased him. He'd known for a long time he was damned to hell, but being with her, kissing her, touching her, being so deep inside her that they became one person, one soul, one being, for that brief moment he'd seen heaven, and he'd never wanted anything more badly in his life.

Not giving words to those thoughts because then he'd be lost forever, he tangled his fingers in her hair, palming both sides of her head to pull her forward.

"Open your mouth," he said gruffly. "But guard your teeth. Teeth are . . . painful and not in a good way."

She smiled just as he pulled her to his mouth, and she parted her lips dutifully.

"Now relax and trust me. We'll start slow and let you get used to it. Play with and tease the head. Especially underneath. Use only your tongue."

She did exactly as he instructed. Too well. He threw back his head at the first tentative touch of her tongue circling the broad head of his penis. This. This was heaven. *She* was heaven. An angel.

She licked and teased, paying special attention to the underside of the flared tip, and then traced the edges of the head, the ridge between it and the length of his shaft.

His breath escaped in a long hiss and his grip tightened in her hair and against her head, but she issued no complaint. She didn't even flinch, but he still forced himself to be more gentle, reminding himself that she was not unhurt. She shouldn't even be doing this. She'd been attacked, shot and then nearly raped by that son of a bitch Bristow. What was he thinking, subjecting her to this when she should be lying in his arms resting?

And yet the selfish part of him couldn't deny himself this one pleasure. The only thing he'd ever wanted for himself. The only thing he'd ever *needed*. He, who needed nothing and no one. But he needed *her*.

Reluctantly he pulled himself from her satin lips and simply sat there, his breaths harsh and loud in the quiet room.

"Just give me a minute, baby," he rasped out.

"Then you like it?" she asked shyly. "Am I doing what you like?"

He bent down, dragging himself to her mouth to kiss her, to show her just how damn much he liked it.

"I don't like it. I fucking love it."

She rewarded him with a smile that stole the breath right from her lungs.

"I want more now," she said.

"You'll get it," he promised.

Once more palming her head and tangling his fingers more harshly than he intended, he guided her back to his straining dick.

"I'm going to start with shallow thrusts to allow you time to adjust. I don't want you to panic. Breathe through your nose. When I think you're ready, I'm going deeper. I'm going to go very deep," he said, clear warning in his voice. Her one chance to back out.

But she didn't so much as hesitate. She only nodded, excitement and arousal flaring in her eyes.

"Trust me," he said. "I'll hold you there and I want you to swallow around the head, milking me. The pleasure is indescribable. But don't panic. I'll know when you need to breathe and I'll pull back. But I'm going to push you, Honor. I'm going to see how much you can take. If at any time it's too much, you need a break or you want me to stop, you squeeze my legs."

His hands left her head long enough to collect her bandaged hands, sorrow once more filling him at the desperation it had taken for her to do this to herself. To actually try and end her precious life.

Carefully, as if they were the most fragile and cherished things in the world, he placed her palms down on top of his thighs, roped with thick muscles, hardened by the many years of relentless training and use.

He pressed her thumb into his flesh, looking at her as he did so. "That's all you need to do. And I'll stop. Immediately."

She frowned and shook her head. "Hancock, I like touching you. I'm sure I'll be squeezing you a lot. There has to be another signal. My hands will never stay still."

He smiled. "Yes. They will. Because I'm telling you they will. Don't move your hands, Honor. Only if you want me to stop. Do you understand?"

She shivered at the demand, the dominance he couldn't keep from his voice. Her submission, what a gift. If only he could have this for a lifetime. Yes, he would absolutely dominate her entire life. He would control every aspect of her life. But there would never live a more pampered, spoiled, cherished-beyond-measure woman than this woman here. His dominance would be of love and his need to protect and provide. Never to punish, to be a controlling asshole. Everything. All things. It would all be for her. His life. His very existence. His only goal to please her and make her happy.

"I understand," she whispered, her eyes glittering with need. Her lips parted and she licked over them as if she couldn't wait another moment for his cock.

He gave it to her, feeding it inch by agonizingly slow inch, stopping to allow her to grow accustomed to his size. He knew without false modesty that he was not a small man. Nor was he average. Women had refused him after seeing his size. Others had groaned, unbelieving of their luck.

To him it was just an appendage. Another weapon in an arsenal he carried with him at all times. Only now was he aware that he could hurt Honor. That he could frighten her. That his size could very well intimidate her and make her think she wasn't capable of pleasing him. As if.

"Okay?" he whispered when his dick was halfway inside her silken mouth.

Her eyes answered for her, glowing brightly, a clear invitation for more. Hell, it was a demand. But her hands remained still, just as he knew they would once he'd made the demand. He also knew that she would never stop him, no matter how far he took things, and he was mindful of that every second.

He paused, withdrew and this time pushed with more force, eliciting a gasp as her cheeks bulged outward. But she quickly calmed herself, exhaling through her nose, and he felt her relax around his girth, sucking him further inward.

He withdrew, and each time he thrust farther, gaining more depth, each time measuring her response, looking for any sign that he was pushing too far. Scaring her. Hurting her. And every time, she gave him a hungry look that told him she only wanted more.

Convinced that she wasn't going to shatter, he finally gave in to the beast inside roaring to take control and find his pleasure. To dominate, take over and take what was his at least for this one night.

Never once did her fingers tighten. Her thumb, instead of pressing into his skin, the signal he'd given her that meant it was too much, caressed him, rubbing lightly in circles, humming around his cock in satisfaction.

Just touching him brought her pleasure.

It baffled him. He didn't understand this—her—this connection. Her easy acceptance of him. Of what he was. Of his needs that many would call twisted. Sick. Perverse. She accepted them as naturally as she would breathing.

He became rougher, though he was ever mindful of every single injury and where he could and couldn't touch her.

But then he could stand no more and he framed her face in his large hands and held her firmly, giving her no choice but to kneel there and take whatever he chose to do. He fucked her hard and long, stopping when he was at his deepest and reveling in her swallowing delicately around the head of his dick, sucking down the sips of pre-cum, merely a precursor of what was to come.

He knew she expected him to come in her mouth, but he had other plans. Primitive. Animalistic. All traits he knew existed within the monster he was.

Then he eased out, letting her catch her breath. He glanced down at her, allowing what he felt to show in his eyes. To let her know that she mattered. He'd said it many times, but this time he gave her the evidence. What he never gave anyone else. Himself, unguarded. His eyes not shielded. She gasped and tears gathered in her eyes, then slowly trickled down her face, colliding with the hands that held her so firmly in place.

"I'm going to fuck you hard, Honor," he said, his voice harsh, laced with drugged passion.

"Please," she softly entreated as the tip of his dick rested on her lips. "Give me everything, Hancock. I want so badly to please you. To give you back what you gave to me. There is *nothing* you can do to make me reject you."

With a guttural cry, he drove hard, almost punishingly to the very back of her throat, stealing her breath. He didn't bother remaining there. He was so close. So very close to coming. And he wanted this. Fucking her mouth. Marking her. She was his for tonight. And she would know it.

He fucked long and hard. She struggled for breath, but quickly adapted and learned how to breathe as he withdrew. When he felt the first burst of semen splash onto her tongue, his iron control nearly deserted him and he nearly stayed there, filling her mouth with his essence.

Instead he allowed her that taste. Just the one. So she'd go to sleep smelling him, his taste in her mouth.

When he withdrew, she protested and her eyes were hurt, shadowed. As if she thought she'd done something wrong. He caressed her cheek with one hand, holding his engorged cock with the other.

He slid his hand down underneath her chin and lifted, baring her neck, and then he began to pump his dick with his hand, hard, nearly vicious. Thick white ropes splashed onto her neck and then he directed it onto her breasts, coating each one, her nipples and then finally her face, pressing his erection to her satiny flesh so it didn't just fly all over her skin, uncontrolled, so it didn't hit her in the eyes.

He smeared his release on her cheeks and then over her lips, coating them like lipstick and then as the last came, he pushed inside her mouth again, deep, hard, and stayed there as he pulsed against the very back of her throat. Spending himself to the very last drop there in the honeyed silk of her luscious mouth.

He could spend forever there.

She licked over his slowly softening shaft, sucking tenderly, as if she knew how hypersensitive he was now that he'd orgasmed. She cupped his balls with one hand, stroking them lovingly as she cleaned every last drop of his semen from his dick.

When he finally slipped free of her mouth, she cupped his waning erection in her palms and pressed a kiss to the head, licking ever so lightly at the slit as she fondled his sac.

Then she looked up at him, her heart in her eyes, tears glistening, tiny diamonds attached to her lashes.

"Thank you," she whispered in a husky voice. "I'll never forget this night. Or you."

CHAPTER 28

HONOR lay nestled in Hancock's arms, her cheek resting on his chest, his chin atop her head. They lay in silence, Honor's arm wrapped tightly around Hancock's waist, wanting to keep him here, next to her, for as long as possible. Every minute that went by was another minute closer to dawn and the end of their night together.

He stroked his fingers through her hair, over and over. Just caressing, absently almost, as if he were pondering something important.

She loved him.

Agony seared through her body, worse than any pain she'd ever experienced. All the injuries, the battering she'd taken in the attack, the bullet she'd taken for Conrad, Bristow's two attacks on her. Nothing hurt worse than loving this man and knowing that in another day's time he would turn her over to Maksimov and she'd never see him again.

It was the hardest thing, and it mustered every ounce of her self-control not to weep for all that was lost. But she refused to give in. Because Hancock was hurting too. She knew it. He was quiet. He hadn't said a single word since he'd gently kissed her forehead after she'd thanked him and had said, "No, my darling Honor. Thank *you*. You are the first time I've ever tasted sunshine."

Then he'd taken her into the bathroom and into a warm
shower where he washed every inch of her body, taking
special care with her injuries. He'd even shampooed her
hair, massaging gently before rinsing the soap from the long
strands. After thoroughly drying her, he'd rebandaged what
needed bandaging, applying antibiotic cream and a numbing
agent to prevent pain. Then he'd finished drying her hair,
taken her into the bedroom and pulled her between his legs
as he sat with his back propped against the headboard, and
he'd combed the tangles.

She was nearly asleep when he eased her down on her
uninjured side and simply wrapped himself around her,
tucking her head beneath her chin, and held her.

But neither slept, and neither spoke. What was there to say
anyway? They both knew what had to be done. What *would*
be done. And she had only one regret. Just one. Not the attack
on the clinic, not her running in constant fear, not Hancock's
initial betrayal, not even Bristow's attack. Because it had all
led to this one beautiful night. No, her only regret was that she
only had this one night.

He'd given her the most beautiful night of her life, but
he'd also shown her what she would never have, and she
craved it as she'd never craved anything in her life. Being
with Hancock? Having his dominance, his caring, protection, his utter devotion to doing whatever it took to make
her happy?

She wanted to weep because as much as she'd wanted
this night, she almost wished she'd never gotten a taste of
what was now forbidden fruit. You couldn't mourn what you
never had.

Hancock was tense, agitated. She could feel his body
vibrating, how tightly he held her. His grip was almost bruising and it was painful at times, but she never said a word, not
wanting to lose his touch. If he thought he was hurting her,
he would immediately put distance between them, and that
she couldn't bear. A little pain was a small price to pay to lie
in his arms for the few short hours they had left together.

She'd asked him for *tonight*. Only tonight. But would he
make love to her again tomorrow night? Knowing that it truly

would be their last night together? That the following morning they'd leave for him to turn her over to Maksimov?

Or would he spend that night hardening himself, turning back into the Hancock everyone but her saw? The machine. The emotionless mercenary who thought nothing of turning a woman over to a man if it accomplished his goal.

Yes, that was the more likely possibility. He would distance himself from her. He'd wake her with those cold eyes and implacable features. He'd treat her as the prisoner she was. Oh, he wouldn't hurt her physically. But he would treat her as a thing. Dispassionately and as though she were of no importance whatsoever. Because it was the only way he would be able to withstand what he had to do. And she knew it hurt him. No one else would know. But she did and would.

That didn't hurt her, that he would harden himself and become a shell of his true self. She knew it was the way he endured—had endured—all these years of loneliness. What hurt her was that she'd never see him again. Nothing Maksimov or ANE would do to her could possibly compare to the agony of knowing love for such a short time, of tasting passion that couldn't possibly be common, of sharing an intimate bond with the real Hancock. The Hancock that only she saw. And would never see again.

Whatever Maksimov and ANE did, she could take. She'd even welcome it because it would give her respite from the very real pain of losing Hancock. And when death came for her, she would welcome it, because then she wouldn't feel at all.

She closed her eyes, a sense of peace enveloping her. Her life hadn't been for nothing. For one magical night, she'd experienced love. She'd loved and been loved in return. This night was worth *everything* that had come before and all that would come after. Because it gave her this. And this was worth dying for.

"I can't let you go."

Hancock's words, guttural with agony and despair, startled her, breaking the heavy silence and the thoughts she'd been lost in.

His hold on her tightened until she could no longer contain the wince. He didn't even notice.

"I can't do it, Honor. I can't. I *won't*. Goddamn it, I *won't* do it!"

He was seething, his entire body tense, his muscles rippling with rage. His face, if she didn't know the man beneath, would terrify her. He looked like what he'd been labeled his entire life. A ruthless, merciless killer.

She gently pried herself away from him, just enough that she could lean up and face him fully, her puzzlement not disguised.

"Hancock?" she whispered tentatively.

She had no idea what he meant. What he was saying. She was utterly confused.

His face was a wreath of torment. Agony blazed in his eyes and he looked as though he bore the weight of the world on his shoulders. Had this been what he'd been thinking of so intently the last hours as they'd lain in silence, him holding on to her as if afraid she'd simply disappear? Had he been planning this all the while, or had he simply made an impulse decision? An irrational bid to hold on to the night as much as she wanted to hold on.

He reached up to touch her cheek and she couldn't help herself. She nuzzled into his palm and turned to kiss it but then returned her gaze to his, questioning. Not understanding what was happening here. Whatever it was . . . it was huge. And it made her very afraid. Not for herself. But for *him*.

"I need you to listen to me, Honor. And I need you to understand. I will *not* give you up," he said fiercely. "There isn't a force strong enough in this world to *ever* make me give you up. Do you understand?"

Her brow furrowed. "But Maksimov . . ."

"*Fuck* Maksimov," he said savagely. "And fuck the goddamn *greater good*. I've been an instrument for the greater good my entire life and I've never, *never* asked for one goddamn thing for myself. I've never *expected* something for myself. I've never had one thing that's all my *own*. Only mine. But I have *you*, Honor. And I will *not* give you up. *Ever*."

Fear was sharp and bitter in her mouth. She stared at Hancock, allowing every ounce of that fear to show. She was terrified. For him. And for what she thought he was telling her.

"But Hancock, if you don't give Maksimov what he wants . . . You've told me who and what he is. He'll *kill* you. He'll hunt you down like some animal. From what you told me about him, about the kind of man he is, I can well imagine that time means nothing to him. That he'll wait months, years, however long it takes, but he'll kill you. No matter how long it takes to exact revenge. He'll wait and he'll strike. I can't, I *won't* let that happen, Hancock. You constantly tell me that I matter. Goddamn it, Hancock, *you* matter," she raged. "*You matter!* You matter to this world. The world needs you. You matter to *me!* You said my sacrifice wouldn't be in vain, that it served the greater good. Then don't let my sacrifice be wasted! I would *never* trade my life for yours. *Never!*"

"And you think you don't matter to *me*?" he roared. "Do you think I'm going to just hand you over to him and walk away knowing that he'll repeatedly rape you, that his men will rape you? Whomever he wishes to reward will rape you. He'll torture you just because he enjoys it. And then he'll turn you over to ANE and every imaginable horror you can possibly imagine, they will do them all to you. When and only when you are so near death that you can no longer withstand their constant brutality, they'll kill you, but it won't be merciful and it will *not* be swift. They'll drag you into the middle of whatever village they occupy and they'll inflict as many wounds as possible so that you die a slow, horrific death, and then they'll leave your corpse to rot and decompose and no one will move you for fear they'll be killed for interfering."

She shuddered at the very real images he invoked. Tears ran down her cheeks. Theirs was an impossible situation and she knew it, even if he didn't admit to knowing the same. They were doomed. They could never be together. If she didn't die, then Hancock would.

"I will *not* trade my life for yours," she repeated, horrible rage building and swelling until it was an inferno. "You are a good man. I don't care what or who you think you are. I see you, Hancock. *I see you*. The world *needs* you."

"And I need *you*," he seethed. "You are the *one* thing I want—need—above all else. I *need* you, Honor. What kind of man would I be if I led you to your rape, torture and eventual slaughter? Do you honestly think I could continue on like nothing had ever happened? Do you think I would survive it? That I could continue on, fighting the good fight, fighting for the greater good when *you* are the greater good and *I* killed you. *I* murdered you. *I* let you be raped and tortured. Do you think I'd sleep at night imagining you in their hands? Do you think the world would be a better place with me in it? I'd turn into a monster unlike this world has ever seen, and I wouldn't give a fuck about the greater good because *my* greater good was destroyed by *me*."

She leaned her forehead to his, her tears dripping onto his face. "What are we going to do?" she whispered brokenly.

"We're going to make the exchange."

Honor looked at him in shock.

"We're going to set it up so that it looks exactly as it should. And then my men and I are going to take out Maksimov. I will not give you to him, Honor. Do you understand that? Do you trust me? *I will not give you to him.*"

She swallowed, the beginnings of hope blossoming, and she tried, oh how she tried, to tamp them down because hope was such a dangerous and delicate thing. So easily broken and yet so easily nurtured.

"I trust you," she said without hesitation.

He leaned in and kissed her.

"Then trust me to do this. I have to go now. I want you to rest. Really rest. And Honor, if you don't, I *will* have Conrad sedate you. I have to get with my men because we now only have a little over twenty-four hours to come up with a completely different plan."

She smiled ruefully. "After the bombshell you just dropped on me, you better go ahead and go get Conrad, because there is no way I'll sleep. I'll just stay up and worry . . ."—her voice trailed off to a whisper, as if by saying the last too loudly she'd somehow jinx them—". . . and hope. I'm afraid to hope, Hancock."

"My name is Guy," he said quietly, surprising her with

the abruptness in the change of topic. "No one but my family calls me that. Well, really only Eden, my sister. Foster sister if you will. My foster father and my two foster brothers mostly call me Hancock. I'd like you to call me by my name, but only when we're alone."

"Guy," she said, testing the sound on her lips. "Guy," she said again. "It suits you. I like it far more than Hancock." She paused a moment before staring at him, locking gazes with him, allowing everything she felt into her eyes, hoping he could see.

He swallowed visibly, mirroring emotion simmering in his own expression.

"I like it far more because you shared it with *me*," she added quietly.

She caressed his jaw, staring at him with the love she felt and hoped he saw it, because she couldn't—wouldn't—say it. Not now. It reeked of emotional manipulation and they weren't out of the woods. Things could go terribly wrong. She would do nothing to make things worse.

He kissed her again even as he was rising to pull on a pair of jeans. "I won't let you down," he said fiercely. "I've let you down time and time again, Honor. But not this time. Not ever again. I know I'm asking a lot when I ask you to trust me. I've betrayed that trust. I don't deserve it from you, but I'm asking anyway. It matters to me. It matters a lot."

She gave him the words, unreservedly, her eyes never leaving his, the words directly from her heart. She might as well have said *I love you* for the way she gave the words. And judging by the fierceness that entered his eyes, she thought he heard the echo of that *I love you* when she told him she trusted him.

And for her, trust was love. Love was trust. They were one and the same for her.

CHAPTER 29

"**YOU** want to run that by us again, boss?" Viper asked, clear bewilderment in his eyes.

His other teammates wore similar confused expressions, but one common thread he found in every reaction he studied was . . . relief. In Conrad's face he found not just relief but fiery satisfaction. He looked like he wanted to physically react and do something absurdly uncharacteristic like throw his hand up and do a fist pump. Conrad, who liked no one, had been won over by a woman with more heart than ninety-nine percent of the men they'd served with. She had his respect and now his protection. Of all the men, Conrad's relief was the most pronounced. It had eaten at him that a woman who'd saved his life was being served up as a sacrificial lamb and he was participating in that repulsive act.

"You heard me," Hancock said curtly, no patience for restating what they'd all clearly heard. "The mission has changed."

"Good mojo," Mojo said, with a more animated voice than his usual monotone. The man actually looked *happy*.

"Not that I remotely object and if I were still in the military, I'd be saying *hooyah*," Cope interjected. "But do we get a clue about what changed since our last meeting a little over twelve hours ago?"

"Everything," Hancock snarled. "We aren't going to use the torture and murder of an innocent *woman* to finally take Maksimov down. I'm fucking tired of the *good of the many* creed and I swear to God, I'll have the balls of whoever says it in my hearing again."

"Fuckin' A," Conrad snapped.

"Good mojo."

"Rock the fuck on, bro," Henderson piped up.

Viper and Cope both nodded their agreement.

"We're going to take Maksimov out by making it appear we're giving him what he wants. And then we take him and any other threat out. I don't give a fuck how messy or clean. And I don't give a shit about dismantling his empire. For once, someone else can clean up the goddamn messes."

"You're on it tonight, man," Conrad said in a dry tone.

"Tell me how Bristow died," Hancock asked abruptly, his tone turning lethal.

Conrad shrugged. "He might still be alive. Or not. I figured a few hours, but he's a pussy. I doubt he lasted more than an hour. More's the pity."

The other team members muttered and expressed their disgruntlement at the idea he would die so quickly.

"His instructions were to drug her for the delivery," Hancock said, turning the conversation back to its original subject.

Conrad's brow lifted. "Is that what you're doing?"

Hancock uncharacteristically paused. Usually his responses were quick, assured. Situation completely in hand and on point. His men picked up on it. He would have been pissed if they hadn't, even as it pissed him off that he'd allowed himself that brief show of uncertainty. His men had been trained to pick up subtleties. It was the smallest of details that saved one's ass.

Hancock sighed. "I am."

The others looked at him in surprise.

"If I thought the other option was the best option, then I wouldn't drug her."

No one asked the obvious question, but it was there in every single face and in their eyes. They waited in silence for their team leader to explain.

"Honor can't know that we're actually pretending to deliver her, and she can't be conscious for more reasons than the fact that Maksimov made it a condition. She's simply too honest. All you have to do is look at her face, into her eyes, and you see the truth. Maksimov would never believe her to be what she *should* appear as. A scared, beaten-down captive about to be turned over to a monster. So I have to drug her, and . . . I have to fucking lie to her."

He said that last with blistering rage, a bitter taste filling his mouth. It was a necessary evil, one that would save her life and, if they were lucky, take Maksimov out in the process. But it didn't mean he liked deceiving her. Again. He fucking *hated* it. *Especially* after what they'd shared the night before. And even more, she'd given him her unconditional trust. The mere thought that for even one moment she could think he'd betrayed her made him sick to his soul.

"We do what's necessary," Viper said, his tone quieter than normal.

"Good mojo," Mojo said by way of agreement.

"You know it's the only way," Conrad said, but Hancock could see the other man's equal dislike of the deception. And his guilt. He could read Hancock. Conrad had always had the uncanny knack of reading his team leader, and he knew just how much Hancock hated what had to be done just as he'd known how much he'd despised the initial mission of handing Honor over and walking away.

"Yes. It is," Hancock said. "Now, we need to come up with a plan. A damn good plan. There is *no* margin for error. Maksimov has to be taken out, and Honor can *not* be harmed in *any* way. She, not Maksimov, is the primary goal. Yes, we're using her as a way to get close enough to Maksimov to take him out. But Honor's safety comes before all else. Even if it means Maksimov escapes us. Again."

"We're on it," Cope said immediately.

And then, as a team, they all turned to face Hancock, at attention, something they hadn't done since they'd left the military.

"You have our word. We will protect Honor Cambridge with our lives," Conrad said formally.

In turn, each of the remaining men repeated Conrad's vow, and Hancock's heart swelled with pride. They were hated, reviled. Their own government, whose dirty work Titan had done for years, had turned on them and tried to execute them. When that hadn't worked, the government had put a bounty on their heads.

His men were *good* men. Good men who'd done terrible things in the name of justice. And for the fucking good of the many. Had saved lives, even the lives of the very people who sought their death. They worked under no banner, no country. They had no true homeland. And they would always be hunted by the few remaining who even knew of their existence.

The very country they had fought so tirelessly to protect—and still protected—had denounced them all. Branded them with the worst insult they could have possibly levied given just how many acts of terrorism they'd prevented. Terrorists. Traitors to their country. The country they would have given their lives for. They were stripped of honor, already declared officially dead before becoming the black ops group Titan and they'd been robbed of their citizenship. They had no home, no place anywhere to call home. No loyalty to anyone save themselves. Their cause, their mission, was still the same. That much had never changed even when everything else had. Protect the innocent. Hunt the evil. Regardless of nationality.

And his men had never once wavered. They'd stayed true to Hancock and to the principles they'd set forth when they were forced to go out on their own. Rogue. Through it all, Hancock had never been able to summon hatred for the country he still considered his, even though she did not claim him as one of her own. He loved America. He loved her people. His hatred was reserved for the few who'd betrayed them and put into motion a decade of eluding assassins, all the while fighting the good fight.

Last night had shaken him on many levels. But perhaps the most profound of all was that for the first time since his country had rejected him, leaving him no place to call home, he'd finally found home in Honor's arms. *She* was home.

And nothing had ever felt so right—so peaceful and soul soothing—in his life.

"I have one more request," Hancock said, as formal as his men had been. "If I go down. If something happens to me, get the hell out of there with Honor. Under no circumstances can she end up in Maksimov's hands, even if it means abandoning the mission and letting the bastard go free. I know our creed has always been to never leave a fallen teammate. But I ask this of you because I would gladly trade my life for Honor's. She deserves no less. She *deserves* to live. She serves a greater purpose and the world is a better place with her in it."

"If we fail, it will only be because we all are dead," Viper said by way of a vow.

The others nodded in agreement.

"We'll get her home," Conrad said softly. "One way or another. I'll protect her with my last breath."

CHAPTER 30

HANCOCK carefully balanced the tray in one hand while he opened the door to his bedroom with the other. He walked in to see Honor dressed as he'd requested in comfortable trousers and a T-shirt. Only her feet were bare and she was perched cross-legged on the bed and gifted him with a welcoming smile that was like a knife to the gut.

He had to remind himself that this was necessary to ensure her safety. To save her life and get her home as he'd promised her. A promise he had every intention of keeping.

He forced himself to return her smile and then carried the tray over to place it in front of her.

"Breakfast in bed?" she asked in mock surprise. "You know, I could get used to such royal treatment."

She was radiant. Happy. Smiling. And her eyes were free of the shadows that had lingered there for so long. They were bright. Shining. And hopeful.

"I want you to eat and drink it all," he said with mock severity, trying to adopt her playful mood.

He knew she'd eventually ask questions. She'd want to know what the plan was. She'd want to know every single detail because she would worry about *him*. So he wanted her to eat and drink before they got into things better left not discussed.

She glanced down at the plate and sighed, picking up her fork.

"Uh-uh," he said with a frown he meant to amuse her.

He gestured toward the antibiotic pills on the tray. "Those first, and drink plenty of juice. Then you can eat."

She rolled her eyes but complied with his request, washing down the pills with several gulps of the juice. Half the contents were gone. Good, but not enough.

He let her eat a few bites of her food, courtesy of Mojo, who was a wizard in the kitchen. He'd made crepes, whatever the hell those were. They looked too damn fancy for Hancock. There were beignets, which Hancock did know and liked. Who didn't like beignets with strong black New Orleans coffee?

And there were fluffy scrambled eggs and breakfast ham along with bacon.

"What did he do, slaughter a pig?" she asked, laughter in her eyes.

He gestured toward the juice. "It's fresh squeezed. Mojo will be offended if any is left."

She nearly choked as she swallowed the food in her mouth. "Mojo cooked this?"

Hancock smiled at her reaction. "He's a man of many hidden talents."

"Obviously," Honor murmured as she drained the juice.

She cut into one of the crepes and took a dainty bite, but she frowned and then quickly tried to cover it up. Hancock pretended not to notice, his heart already sinking.

She toyed with the eggs a moment, speared a forkful and lifted it toward her mouth, but then slipped her free hand over her stomach and let the fork drop with a loud clatter.

"Hancock, I feel sick. I haven't eaten hardly anything. But I feel . . ."

She swayed, her face paling as she pressed her palm harder into her stomach. He saw her throat working as if she were trying not to vomit. He immediately reached forward to rub her back in an effort to soothe her and hopefully settle her stomach.

She flinched and then looked up at him with so much

horror and hurt in her eyes that it was like a knife to the heart.

"What's wrong?" she asked in a stricken voice. "What did you *do* to me?"

He cupped her face firmly when she resisted, and he pulled her into a gentle kiss, pouring out all the emotion he'd never allowed himself to feel until *her*.

He tasted her hot tears. Felt her keen sense of betrayal as if it had been done to him, and it only made him hate himself more for what he knew he had to do.

Kissing her again, he whispered against her lips, "Trust me, Honor. Don't fight it. Just go to sleep now. Just go to sleep."

"Am I dying?" she asked in a choked voice, tears silently streaking down her cheeks. "Kiss me," she whispered, eyes bright with those heart-wrenching tears. "Kiss me one last time before I go. Pretend this once, for me."

It broke his heart that she thought he'd pretended passion with her. That he'd used her, manipulated her emotions and tricked her into trusting him. Believing in him.

But he gave her what she wanted—what he wanted, savoring the sweetness of her mouth one last time before they had to go. Then he drew away, gazing intently into her eyes so she would know he was sincere.

"No, baby," he said tenderly, stroking a hand through her silky hair. "Just trust me. Just this once. *Trust me*. Death doesn't come to the innocent this day."

But her eyes had already closed and had he not had his hand against her head, stroking her hair, she would have listed to the side, already unconscious. He swore violently, tears burning his own eyelids. She'd slipped under not only thinking she was breathing her last breath, but that he had been the one to poison her. His final betrayal when she'd offered him her trust time and time again, only for him to break it over and over.

So much regret surged through his body, heart, mind and soul. For a moment he simply gathered her in his arms and held on, burying his face in her soft neck. He inhaled deeply, wanting to savor this one moment in time when there were no impossible barriers between them to breach.

He grieved silently, holding the woman who'd forever changed the course of his fate—his destiny—the very direction of his entire future. And then he once more reached for and embraced the familiar, icy chill of indifference. He made the transition from a man with humanity, a soul, to an emotionless killer. A machine programmed to carry out the mission at all cost. Or die trying.

Without a word, he bent and carefully gathered her in his arms before rising with her. He strode to the door and into the hall where his men waited, having shed any remaining vestiges of his deep connection to Honor, refusing to contemplate that he could very well *be* taking her to her death.

They all had grim expressions, having no more liking for the task than Hancock did. But they had no choice. It was their only chance to save Honor. And finally take down Maksimov. God help them all if they failed.

God help the world if Honor was lost and Hancock survived. Because no one would be able to stop him. Not even the devil himself.

CHAPTER 31

THE members of Titan crept silently through the brush, circumventing the route Maksimov had outlined so they'd surround him and come in behind him where he thought he would be safe. They'd spent countless hours, considering every angle, every possibility, preparing for the worst-case scenario and the easiest. After all, sometimes the path of least resistance was . . . just that.

For the first time, Hancock didn't lead his men as he always did, placing himself between him and his team. His team—their safety—was his responsibility, but today Honor was his sole objective.

The others encircled him and Honor, forming a protective barrier around him and the unconscious woman he held so carefully in his arms. He'd ensured that the drug he'd given her was strong so there was no chance she'd regain consciousness until it was all over with and she'd awaken in his arms, safe with the knowledge that it was over. That Maksimov was no longer a threat and she was finally safe. Beyond the reach of ANE.

And well, a few planted seeds, leaks to the right media outlets, and a sensational story would spread like wildfire that Honor Cambridge had died at the hands of ANE. It would save face for them and appease their sense of dishonor. Their public image was everything and as long as Honor kept a low profile, she would be safe within the confines of the United States.

But they were going to have a serious come-to-Jesus meeting about her vow not to let ANE disrupt her work. She was never going back to her old job. Over his dead body would she put herself in that kind of jeopardy again, and he knew he'd have allies with her family.

She'd told him that they had desperately tried to dissuade her from going but that in the end, they'd supported her decision. When they knew the truth—and they would know the full truth, minus the gory details that did them no good to dream about at night—they would ally themselves with him and be just as determined to keep her out of harm's way.

A prickle of alarm, a shift in the air, brought unease knotting Hancock's gut. And he always listened to his gut. Even as he shifted Honor from the cradling position he held her in to carefully place her in a fireman's hold so he could free the hand that already gripped the stock of his pistol, he heard Mojo's muttered "Bad mojo."

A sentiment shared by his other teammates as they stopped and sniffed the air like predators on the hunt. Or prey, measuring their opponent.

Pain seared into Hancock's left shoulder, leaving him breathless as hot blood scaled its way down his arm and side. Damn it. He'd made a rookie mistake. With Honor cradled in his arms, no one had a clear shot at him without risking hitting her. When he moved her, it left his entire left side exposed.

He staggered to his knees, ensuring that he took the brunt of the fall so Honor wasn't jarred into consciousness. The very last thing he needed was her awake and aware, convinced he'd betrayed her and given her up to the enemy. And who was to say he hadn't done just that, fuck it all.

His arm went numb as he tried to stumble upward and right himself so he could position himself over Honor, but his rifle fell from his hand's useless grip. His knees hit the ground, jarring his entire body painfully, and his men erupted in gunfire around him, with shouts of "Get down!

Get down! Sniper! Six o'clock. Cover Hancock, damn it! He's down!"

He fell forward, rotating as best he could so he absorbed the impact, not Honor. She was little more than a rag doll lying beside him, his arm curled tightly around her.

The world around him was going to hell. Ambush. Some of his men had been shot, some already dying.

"I'm sorry," he whispered to Honor, his voice barely audible. "I'm so sorry, Honor."

The firefight was fierce and unrelenting. His men gave as good as they got, but Hancock couldn't spot Maksimov anywhere. And all he could do was try to keep Honor covered as best he could and somehow maneuver his now-useless arm so he could get a grip on his gun, now slippery with his own blood and the only goddamn means he had of protecting Honor.

From seemingly a mile away, Hancock heard Cope shout, "Mojo!"

Hancock closed his eyes. Goddamn it, *no!* Mojo had obviously taken a hit, and by the frantic note in Cope's voice it was bad.

Grief consumed him when he heard Viper's equally impassioned plea. "Mojo! You stay with us, goddamn it. Don't you dare let go. Do you hear me? Fight, damn it! You fight!"

Copeland scrambled over and dragged Mojo behind thick rock outcroppings that provided natural cover and only one way in or out. Anyone coming in would meet with the end of Cope's rifle and he was in a cold-blooded rage, ready to take out every single one of the bastards.

"Mojo, man, hold on. Speak to me," Cope begged, shaking his teammate.

Blood bubbled and was frothy coming from Mojo's lips, and Cope knew that wasn't good. A hit to the lung.

As Viper pleaded with Mojo to hold on, Mojo whispered, "Good mojo."

Then he smiled, to the shock of his teammates. Mojo *never* smiled. He turned to his teammate with tears streaming down his face. A face carved with emotion they'd never once witnessed. Stoic and reserved. Never had much to say. He was overcome and could barely speak around the tears clogging his throat.

"I always figured I'd go to hell for all I've done in my time on earth. But this *has* to be heaven. It's the most beautiful thing I've ever seen."

There was awe in his voice, and then his words trailed off and his gaze became fixed, but there was such an expression of peace that it choked Cope up, and he laid his head on Mojo's chest as Mojo took his last gasping breath.

His eyes fluttered closed and he suddenly looked so much younger; the lines of age and of the horrors they'd seen and participated in eased, leaving smooth skin of youth in their stead. His lips curved upward almost as if he were holding his arms wide, welcoming death like a long-lost lover.

Hancock felt a kick at his leg and stiffened, his grip on Honor tight, so tight it would leave a bruise. He'd never been more afraid in his life. He was absolutely unable to protect her. There was nothing he could do to prevent her from being taken from him. And God help him, but he'd tear the world apart to find her again.

"Well, maybe I was wrong." A heavily accented Russian voice made him stiffen, his arm imperceptibly tightening around Honor. "Perhaps he didn't form too much of an attachment to the girl and my informants were wrong."

Of course Maksimov would have more than one mole reporting every movement made in Bristow's household. Whom had Hancock overlooked? He'd sniffed the first out quickly, but how had Bristow gained any knowledge of his "attachment" to Honor? Unless . . .

No, he wouldn't even allow for the seed of doubt. His men were solid. They wouldn't betray him. There was someone else in Bristow's operation who'd been feeding Maksimov information, and it was Hancock's own goddamn fault for losing his shit when Bristow had tried to rape Honor a second time and having the asshole killed. That would have tipped off Maksimov in a big way, because he would know of icy Hancock. The one with no emotions, no feelings. As cold as an iceberg and absolutely incapable of human feelings or reactions. Maksimov's informant would have left out no intel that was useful to Maksimov.

"Perhaps the idiot Bristow intended to kill her or use her in such a manner that neither you nor ANE would want her," suggested Ruslan, Bristow's second. "You've received all the intel on him and his men. You know that they take their missions seriously, and you wouldn't have paid Bristow for damaged goods, which means he and his men wouldn't have been paid either. He's a mercenary. I doubt he was interested in anything more than a paycheck."

"Perhaps," Maksimov reluctantly conceded. "He did as I asked and drugged her, and it does appear as though he was set to deliver her to me. Ah well, it never pays to be too careful."

Maksimov sounded perplexed and a little amused at the notion he could be wrong. He toed Hancock's body and then bent to pry Honor away from him. Honor was lifted and Hancock's hand trailed down her body to desperately latch onto her hand, holding for the briefest of moments before it was pulled forcibly from his grasp.

"No, I wasn't wrong at all," Maksimov said smugly. He appeared in Hancock's blurred vision above him. "I wonder what you thought you were doing by hand-delivering the girl to me?" He laughed and then leveled a pistol at Hancock's chest and rapidly fired a shot.

Despite the Kevlar vest Hancock and all his men wore, at such close range and with the fact that Maksimov was using what on the streets were called "cop killers," meaning they could penetrate a bulletproof vest, while he didn't feel like the bullet had penetrated his skin, it damn sure felt like he'd broken some ribs. Or something vital. It was like being hit by a pitchfork from hell. Apropos, since soon he'd be at the gates of hell. The gates would be flung wide and he'd be welcomed like a lost child or an escaped sinner who'd been judged and found guilty several lifetimes ago.

For so long, he'd embraced the notion that he'd lost all semblance of humanity and was the emotionless ice man everyone thought him to be. Because it meant never feeling remorse. It meant never feeling loss so devastating that it threatened to consume him and eat at his soul until there was nothing left. Anything at all was worth not feeling that. He knew that now, because he felt it *all* now. And it was worse than any mortal bullet wound would ever be. The world faded to black around him and a single tear trickled from the corner of his eye over his temple to disappear into his hair.

It was becoming hard to breathe, and the pain in his chest was unbearable, whether because of the bullet or the weight of his despair he wasn't certain. Probably a healthy dose of both.

He'd failed his men. He'd failed his country, though it neither claimed him nor embraced him. He'd failed countless innocent lives. He'd failed himself but most of all, he'd failed the one thing that mattered to *him*. Not the fucking greater good bullshit creed. Because Honor *was* the greater good. She was the very *essence* of the greater good. Of what their creed *should* stand for. What it should have always stood for.

And now an innocent would be doomed to hell, a place where no angel's wings should ever be singed by greedy, licking flames, preventing them from flying into the heavens where Honor belonged.

CHAPTER 32

THE mood was unusually relaxed in the KGI war room. Sam was holding a "staff" meeting, though the others teased that it was just an excuse to get everyone together for Swanny and Donovan to demonstrate their mad cooking and grilling skills.

They hadn't drawn a mission in four weeks. Four peaceful, blissful weeks they'd spent with their families. Their wives, children, the people they cared about. Good times.

Laughter sounded when Garrett dropped an F-bomb and was immediately threatened by at least three of his men, knowing that Sarah was even more strict than ever now that they had a baby girl and she didn't want her child's first word to be *fuck*.

As the laughter died down, a phone rang and a round of groans sounded. Sam cursed vehemently, more than taking up the slack for Garrett in the swearing department. The secure line had to ring *now*? Today of all days? When the weather couldn't be more beautiful. Autumn on Kentucky Lake. The wives all on their way to the central gathering point, Marlene and Frank Kelly's newly constructed and recreated replica of the house the six Kelly brothers had all grown up in. The new heart of the KGI compound. Now all that remained outside the secured facility was the lone hold-out, Joe. Well, and the team members. But of the Kellys, only Joe still lived in Sam's old cabin, calling it the perfect bachelor pad, and if he didn't spend too much time inside the compound then he would escape his mom's and sisters-in-laws'—whom he adored beyond reason—hatching plots for his eventual downfall.

Goddamn it all to hell. Sam had looked forward to spending time with his precious wife. His beautiful Sophie and her mini-me, Charlotte, or Cece as she was lovingly dubbed by her doting aunts, uncles and grandparents. And his baby son. He took the time every single day, no matter where in the world he was, no matter how grim or dire the circumstances, to thank God for the miracle of his family. He still marveled at all that was his, and he knew his brothers and many of the members of his team did as well. Rio, a team leader. Steele, another team leader. Nathan, co-team leader with his twin brother, Joe, who also happened to be the sole surviving unmarried Kelly chick under Mama Kelly's watchful eye.

KGI had undergone many traumatic events over the years. Things that would have crippled and destroyed a lesser family. But the Kellys were tough, resilient, all qualities inherited from and instilled in all their children—blood or not—by Frank and Marlene, the patriarch and matriarch of the ever-expanding Kelly clan. The very heartbeat of the entire family.

Marlene's reach extended not only to her birth children but far beyond. She had a penchant for adopting strays, as her sons teased her, a term she took offense at. But she'd taken many under her wing. The now sheriff of Stewart County, Sean Cameron. Rusty Kelly, whom his parents had adopted even though she hadn't been a minor when the adoption had occurred. But it had meant more to her than anything else in her young, troubled life, and Sam knew without a doubt that his mother had saved Rusty's life.

Swanny, who'd come back as wounded and suffering as

Nathan had after months of captivity when a mission went FUBAR. All the KGI team members, including the leaders, and they didn't even bother trying to deny it. They could protest and pretend to be exasperated, but they loved Ma's mothering just as her own sons did.

And Maren Steele, Steele's wife and mother of their daughter. She, too, was one of Marlene's adoptees.

He found himself angry as he stalked toward the secure sat phone for disturbing what should have been a perfect day. A day to remember their blessings and revel in them. Simply enjoy living and loving and being the family unit they were. Or maybe he was just getting too fucking maudlin in his old age. Finding the love of your life and then watching her grow heavy with your children had a man rethinking every priority he thought ever held importance.

"Sam Kelly," he snapped. "And this better be goddamn important."

"Kelly," the brisk acknowledgment came, and there was a brief tingle of recognition that flickered through Sam's mind, but he couldn't place the voice to save his life.

"You have me at a disadvantage," Sam said, an edge to his voice. "Who are you and how did you get this number?"

The voice sounded dim. Haggard. Like he'd been to hell and back and was only barely living to tell the tale. "I doubt you'd remember my name, but you'd know my team leader. I'm Conrad. I work for . . . Hancock."

"Fuck!"

The entire room came to attention. Silence was immediate as every single member of KGI crowded in close, watching Sam's every movement, his body language, and straining to hear what was being said on the other side.

"And why are you calling me—us—since I assume you aren't calling to have a personal chat with me," Sam said bluntly.

"Look, I don't have much time. *He* doesn't have much time. Most importantly, *she* doesn't have *any* time," he said in a voice that turned savage in a split second. "I'm not interested in dick sizing or having a pissing match. I—we— need your help. As much as you can give. And I need you to move out now. I wouldn't ask this if it weren't a matter of life and death, and not just Hancock's life, which may or may not even be an issue, or even the man we've already lost. But there is an innocent woman even now in the hands of Maksimov, a man we've been close to shutting down on two previous occasions, but we forfeited our mission to save two of your women and one of your children."

Rio stiffened and extended his hand for the phone. It wasn't a request. Sam handed it over without question, but he pushed the speakerphone button so they'd all be in the loop. Rio used to lead Titan. He knew this man, and Sam trusted Rio and his instincts. Rio wouldn't guide them wrong.

"This is Rio," he said.

"Rio, it's Conrad."

Relief was evident in Conrad's voice.

"I don't have a lot of time to explain," Conrad continued. "But it's bad, Rio. Real bad. We had Maksimov in our sights. Again. We had something he wanted very desperately, and all we had to do was hand her over and we were in."

"She?" P.J. and Skylar echoed at the same time, scowls darkening their faces. "Is that how you win your battles at Titan?"

"She was never supposed to be within a mile of Maksimov," Conrad said, impatience simmering in his voice. "Look, do you have your doctor on hand? If she can't tell me how to help or fix Hancock, he's going to die. And goddamn it, we need your . . . help."

Any other time, such a statement would begin an endless chain of torment, sly innuendo, smugness and arrogance that would end in bloodshed on both sides. All in good fun, of course. Except that there was very real animosity between the two groups. But they also owed Hancock, and Sam paid all his debts. Every last one. And they owed Hancock big.

"Maksimov has her now," Conrad said painfully. As though he gave a damn. Like he had a heart.

The others stared at one another in astonishment. The members of Titan were not known for their humanlike qualities. It was questionable as to whether they were even human at all except that Rio had once led the team, and he was evidence that there were at least some vestiges of what made up a human being.

"Stay on the phone, Conrad," Sam said in a crisp, take-charge tone. "Brief us on what we need to know while I send for Maren. Then I'll put her on the phone with you so she can assess the damage based on your findings and guide you through what has to be done."

"I'll make the call," Steele said. "She's two minutes away at regular speed. She'll be here in less than one. I guarantee it."

And so Conrad gave them an abbreviated, terse, to-the-point sterile recitation of their mission, their integration into Bristow's organization and how Honor became collateral damage but at the same time provided them their best opportunity they'd had in all the long years they'd spent hunting Maksimov.

KGI was well aware of who and what Maksimov was and that most governments feared him and stayed well out of his way. They also knew of Hancock's previous run-in with him when Maksimov had nearly beaten Hancock to death for getting Maren out danger and back to KGI—and Steele.

"He couldn't do it," Conrad said quietly. "He stayed the course until the day before we were set to deliver her to Maksimov and he refused to do it. His exact words were *fuck the greater good*. That Honor *was* the greater good and he was goddamn tired of fighting the good fight for a country that neither claims us nor welcomes us, for protecting the very people who have tried to assassinate us. And for what? What does it get any of us? We have no home, no homeland. No one who claims us. We don't even exist. We're fucking ghosts expected to clean up messes no one else will and take out the garbage that preys on the innocent. Well, fuck that. Honor Cambridge took a goddamn bullet for me. *Me*. A man who betrayed her by making her believe I was her salvation. That I rescued her from a terrorist organization that I planned to turn her right back over to. She has more fire, courage, heart and loyalty in her little finger than most of the men I've ever served with. So yeah, fuck the greater good and fuck Maksimov. We need your help, because over my dead body and over the dead body of our fallen brother and above all for Hancock—who's sacrificed far more than any of us will ever know, if he lives through this—will I not see Honor safe and returned to her family. And I'm not too proud to beg if that's what it takes, because I owe Honor Cambridge more than I can ever repay her and I'll be damned if her repayment is rape, torture and pain from Maksimov only to then be turned back over to ANE to be endlessly brutalized and kept alive for as long as possible so she suffers so badly that she begs, she pleads, she *prays* for death because only then will she be truly free."

"I'm with him," Skylar muttered. "Fuck the goddamn greater good. Especially when it means an innocent woman, whose only crimes were giving aid to people nobody else in the world gives a fuck about and being in the wrong place at the wrong time, is punished."

Donovan scowled, his legendary regard for women and children coming roaring to the forefront. He looked ready to take on an entire fucking army and take apart anyone who would so abuse a helpless woman.

"Just how the hell do we know that if we help you recover Honor Cambridge, we aren't just finishing the job you started—and evidently failed to complete? I—KGI—won't be used to send an innocent woman, *any* woman, to a fate worse than death and we all know that Maksimov, ANE, take your pick, would be a nightmare of unimaginable agony and degradation."

"Fucking Bristow tried to rape her before passing along the used goods to Maksimov," Conrad said in a brittle tone that in no way belied the fury laced in every word. "To save herself—or hell, maybe she really did want out—she slit one wrist and then the other and then she faced that motherfucker down holding the knife to her throat after he'd savaged her and told him if she died, then so would he, because Maksimov would kill him for not following through with his promise to deliver her to him."

"Holy fuck," P.J. breathed, her eyes darkening, shadowed by the past, likely not even realizing she trembled against Cole, whom she leaned into, again, likely without being cognizant of it. She was not a woman who ever showed vulnerability in front of others. Especially her team.

"Did you kill him?" Garrett asked calmly.

"Fuck yeah, I did, and I made damn sure it wasn't quick and it sure as hell wasn't merciful. Hancock would have done it himself. He wanted to take him apart with his bare hands, but he was the only one who had a prayer of talking Honor down, and he did. But if you could have seen him in that moment, if you could have seen him when he gave the order that the mission had changed, you would not question his—our—motives in the least bit. She means something to all of us, Kelly," he said, using the common address for them all. "She's ours and we are not giving her up to that sadistic piece of shit. All we wanted was to give the appearance that we were making the exchange and we were going to take him out. Fuck making it clean and tidy, building evidence, dismantling his empire and allowing countries to fight over who got what of his seized assets. We wanted his goddamn ass dead and that was all that mattered to us.

"He had more than one mole in Bristow's organization. We knew of one. We killed Bristow because we no longer needed him and even if we had, after what he did, he was a dead man walking. But Maksimov still wasn't quite sure and so he showed himself when they ambushed us. Hancock betrayed his emotions for Honor when he tried to keep Maksimov from taking her from his grasp. A sniper had already put a through-and-through in his left shoulder. This time Maksimov shot him in the chest with a cop killer at close range, and he's not doing good. Not good at all. I've already lost a damn good man and goddamn it, I won't lose Hancock. And I sure as fuck am not losing Honor Cambridge to that twisted asshole who thinks he's a god."

Maren burst in, her glasses askew, her hair in disarray as if she'd run the entire way. Steele immediately took Olivia from her arms and gently guided her toward the phone.

"Conrad, Maren Steele, our team doctor, is here and you'll give her the rundown so she can see if there's any hope for him."

"I'm more interested in knowing if there's hope for any of us. Especially Honor," Conrad ground out.

"Cool your jets. We've got to think about this for more than three seconds. Talk to Maren. Let her help you help Hancock."

At Hancock's name, Maren's head jerked up, her eyes widening in concern. Steele's hand slipped comfortingly around his wife's nape, his expression grim.

"They need you honey. Hancock needs you." He sighed, knowing despite his misgivings over the man, he owed his wife's and daughter's lives to him, just as Rio did. "It doesn't look good," he added quietly. "You need to talk quick and help his man any way you can while we prepare to roll out."

Maren briskly took the sat phone but turned off the speakerphone, much to Sam's chagrin. She frowned at him and shook her head. "I need to think, damn it, Sam."

She pushed away from the others, talking in urgent, hushed tones, her questions calm and efficient, not allowing Conrad to panic.

"What the fuck, Sam?" Garrett asked in a low voice. "This is some deep shit. This goes deeper than even we're up for."

"What else can we do?" Rio asked simply, his dark eyes flashing. "I get that Hancock is a wild card. But he's got a code. It may be fucked up to you and me, but he is an honorable man. Before you laugh me out of the war room, just remember that he could have taken Grace at any time. I carried her halfway out of the mountains attached to my back, and she walked the rest of the way in unspeakable agony until she wanted to die from it. Me and my men were in no way prepared to ward off a full-scale attack from Titan. Instead? Hancock gave me a pass. Said it was my only one, but it was bullshit. Saving face. Looking like he owed me because I saved his life. It was what we did as a team. No one kept score. That was bullshit. We did what we had to do and we offered no apologies or thank-yous. And then he warned me. He gave me everything I needed to know about who and what was after Grace. All he didn't give me was why, and you want to take a guess why that was?"

"No, but I'm sure you'll tell us," Donovan said in a weary voice.

"Because he knew Grace was too goddamn weak to heal a kitten. That she'd likely die if he brought her to Farnsworth right then and forced her to attempt to heal his daughter. So he bided his time, waiting, knowing damn well she was in good hands with me. And when he knew she was well enough to have a chance to save Elizabeth, then he took her. He never hurt her. Never laid a hand on her. But she was also fucking fierce and he admired that about her."

"Is this going somewhere, because the clock is ticking," Garrett snarled.

"Yeah, it is," Rio snapped back.

"Let him speak because I have a hell of a lot to say too," Steele said in a frigid tone.

"Only when he was certain Grace had a good chance of surviving Elizabeth's healing did he take her in. He could have taken out Farnsworth at any time. Why wait? Why would a mere child matter to him?"

Joe cleared his throat. "It wouldn't appear an innocent woman means much to him."

"He wanted to save Elizabeth," Rio said quietly. "And he wanted to save Grace. I didn't figure it out until the whole thing with Maren went down, and I only told Steele. But you all know. I've told you. Titan was the real deal. Failure was tantamount to dishonorable death. And yet he gave up his chance to nail Maksimov for good because he feared for Maren to stay another night as Caldwell's prisoner. She was pregnant, scared out of her mind, and so he called me and he pulled her out."

"I think this is where I take over," Steele said pointedly, glancing at his wife, his eyes briefly haunted as if he were reliving the experience all over again.

"He showed up at my home beaten to hell and back. Never seen a man so badly beaten, and it was because he let Maren go and could no longer control Caldwell. Maksimov was sending him a message. *Don't fuck with me. Ever.* And then he took a bullet for my wife, my child," Steele seethed. "And when the chopper went down, he covered her body with his own, and I still don't know how the hell he survived."

"That's because the fucker has nine lives," Garrett said darkly. "Okay, I get it. We have to go in, but we don't go in not knowing what the fuck we're up against. This is bigger than anything we've ever taken on. Maksimov's reach extends around the globe. I don't trust anyone who isn't in this room, and that's fact."

Maren's voice rose in agitation. "Of course I wouldn't expect you to have a chest tube in a field kit. You're not a surgeon. You'll just have to find something you can sterilize and use as a chest tube. Isn't that what you're trained to do? Adapt and overcome?"

Her response was greeted by a raucous round of *hooyah*s, *oorah*s and "Oh hell yeah, that's our girl."

Steele scowled but looked absurdly proud of his petite wife with so much ferocity in such a tiny body. "My woman. Not anyone else's."

"I don't think it's as bad as you think it is," Maren said soothingly to the man on the phone.

"He can't fucking breathe and he's bleeding like a stuck pig!" Conrad bellowed loudly enough for the rest of the room to hear. "How can it not be as bad as I think it is?"

Steele wrested the phone from Maren's grip despite her heated protest and a glare that promised retribution.

"You will watch the way you speak to my wife, and you will treat her with the utmost respect she deserves. She's damn well earned it," Steele said in a dangerously soft voice. "If she says it's not as bad as you think, then it's not. So shut the fuck up and start doing what she tells you or you're going to have yourself an even more fucked-up mission."

Maren rolled her eyes and yanked the phone back down, explaining the need for a chest tube to drain the blood and air that prevented his lung from reinflating. While the bullet didn't penetrate Hancock's chest, only the vest, the impact was great enough to break ribs and damage his lung. The bullet to his shoulder was a clean through and through and all that was needed was to ensure there was no further loss of blood and get an IV started immediately to replenish the lowered blood volume. And she instructed Conrad to start him on antibiotics, since the risk of infection was great given the conditions.

"Are we really all just going to risk our lives for Hancock?" Dolphin asked, as if he couldn't quite grasp how such an ordinary afternoon had become something out of some bizarre government conspiracy theory.

Dolphin had more reason than most to dislike the man. He'd been shot by a sniper, though he knew it wasn't intended to be a kill shot, nor had it been, when Hancock had made his move and taken Grace from KGI. Dolphin had a long memory and he tended to especially remember things that took him out of action for prolonged periods of time.

At Dolphin's question, Maren's frown deepened and she lowered the phone, pressing it to her thigh so she wouldn't be overheard.

"Somehow I think Eden would have a different opinion," she said softly. "As do I. He saved me. *Three* times. He took care of me. You, *none* of you, spent all those months with him that I did," she said, not sparing a single person in the room her piercing gaze. "He was . . . *kind.* Caring even. Even when he was scary as hell, he was also very gentle with me, and he told me he wouldn't allow any harm to come to me or my child. He could have died because he saved me. He nearly *did.*"

"I owe him much," Steele said gruffly. "I owe him *everything.*"

It was obvious just how much he hated expressing his vulnerability and revealing the shadows that still occasionally haunted his eyes when he recalled just how close he'd come to losing Maren and Olivia.

"So do I," Rio affirmed. "What he did more than compensated for me saving his life. Saving a teammate's life isn't some goddamn favor. It's not recorded on a scorecard. It's your fucking *job* and if you get your teammate killed, you get one ginormous F on your report card."

"We all owe him." Swanny spoke up in a quiet tone. He swept his gaze over the room. "He's Eden's family. Which now makes him my family. And if all of you were speaking the truth about the fact that *we* are all family, then that makes Hancock your family as well. Eden will never forgive you and neither will I if you leave him to die. That isn't who we are. It never has been and I pray to God it will never will be."

"When you finally speak you take no prisoners," Sam said in a sour voice.

"Fuck!" Garrett exploded, knowing they'd been had. "Fuck, fuck, fuck, fuck, *FUCK!* And furthermore I don't give a flying *fuck* who tattles to Sarah. If this doesn't call for a hundred F-bombs, then what does?" He made a show of pulling the hair on the sides of his head. "Goddamn fucking Hancock. Swear to God, if even one of us gets killed saving his sorry ass, I'll undo all Maren's handiwork and kill the bastard myself."

Donovan held up his hand. "No one ever implied we would turn a blind eye on this matter. The decision will be who goes and who stays. Not whether we act or not. That's a given. What I won't do for anyone or any mission is make taking part in the mission mandatory. No one is going to be sent into a situation with sketchy intel with no idea just what we're up against."

Maren had resumed giving instructions to the man tending Hancock in a quiet voice, but she kept a wary eye on the proceedings around her, as if not trusting them not to take her along. As if she were staying behind under lock and key when Hancock had saved her life three times. She owed her entire world to him and it was a debt she could never hope to repay in a thousand years.

"This mission will be volunteer only," Donovan said quietly. "I'm going."

"I'm in," Rio says. The rest of his men quickly followed suit. Terrence went back far enough with Rio that he had been part of Titan when Rio had trained a new recruit called Hancock, though not many people were privy to that information. Rio doubted even Sam knew it. With everyone ever associated with Titan marked for death, it would be a death sentence to the members and families of KGI.

Rio wasn't stupid, though. He had an insurance policy of sorts. A get-out-of-jail-free card. He had enough damning information on high-ranking government officials, domestic and abroad, and he'd made it very clear that if he were to ever die under any circumstances, the information would be made public and entire countries would crumble. This card he held could come in very handy in just this sort of situation and could very well save Hancock's ass, provided he kept his nose clean in the future.

"I'm in," Steele said. "My team makes their own decisions." He no longer looked to P.J. when missions involving such horrific circumstances came down the pipeline. He respected that she knew herself well enough to know what she could handle and what she couldn't after her ordeal at the hands of three rapists.

And it was equally clear she was grateful to her team leader for not singling her out and drawing attention to her past.

"I'm in," she said firmly. "I will never allow another woman to endure what I had to endure if I can stop it."

Her team—and the others—looked at her in surprise. Pride shone in her husband's eyes. Cole. For so long, she never spoke of it. It was an unspoken rule. It was there. Always there. But never acknowledged aloud. Until now. Cole squeezed her hand and whispered softly in her ear so only she could hear.

"I'm so damn proud of you, P.J. I thank God every day that you chose me. That you love me. And that I'm married to the strongest damn woman I've ever known."

Faint color dusted her cheeks, but over time she'd grown accustomed to him displaying his love and affection and admiration for her in front of others, though it had taken a lot of adjustment on her part.

"No one should ever have to suffer such degradation and humiliation. No one should ever feel so ashamed that they literally want to end their ceaseless suffering by taking their life. And yet she apologized for almost fucking up the mission," P.J. said, terrible rage blazing in her eyes. "She apologized for being *weak*, for fuck's sake, and not being able to save all those people because for that one moment she only wanted to die so the pain would finally end. No wonder Hancock can't and won't hand her over to Maksimov. Swear to God if he did, there wouldn't be a safe place on this earth for him because I'd hunt him down and I'd repay in kind every hurt done to her."

"Singing to the choir, sistah," Skylar said, anger dulling her usually sparkling and infectious smile and gaze.

Nathan and Joe exchanged glances, then looked to their team, where Swanny stood tall and rigid. Before the twins could say anything, Swanny stepped forward, defying the precedent set by Rio and Steele's team of waiting for their team leader's decision before falling in behind him.

"I'm in," Swanny said in a determined voice.

"So are we," P.J. said, as she and Cole stepped forward, P.J.'s hand clasped tightly in Cole's. There were flickers of surprise at P.J.'s lack of hesitation. It wasn't a secret that she'd love to get Hancock between the crosshairs of her scope for one of her team members being shot by Hancock's team when the mission to save Grace went all to hell. She'd sworn to kick his ass if she ever met up with him in a dark alley somewhere.

Zane and Skylar stepped up on either side of Swanny, not even voicing what their action implied. There was no need. Their actions did all the talking for them.

"I think we have mutiny on our hands," Joe said with a wry smile.

Nathan shook his head. "Like our team is going any-where without us?"

All attention turned to Sam and Garrett, the only two who hadn't spoken up.

"Fine. I'm in," Garrett said, throwing up his hands amid more muttered F-bombs.

Sam sighed. "Do you all honestly think I'm letting you infants go off on your own? Fuck that. I'm in. If only to save your goddamn asses."

A round of flipping the bird erupted, breaking the strain so evident in the room. Then Sam issued the order for them to load and go. Hancock didn't have much time, judging by the grim lines marring Maren's delicate, feminine features.

"And just so you know, I'm in," Maren said in a voice that rivaled her husband's demanding tone. "Olivia can stay with Marlene."

You could have broken a stone on Steele's face as he grappled with the knowledge that he'd be putting his wife—his entire life—in harm's way. But he also knew that Maren was Hancock's only chance at survival. With a resigned sigh that said he didn't like it one bit, he gave a clipped nod and was rewarded with a loving smile that melted the big man to his toes.

Sam gave the motion to move out. He planned to call Resnick when they got in the air and ferret out as much information as possible. Resnick would cream himself if he thought he had a shot at taking down Maksimov *and* ANE. Sam wasn't above calling on the two black ops teams at Resnick's disposal either, because they were going to need all the manpower they could muster if they had any chance of recovering Honor. Whether she still lived was a huge question mark, but if she was already dead, Hancock wasn't going to be any more alive than she was, if Conrad could be believed.

Maren still had an open line to Conrad, patiently instructing him as his frustration mounted at the helpless fury he felt over being unable to do more to stabilize Hancock. But Maren assured him that once the chest tube was properly inserted, Hancock's breathing would become easier and less labored; he would be stable for the few hours the flight would take them, and then she could fully assess the damage. And then sorrow filled her heart, tears threatening, which she immediately hid from Steele because he *panicked* if she cried.

And then, because he *had* seen them, she hastened to give the reason—sympathy—that had prompted her horror that this could have been Steele not returning from a mission. Or any of the other KGI members.

"I'm sorry about the loss of your teammate," she said to Conrad, her sorrow genuine. "I will do everything in my power to save Hancock."

"Thank you," he said gruffly.

"Honey," Steele said, sliding his big hand gently over her leg and squeezing. "It won't be one of us. I need you to believe that."

She looked up at him and then at them all, tears glistening on her eyelashes. "But it could be," she whispered.
"There's always the chance that I'll get a phone call like this
one and it will be about one of you, and I love you all dearly.
I can't lose any of you, even as I know this is what you have
to do. What we have to do. Just promise me you'll be careful.
And promise me you'll get that poor woman out of the hell
she's enduring. Hancock protected me from that, but he can't
protect her now."

CHAPTER 33

HONOR came sluggishly to awareness, confusion and alarm vying for equal control of her state of mind. Her head ached vilely and she tried to lift a hand to massage her temple but found herself unable to.

As her vision cleared, horrific pain—a keen sense of betrayal—sliced her into tiny ribbons until there was simply nothing left of her. Just a vague nebulous being that hovered somewhere between life and death in the spirit world. Purgatory.

Hancock had promised her he wouldn't give her to Maksimov. Hancock had drugged her. Hancock had handed her over to Maksimov in a simple business transaction. Hancock was nowhere near this place, wherever it was.

She wondered just how gullible she'd been. All that crap about being sacrificed for the greater good. That because of her sacrifice, Maksimov—and ANE—would be taken down, no longer a threat to hundreds of thousands of innocent lives. It seemed to her that this was merely a mercenary exchange. For money. Hancock had never denied being a mercenary.

But why be so . . . cruel? So inhuman? Why even pretend kindness and caring when he possessed neither? It wasn't as though she could have escaped him anyway. So why all the bullshit? Why even make the effort to comfort her at all? She would have preferred brutality, rape even, over what she thought to be something beautiful and . . . genuine.

Maybe it was how he dealt with his conscience, but then he didn't have one. He didn't have a heart or a soul. So why? The question reverberated in her mind until she wanted to scream her frustration. Why be kind to her? Why pretend tenderness? Why pretend that she mattered? And for God's sake, why give her false hope?

That was the cruelest of all. To give her even a moment's hope that what she'd accepted as her fate wasn't to be after all.

She looked wildly around her, trying to discern her surroundings, anything to get her mind from its soundless screams of grief and agony. But what she found only added to her terror and sorrow.

She was in a . . . cage. Wrists and ankles manacled like an *animal*. The space was so small that she was forced into an uncomfortable position, her body contorted like some magician's feat.

So stupid. So foolish. So naïve.

How Hancock must have laughed at her innocence. How he must have delighted in knowing he'd one-up Maksimov and even Bristow by being the one to have her first. The innocent little virgin. The supposed gift he was so humbled to have received. Sorrow vied with regret. So much regret that there was no room for fear over her fate. She was resigned to it after enjoying a brief respite. A short window of time where she'd allowed hope to bloom. She'd been so very foolish to foster the forbidden. She knew better and yet she'd allowed hope to grow, unchecked within her heart, encompassing her very soul.

Her breath stuttered erratically over her lips as she glanced around her prison. She was in a tiny cage suspended from the ceiling, so even if she did somehow manage to wrest free of the manacles digging into her skin and get the cage open, she was at least a dozen feet above the floor. Not that she'd ever be able to free herself anyway. The restraints had torn her skin, and her hands and feet tingled from the decreased blood circulation forced by the tightness of her bonds.

The height was dizzying, but her fear of enclosed spaces was even more crippling. Having spent an entire night trapped under the rubble of the clinic that lay around her in ruins had given her an intense phobia of tight, enclosed and airless places, even though the cage was well ventilated.

Sudden unexpected pain screamed through her body—but no, the high-pitched shriek came from her, the sound of someone in unspeakable agony. Her skin was on *fire*. She could feel the horrible licks of the flames consuming her. Was she being burned alive? A vague recollection of something like a cattle prod, an instrument that when touching her skin delivered a shrieking electric shock that set her nerve endings on fire, drifted through her shattered memories. For a moment it was as if she simply short-circuited because she had no idea what had just happened. Only that it hadn't been the first time it had been done to her.

Then she saw him. The man who must be Maksimov. He held a long rod that he'd pressed to her skin, delivering a devastating electric shock that still had her nerves jumping and quivering. She was in no way in control of her body, her muscles giving involuntary jerks and spasms.

She huddled there, weeping, not just from the shock delivered to her body, but from the ultimate betrayal Hancock had handed her. It was her fault for offering him her forgiveness. For giving him her trust when he'd *proven* he wasn't deserving of it.

But it didn't make the agony any less. He had done what nothing or no one else had been able to do.

Hancock had broken her.

Not the clinic bombing. Not ANE. Not Bristow's two attempts to rape her. Not even this asshole standing by her cage, a predatory gleam in his eyes. He enjoyed pain—inflicting pain. He thrived on it. If she could see any lower than his face, she was sure he'd be aroused, just as Bristow had been when he'd hurt her.

But neither of those men, Bristow or Maksimov, had broken her or would break her.

Hancock had broken her, and she no longer cared whether she lived or died. She no longer cared what was done to her because nothing could equal what had *already* been done by Hancock's hand.

"I think I may keep you for a while before I let A New Era know of my precious find," he mused, studying her as he circled the cage. "You're surprisingly strong. For a woman," he added with a sneer that conveyed all the disdain he obviously felt for the "weaker" sex. "I think you will provide me many days of entertainment. You'll be a challenge and I do so enjoy a good challenge. But I'll break you. You'll learn what is expected of you."

"You can't break me," Honor said softly, speaking for the first time.

Her tone was absent, disinterested almost, as if she were thinking of something else and he was a mere distraction. He wouldn't like not being able to command absolute focus and attention. He was a man well used to deference from everyone. Well, too fucking bad because he wasn't getting it from her.

He looked faintly puzzled, as if he sensed something other than defiance, which such a statement would normally be construed as.

"And why is that?" he asked in a mild tone that told her she hadn't pissed him off. Yet. No, he was genuinely curious.

She found his stare and knew hers to be vacant. Hollow. Lifeless. Already gone. His eyes narrowed as if he too saw what she knew to be there. And for some reason unknown to her, she got the impression that it bothered him. Which was laughable given he thrived on making others suffer so much that they became as lifeless and as hopeless as she already was, and he'd only just begun. Perhaps he was merely angry because he wasn't the reason that she was already far gone from this world—and reality.

"Because you can't break what's already broken," she whispered through numb lips.

He pondered her words for a moment and maybe she imagined it, but she could swear something in his gaze shifted and softened. Maybe she was just finally losing the final pieces of sanity that had seen her through this far because they were no longer needed. She needed no shield. No protection.

If only . . .

She didn't even bother feeling shame or regret for not having succeeded in taking her own life. If she'd had any inkling of Hancock's coming betrayal, she would have sliced through her carotid artery in a heartbeat to deprive them all. Hancock, Maksimov and ANE.

He flipped a switch that caused the cage to lower closer to the floor, and then he reached through one of the bars, his fingers lightly caressing the bandages of her wrists, studying them.

"I don't suppose you can," he murmured. "But I guess we'll see then, won't we? But, woman, do not think to defy me. You will instantly regret it."

She gave a faint ghost of a smile, one that matched the hollowness of her eyes, and as much of a shrug as she was able in the confines of her tiny prison. "I have no reason to defy you. My fate has been sealed. I know what my destiny is to be. I have no *reason* to live, so why make my eventual death worse by fighting the inevitable?"

He frowned again, as though he had no idea of what to make of her. As though he'd never come across someone like her. And judging by the expression on his face, he didn't much like puzzles he couldn't solve.

Any idiot could figure her out. It didn't take a rocket scientist to know when a person had already been driven past their limits. That she was already a hollow shell of a human being. Nothing could touch her no matter what was inflicted on her from now until whenever monsters tired of their sick, torturous games and finally gave her eternal rest and . . . peace.

She closed her eyes, imagining resting with the angels. She could almost feel the soft brush of their wings and the comfort of their protective embrace.

"Soon," she whispered to herself. "Soon."

CHAPTER 34

AS soon as KGI boarded the jets, Sam pulled out his secure phone and punched in the series of numbers that would get him to Resnick no matter what time of day or circumstances. Resnick answered on the second ring, his voice wary and alert.

"Sam," he said by way of greeting.

"Adam," Sam returned dryly.

"Now that pleasantries have been exchanged, to what do I owe this unexpected honor?"

His voice was laced with heavy sarcasm, which Sam ignored. Needling Resnick, just like needling Hancock, was taking enjoyment where he could, but this was business and there was no room or time for fucking around.

"I'm not calling in a favor," Sam said.

"Thank fuck for that," Resnick muttered. "I've learned your favors have a pattern of me nearly getting killed."

"You're still alive," Sam pointed out. "Look, what if I told you that we're about to take Maksimov down for good and there's a good possibility that we'll take A New Era down with him."

There was a strangled choke as if he'd just inhaled a drag from his cigarette and it poured out of his mouth and nostrils in an excited rush. "You're shitting me. No fucking way. You're out of your goddamn mind."

Then his voice became suspicious. "We've been after Maksimov for years. Hell, everyone has been after that bastard for years, and *no* one has ever gotten close enough to him to bring him down without dying."

"You're acquainted with Titan," Sam said mildly, knowing the reminder would only piss Resnick off. "Hancock in particular. And Hancock has been hunting him for a very long time. He's gotten close on two occasions only to let him go to avoid getting an innocent killed."

Resnick snorted. "Hancock would sell out his own mother to achieve his mission."

"And that's where you're wrong," Sam said, his voice deadly soft, suggesting insultingly that Resnick didn't know fuck-all about Hancock. "Maksimov fucked up big this time. He has something very valuable to Hancock, and trust me when I say Maksimov is a dead man."

"Tell me how Maksimov gets us ANE." Excitement edged Resnick's voice and Sam could hear the inhales and sharp exhales of repeated cigarette drags.

"Can't promise anything, but what Maksimov has that Hancock wants is also what ANE wants and will pay a lot of money to get. The plan was to stage the exchange, take out Maksimov and then set up a similar exchange with ANE."

"A FUBAR then," Resnick accurately guessed.

"Exactly.

"What is it that Maksimov has that both Hancock and ANE want so desperately?" Resnick asked.

"A woman," Sam said quietly.

Resnick groaned. "Fuck me. A woman? You Kellys and goddamn women. Swear to God." And then as if what Sam had truly said sank in, shock registered. "Hancock has lost his shit over a *woman*?"

There was a long pause as Resnick took his time to sort through all the *what the fucks* Sam knew were circling his mind.

"Okay, so as shocking as it is that Hancock would lose his shit over a woman, what the fuck could ANE possibly want with this same woman?"

"Honor Cambridge ring a bell?" Sam asked.

"Of course. She was killed in an attack ANE took credit for. It was a relief center. Mostly Western volunteers and doctors and nurses."

"She survived."

"The hell she did," Resnick sputtered. "There were no survivors."

"She lived," Sam said quietly. "Not only did she live, but she evaded capture for over a week. She made ANE look like weak fools. They lost a lot of face and she became a beacon of hope to an oppressed people. ANE wants her and they want her bad. ANE fucked Maksimov over in a deal. Not ever a good idea. Bristow, the man Hancock was working for undercover as a way to Maksimov, learned of Honor's survival and sent Hancock to get to her before ANE did. Bristow wanted favor in Maksimov's organization. So he was going to give Honor to Maksimov, and then Maksimov was going to give Honor back to ANE for a hell of a lot more money than they originally fucked him out of."

"Okay," Resnick said thoughtfully. "That all makes sense. Right up to the part about Hancock losing his shit because Maksimov has the woman Hancock planned to hand over to him from the very start."

"Look, you know everything I do at this point except that Conrad, Hancock's second, said the night before the exchange was to take place, Hancock called the whole thing off. Came up with the idea of staging the exchange but ambushing Maksimov and executing him on the spot. He didn't give a fuck about Maksimov's connections, what he could lead Interpol, the CIA and God only knows who else to. All he wanted was Maksimov taken out and for Maksimov to never get his hands on Honor."

"Obviously things didn't go as planned or you wouldn't be calling me," Resnick said grimly.

"Hancock lost one of his men. Several are injured. Hancock is touch and go. I don't even know if he's alive at this point. But his second called and asked for our help. They want Honor out of Maksimov's hands, and they don't care how it's done. He's a sadistic son of a bitch and every hour she's with him will be hell."

"I'll send Kyle Phillips's team and two others. You're going to need all the manpower you can get. I assume you have every available man on your end."

Sam didn't dignify that with a response.

"I'll send you the coordinates and I need your men wheels up in half an hour tops. And Adam?"

"Yeah?"

"Two things. We're operating blind here, so I need every single piece of intel you have on Maksimov. I don't give a fuck how classified it is. I need it and I need it yesterday if we're going to save her and take the Russian down."

"Done. The other?"

"Honor Cambridge did die in that attack. You can *not* leak that she lived. Not yet. If we manage to get to her in time to save her life and get her back home to her family, then it can quietly be revealed that she was rescued by a joint special forces operation."

Resnick snorted. "As if that kind of information will ever be low key or quiet. It will be a media circus."

CHAPTER 35

THE rural, rundown cabin in Bumfuck, West Virginia, where Titan had taken refuge smelled of blood and death. Resnick had complained that no wonder no one had been able to find Maksimov when he was meeting people in such a back-woods place.

Rio led the way inside, because he was known to Titan. Although that hadn't saved him from an overeager trigger finger one of the last times Titan and Rio had butted heads.

Conrad met Rio at the door, pain in his eyes. "Mojo," he choked out.

Rio closed his eyes a moment. He'd liked Mojo. Quiet but tormented like so many others in the ranks of Titan. But Mojo was loyal to his bones, and his death hit Rio harder than he would have imagined after so long.

He'd given that life up. A life forever in the shadows, always skating the thin edge between right and wrong. Sometimes, wrong was right. And sometimes right sucked. But now, seeing the men who used to follow him as they now followed Hancock brought back many of the things he'd tried to forget.

"I'm sorry," Rio said, allowing the sorrow he felt to creep into his voice. "He was a good man." He glanced toward the floor, where Conrad had been working on his team leader. "Hancock?"

Conrad walked back to where Maren was already looking Hancock over. Conrad had given him pain medication but not enough to suppress his respirations too much because there was no way to know the extent of the damage to his lungs. A CNS depressant could be lethal to weakened lungs and too-shallow respirations.

Maren bent over Hancock, and he turned dull eyes on her that briefly lit with recognition. And relief.

"Maren. Thank God. Need you." He licked dry lips. "They have her. Didn't save her like I did you. Have to," he said painfully.

"Hancock," she said with mock severity, her hand on her hip. "What have I told you about playing with guns?"

Steele had silently glided to his wife's side the moment she'd moved toward Hancock, and he saw Hancock smile. The bastard actually smiled, but just as quickly it was gone and his eyes flashed with so much pain and grief that it took Steele's breath away. And it took a hell of a lot to elicit that kind of reaction from Steele. Maren had seen it too because moisture rimmed her tenderhearted eyes. While the rest of KGI had an . . . interesting . . . love/hate relationship with Hancock, Maren liked him and made no bones about the fact. He had her loyalty, and well, she was a hella fierce woman when she gave her loyalty.

"How bad is it?" Hancock asked bluntly through a tightly clenched jaw. He had to be in a lot of pain. Perspiration glistened on his forehead and he was pale, with deep grooves etched into his face. He suddenly looked a hell of a lot older, when before he had had a timeless look about him. It was part of his chameleon ability to blend, to look anywhere from midtwenties to midforties or anywhere in between. Right now he looked exhausted and sick to his soul.

"I need to be on my feet. I don't have much time." Sorrow flooded his gaze and to Steele's continuing shock, a shimmer of tears glistened in the hardened man's eyes. "I may already be too late," he said hoarsely.

"You'll live," Maren said lightly. "Conrad did an excellent job with the tools he had. He's to be commended. He saved your life."

"I only did my goddamn job," Conrad snapped, pissed that saving his team leader would be heralded. As though he would have made any other choice.

Steele's head whipped in Conrad's direction, his eyes as cold and as flat as Hancock's typically were. "Watch how you speak to my wife," he hissed.

Conrad's eyes were bleak. "I meant no disrespect, Dr. Steele. But he's my leader. I'd give my life for him."

"Stand the fuck down, Conrad," Hancock snapped. "We don't have time for this shit." Then he looked at Maren, catching at her hand, squeezing her fingers in what might have been construed as an affectionate gesture if Steele didn't know better.

"Level with me, Maren. I've got to get to her. Every hour . . . Every goddamn minute she's in his hands . . ." He broke off and closed his eyes but not before his grief and fear was broadcast throughout the entire room, leaving the KGI members to look on in astonishment.

They were witnessing something more momentous than watching Steele, formerly the ice man, be taken down by a petite blond blue-eyed woman and a precious baby girl who looked just like her mama.

The looks ranged from bewilderment, to amusement, to disbelief and outright "what the fuck?"

P.J. didn't look haunted, as one might expect. Yes, it had taken time for her not to react to the knowledge of a woman being abused, but she'd become more adept at hiding her reaction.

Then Hancock's gaze settled on Resnick and flickered dispassionately over the teams standing behind the man who dangled an unlit cigarette from his lips. That gaze went back to Sam, studying and measuring, asking the silent question.

"He can be trusted," Sam said. "We need all the firepower we can get. It's not going to be a walk in the park to take Maksimov down, but first we have to find him, and that's where Adam has proven himself to be particularly useful in the past."

"You should know," Resnick said in a sour tone. "You shot me and hacked into my computer."

Hancock didn't bother giving fake remorse. They all knew that their jobs made for less-than-desirable missions, and every single person in the room had been forced at one time or another to go against their personal code in the name of good.

Hancock ignored Resnick's dig, and his gaze found Maren's again. "Cope is hurt. I need you to look at him. Viper too. You said it yourself. I'm not dying. Yet. Take care of them."

Then he gazed fiercely at Rio and included Sam, who stood beside Hancock's former team leader. Though Sam led KGI, it didn't bother him for Hancock to look to Rio. Rio had been to Hancock what Sam was to Rio and the rest of KGI.

"The priority is Honor. I don't give a fuck about Maksimov. Another day. Another time. There'll always be another time. But not another Honor. She has to come first. Swear it. She has to be the priority."

Rio knelt and grasped Hancock's uninjured arm in the grip of one warrior to another.

"You have my word on it, brother."

It was the first time Rio had acknowledged the once strong bond between himself and the man he'd trained. And Sam knew how Hancock felt. Every man in the room knew how he felt. They'd all been in the position of knowing the woman they loved had to come before all else. The mission. The greater good. That in some cases, the good of the one did goddamn well outweigh the good of the many.

"I'm already on locating him," Resnick interjected. "He could goddamn be anywhere, but I'm working on the logistics given our present location and what I know to be some of his hidey-holes. The problem has never been not knowing where Maksimov is, but rather being able to nail the bastard down. He's a fucking escape artist. There one moment, gone the next."

"I was arrogant," Hancock admitted painfully, looking up to find Swanny. His brother-in-law of sorts. "I should have put a tracking device on her like you did Eden. There just wasn't much time and I was so sure I could just take him out and Honor would never even wake up."

"Why did you drug her?" P.J. asked angrily.

Her teammates eyed her warily, and Cole's expression turned grim even as he gathered his wife close to his side.

"You made her helpless and you didn't plan for the worst. You always plan for the worst," she said hoarsely.

Hancock closed his eyes. "I had no choice. I was working without a net. No backup plan. It was the way Maksimov wanted her delivered, and I had to make it look good or we would have never gotten close enough to take him out. Not that it did us any good."

His tone was bitter and filled with self-condemnation.

"I found his mole buried in Bristow's organization, but there was obviously another. That or one of my men is or was dirty, and I can't believe that."

"You know you can't assume anything," Rio said bluntly, reprimanding his former man.

"You know them too, Rio. You look at them. You look at their faces and see how they feel about Honor. Then you tell me one of them sold her—us—out."

"What's the damage to him, Maren?" Steele asked, interrupting the tense exchange. "Is he up to this? Because I have no qualms about sidelining him if I think he's going to get any one of us killed."

"Free-floating piece of broken rib," she said briskly. "The vest saved his life, but at such close range, and with the caliber bullet used, he's fortunate the bullet didn't go right through the vest. Conrad alleviated the pressure on his lung and drained the fluid and air so it could reinflate. Not saying he could go to war, but he'll do. Provided he rests and doesn't move until go time."

Hancock nodded, surprising Sam with his acquiescence. Judging by the paleness and sweat, Hancock was suffering far more than he was letting on. But his physical suffering paled in comparison to his emotional pain.

"Then let's get to tracking down this motherfucker and take him out," Garrett said, speaking up for the first time.

Every single person in the room—KGI, Titan and Resnick's teams—all echoed the sentiment in unison. There was an innocent woman in the hands of a monster, and while that was reason enough to stage the takedown of one of the world's most dangerous men, this wasn't just any woman.

She was the only woman Hancock had ever shown any vulnerability over, and that made her even more important.

CHAPTER 36

HONOR lay in her cage, curled into an unfeeling ball. She sensed Maksimov's frustration, his mounting rage. And his puzzlement over her ability to withstand his repeated attempts to hurt her. But she simply felt nothing at all. It was hard to hurt someone who simply didn't care and no longer had anything to live for.

She wasn't a fool. There would be no rescue. When Maksimov grew tired of his games, he'd resort to getting the only thing from her he could. Money. From ANE. She knew it would be soon because with every passing day—and she'd lost count of them—he grew more agitated and disappointed that his prey didn't give him the satisfaction he'd counted on.

She sensed the change in him this morning when he strode into the tiny, windowless room where her cage was suspended from the ceiling. He hadn't bothered giving her food and water. She couldn't have eaten anyway. She would have thrown it all up. But water, she'd sell her soul for, but then she remembered she didn't have one.

Dead people didn't have souls or anything else.

"You've proved a disappointment," he said in a churlish tone. Almost like a child deprived of his favorite toy. But then he was nothing more than a spoiled bully, unused to not getting his way.

He was used to being feared to the point of being able to bend and manipulate people to his will, and he'd utterly failed with Honor.

"I'll be going out for a while," he said with a sinister smile that might have once scared her. "ANE is very anxious to get their hands on you. You'll be going on a trip soon. I believe you're familiar with the destination. At least you won't have an issue with the language barrier."

She didn't react. Wouldn't give him the satisfaction. Besides, this brought her one step closer to death, so she welcomed it. She'd expected him to keep her several more days, determined to have his fun and more importantly win the battle of wills he thought ensued between them.

If he only knew. There was no battle. She had no reason to fight. All she wanted now was to rest. And hope to find peace in the next life, though her beliefs had been badly shaken and she was no longer sure what awaited her upon death. She'd witnessed evil winning too many times to be so sure that goodness existed. That it triumphed over all. And that those who fought the good fight were rewarded in final rest.

He didn't even bother with a parting shot. No attempt to make her cry out in pain. Perhaps he knew he wouldn't be any more successful than he'd been with all the other attempts.

He simply turned on his heel and stalked from the room, slamming it behind him. She heard the hiss of the airlock, sealing the room. It was an impenetrable room with fortified walls. Likely underground, though she was only guessing by the dank smell and the fact that there were no windows, just fluorescent light that stayed on at all times, ensuring that she was never able to seek solace in the soothing embrace of the dark. Just another attempt to break the already broken.

She fixed her gaze on the far wall and began making patterns in her mind, creating a swirl of color and calling back memories of her family, a ritual she indulged in constantly, especially when Maksimov was tormenting her. She was building a wall around herself because worse was to come and just because she welcomed it, wanted it, would be relieved when death finally claimed her, didn't mean that she was going to go out screaming, begging, sobbing.

She might have no pride any longer, but it wasn't about pride. It was about not letting them have that ultimate victory of seeing and enjoying her torture. She'd go as silently and as peacefully as one ever went to their death.

That was her promise to herself. And to her family.

"THE problem, as I'm sure you know, Hancock, is that gaining access to one of Maksimov's holdings isn't the problem. He's a cagey, paranoid bastard with hidden nooks and crannies that can easily be overlooked when they're right under your nose," Resnick said.

Hancock nodded, moving slower than he'd like. He still labored for breath, but his absolute focus was on finding Honor, and this was their third search. They were running out of time and he was choking on his despair.

"I've got movement in the north wing."

There was uncharacteristic excitement in P.J.'s voice when it came over the com. She, Cole, Skylar and two of Resnick's snipers surrounded the holding while the others had fanned out, taking position at every possible entry point.

Explosives had been set on two concrete walls to blow a hole, giving them additional entry points. All they waited for now was go time.

"South too," Cole said, checking in. "Looks like guards."

Hope curled in Hancock's gut despite his best attempt not to set himself up for disappointment. Again. But the other holdings they'd scouted were deserted. This was the first that showed any signs of life.

"We need a count of heat signatures," Hancock broke in.

Yeah, he was down, but he wasn't out, and he wasn't taking a backseat in this. This was his mission. His fuckup. He was getting Honor back no matter what it took.

"I got three here," P.J. reported in.

"Two here," Cole said.

"There's movement in the courtyard," Edge said quietly. "Looks to me like they're getting ready to move out."

Hancock's heart accelerated as did his breathing, and he paid for it when his lung expanded too rapidly and pain speared through his chest. But he ignored it because if there was movement, it meant that Honor was likely here and Maksimov was preparing to turn her over to ANE. He wasn't too late.

Sorrow ate at his gut. Not too late to save her from the clutches of ANE but days too late to save her from whatever Maksimov had done to her.

Turn it off. Steele had told him to turn it off, and the man had experience in having to do just that. He'd nearly lost Maren and with it his iron control. Hancock did Honor no good by losing it. He was of no use to her mad with grief. He could get her and the others killed.

"Hold your positions," Sam ordered. "Vehicle coming in the front gate. As soon as I give the all clear, we go in hot. We need to make it fast. Don't give a shit how clean. Just make damn sure Honor isn't caught in the crossfire."

Everyone had their orders, so radio silence ensued. The snipers would take out their targets as soon as they could be sure Honor wasn't in the way.

"I've got one heat signature completely still and seemingly suspended in midair," Skylar said quietly.

Hancock knew she wouldn't break radio silence unless she was sure this was Honor.

"Give me a minute to get a better sight line," she said. Then she swore, and Hancock's blood froze.

"It's below the house. And the signature is faint. I'm betting on a basement secure room. Reinforced walls. Just the kind of place a prisoner would be kept."

It was the fact that Skylar had said the heat source was completely still that panicked Hancock. And that it was faint. But no. Heat meant life. And if Skylar was right and it was a subroom with reinforced walls, that would explain the faintness of the signal. But not the stillness.

But she was alive, and that was all he could focus on or he'd lose his mind.

"Give me cover," Hancock said quietly. "The subfloor is mine."

Rio swore. "Not without backup. Don't even argue with me."

Hancock smiled faintly. "You don't lead me anymore, Rio."

"That doesn't mean you still aren't goddamn mine," Rio said in a savage tone.

"Rio and I will have your six while the others clear a path," Conrad said, siding with Rio.

"Vehicle is stopped. Three men. No one else. They're all inside. We need to move now," Nathan said.

"Go," Sam barked.

And all hell broke loose.

Gunfire erupted. Explosions rocked the earth, nearly knocking Hancock to his knees, but Rio and Conrad were there to anchor him as they rushed inside the house, looking for the way down below the main floor.

Resnick's teams flooded the rooms, taking down every target in their way. Hancock's only focus was on finding the way down. Rio and Conrad flanked him, but he didn't slow or wait for their cover. He carried an assault rifle in one hand and a pistol in the hand on the side where he'd taken a bullet to his shoulder.

An initial sweep of the downstairs brought them exactly nothing and Hancock swore viciously. What were they overlooking?

"Calm down and focus," Rio said quietly. Then he said into the com, "Sky, can you give us a position of the heat signature in the sublevel? We aren't coming up with shit. We need your eyes."

"Center. Dead center," came Skylar's calm response. "You're standing right over it. It's there."

Hancock dropped to his knees, as did Conrad and Rio, and they felt along the floor for any sign of an entry. Then Hancock's gaze rose and scanned the walls. A switch, of course. There wasn't an obvious doorway and the flooring was seamless.

"Get the switches," he barked to Conrad. "Try them all. There's a row of half a dozen on the right side of the room. One of them has to open the subfloor."

Conrad hurried and one by one began flipping the switches. On the last one, Rio nearly stumbled and fell right through the floor when a section smoothly began to slide open, revealing a set of stairs.

Hancock wasted no time. Light was beaming upward, the tiny room flooded with bright light. He stormed down the stairs, prepared for the worst, but not even that could have prepared him for what he discovered.

His knees locked and his stomach lurched when he saw the impossibly small cage suspended from the ceiling and Honor's body curled into a tight ball, barely fitting into the prison.

The cage began to lower and he glanced over in surprise to see Rio flipping a switch that made the cage slowly descend from the ceiling.

Hancock rushed forward, his heart in his throat, and then it was nearly torn out of his chest when he got a good look at her.

Her wrists and ankles were raw and bloody, her skin torn from the too-tight manacles. Why? She would have no way of escaping the cage. But then Maksimov enjoyed inflicting pain and misery.

Oh God.

He made a sound of a wounded animal and didn't even realize it had come from him.

Honor was a mess. Her hair a mass of tangles, face bruised and bloodied. Worse, on the floor beneath where the cage had been suspended was a fucking shock probe. And there were burn marks covering her body where Maksimov had obviously shocked her repeatedly.

Tears blurred his vision and he roared with pent-up rage, his entire body shaking. He grabbed the bars as if by sheer will alone he could break them and free her.

He was unstoppable. Rio and Conrad quickly saw the futility in trying to calm Hancock and instead searched for a way to open the cage. When they finally found it, Hancock had bloodied and skinned a good portion of his flesh from his hands in trying to break her free.

Hancock flung open the door but then stopped, his frustration at a boiling point.

"The key," he rasped. "Where the fuck is the key to get her out of these fucking cuffs?"

Conrad didn't say anything. He just pushed forward,

pulling a lock pick set from his fatigues, and set to work freeing Honor from her restraints.

So wrapped up in trying to find and free Honor, Hancock hadn't even noticed until now that her eyes were open. He froze, staring down at completely lifeless eyes. No spark. Dull as death. Absolutely no reaction, no evidence that she even knew they were there.

He tentatively caressed her cheek, afraid that she might well shatter if he touched her.

"Honor?"

His voice was hoarse, laced with worry and choked with tears he couldn't control. They streamed down his cheeks and he lowered his face to her hair as Conrad set to unlocking the last manacle holding her ankle.

His entire body heaved as his tears soaked into her hair.

"She's free," Conrad said in a low voice. "Let me carry her, Hancock. You know you aren't strong enough. And if she wakes and sees you like this, you'll scare the shit out of her."

Hancock reluctantly agreed but not for the reasons Conrad outlined. Hancock knew that if Honor regained awareness and saw Hancock, she'd look at him like the betrayer he was. Like the failure he was. Like a man who'd broken his promises to her time and time again.

"Only until we get to the plane," Hancock said fiercely. "Then I want her to have pain medication and a sedative. I don't want her to wake up this way. Not here. Not on the plane. I want her to wake up in a place she knows she's safe."

"I'll take care of it," Conrad said, understanding the torment Hancock faced. "And Hancock, we all failed her. Not just you."

"I betrayed her," Hancock said savagely. "I was the one who promised her I wouldn't give her to Maksimov, that I'd find a way. I was the one who drugged her and didn't tell her what we were doing. I'm the one who she thought betrayed her when she woke up with Maksimov's hands on her. This is on me. Only me. And it's me who's going to have to live with it for the rest of my goddamn life."

CHAPTER 37

"I just struck *gold*," Donovan said, gleefully doing a fist pump as he leaned back from where he'd been feverishly hacking into Maksimov's encrypted computer files.

The plane had lifted into the air an hour ago and Honor lay in the small bedroom, sedated, while the others had sprawled in the sitting area on chairs, the couch and even the floor.

One of Resnick's teams had taken the other jet so they could keep close watch on Honor's family. Sam had sent word ahead to Sean to lock down the compound, and that under no circumstances was anyone to go in or out of the secure area.

It had already been decided that Nathan and Joe's team would remain at the compound to ensure the safety of the family while every other available KGI member along with Titan would go after Maksimov.

"Spill," Hancock growled.

He was the only one not seated and the one who needed to be resting the most, but he paced the small confines of the sitting area, his gaze going often to the door to the bedroom where Honor slept, which was left ajar just in case she awoke and panicked.

"If it were anyone else, I'd suspect a trap," Donovan said.

"But Maksimov is an arrogant bastard who truly believes he's invincible and is unstoppable. I have the coordinates, the place and the time he's making the exchange with ANE and he's gone ahead already. It's why he wasn't here. He's negotiating with ANE and milking his 'find' for all its worth. He sent his men to bring Honor to him—and ANE. We have a dream scenario here. We can take them both out at the same time. We'll never get another opportunity like this, so we have to go in and get it done."

Sam frowned. "We don't have the manpower for that kind of op. We're good, but we're vastly outnumbered and without the team guarding Honor's family and Nathan and Joe's team locking down the compound, we don't have a chance in hell of taking both Maksimov and ANE out."

"That's where you're wrong," Resnick said fiercely. "I'm going all out on this. I have four SEAL teams I'm calling in. I have the two black ops teams, and I'm bringing three special forces units and the best of the best, army rangers and several airborne units. They won't know what hit them. Uncle Sam would like nothing more than to kill two birds with one stone, and they'll give us whatever the fuck we need to take them all down. For this mission? They'll give me the fucking keys to the kingdom. And that's a fact."

"You'll need bait," P.J. said thoughtfully. "Without evidence of Honor, we'll never get close enough to take them out."

"No!" Cole exploded in fury, knowing exactly where she was going with this. Hancock could see the raw pain in Cole's eyes and knew he was remembering the last time KGI had used bait—P.J.—and the horrific results. She'd been raped and brutalized and every single member of KGI still carried the weight of their guilt, but no one more than Cole.

"It is *not* an option," Cole said in an icy, furious tone. "I will not risk you again, P.J. You can't expect me to let you. Not after . . ."

He broke off, the words choking and dying in his voice, but tears glittered harshly in his eyes.

"Of course she can't," Skylar said in a soothing voice, putting her hand on Cole's arm, squeezing in a comforting gesture. "P.J. looks nothing like Honor. It would never work."

Relief made Cole go weak in the knees, and he dragged P.J. against his side, burying his face in her hair, and she let him, a testament to just how upset she knew her husband was.

P.J. was not a woman to allow herself to seem weak or in need of protection or comfort in front of others. She was a fucking fierce warrior. Honor was every bit as fierce, just in a different way.

"I would be the logical choice," Skylar said calmly.

The entire cabin exploded with a chorus that ranged from *Hell no* to *Over my dead body!* Edge stood, the big man seeming to take up the entire space of the already cramped cabin, his eyes glittering with rage.

"You will *not* do this, Sky."

"You aren't my team leader, Zane," Skylar said gently, using his real name.

The two roomed together and were close friends. Best friends. There was nothing romantic to their relationship. It was more one of close siblings. But that didn't mean Edge wasn't fiercely protective of her.

"No, but we are," Nathan said in a hard voice, thumbing his chest and then in Joe's direction. "And we aren't risking you as fucking bait. Never again will we put someone in the position P.J. was forced into. She paid the ultimate price and we damn near lost her. We will *not* lose you. And that's an order."

Skylar sent them all an exasperated look. She and P.J. exchanged quick looks of sisterhood and the equivalent of a mental eye roll. They were highly trained, lethal weapons, equal to their male counterparts in the KGI organization, but above all, KGI cherished and protected their women. All of them. Wives, sisters, mothers. And even their teammates.

"If we needed a male to use as bait, would any of you even hesitate to volunteer?" Skylar challenged. "I distinctly remember Nathan taking the place of the pilot of the plane that was going to fly Maren and Caldwell to wherever the fuck he was taking her. No one made any bones about risking him."

The KGI men exchanged uneasy looks because they were well and truly fucked. If they insisted on not risking Skylar, it sent the wrong message. That she wasn't an equal when she was in every possible way. That they didn't trust her to be able to take care of herself and do her job.

"Just listen to me before you hand down your decree from on high," Skylar said with heavy sarcasm.

"Honor is small. We're almost exactly the same height. She's thinner than me, but she's been through hell so that's to be expected. But we're both blond and I don't have to get up close and personal for them to get a detailed look. They just need to see who they *think* is Honor trussed up like a Thanksgiving turkey about to be delivered to ANE.

"We bruise me up. Not literally," she added hastily when every single expression in the plane blackened to rage. "Makeup is a useful tool. We make me appear as she was when we found her. And I'll pretend unconsciousness, which they would expect since they seem to have a predilection for drugged women," she added in disgust.

"The point is, me being Honor gets us in. The rest is up to us, Resnick's teams and whoever the hell else Uncle Sam decides to send. You know it's a damn good plan and if you'd set aside your manly thirteenth-century egos for two seconds, you'd recognize that it's the only way we achieve our objective."

"Well fuck," Garrett muttered.

Edge didn't look any happier than he had in the beginning, but he pressed his lips together, obviously refusing to give voice to the torrent of objections he wanted to launch.

"She's right," Sam said quietly. "Goddamn it, I don't have to like it—I don't like it. I fucking *hate* it—but she's right. But I want her covered at all times."

P.J. reached over and squeezed Skylar's hand. "Thank you. I didn't intend for you to do it. I wasn't setting you up to be the bait. I would have done it, dyed my hair, whatever. But . . ."

She looked embarrassed and vulnerable, enough so for Cole to slide his hand around her nape and squeeze gently in comfort and support.

"I'm not sure I *could* have done it," P.J. admitted. "I don't know if I could trust myself not to freak out, and that shames me, especially since I'm *relieved* that you'll be doing it and not me. It makes me a fucking coward," she added in disgust, emotion glittering brightly in eyes that were usually unreadable.

Hancock had had enough of this brave woman browbeating herself when she was one of the fiercest women he'd ever known. He stalked over to her, ignoring the fact that Cole immediately bristled and tried to maneuver P.J. behind him.

Hancock stopped in front of P.J. and knelt so he was on eye level with her.

"Don't you *ever* call yourself a fucking coward," he said, allowing every bit of his pissed-off tone to be heard. "You have the heart of a warrior and you are one of the bravest people—that's right, *people*, not women—I've ever known. I have no doubt you could take down every single one of your team members in a fight and they know it. We all know it. What you did, what you went through was the most selfless act I've ever witnessed. Until Honor . . ."

He trailed off as sorrow filled his voice.

Cole looked stunned by Hancock's impassioned defense of P.J. Respect glimmered in his eyes as he and Hancock exchanged a look of understanding. The rest of KGI didn't look any less astonished. Except Rio, who looked as though he would have expected nothing less.

Hancock collected himself, because he wasn't finished. He abruptly got up and then went to where Skylar sat, and as he had with P.J., he knelt and took both her hands in his, making sure his touch was gentle and not bruising because of the seething rage imprinted in his bones.

"Thank you," he said in a low voice. "For risking yourself for a woman you don't know and for a dishonorable man who has caused much trouble for all of you in the past. I don't deserve the help you are unconditionally offering, but you have my heartfelt gratitude—and know this."

He paused and speared her with his gaze, stared until he was sure she was looking directly at him, seeing him. The heart of him.

"If there is ever a time when you need help. If you need anything at all, you only have to contact me. I'll come. No matter what. I can never hope to repay my debt to you all, but I can only try."

Skylar surprised him by leaning forward and wrapping her arms around him, hugging him carefully, ensuring she didn't cause him further pain. He went stiff, caught totally off guard and not at all sure what he was supposed to do. Nobody hugged him. Except Honor. And his sister.

"It will be all right, Hancock," Skylar whispered close to his ear. "All is not lost. You've given up and you can't do that. Is she worth fighting for? If so, then *fight*. Do you hear me? You fight, Guy Hancock."

He hugged her back and rested his chin atop her head.

"You're a very special woman, Skylar," he said, weariness creeping into his voice.

"Go to Honor, Hancock," Donovan said quietly. "Your head isn't in the game right now. You need to reassure yourself she's okay. We'll keep you in the loop. We aren't benching you, though God knows you're in no shape to be doing anything but lying in a hospital bed, but if it were Eve or any of our wives, we wouldn't stand down even if we were at death's door. You have my word, you will know everything."

"The very last thing she needs is to wake up and see me," Hancock said bleakly. "I won't hurt her any more than I already have."

"She's out," Conrad said. "She's not going to come around anytime soon. Stop torturing yourself. You and I both know this *wasn't* your fault."

"The *hell* it wasn't," Hancock said in a savage tone that made the others flinch at the raw pain in his voice.

Conrad was wrong and Hancock knew it. It *was* his fault. He'd betrayed her and he'd failed her and that was unforgivable. But he took Conrad at his word that he'd sedated Honor so she wouldn't waken until she was in a safe place, and he *needed* to see her. To touch her even though he didn't deserve either. But he had to know just how badly Maksimov had hurt her.

He nodded curtly and then quietly slipped into the tiny bedroom where Honor was huddled on the bed. Even unconscious, she was in a protective ball, curled into herself, so vulnerable looking that his grief was a tangible ache in his chest.

He loved her. He fucking adored her. He'd never loved anyone except his foster family, Eddie and Caroline Sinclair, the parents he never had. And his brothers, Raid and Ryker, and his precious baby sister, whom he'd also let down. It seemed he was forever hurting the people who mattered most to him. How could he ever look Big Eddie Sinclair in the face again after all he'd done? Before, he'd always known that his actions were a necessary evil.

But Honor was something he'd been utterly unprepared for. She'd slipped past his carefully erected barriers and somehow she'd become a living, breathing part of him. His other half. Now he understood what drove the Kellys in their absolute protection of their women, their wives. Because he felt it himself. But the Kellys hadn't done to their women what Hancock had done to Honor, what he'd planned to do in the beginning with no regret or remorse.

Now, those were two emotions he'd keenly feel the rest of his life.

He slid onto the bed, moving inch by inch closer to her so he could smell her, feel her heat, touch her. It seemed an eternity before he finally had her nestled in his arms, and then he finally allowed himself to relax.

He buried his face in her matted hair, uncaring of the scent of dirt and blood. And then he wept. He wept for all he'd been given and for what he'd so callously discarded and betrayed. What was now lost to him forever.

Honor had changed him. She'd changed him on a fundamental level and though she now hated him, he would live the kind of life going forward that she would have wanted him to. He wanted to be the man she'd thought him to be. The only person who'd ever seen past the darkness that was ever present in his soul. He was done with Titan. Done with fighting for the greater good. He was finished being a man who didn't even look at himself in the mirror because he no longer recognized the man staring back at him.

She'd given him the gift of herself, the very best part of him, and he'd thrown it away. All for the greater good.

CHAPTER 38

HANCOCK stiffened, coming to instant awareness when he felt Honor stir against him. Damn it! He'd drifted off, needing sleep and healing, but he hadn't intended to stay this long. And she wasn't supposed to regain consciousness until she was returned to her family. He didn't even have another syringe so he could quickly inject her so she didn't come to awareness.

He gazed anxiously at her, hoping she was just restless and would succumb once more to the drugs in her system. But he wasn't that fortunate.

Her eyelids fluttered sluggishly and then she saw him. He tensed, awaiting her condemnation, her hatred, bracing for everything he deserved. But she simply stared at him with dull, lifeless eyes and didn't react at all. Nothing. Fear skittered up his spine because she simply wasn't there.

"I should have known," she said in a monotone. "That you would be the one bringing me to ANE, not Maksimov. Ironic, isn't it? You 'save' me from ANE and you're the one to return me to them. Full circle."

Saying nothing further, she turned, struggling, emitting gasps of pain that her movement caused as she turned away from him and curled once more into a protective ball, shutting him out, retreating into herself and a place where she couldn't hurt anymore.

His torment was tearing him with its vicious claws. He felt every word to his tainted soul. He ached to hold her. To comfort her. To tell her all that was in his heart. But she wouldn't believe him. She'd never believe him. As with everything else so precious he'd lost, he'd lost her trust as well.

He nearly put his hand on her shoulder, drawing back at the last second, because he didn't want to cause her further pain and he had yet to determine the extent of her injuries.

"What did that bastard do to you?" he demanded, barely able to keep back the roar of fury that threatened to erupt.

One small shoulder lifted in a shrug. "Does it matter?"

"Yes, it goddamn matters! What did he do, Honor?"

She stiffened and he could feel her pain radiating from her tightly curled body, and it made him want to weep like a baby.

"You should know, Hancock," she said, her tone weary, as if her barriers were slipping, as if the shields she'd constructed and the alternate reality she'd created in order to survive were slowly crumbling. "You told me what Maksimov would do. Just as you told me what ANE will do. Do you want all the gory details? Will it make you happy to know that I suffered? Are you concerned that he *didn't* do all the things you said he would?"

He couldn't breathe. His heart weighed a ton in his chest. Fear as he'd never known paralyzed him and he couldn't speak. Couldn't think. Couldn't get past all he'd told her that Maksimov and ANE would do. Things he'd sworn to her he wouldn't allow to happen because he was pulling the plug on the mission. And she thought it had all been a lie.

"*What did he do?*" Hancock asked hoarsely, his voice thick with tears and so much emotion that it overwhelmed him, consumed him, rendered him incapable of the simplest of processes.

"Nothing worse than what's been done before," she said, as if it didn't matter. "He didn't hurt me, Hancock. *You* did that. *You* destroyed me. And I guess, in a way, I have you to thank. Because you hurt me in a way no one has ever hurt me, and the things Maksimov did paled in comparison. It hurt. I know it did. I mean it had to, right? But I didn't feel it. Because the dead don't feel. And I died the day you betrayed me. So whatever ANE has in store for me, I welcome. Because it won't matter. Nothing matters anymore. And as with Maksimov, I can at least deprive them the pleasure of hearing me scream. Of hearing me beg. Because it will *never* happen. They'll delight in breaking me, but as I told Maksimov when he smugly informed me that *he* would break me, you can't break what's already broken."

Hancock's heart shattered into tiny razor-sharp shards, inflicting permanent wounds he'd never recover from. He was bleeding on the inside. And it would never stop. Tears streaked down his cheeks, grief consuming him until there was simply nothing left. Just as Honor had said there was nothing left of her.

Broken.

He'd broken her when nothing else had been able to.

He'd destroyed this precious gift.

"I know you don't care what I want," she said in a tired voice. "But I *do* hurt, Hancock, and I know I don't have much time until the end begins. Will you at least leave me in peace? Will you give me that at least? Seeing you, talking to you has destroyed the void I worked so hard to build. A place where nothing and no one can hurt me, touch me. Where I feel no pain. I feel . . . nothing. And I need that. You've gotten what you want. Will you please just leave me in peace so I can try to prepare myself for what is to come?"

Hancock rolled away, not daring to look back at her, knowing it would kill him. She was hurting. No matter that she'd said Maksimov hadn't hurt her, she hadn't meant it in the way he had. She'd only meant that *Maksimov* hadn't been able to break her because Hancock had already done that.

He strode into the sitting area, and he knew everything he felt must be reflected in his eyes, his face, because the others visibly recoiled from whatever horror they saw in him.

He focused his attention on Maren and tried to be calm and composed when he was dying on the inside. Bleeding out from the thousands of cuts caused by his shattered heart.

"She's hurting. I don't know what he did to her, and she hates me. But she's hurting and I need you to look her over. She needs pain medicine, and Maren, I want her sedated. She's . . . broken. I broke her," he choked out. "*I* did. Not Maksimov. Me. Every second she's conscious, she's hurting, dead on the inside. Please give her peace. For me. Please."

Maren's face was stricken and she, as Skylar had done, wrapped her arms around him and hugged him gently. He could feel the dampness of her tears soaking into his shirt. For him. God.

He gently tugged her away and then looked at her with dead eyes.

"Do not defend me, Maren. Don't try to explain anything to her. If she thinks you are anything to me other than someone I paid to get her cleaned up before she's turned over to ANE, she won't trust you and she'll refuse treatment, pain medication and especially sedation. Please, just make her as comfortable as possible and try to find out what that bastard did to her. I have to know. Goddamn it, I have to know because it will be my sin to bear for eternity."

"But . . ."

"Please. For her, Maren. Do this kindness for her. I don't deserve any, but she does. Make her think you hate me. That I kidnapped you and forced you to see to her injuries. Do whatever it takes to convince her that you are in no way sympathetic to me or she won't cooperate."

Maren sighed but then nodded, going over to collect her medical bag. She cast one last sorrowful look in Hancock's direction before disappearing into the bedroom.

Hancock turned to Resnick. "I have no right to ask you for anything, but I want your best team protecting Honor at the safe house. Tell her the U.S. military intercepted me—she believes I'm the one delivering her to ANE—and rescued her and that she's safe and on U.S. soil but until Maksimov, ANE and . . . I . . . are taken down for good it's not safe for her to be with her family. It's not safe for her family to know she's alive. Explain the danger to her and to her family and that her family will also be guarded and protected, and that when the danger is no more, your team will take her to her family."

"Consider it done," Resnick said without hesitation. "And just for the record, Hancock. You aren't the heartless bastard you want the world to believe. Mind you, I didn't appreciate being shot, but I know now the reasons why and it was a righteous mission."

"You're wrong," Hancock said coldly. "I am exactly that and a whole lot worse."

CHAPTER 39

ALL eyes flew to the door to the bedroom an hour later when Maren stuck her head out. Hancock's stomach bottomed out because Maren looked as though she were on the verge of shattering. Steele was up and across the space before Hancock could ask about Honor.

"Come inside with me, please, Jackson," Maren asked in a tearful voice.

She was the only one who called him by his first name, and it sounded odd when *Steele* fit the man's personality to a T.

Hancock stood to protest, but Maren held up her hand. "She's resting peacefully. She won't be aware of Jackson's presence. I . . . I need him for a moment."

Steele pressed in close, enfolding his wife in his arms, pushing them both into the room and closing the door behind them.

Maren burst into tears, burying her face in her husband's broad chest.

"Don't cry, baby," Steele said in a desperate voice. It was a well-known fact that his wife's crying brought him to his knees and made him as helpless as a newborn baby.

"She's hurting so badly, Jackson," she choked out. "They both are. Hancock was right. She's *shattered*. She's not there. There's no fight left in her. She wants to die."

Steele held her, stroking his hand up and down her back, offering her comfort he knew she wouldn't find. She was good to her toes. Tenderhearted and sweet. Light and sunshine. All the things he wasn't but experienced through her. With her. God, what had his life been like before her?

He glanced over his wife's head to where Honor lay curled into a protective ball on the bed, and he winced. She looked like hell.

"What did that bastard do to her?" Steele asked, his voice dangerously low, rage rolling from him in waves.

"He tortured her. He used a cattle prod on her frequently. She has marks all over her body. She's bruised. She's been beaten. But Jackson, that's not the worst of it. She'll recover from her injuries. But she's broken. She's simply given up. She doesn't care. She doesn't hate. She doesn't love. She isn't angry. She's incapable of feeling anything. She's an empty shell, already dead except that only her heart still beats. But in every way that counts, she's already gone.

"She isn't afraid of being turned over to ANE. She accepts it. She welcomes it. God! She simply doesn't feel anything. I don't know if she'll survive this. She tried to kill herself when Bristow tried to rape her. Both wrists are stitched and the cuts are deep. When she realizes she's not being turned over to ANE, I fear she'll simply finish the job and end her physical life, because her soul is already dead."

"Son of a bitch," Steele said, rubbing his chest at the sudden ache that gripped him. "That woman has been to hell and back. She survived in the face of impossible odds. She fought. She never gave up. But she obviously loves Hancock, and his perceived betrayal was able to do what nothing else could. Defeat her."

Maren raised her tearful gaze to Steele's. "And how can I walk out there and tell Hancock everything I just told you? Did you see him? As dead as she is, as devastated as she is, he is every bit as dead on the inside. He won't survive this any more than she will."

Steele cupped her chin gently in his hand and pressed a kiss to her lips. "You don't."

"He won't accept that," she said. "He'll lose it. He's

already torturing himself with what Maksimov did to her. Not knowing is killing him."

"You give him the basics. You tell him of her injuries. But everything you just told me, you don't tell him. It accomplishes nothing, and in fact, it could compromise our mission in a huge way. Because he will completely lose it if you tell him everything you told me. He will be unstoppable. A liability. His only goal will be to take out the man who hurt her and the men who *will* hurt her. He won't care if he dies. As you said, he's already dead. But he could get a hell of a lot of us killed. We need him as calm and as focused as possible, so tell him only what you need to tell him and nothing more. I will *not* lose a single member of KGI because Hancock has lost his tenuous grip on his sanity and put our entire mission in jeopardy."

She sighed, leaning into him. He wrapped his arms around her and simply held her, knowing that was what she needed most right now.

"You're right, of course," she said. "But God, Jackson. It hurt me to see that young woman so defeated and accepting of her fate. I want so badly to cry for her."

He smiled. "Honey, you *are* crying. You've cried all over me."

She sniffed. "You weren't supposed to notice that."

He took her hand and squeezed. "Let's go give Hancock a report before he tears the plane apart."

"I love you," she said in an aching voice. "I think part of the reason I'm so devastated for Honor is this could have been me."

Steele hugged her to him, tremors running through his body. The memory of just how close he'd come to losing her never left him. There wasn't a day he didn't think of it, that he didn't remember the moments when he thought he had lost her. Because, God, there had been more than one.

"I love you too," he said gruffly. "You and Olivia are my life."

"And it hurts me to see Hancock this way," she said in a pained voice. "He's a *good* man. He's not the man everyone thinks him to be. He's not the man *he* believes himself to be, the man he's convinced himself he is. He took care of me the entire time I was in captivity. He protected me and he was gentle and *caring*. He offered me reassurance and comfort when he knew I needed it the most. Never once did he threaten me, and he gave up his mission to save me. And then he saved me again. He was willing to *die* for me. He doesn't deserve this, Jackson. Neither of them do."

He stroked a hand through her hair, knowing full well he owed Hancock a debt he could never possibly hope to repay. Because of Hancock, he had Maren and their precious baby girl. No, Hancock didn't deserve the pain of losing the woman he loved and he hoped like hell that somehow, someway, things would work themselves out and that two people dying slow deaths could somehow find their way back to one another so they could be whole again.

CHAPTER 40

WHEN the plane landed at the airstrip where the teams would split up, one taking Honor to the safe house and standing guard over her and the others to rendezvous to plan the mission to take Maksimov and ANE down, Hancock insisted on carrying Honor to the jet she and Resnick's team would fly out on.

He requested a few moments alone before the others boarded, and they granted the request. The mood was grave, and sorrow pervaded the entire group.

Reverently, Hancock laid Honor on the couch, ensuring that she was as comfortable as he could make her. His hands drifted over the torn flesh at her wrists. On top of the sutures from when she'd cut her own wrists, the skin was ripped and raw from the manacles that had dug so deeply into her delicate flesh.

He palmed her forehead, stroking his fingers through her tangled hair, and he simply drank her in before leaning down to press a kiss to her still lips. He inhaled, savoring her smell, her taste, imprinting it into his heart for all time.

Grief bore down on him, so heavy he couldn't move. Wherever he went in his meaningless life, he would forever carry a piece of her with him. That piece being the best—the only good—part of him.

"I'm so sorry, Honor," he whispered. "I love you. I'll always love you. Only you. There'll never be another I love as I love you. I'm so damn sorry I couldn't be the man you needed. That I couldn't be a good man for you. I hope you find happiness. That I haven't forever destroyed something so very precious. The world needs more people like you, Honor. It needs your kindness, your spirit, fire and courage. And your compassion. All the things I lack, but just for a little while got to experience what those things felt like through you. Be happy, my love. And live. *Live.*"

Knowing if he didn't walk away now, he'd never be able to, he reluctantly rose, allowing his fingers to linger in her hair, trailing down to the very end of the tresses until finally they fell away. He felt the loss as keenly as if she'd died.

He'd never touch her again. Never kiss her, hold her, be enveloped by her sweetness, nor would he ever see her radiant smile that rivaled a sunrise.

Closing his eyes, he turned and walked to the front and then down the steps to the paved runway. He knew what he looked like. Why the others refused to look at him. Because what they'd see was something terrifying. Too terrible to look upon. He'd never look in the mirror again, because without Honor, he knew he'd only see a soulless monster who'd robbed an innocent of everything.

"Let's go," he said in a voice he didn't recognize.

CHAPTER 41

HONOR began the slow climb to awareness, signaling she was once again shrugging off the effects of a sedative. She'd been so adamant in the beginning about not being given them, not wanting anything to impair her. She needed sharp reflexes and clear thinking.

Now? It was a welcome respite and it really wasn't so different from her nondrugged state, so she couldn't really bring herself to care.

She opened her eyes and discovered she wasn't on a plane anymore. She was in a bedroom. A nicely furnished bedroom with a really comfortable bed. A hysterical laugh began in her throat, but she stanched it. It reminded her of when she'd awakened in Bristow's house, thinking she was safe, rescued.

She would never make that same mistake again. Never be so trusting and naïve.

A sound had her slowly turning her head in its direction, disinterest reflected in her movements.

A tall, well-muscled man in a military uniform stood just inside the doorway. When he saw she was awake, he took a few steps forward but maintained a distance between himself and the bed. As though he feared scaring her? She had to bite her lip to prevent the hysterical laughter from bubbling up from her throat. She was beyond the frightened stage. Now she was simply accepting of her fate.

"Miss Cambridge, I'm Kyle Phillips of the United States Marine Corps. We intercepted an attempted exchange between a Russian arms dealer and a terrorist organization, and realizing you were a prisoner, we took the necessary steps to rescue you and get you back to the U.S."

She merely blinked. Did he expect her to believe this bullshit? Furthermore, why bother to lie? Apparently monsters liked to play psychological games. Hancock was certainly a master at it.

"Until the terrorist organization is dismantled and Maksimov is eliminated, you'll be under constant surveillance and around the clock protection. You are not a prisoner. You're free to go anywhere in this house you wish. We also believe there to be a credible threat to your family, so until that threat is eliminated, we've arranged for their protection as well. But it's imperative they not know you're alive until after—"

"Yeah, yeah," Honor muttered. "Until after all the bad guys are dead. Here's a clue. They'll never be dead. They were never *alive*. You can't kill someone who doesn't have a soul."

The man, Kyle, as he'd introduced himself, frowned and studied her, something resembling concern reflected in his eyes.

"As soon as I'm given the go-ahead, I'll take you to reunite with your family personally. You have my word."

"Words are meaningless," she said bitterly.

She turned back over, blocking him out, surprised she'd even bothered to say anything at all. For a moment she'd actually felt . . . anger. Something other than the dullness that had pervaded her entire mind. And she didn't like it. Not at all. A crack had developed in her hard fought barrier against emotion. An impenetrable fortress surrounding her so she felt . . . nothing. Or so she'd thought. Would it disintegrate now when she needed it the most?

Too bad someone hadn't swooped in with the handy-dandy syringe with a sedative. Then she could drift away again. To nothingness.

Instead, she closed her eyes and began mentally

resurrecting the walls she'd so painstakingly built during her captivity, embracing the sensation of the black void.

"WHEN the fuck can I bring her home?" Kyle Phillips snapped to Sam Kelly.

"As soon as we fucking blow Maksimov and ANE all to hell," Sam bit back.

"She's wasting away," Kyle said with pronounced frustration.

There was a brief pause. "What do you mean? You told her she was rescued and that she and her family are being protected and that as soon as Maksimov and ANE are eliminated she's going home, right?"

Kyle made a sound of impatience. "Do you honest-to-God think a woman who has been shit on and lied to at every turn is going to just accept that one minute she's on a plane with a man she believes is delivering her to a terrorist group and then she wakes up and the Marines swooped in and rescued her, but oh by the way, you can't go home yet, but you will. Eventually."

"Describe 'wasting away,'" Sam barked.

"You think I'm bullshitting you," Kyle said, pissed now. "She won't eat. She won't drink. Goddamn it, I had to have one of my men hold her down so I could insert an IV so I could at least keep her hydrated. Yeah, that was fun. Terrorizing and bullying a woman who has already been to hell and back is right up there at the top of my list of duties. Hell of a way to serve one's country, isn't it?

"She doesn't talk. She doesn't respond. The lights are on but nobody is home, and that is *not* a figure of speech. She's going to die, Sam. If something doesn't change and change *soon*, she's going to die. And the hell of it is, she's waiting for it. She *wants* it. You have to *care* enough to fight to live, and she doesn't give a shit what happens to her."

Sam let out curses that would have blistered most hides. For Kyle, it was just another day in the field.

"Go time is tomorrow," Sam said, and Kyle knew he wasn't supposed to have told him that. "You do whatever you have to do, but you keep her alive until tomorrow, and then I'll call and you get her the hell back to her family. She's not going to believe anything until she sees it."

"*Now* you figure it out," Kyle muttered.

HANCOCK stood over Maksimov's bloodied body with so much hatred that the man's eyes were filled with terror and also resignation. None of the blood was courtesy of Hancock. When the attack had been launched, Maksimov had shoved several of his men in front of him, using them as shields. The result was Maksimov wearing the blood of five men behind whom he'd hidden like the coward he was.

Resnick and KGI were true to their word, and Maksimov had been left for Hancock alone. Even now Resnick was tasking the military team with rounding up the terrorists who'd survived and doing a body count of those who hadn't.

No one but Resnick, KGI and Hancock himself would ever know how Maksimov met his end.

Hancock wanted to take Maksimov away and make his death a long, excruciating, merciless death. Torture him as he'd tortured Honor. The burn marks on her body, the mangled and shredded skin on her wrists from the manacles that had to be pried out of her wrists because they were so deeply embedded were vivid images in his memory, and he wanted to repay Maksimov in kind.

It was what Hancock would have done years ago, hell, even a *month* ago. But that was before Honor. Before he'd actually seen and experienced *goodness*. He wanted Maksimov to suffer as no man had ever suffered. He wanted to return all that Maksimov had done to Honor tenfold. But that made him no better, no different than the monster who'd brutalized Honor and countless others. He didn't want to be that man anymore. He wanted to be a man Honor would have been proud of. He wanted to be worthy of her. He wanted to *be* like her.

"You deserve no mercy for what you have wrought," Hancock said in a voice that seethed with both anger and grief. "But I am better than you. And I won't lower myself to your standards. I will not *become* you."

He turned, sparing only a quick glance at the men who'd stood guard. Who'd saved Honor. Who even now were prepared to turn their back on what he wanted to do to Maksimov and swear ignorance of his fate. *Good* men whom he would have dragged into hell with him if he'd carried out his vengeance.

"Hand him over to Resnick. I have no use for this pathetic piece of shit," Hancock spat, ignoring the looks of surprise and . . . respect. He walked past them and kept walking, only wanting to be away from this place and the memories that burrowed insidiously into his mind. Closing his eyes to all he'd gained—and lost—in such a short amount of time. A lifetime.

"Hey, hold up," Rio said, jogging after his former teammate.

Hancock stopped, but all he wanted to do was just go. To be left alone.

"Want a ride to Honor's place? By the time we get stateside, she'll be at her family's house."

For a moment he couldn't breathe for the pain splintering through his body, heart, soul.

"No," he finally said in a low voice.

Rio shot him a look of surprise. "What the fuck, man? You're walking away?"

Hancock turned on him, his features savage as anger rushed hot through his veins.

"I betrayed her. I broke so many promises I can't even count. I don't deserve her and she certainly deserves a hell of a lot better than me. She hates me but not more than I hate myself."

"Don't do this, man," Rio said, his eyes dark with sympathy. "Don't do something you'll regret for the rest of your life."

"Too late," Hancock bit out, and he turned and walked away.

CHAPTER 42

KYLE Phillips stood in the living room of Honor's parents' home facing her entire family. Her mother, father, four brothers and her sister. There was stark grief in their eyes because he knew they assumed the worst.

The news had broken just the night before that the terrorist group responsible for the attack on the relief center Honor had volunteered at had been completely taken out by a joint U.S. special forces unit and SEAL teams. Her family was fully prepared to be told that their daughter's death, although already broadcast over the news for endless days and nights immediately following the attack, could now be officially confirmed. There'd been no survivors, according to reports, though Honor's body had never been returned. It was through that, that her family had clung stubbornly to hope. But now? They fully expected official confirmation of Honor's death.

After formally introducing himself, Kyle asked them to sit and waited until they complied before he said what he'd come to say. There was no easy or delicate way to say what he had to say, and he wasn't one to tiptoe around an issue. It was a lot less time consuming to get straight to the point.

"Your daughter is alive," he said, no inflection to his tone as he took in all their faces and the sudden change from resignation to wary hope.

There was complete silence. Stunned expressions. Shock. And then it seemed to register what he was telling them. Her mother burst into tears as did her sister. Her brothers rocked forward, faces in their palms, and her father went ashen.

"W-what?" Mandie's voice quivered as she stared at the Marine in disbelief. "But we were told she was dead. The whole country was told she was dead. It's all the news has talked about since the attack on the relief center where she worked. What on earth are you saying?"

"She survived," Kyle said quietly. "I understand this comes as a shock . . ."

He got no further before he was bombarded with questions.

"Where is she?" Honor's mother said hoarsely, tears streaming down her cheeks.

"Is she all right?" her father demanded. "Why isn't she *here*? Why are you here and not her? What aren't you telling us? Is she hurt?"

"Why the hell weren't we informed before now?" Brad bit out angrily, his eyes ablaze with relief but also suspicion.

Kyle held his hands up to silence the torrent of conversation.

"I need you to listen to everything I have to tell you. It's very important and it's why I arrived first. She's on her way here now. She's not very far out, but I needed to come ahead to . . . prepare you."

"Prepare us?" Honor's mother whispered, her voice thick with tears, and now fear.

Sensing the importance of what Kyle had to say, everyone went silent and leaned forward, concern etched into their every feature.

Kyle gave them the details—most of them—of Honor's escape and recapture. He gave an accounting of everything that had happened. Except anything relating to Hancock. Hancock was Honor's to either reveal or not, but he'd not take that choice from her.

"I had to force an IV on her while we waited until it was safe to reunite you with her. She gave up," Kyle said in a pained voice. "She was fierce. Brave. Courageous. I've never met her equal. But in the end, it was simply too much. Too much pain and torture and worse, the final loss of hope that had kept her sustained for so long. She doesn't believe I'm telling her the truth, that she's free. She believes me to be taunting her—psychological torture—delaying her eventual *physical* torture and death that she'd come to accept. She's broken, ma'am," he said to her mother.

In a quiet voice, he told them what they had already deciphered for themselves. "Your daughter is not the same young woman she was when she left here, and I want to prepare you for that. She's retreated deep inside herself. She's starved. Refuses to eat. I had to force the IV or she would have already died. She's wounded in multiple areas, in multiple fashions. She's going to need your love, support and, above all, your patience. She needs medical care. But most of all, she needs a reason to *live*."

"Oh my God. Oh my God," her sister said, her sobs echoing through the room.

"She's alive!" one of her brothers exclaimed. "She's coming home!"

"We'll help her," her father vowed. "Whatever she needs. Whatever it takes. I will not have the miracle of my daughter back only to lose her again. I won't let it happen."

"There is nothing I won't do for my baby," her mother said fiercely. "Nothing."

Kyle nodded. Yes, he thought. Her family would bring her back. He could see the love and resolve in their eyes. They were fierce. He could well see where Honor got it from.

But who would save Hancock?

HONOR cautiously opened her eyes and then slammed them shut again, fear shuddering through her fractured mind. Hope—something she'd been denied time and time again until she'd refused to allow herself to even entertain it—was insidiously creeping through her veins, accelerating her pulse until she was nearly breathless. She shook her head. No. Not again. Never again. She'd given in to hope one last time and it had destroyed her completely. Some lessons were learned the hard way.

When the SUV turned onto Oakwood Street, she lost any and all of her carefully constructed control and burst into tears. Her hands flew to her face, covering the guttural sobs tearing from her throat. She rocked back and forth as they drew closer and closer to . . . home.

"Stop!" she cried. "Oh God, please stop!"

The driver immediately slammed on the brakes and Honor bent over, putting her head between her knees as she struggled for breath, panic scraping her insides raw.

Kyle Phillips, who had returned to their "waiting" point and slid into the seat beside her, giving the driver the order to go, put his hand on Honor's back and rubbed up and down and then in gentle circular motions.

"Honor? Are you going to be sick? Are you all right? Come on, honey, you have to breathe for me."

"I can't go in there," she wept.

She lifted her tear-drenched gaze to Kyle's surprised one.

"I don't understand," he said, clearly puzzled by her reaction. "They know you're coming, Honor. It's why I made you hang back. I wanted to prepare them. I didn't want to just spring you on them."

"They can't see me this way," she cried. "Look at me!" She made a sweeping motion of her emaciated body, the still-healing wounds, the fading burn marks and the still very vivid gashes on her wrists, a match to the ones on her ankles, but at least those were hidden.

"This will kill them," she whispered. "I can't do this, Kyle. Please, if you have any compassion, any mercy, you'll tell them I'll talk to them on the phone. And I'll see them. After I heal. I'll eat. I swear it. I'll do whatever you tell me to do. But please, God, don't make me go in there like this."

Kyle looked gutted, his eyes swamped with so much sympathy and understanding that it spurred another round of gut-wrenching tears.

Gently, he pulled her upward and then into his arms, hugging her to his chest, rocking back and forth in a soothing manner.

"I understand how you feel, Honor," he said quietly. "I swear to you that I do. But, honey, they know what to expect."

"You *told* them?" she asked in a horrified voice.

"Not everything," he said even more gently. "Only what pertained to your physical and psychological condition. I never mentioned Hancock. That is yours to tell or not. But think of this from their point of view, Honor. They've just been told that the daughter they thought was dead is very much alive and will be home shortly. Of course they're upset and angry that you endured so much. But what they want, what they need most right now, is to see you. To hold you. To have proof that you're alive. You have *nothing* to be ashamed of."

He tugged her away from his chest so he could cup her chin. He rubbed his thumb over her cheek and forced her to look into his eyes.

"Now, show me the Honor Cambridge who escaped and evaded capture by the most powerful and ruthless terrorist group in the Middle East. You will not walk into your home ashamed with your head down. Your family is overcome with joy. They are even now counting the seconds and watching for our vehicle to pull into their driveway so they can see you. Touch you. Hold you. And tell you how very much they love you. Would you deny them that?"

"No," she choked out. "I'm sorry. I'm sorry I didn't believe you. You were kind to me, but I learned that betrayal follows kindness, and so I wouldn't acknowledge you. I couldn't. It was the only way I could survive because I couldn't allow myself the one thing that had the power to completely destroy me. Hope."

"Shhh, you will not apologize. I would serve with you any day of the week, Honor Cambridge. You have the heart of a Marine, and that's a fact. Now, can I tell Anthony to resume driving?"

She smiled and then impulsively hugged him, craving what she'd long been bereft of. Human touch. Contact. Comfort. Not since . . .

No, she wouldn't go there. What she'd shared or rather what Hancock had taken from her didn't count. Because it wasn't real.

As if sensing her need for that contact, humanity, he

hugged her back ever so gently but no less encompassing and for long moments he merely held her, allowing her to clutch at him while she collected herself.

Finally she pulled away and braced herself, and allowed hope and relief to flood the very depths of her hollow soul.

Excitement began to burn as she caught sight of her house at the end of the cul-de-sac. She half expected her entire family to be on the front lawn waiting, but Kyle had said he'd gone ahead to prepare them, which likely meant he'd told them how fragile she was.

When they pulled to a stop behind her mother's familiar minivan, Honor sat, frozen to her seat as she hungrily drank in the sight of what she thought she'd never see again. Uncertainty gripped her and her palms grew sweaty, and she recognized the signs of yet another impending panic attack.

Kyle reached over and took her hand, squeezing reassuringly.

"I'll be with you the whole time," he said quietly.

She smiled at him. Really smiled, and he seemed delighted.

"Thank you," she said sincerely.

"Forgive the corny thing I'm about to say, but it has truly been an honor to know you, Honor Cambridge."

She squeezed his hand back and then drew in a deep cleansing breath, the wheeze floating away as her lungs opened fully, allowing her to breathe easy once more.

"Let's do this," she said.

CHAPTER 43

CYNTHIA Cambridge threw up her hands, despair radiating from her eyes as she faced her family—minus Honor, who was holed up in the library, her sanctuary. Everyone had gathered. Brad had come from work, no questions asked. Keith had secured release from fall training from his team the minute he'd received the news of Honor's return home, and he had yet to return. Tate and Scott owned multiple local businesses and both made their homes nearby so they had been there in minutes. Mandie, like Keith, had yet to return to her job.

They all looked to their mother—wife—worry tight in their chests. Cynthia looked worn and haggard, so much grief in her expression that they all feared the worst.

"This has to end," Cynthia said, near tears.

Mike, her husband, pulled his wife into his arms, his distress as great as hers, though he held it tightly reined because he sensed just how close his beloved wife was to her breaking point.

"She's not getting better. She's sick. She won't talk about it—anything."

"We knew this wouldn't be easy, Mom," Brad, her oldest son, said.

He was in uniform and had come when his father had

called, telling him he was needed at home. His deputies could hold down the fort in his absence. Family—his sister—was more important.

"She's recovering physically," Tate said cautiously. "A breeze would have knocked her over when she first came back. She's gained weight. She's eating."

"I agree with Mom," Mandie said firmly. "She's recovering from her wounds, her injuries. In fact, you can barely see them. Except her wrists," she added with a frown.

The Marine who'd brought Honor home to them had said that her wrists and ankles had been so tightly manacled that the metal had to be pried from her flesh. But there were underlying wounds. Cuts that had been stitched. They didn't know, but they suspected . . . However, no one ever mentioned it because it meant acknowledging just how bad it must have been for Honor to have tried to take her own life. And it was more than they could bear to have it confirmed that she'd been so desperate as to try to end her misery.

"But she *is* sick," Mandie continued. "Something's wrong with her. She can't keep anything down. She's pale and so fragile. I'm worried. *Really* worried. I think we should take her to the doctor."

Her father sighed. Honor had refused to go back to the doctor after the preliminary examinations, treatments and vitamin regimen she'd been placed on. She'd refused counseling, even though all of them urged her to talk to someone, because she wasn't talking to them. And if something didn't give soon, she was going to shatter, and he wasn't sure they'd get her back this time. If his wife and daughter planned to take Honor to the doctor, they were going to have one hell of a fight on their hands.

"We've all been careful with Honor. Maybe too careful," Cynthia acknowledged. "But now we have to present a united front and give her no choice. Mandie and I are taking her to the doctor. I've already called the clinic, and they'll see her today."

"And you wanted us here for the extra muscle," Keith said wryly.

"No. For support," his mother corrected. "We love her

and I refuse to let her waste away into nothing. She may hate me, but at least she'll be alive to do it."

"I will never hate you, Mom," Honor said quietly from the doorway of the kitchen.

They had been so absorbed in their discussion and concern, they hadn't heard Honor enter the kitchen.

"I'm sorry I've worried you. All of you," she added, sweeping her glance over each family member, sorrow and apology bright in her eyes. "If going to the doctor will ease your worry, then I'll go. I'm sure it's just a stomach bug or something. After everything else I've had happen, this hasn't even registered on my radar," she said honestly.

Brad's features darkened into a mask of hatred at the mention of all his sister had suffered. He was the sheriff, sworn to uphold the law and seek justice. By the book. But by all that was holy, if he could have gotten his hands on the bastards who'd tortured Honor, he'd have killed them in cold blood and suffered absolutely no remorse.

"I'm going too," Mandie said, sliding her arm through Honor's and then offering her sister an affectionate squeeze. "No way I'd leave you to Mom's mercy alone. She can be ruthless. She'll probably have the poor doctor stammering his way through the exam."

Honor smiled. Mandie could defuse any situation with her wit and humor. It was one of the many reasons she loved her sister so dearly. She loved them all, and she realized, to her shame, that she wasn't the only one suffering. She'd been selfish and self-absorbed while her family were clearly at their wit's end.

"I *am* sorry," Honor said, sincerity ringing in her voice. "I didn't mean to be such a burden to you all and worry you so much. I've been selfish."

Her mom rounded the corner of the island and caught Honor in a fierce hug.

"You are *not* a burden. You are *not* selfish, and I won't have you saying so. You're our baby, Honor. The heart and soul of this entire family. Always the peacemaker, always the first one to smooth things over. The first to offer a hug. You've always known what everyone needs and given it without hesitation. You have the most generous heart of anyone I know. Of course we worry. Because of all people you didn't deserve what happened to you!"

Tears fell freely and Honor could no longer tell if it was her mother hugging her or Honor hugging her mother.

And then Brad gently pried them apart and enveloped Honor in his arms. Always the big brother. Her protector. She'd been his shadow since the day she learned to walk as a toddler, and he'd never minded, had never been too busy for his baby sister. How she loved them all. She'd missed her family. The closeness. The unconditional love of a tight-knit family unit.

"I'm angry," he said in a low voice against her ear. "I see shit every day and nothing compares to what was done to you. Goddamn it, you of all people didn't deserve this. You are everything that is good in this world, Honor. Not one of us could have done what you did. Give selflessly of yourself to help people no one else would help, knowing and accept-ing the risk, knowing it could mean your life. Burden? You are a *gift*, baby girl, and don't you ever forget it. I love you above all others. I always will. From the day you were born, I knew you were something special and that you would accomplish great things. I just never imagined the sacrifices you would have to make in order to answer your calling."

Honor's eyes watered, when she hadn't cried since the first time she'd come home to her parents. She knew they worried that she was in denial. That she wasn't dealing with her demons and only suppressing them. But the truth was, she was numb and grieving for what they knew nothing of. God, if only the torture and abuse were all she had to deal with. But she'd *never* get over Hancock and his betrayal. God help her, but she loved him still. After everything he'd done, the promises he'd broken, making love to her and making her believe he felt for her what she felt for him. She couldn't bring herself to truly hate him, and that made her angry. *Furious.*

"If we're going to make the appointment, then we need to get moving," her mother said briskly, wiping away her tears and slipping into mom mode. "I'll expect the guys to take care of dinner tonight since my daughters and I won't be back until late. They're working her in as the last appointment of the day."

Tate gave a lazy grin. "I think we can handle that."

TWO hours later, Honor walked numbly back into the waiting room where Mandie and her mother sat. Her mom hadn't been pleased that Honor had insisted on seeing the doctor alone and so wasn't privy to the doctor's diagnosis. But Honor knew that her mom would have harangued the doctor and they would *still* be in the exam room if Honor hadn't put her foot down and made her mother and sister wait outside.

Her mom and sister immediately picked up on Honor's somber, shocked demeanor, and they both bolted from their chairs and surrounded her immediately.

"Baby, what's wrong?" her mother demanded.

Honor held up a shaking hand. It was all she could do to keep what little control she had in check and not shatter in front of the entire waiting room.

"Please, not here," she whispered. "Please, let's just go home. I'll tell you everything there. But not here. *Please.*"

Her mom's mouth set into a mutinous line, but Mandie, sensing how dangerously close Honor was to breaking down, wrapped a supportive arm around Honor's waist and began walking out of the clinic and into the parking lot.

"You drive, Mom," Mandie said firmly. "I'll sit in the back with Honor."

Honor squeezed Mandie's hand when she slid into the backseat with Honor and offered her a silent thank-you that she knew held unshed tears.

Mandie squeezed back and then whispered as their mother started the engine, "Whatever it is, Honor, we're behind you. We'll get through it together. Don't worry. You're home now and you're never going to be away from us again."

Honor leaned into her sister, surprising her with her need for comfort. Honor had been distant with all her family, only giving them the affection *they* seemed to need but never seeking it out for herself.

Mandie hugged her tightly, meeting her mother's worried gaze in the rearview mirror. Cynthia, always a careful driver, broke every traffic law in her bid to get her daughter home as quickly as possible.

Her father and brothers would be waiting. While Cynthia had banned them from going, they'd been firm when they said they'd all be there when she returned. How could she face them with what she had to tell them? What she'd never told them. Now, they would have to know every shameful aspect of her ordeal.

They pulled into the drive and Honor quickly extricated herself from her sister's fierce hold and hurried inside. As she'd known, her father and brothers were in the living room, doing little to disguise their impatience and worry.

Mandie and her mother came in behind her, and her father and brothers looked expectantly at her. It was simply too much.

She burst into tears, to the horror of her brothers, especially Brad, and then she rushed by them, yanking open the door to the back deck. She fell back into the swing she'd always found comfort in growing up, and the tears flowed.

"What the hell is wrong, Cynthia?" Mike demanded, his gaze even now staring in the direction of where Honor had disappeared.

"I don't *know*," Cynthia said in frustration. "She didn't say anything. She looked like a ghost when she came back into the waiting room, and when I asked her what was wrong, she said, 'Not here.' She begged me not to talk about it there. She said she'd tell us when we got home."

"Let me go talk to her," Brad said in a low voice.

Brad had always had a close relationship with his youngest sister. He'd known from a very young age that she was special. Different. Tenderhearted and good. Never having a bad thing to say about anyone, and she would do anything for anyone in need.

He'd been the strongest objector to her going to the Middle East, but he'd also understood her drive. But he hadn't wanted her there. He wanted her here where he could protect her. Where no harm could come to her. And the very thing he'd feared the worst had come to pass.

But she was alive. She was their miracle. But now she was hurting and had retreated even from her family when she'd never been anything but honest and open. Whatever was wrong was worse than what she'd already confided in him, and *that* terrified him. What could possibly be worse than what she'd endured? He faced horrific circumstances in his job as a cop, but he was always able to shake fear's hold on him. Now? Fear gripped him, paralyzing him. It choked him until he could barely breathe.

Not waiting for anyone to object, he turned and followed Honor's path to the back porch, and when he stepped out, hearing and seeing her sobbing as if her heart were breaking—had already broken—emotion knotted his throat and he struggled to keep his own tears at bay. Because Honor needed his strength. Now more than ever.

Quietly so as not to startle her, he eased into the swing beside her and tucked her fragile body against his side.

"What's wrong, baby girl?" he asked in a gentle tone. "You know you can talk to me about anything. Whatever is wrong, we'll fix it."

"I can't fix this," she said, sorrow thick in her voice. "No one can. I'm pregnant, Brad. Oh God, I'm *pregnant*."

He sucked in his breath, his expression stricken at first and then murderous. "You didn't tell us . . . I mean, you didn't tell us much at all. Just the pain and torture. You didn't say you'd been *raped*."

Grief simmered in his eyes and he leaned over, pulling her into his arms, holding her and rocking her back and forth, his body trembling with sorrow.

She burrowed into his arms, soaking up his strength and love. Always her big brother and protector.

"I wasn't raped," she whispered. "Some tried but the man . . . the man who is the father of my child protected me. He made sure they didn't rape me. But . . . he betrayed me. I *trusted* him. He told me he was taking me home, that I would be safe and that he would be with me all the way. But then he drugged me and turned me over to Maksimov and I don't understand *why*. Why deceive me? Why make me think he cared? Why seduce me and tell me he would get me back to my family and then drug me? I woke up a prisoner of a man who tried to rape me twice. And then he turned me over to a man who tortured me. Shocked me. Beat me. He wanted to break me, but I was already broken. Hancock did that. No one else.

"Until then I was strong. I refused to give up. I fought, and I wasn't going down without a fight. But when he betrayed me, I gave up. I no longer had anything to fight for. I didn't care. I had nothing to live for, and I never wanted my family to see me so weak and shattered."

"Oh, honey," her brother said in an aching voice muffled by her hair. "I'm so sorry for all you went through. Are still going through," he amended. He kissed the top of her head and simply held her for several long moments, allowing silence to descend as her sobbing quieted. He gave the swing a gentle push with his foot every now and again, soothing her. Not pressuring her to say more than she was willing. Just waiting for her to talk to him in her own time. Though secretly he wanted to track down the damn Marine that had returned Honor and grill him about this Hancock guy. In particular, where Brad could find him. And then he wanted to exact some old school justice that would forever ban him from a law enforcement career.

It would be worth it.

He sighed as he stroked her back. "I know this is a shock. And I know you've been through the unthinkable. But you have options, honey. If having this baby hurts you, is a constant reminder of pain and betrayal, you can terminate the pregnancy. You can give it up for adoption. You can do whatever is best for *you*. Do you understand that? For *once*, think of yourself. There's no crime in that. Especially with all you've endured. No one would blame you. No one would condemn you."

"No!" she said fiercely. "This child is innocent. This baby did *nothing* wrong and I refuse to be so selfish as to refuse to have it because it brings back painful memories. This child—*my* child—deserves life and I won't give it up. I'll go away. I don't want to shame you and the rest of my family. None of you deserve that."

"The hell you will," Brad said savagely. "You need your family now more than ever, and if you think for one moment that we will allow you to leave because you don't want to shame us, then you're out of your goddamn mind. Never has there been a more courageous, giving woman than you, and I'll be damned if you bear this alone. Your family will be with you every step of the way. *I* will be with you every step of the way. Shame us? Never has a family had more reason to be proud of a daughter and sister than we do. And I don't give a damn what others think or say. I'll stand behind you and my niece or nephew all the way and fuck anyone who has *anything* to say about it."

"Your brother is right," her father said from behind them.

Honor turned and bowed her head when she realized the entire family had followed Brad to the back porch and had heard every damning word.

"You will not bow your head as though you have some-thing to be ashamed of," her mother said fiercely. "You were a victim. This is not your fault. This is not your doing. And by God, we will *all* be with you every step of the way."

Honor lifted her gaze to see the same determination in every family member's eyes. And she burst into tears all over again.

Mandie walked forward, taking the only other seat on the other side of Honor so that Honor was sandwiched between her and Brad.

"Will you tell us about it now, Honor? We've known that you've been holding back. That something hurt you terribly, but you've refused to speak of it. You can only go so long before you break."

"I'm already broken," Honor said bleakly.

Brad cupped her chin, forcing her gaze to his. "The hell you are. You're one of the strongest women I've ever known. You may be down but you aren't out. Not by a long shot. And if you'll let us help you, if you'll confide in us, we can help you. You can't keep this bottled up any longer. Lean

on us, honey. That's what family is for. You'd do the same
for us and you know it. You'd never accept silence from one
of us if you knew we were hurting, and we're damn sure not
going to accept it from you. I believe in you, Honor. Even
if you don't believe in yourself right now."

She leaned into him, hugging him, wrapping herself
completely around him, holding on for dear life. She
squeezed her eyes shut as more tears streamed soundlessly
down her cheeks. Her muffled "I love you" was returned
gruffly by Brad.

And then she told them every single part that she'd left out.
About her falling in love with Hancock and his promise, after
making love to her, that he'd find another way. That he wouldn't
sacrifice her for the greater good. And that he'd lied and how
that, not anything else done to her, had destroyed her.

When she was finished, she was exhausted and nause-
ated. Her family was furious, their rage evident in their eyes,
their expressions and their words.

But they surrounded her with their love and unconditional support. Plans were made. OB visits were divided up
so that one of her family would always be there with her.
Her father immediately began planning an addition to Hon-
or's bedroom so the baby would have a nursery but always
be close enough that Honor could hear the infant.

Honor's hands slipped down over her belly to the slight
bump there she'd assumed was a result of her gaining back
badly needed weight after she had nearly starved herself.
According to the doctor, she was right at four months along.
How could she not have known until now?

Looking back, all the signs and symptoms were there.
Overwhelming fatigue, nausea, tenderness in her breasts
and being overly emotional. But after what she'd been
through, how could she have thought it could be anything
but the fallout from that?

In some strange way, she welcomed the thought of having
Hancock's child. A piece of him that would live on through
her. The very best part of them both. And if it was a boy,
she would raise his child to be the man Hancock *wanted* to
be but thought he could never be. He would have Hancock's

drive to protect others, and he would have his mother's strength and courage.

If it was a girl, she'd have the thread of steel that infused Hancock's will and his determination for justice. And Honor would teach her to never undervalue herself. To follow her heart and her dreams and to never avoid the road less traveled.

She would cherish this child as the gift it was. Her only regret was that Hancock would never know his child and never know that he was capable of loving and protecting and that he would never hurt what belonged to him.

His child was his blood. Honor wasn't. While he could sacrifice Honor for his mission, she knew that he'd never sacrifice his own flesh and blood.

CHAPTER 44

HONOR'S mother appeared on the back porch, a frown on her face. "There's a man here to see you. He says it's important."

Honor glanced up, trepidation skittering up her spine. But no, she had no reason to fear. Her family was here. Nothing would happen to her.

"Show him back here," Honor said in a low voice. "And please. Give us privacy until I know what it is he has to say."

Her mother looked as though she'd argue, but resolve was centered in Honor's eyes and so, tight-lipped, her mother nodded and disappeared, leaving Honor to wait and worry over her unexpected visitor.

A few moments later, the door opened and for a moment she refused to look up. Then she swallowed, refusing to be the coward she'd been for so long, and she lifted her gaze, shock hitting her like a bolt of lightning.

"Conrad?"

He nodded grimly.

"We will be just inside," her mother said, more to Conrad than to Honor. It was a clear warning, one that brought a small smile to Conrad's lips.

"I have no intention of hurting your daughter, Mrs. Cambridge," Conrad said gently. "But I would like to speak to her privately."

Cynthia nodded and reluctantly withdrew, though Honor knew the entire family would be gathered just inside the doorway, watching them the entire time.

"You look like hell," he said bluntly as he took a seat across from the swing Honor occupied.

"I could say the same for you," she said dryly.

"Touché," he said wryly. "But *you* concern me, Honor. You don't look well at all."

She arched one eyebrow. "Why are you here, Conrad?"

"I came for many reasons," he said. "I came to thank you for saving my life. I came to apologize for failing you. But the most important reason I came is to tell you that Hancock did *not* betray you, Honor."

She stiffened, her gaze becoming hard and impenetrable. "I have no desire to talk about Hancock. If that's all you've come to talk about, you can leave now."

Conrad's expression became as hard and as determined as hers. He leaned forward, his features savage.

"I will not leave until I say what I have to say. What you do with what I have to tell you is solely up to you, but I *will* tell you what really happened."

Honor closed her eyes as grief consumed her all over again. In the weeks since she'd discovered she was pregnant with Hancock's child, she'd worked so hard to put Hancock and his betrayal behind her. To look forward, not back. To concentrate on the tiny, innocent life inside her that she'd protect with her dying breath.

"Say what you have to say, then," she said hoarsely. "Then get out."

"You know he changed the plan. That we stayed up all night planning an alternative. And then he drugged you and he hated it. He loathed himself for what he knew he must do. For two reasons: One, Maksimov ordered you drugged and we were forced to carry out the charade. And two, if you were conscious, there was no way Maksimov would see what we needed him to see. You're too honest, Honor. There is no way when Maksimov looked at you he would've seen the terrified, beaten down, and broken captive that he'd expected. He'd've seen the courageous, defiant woman who'd spit in his eye before ever allowing him to intimidate her."

"Which he did," Honor pointed out. "I'd call that a waste of a good night's sleep."

Conrad shook his head. "You don't understand. He *couldn't* tell you the plan. God, he wanted to. He hated the idea of deceiving you when you'd given him your trust. When he'd vowed not to betray your trust. But too much was riding on you *not* knowing. You had to have no knowledge or it could compromise the entire mission and it could get us all killed. And Hancock made it clear that you were the sole priority. That even if it meant letting Maksimov get away, you were to be protected at all costs."

Honor sent him a puzzled look because she didn't understand any of it.

"We planned an ambush. The original plan, you see, was to turn you over to Maksimov as a way of gaining access to him. To finally be part of his inner circle after years of working through middlemen like Bristow. He would turn you over to ANE while we worked to systematically dismantle his entire operation from the inside. Every player, every source of crime. We wanted his entire network destroyed, and then we were going to take him out. And that was going to take time. A lot of time. You would have been dead by ANE's hands before we completed our destruction of Maksimov's entire organization.

"But Hancock decided against that. Bristow set up the exchange and Maksimov dictated the terms, but we planned an ambush. We were only going to get close enough to take Maksimov out and then get you the hell out of there no matter what it took. He didn't care that the connections would still be there, that someone else would simply pick up the reins of Maksimov's empire. He only wanted him taken out and you safe and then he was going to walk away. With you. And let someone else take on the task of taking down Maksimov's vast empire."

"Then how . . . ?"

Her brow furrowed, not understanding any of it. She'd awakened in a cage, Maksimov taunting her. He'd tortured her for *days*. And then she'd awakened on a plane with Hancock, who was taking her to ANE.

"Maksimov obviously had more than one mole planted in Bristow's organization. We took out the one we were able to ferret out. And he would have reported Hancock losing his shit and killing Bristow when he tried to rape you. So he ambushed us instead of the other way around. We lost Mojo," Conrad said painfully. "Viper and Cope were both badly injured and Hancock was shot twice. He nearly died and even then, Maksimov had to *pry* you from his grasp. Hancock called in every favor ever owed to him from an organization where much bad blood exists. We aren't direct enemies, but neither are we allies. Hancock didn't care. He had no pride when it came to you. He begged them to help him find and save you. He tortured himself endlessly, knowing you were in Maksimov's hands, and there wasn't a damn thing he could do about it. He blamed himself. He *believes* he betrayed you. That he failed you. Every single thing you believe of him, he believes it too. But he *didn't* betray you, Honor. The mission was FUBAR. We lost much and yet he wouldn't stand down when he desperately needed to be in a damn hospital."

Honor shook her head in bewilderment. "I don't understand." It seemed it was all she was capable of saying. It was too much to take in, to have what she'd believed and grieved over for months change in seconds.

"He loves you, Honor," Conrad said gently. "Hancock hasn't ever loved anyone in his life except his foster family. He's never *been* loved by anyone except his foster family. He's never felt he *deserved* to be loved. He believes himself to be a monster. He believes himself to be *worse* than Maksimov. He's dying with every passing day. He's grieving, tormenting himself, loving you and yet knowing he's not worthy of you, that he doesn't deserve you. He let you down. He betrayed you. He allowed Maksimov to hurt you and he will *never* forgive himself for that."

"Why are you telling me all this?" she whispered.

"Because I believe you're hurting just as much as he is. I believe you love him as much as he loves you. I believe you're *both* dying and that you've given up. And I know you're the only one who can save him. I couldn't allow you to believe what he wouldn't even defend himself against, because he believes it all. That he betrayed you. Let you down. Hurt you. Manipulated you. Lied to you. But Honor, you didn't see him when he told us the mission had changed. You didn't see the determination in his eyes when he told us that *you* were the sole priority, that your safety took precedence above all else. He didn't give one fuck about the mission or whether he was successful in taking Maksimov down. He tried to do the honorable thing and spare you but still take out a serious threat to thousands of innocent lives. And he lost *everything* as a result."

Tears spilled down Honor's cheeks and she hugged herself, rocking back and forth in the swing.

"Why didn't he explain? On the plane. After he'd freed me from Maksimov. Why did he let me believe he was delivering me to ANE? Why didn't he at least try?"

"Because you believed it. You weren't there, Honor. You were a million miles away and you wouldn't have heard a word he had to say. And it's hard to defend or explain when you feel that you *are* guilty of every single sin you accused him of. He didn't defend himself because he knew he was guilty of the crimes committed against you. And he loves you as much as he hates himself."

"Where is he?" she demanded.

Conrad closed his eyes. "I don't know. He disappeared after Maksimov and ANE were taken down. Titan is no more. We all walked away. We're done. He's a lone wolf, Honor. He's gone off somewhere to die a slow, painful death because he can't live with what he did to you. But I know this much. He loves you with every breath in his body. I've worked with him, followed him, been loyal to him for over a decade. And before you, every single characteristic attributed to him was true. He was more machine than man. No emotion. He had his own code and he lived by it. The greater good. And sometimes that means sacrificing innocents. He hated it, but knew it was a necessary evil.

"But you changed everything. You changed *him*. Suddenly he *wanted* to be the man you saw when you looked at him. He wanted to be better. For you. You showed him how to love. How to feel. How to be human. And he'll never love again. He'll love you forever just as he'll hate himself for eternity for what he did to you."

"Then how can I find him?" she asked in frustration. "Damn it, Conrad, you can't come here and tell me all this and then walk away without giving me *something*. I won't let him do this to himself. I won't. I *love* him. Do you have any idea how much it hurt when I believed that he'd used me, that he'd betrayed me and allowed Maksimov to torture me?"

Conrad's eyes were haunted. "I failed you too, Honor. Not just Hancock. We all failed you."

"Bullshit," she said angrily.

Sorrow swamped her eyes. "I'm so sorry about Mojo. He was a good man. He didn't deserve to die because of me. Because Hancock changed the mission. Are Viper and Cope okay now?" she asked anxiously.

Conrad smiled gently, reaching for her hand to give it a light squeeze. "Always worried for others. You are a remarkable woman, Honor. My life is better for having known you. And if you can save Hancock, you will have my eternal gratitude. Yes, Mojo was a good man, but he died peacefully. He was given redemption, something none of us ever dreamed we would be given. And Viper and Cope are fine. I don't know where Hancock is, I swear it. But I can point you in the direction of people who might know or at the very least can help you find him."

She leaned forward eagerly. "Tell me."

"I'll bring you there myself," he said. "I won't send you off without protection. And it's not far at all. Dover, Tennessee, just a few miles south of the Kentucky border. How soon can you be ready?"

She was already rising from the swing. "Give me five minutes."

Conrad smiled to himself as he watched her stalk away, her eyes fierce with purpose. The dull, lifeless look that clung to her like a second skin had evaporated and she looked like the Honor he'd first met. Full of fight and fire. Courage and bravery.

If anyone was going to save Hancock, it was going to be her. He almost pitied the man. Almost. Because he was never going to know what hit him when Honor Cambridge ran him to ground.

CHAPTER 45

HONOR'S family made it clear that she was going nowhere with a man they didn't know, and she damn sure wasn't going alone with Conrad. Brad insisted on accompanying her, and Conrad and she were equally insistent she was going alone.

An argument broke out, and every single member of Honor's family refused to allow her to leave without them.

"This is something I have to do," Honor said quietly.

"I realize you don't know me and have no reason to trust me," Conrad said in a calm voice. "But I will protect Honor with my *life*. You have my word. And where we're going, there is no danger to her. She will have an entire army of men surrounding her at all times. This is important to your daughter. She needs to heal, and that is exactly what I mean to make happen. If you love her, and I know you do, and if you trust her, which I know you do, then let her do this. She needs this if she's ever going to come back whole."

"I don't have much time," Honor said impatiently. "Trust in me to know what I'm doing. I'll keep in touch. Conrad will keep you informed. But I have to do this if I'm going to survive."

There were shocked and worried expressions on every one of her family's faces, but also resignation, much as there had been when she'd been so determined to go to the Middle East to help those in such desperate need.

They all gathered around her, hugging her, tears shed as they kissed her and told her they loved her. And then Brad leveled a hard stare at Conrad.

"I know your kind. I know the things you do in the name of justice. I'm not judging you. But you protect my sister. You keep her safe and if things go bad, you get her out. I don't care what she wants or says. You get her back home where she belongs."

Conrad came to attention, a signal of respect for the lawman.

"I'd give my life for her," he said truthfully. "She saved my life, and I repay my debts. I swear to you that she will be safe with me."

Honor gave each of her family one last hug, and then she urged Conrad out of the house so they could be on their way.

"How far is it? Are we driving or flying?"

"We'll fly. KGI has a private landing strip in their compound and it's secure. It's not only the fastest way, but also the safest."

Relief staggered her. Now that she knew, every minute was agony. Every moment apart from Hancock seemed an eternity.

HONOR swallowed nervously as one of the men who'd met them at the landing strip and driven them to the "war room" punched in the access code and the doors slid open with speed that made her blink.

She'd purposely worn baggy, oversized clothing because at approaching five months pregnant, her pooch had developed into a tight ball. But all the weight loss and starving she'd done was in reality making her pregnancy look like her regaining her normal weight and size.

Besides, she wanted Hancock to want *her*. She wanted him to love her independent of anything else. And she knew, regardless of whether he loved her or not, whether he wanted her or not, he'd never turn her away if she was pregnant with his child.

It wasn't in her nature to deceive, but she refused to manipulate him or force him to make a decision he wouldn't have ordinarily made by revealing she was pregnant until she knew the outcome of her come-to-Jesus meeting with Hancock.

As soon as she was herded into the main area, she could see that apparently everyone who worked for KGI had turned up for the occasion. It only took one person to tell her how to find Hancock. Not a room packed full of kick-ass operatives.

Anger suddenly gripped her. She was tired of being endlessly intimidated by soldiers, mercenaries, terrorists, assholes, whatever. If they thought to intimidate her they could all kiss her ass.

She narrowed her eyes and stepped from behind Conrad's protective position.

"Look, is it that all twenty or so of you all know where Hancock is, or are you just fucking with me and trying to intimidate me? Because if this is all you've got, bring it on."

She was greeted by broad smiles, some outright laughter, and she could swear she heard a female voice saying, "You go, girl."

One of the men stepped forward with a smile. He had muddy blond hair and the clearest blue eyes she'd ever seen. He extended his hand and she had no choice but to reluctantly take it.

"Miss Cambridge, it's an honor to see you again. I'm Sam Kelly."

She looked at him, faintly puzzled, but then realized he would have been on the mission to rescue her from Maksimov. Which meant that she was facing an entire room of people who'd seen the way she was when they'd gotten her out.

Her back went up. She refused to feel shame for that. She was going to stop feeling humiliated about things she had no control over, and she was going to stop being so easily intimidated and stop acting like a timid freaking mouse. Maybe she could take lessons from the only two female members of KGI. They certainly didn't look like scared mice.

"Who can tell me where to find Hancock?" she demanded, donning her most ferocious look. The one Brad told her made her look like a really cute kitten hissing for the first time.

She pulled at her hair in exasperation, not even waiting for an answer.

"What is with men making arbitrary decisions, thinking they know all the answers to the universe? What is with them torturing themselves because they think they've betrayed or hurt someone, and yeah, while it might look to the person that they'd been screwed over, the man knows it but doesn't bother to *explain* because *he* believes he *is* guilty of betraying her and hurting her. So he goes off in some giant manhurt and broods and sulks and God only knows what else men like you do," she said with a sniff of disdain. "But I know what Hancock *isn't* going to do, and so help me if one of you doesn't cough up some information fast, you are *not* going to like the results."

The others had watched her with open mouths in obvious befuddlement, but by the time she got to the end of her tirade, they started laughing until tears rolled down their faces. She was furious with them for laughing like hyenas when her life was on the line. Her future. Her child's future. And Hancock's.

Garrett wheezed. "Oh God, he's never going to live this down. I'll torture that bastard the rest of his life over this. How priceless is this?"

Honor gritted her teeth and stalked over to get right into the big man's face. She nearly mowed him over, and would have, but his back bumped against the wall, effectively trapping him.

"What is *wrong* with you, laughing at a time like this? You're being a complete asshole."

Garrett gave her a meek look. "I'm sorry, ma'am. I meant no disrespect." He rapidly looked at his teammates, begging for help. They just laughed even harder.

Honor threw her hands up. "This is pointless. I wasted an entire day by coming here. Fine. I'll find him myself. No thanks to you."

She stalked past them all, Conrad falling in behind her, as she headed for the door. Sam caught her arm and gently halted her, his eyes still full of mirth, but he made a concerted effort to be serious and sincere.

"We honestly don't know where Hancock is, but I just might know someone who can help. Give me two seconds to make that call?"

She studied him a moment, saw that he was all business now. Finally someone with some damn sense. She nodded.

Sam picked up the phone and punched one digit, obviously a contact.

"Eden, honey? This is Sam. I need you to come to the war room as soon as possible. Can you do that? It's important."

There was a brief pause and Sam smiled. "Thanks, Eden. You're the best."

"Joe, step out and meet Eden so she won't feel awkward coming to the war room," Sam instructed.

Donovan glanced at the surveillance cameras that gave viewpoints of over thirty areas. He grinned. "No need. Swanny's with her and he doesn't looked pleased that he wasn't included in the invite."

"God save us from newlyweds," Joe said in disgust.

Everyone in the room shot him knowing grins from all directions.

"Oh your time is coming, baby brother," Garrett said smugly. "And I predict you're going to fall harder than all of us put together."

Joe lifted his middle finger amid laughter from everyone else.

P.J. and Skylar, the two female members of KGI, had made their way to where Honor stood, either out of solidarity so she wasn't surrounded by so much testosterone or because they were simply being nice.

"How are you doing, Honor?" P.J. asked quietly. "Really."

There was something in this woman's eyes that told Honor she'd seen and endured horrific things and that she knew what Honor was going through and had gone through.

She smiled, though it felt more like a grimace. "In the beginning, not so good. But now . . . I'm hopeful. If I can get a certain arrogant male to pull his head out of his ass, things will be great."

Skylar hooted with laughter, drawing suspicious stares from her male teammates. She just gave them an innocent smile that in no way allayed the nervousness in their eyes.

P.J. still regarded Honor seriously. "No matter how it goes, what happens, whether you're able to make Hancock see reason, that man loves you. Every person in this room can tell you how much he loves you. Hancock is a hard man. No one here would have thought he was capable of loving *anyone*, but over time, we began to see bits and pieces of humanity and we realized that Hancock was a product of his training, and he's lethal, but he has a heart. He's a good man, Honor."

Honor smiled. "I know. And thank you." She touched the other woman's hand. "That meant a lot to me. And I'm glad I'm not the only one who sees past the facade."

The door opened and Honor's heart jumped when an absolutely stunning, tall blond woman walked gracefully inside, flanked by a man a few inches taller than her with heavily scarred features and a muscled body that rivaled that of any of the males already in the compound.

Eden's eyes widened when she saw that all of KGI was assembled, and she glanced fearfully at the man at her side, who Honor assumed was her husband. He pulled her into his side and pressed a kiss to her temple.

"It's okay, honey," he reassured.

Sam walked over and gave Eden a warm hug. "Thank you for coming so quickly. There is someone here who is very anxious to run Hancock to ground, and we wondered if you could be of any help to her?"

Eden's brow scrunched in confusion, but before she could scan the room for the source of the "she" who needed her help, Sam pulled her to the side and spoke to her in low tones that didn't carry to the others.

At first Eden looked stricken. Then tears glittered brightly in her unusually colored eyes and then she smiled, relief so stark in her expression that Honor wondered what on earth Sam was saying to her.

When Sam started to lead Eden to where Honor still

stood, Eden flew around him and then threw her arms around a stunned Honor. Eden hugged her fiercely and a shudder of emotion quaked through the woman's body as she clung to Honor.

When she finally pulled away, she was smiling broadly, a sheen of tears in her eyes. Honor looked at her in complete bewilderment when Eden took both Honor's hands in hers and held on nearly as tightly as she'd hugged her.

"You have no idea how long I've prayed for this day," Eden said, emotion thick in her voice. "Guy was so lost as a young boy. My mother and father took him in. He was every bit as much their son as my two older brothers, Raid and Ryker. My family is the only family Guy has ever known."

She turned and beamed at the rest of KGI, and they all groaned. She turned back to Honor, a smug smile on her face.

"They're just pissed because Guy is my family and now KGI is my family, which makes Guy and KGI family. A fact that neither are particularly thrilled about. But they'll get over it," she said cheerfully. "Especially now that you're here. You're going to change Guy's life."

"She's already changed it," Conrad said, speaking up for the first time.

The other members of KGI scowled at Conrad as if only just remembering he'd accompanied Honor. Honor scowled just as fiercely at them.

"Don't you *ever* look at him like that. He's *my* family and Guy is going to be my family, which will make Eden family and by proxy you as well. Therefore Conrad is now also your family."

Conrad looked poleaxed. His look of astonishment was comical. KGI just chuckled, and she heard mutters about women ruling the world.

"I know you're in a hurry, so I won't delay you any longer," Eden said to Honor. "Guy is at my father's house with my two brothers, and according to them, he's been in such a black mood ever since he arrived that they're ready to murder him in his sleep."

Honor looked to Sam, her heart in her throat, and his entire gaze softened.

"Will you take me to him?" she asked hesitantly.

Sam closed the short distance between them and enfolded her in a hug. "Of course, sweetheart. Just as soon as the jet can be fueled and ready to go."

Then he turned and grinned at his brothers. "So who wants to go witness the greatest takedown ever known to mankind?"

A chorus of whoops, *hooyah*s and *oorah*s exploded through the room, and Honor looked at Sam with even more bewilderment. Were they all crazy?

He smiled. "Don't mind us. We've waited a long damn time for Hancock to prove he's goddamn human after all."

He turned to Eden. "Call your father, honey, and tell him to sit on Hancock and not to let him out of his sight until we get there."

Then he barked a series of orders so they could be in the air in no more than a half an hour.

BIG Eddie Sinclair got off the phone and turned to his sons, Raid and Ryker.

"That was Eden," he said in a puzzled voice. "She wants us to sit on Hancock and make sure he goes absolutely nowhere until she gets here. She says she has the cure for what ails him."

"Well, thank fuck someone does," Raid said darkly. "I've had all the self-loathing and pity a man can take."

"A-fucking-men," Ryker said in a fervent voice.

CHAPTER 46

EDEN led the way to the front door of her family's home. It was a good thing dusk had fallen, because there was no way they wouldn't have drawn attention with over twenty badass operatives trailing Honor, Eden and Swanny, who never left his wife's side.

The door opened before Eden could even knock, and standing in the doorway was a man Honor assumed was her father and her two older brothers. Guy's family.

The three men's gaze swept from Swanny to Eden and then finally settled on Honor, shock reflecting in their eyes.

The older brother shook his head. "No way," he murmured.

"No fucking way," his younger brother agreed.

Eden's father smiled when before his features had been etched with worry and grief. He suddenly looked younger, the deep grooves easing as he stared at Honor.

"Well, I'll be damned," he said in an awed tone. "Never thought I'd see the day."

It just pissed Honor off and she put both hands on her hips, glaring down the male members of Eden's family.

"What is *wrong* with you people? Treating Guy like he's not human or capable of humanity. I don't know which is worse. Him believing himself to be lacking a soul or his family believing it."

Eden's brothers burst into laughter, but her father's entire grizzled face softened. He took the two steps toward Honor and pulled her into a bone-crushing hug that had her holding back. She might have disguised her pregnancy well, but a hug that hard would reveal the taut baby bump she carried.

"Welcome to the family, my dear. We've waited a very long time for someone like you to turn Hancock's world upside down. My name is Eddie and these are my sons, Raid and Ryker." He pointed to indicate who was who.

And then as if just noticing the horde of burly men standing several feet behind Eden, Swanny and Honor, Eden's father gave his daughter an inquisitive look.

"Eden? Who are all these people in my front yard?"

"Oh, they're here to witness Guy's downfall," Eden said cheerfully. "It's dark so you can't see them, but they're KGI."

"Nathan? Joe?" Ryker asked as he stepped in front of his dad to see who all had accompanied Eden and Honor.

Eddie's face lightened in recognition as he saw the rest of his son-in-law's team step forward to greet the Sinclairs.

Skylar was forcibly hugged by Eddie and Ryker while Zane exchanged handshakes with the men.

"It's good to see you, sir," Joe spoke up. "As for why the entire KGI organization is here? There was no way in hell we were going to pass up the opportunity to witness Hancock brought to his knees by a woman barely over five feet. We intend to make sure he never lives it down. Not even Steele provided this much entertainment when he got his balls served on a platter to him by his wife."

"Fuck you," Steele said rudely from the shadows he hadn't yet emerged from.

"Hello?" Honor growled, impatience and frustration evident in her voice. *"Where is he?"*

"I'll be more than happy to take him to you myself," Raid said smugly.

"Well, come on in," Eddie said to the large group assembled. "I suppose we'll see the two of them eventually. We'll be much more comfortable in the living room."

Leaving the others, Raid led her up the stairs and down

a long hallway to the room at the very end. He paused and then looked down at her, his expression utterly serious.

"If you can bring him back to us, you will forever be in my debt. He's given up, Honor. He has absolutely no will to live, and he's in so much pain that I can't even bear to look at my own brother."

"Oh, he's coming back," she vowed. "If I have to knock him out, tie him up and drag him back home, I'm not leaving here without him."

Raid chuckled and leaned down to kiss her brow. "You know what? I believe you, little sister." Then his expression became serious again. "Do you want me to go in first?"

She rolled her eyes. "Guy would never hurt me. You should be worried I'll hurt *him*. But, no. This is private. I don't want anyone in there but me and him."

Raid nodded and started back down the hall. She waited for him to disappear before she turned back to Guy's door. Her hand hovered over the knob, afraid the door would be locked and he'd refuse to let her in. Then she shook her head. There were over twenty people downstairs who could easily break down the door. One way or another she was going in.

To her relief, when she quietly twisted the knob, it was unlocked and the door opened a fraction. Still, she hesitated, because for all her bravado and determination, she was terrified he wouldn't even look at her. Acknowledge her. Listen to her.

From inside came an irritated growl. "I said to leave me the fuck alone. What don't you interfering assholes understand about that?"

Honor shoved open the door all the way, stomping into the bedroom, her hands on her hips. When Hancock saw her he nearly fell off the bed. He scrambled to sit up, his face drawn with shock. And then so much grief and regret and self-loathing replaced his initial shock and it nearly brought her to her knees.

In that moment she knew she would have to be the strong one. She couldn't allow an ounce of past hurts in her eyes, because it would destroy him and he'd never listen to her. He'd never *hear* her. He'd drive her away, convinced that he'd only hurt her again and again. At least one of them had sense, and it wasn't him at the moment.

So instead of throwing herself into his arms like she ached to do and cry for all that had been lost and how much she loved him, she was going to have to dish out some tough love.

"Is that any way to speak to your family?" she demanded, her foot tapping on the floor in reprimand.

"Honor?"

His voice was shaken, so hoarse that her name was nearly indecipherable, his eyes ravaged by grief and pain. So much hurt that her throat closed up on her, rendering her momentarily unable to speak. She forgot all about tough love and being the bitch.

She couldn't stand the distance between them any longer, and she flung herself at his body so he had no choice but to catch her or be bowled over by her. Her hands came to rest on his cheeks as she stared down at the stirrings of hope in Guy's eyes. He swallowed and then looked away, as if refusing to even entertain such an emotion, but she wouldn't have it. She too had refused herself hope, and she'd been wrong. She should have fought, like she was prepared to fight now. It was a battle she couldn't lose or it would destroy her. She *wouldn't* lose.

She firmly guided his face back to hers and simply stared him down until he finally, reluctantly lifted his eyes and met her gaze.

"Yes, it's me," she said in a husky voice. "And I have to tell you, Guy Hancock, I am not very happy with you right now."

"Why *should* you be?" he asked in a pained voice.

She made a sound of exasperation. "You didn't betray me, and we both know it. Or you should. If you weren't so bent on convincing yourself that you're this horrible monster, you'd realize you did *not* betray me."

"How could you possibly think I didn't?" he asked incredulously.

She rolled her eyes. "Well of course in the beginning I thought just that. But, gee, if someone had troubled himself to tell me what really happened when you let me believe you were flying me to give me to ANE—something else I'm extremely pissed about, by the way—neither of us would have suffered for the last several months."

"I lied to you. I drugged you, something I swore I would never do again. And I failed you, Honor. I let that bastard get to you and he tortured you for *days* before I could find you."

"Did it ever occur to you even once to tell me what happened and allow *me* the luxury of deciding whether you betrayed me or not? Instead, you played judge and jury *for* me. You were so convinced that you had done exactly those things that you decided for *me* that I was never going to know. That is the *only* thing I'm angry with you over. Well, not even angry, but hurt. You hurt me, Guy," she said painfully. "For five long months I hurt. I couldn't sleep, couldn't eat. It's the God's truth, I wanted to die. I gave up. I didn't want to live without you. Can't you understand that?"

Her voice was pleading. Precariously close to begging, but God, she had no pride whatsoever when it came to this man. She'd crawl if she had to. Anything to make him come back to her. To love her as much as she loved him.

He stared at her with those haunted eyes, and he clearly had no idea how to respond. He was so assured of his guilt that no, it hadn't occurred to him to give *her* the choice of judgment.

He simply ran his hands over her face, her lips, her neck, shoulders, over and over as if he really didn't believe she was here.

"You hate me," he whispered in a tortured voice. "God, I hate *myself*."

"Look at me, Guy," she said tenderly. *"See me."*

He stared into her eyes for what seemed an eternity before it seemed to register with him. There was no hatred there. No fear. No sense of betrayal or hurt. Only love. And tenderness, compassion and a vow to always protect him. That he'd always be safe with her. His heart would always be safe with her.

"I don't hate you. I *love* you," she whispered fiercely. "I love you. And you don't get to decide for me. You don't get to tell me that I don't love you. There is *nothing* you can do to make me not love you."

Thin rivulets trickled down his cheeks. His nostrils flared with every inhale as if he fought a vicious battle for control, not to completely break down.

She framed his beloved face in her palms and looked directly into his eyes.

"Now, listen to me, Guy, because this is important. It's *everything*. Do not interrupt me until I am finished. Do you understand?"

He gave a chopped nod, and she pondered whether her telling him not to interrupt was even necessary. He wasn't capable of saying a thing at the moment. He was simply too overcome.

"Now, if you walked away from me because you don't want me and you don't love me, then I have to accept that."

He made a strangled noise in his throat, and she shot him a warning look, reminding him of his promise. But he didn't look happy at all. He looked pissed, fire blazing in his eyes.

Good, she thought savagely. She'd take his anger and rage over the soulless look in his eyes any day of the week.

"However, if you walked away from me because you thought I hated you, because you truly believed you betrayed me, lied to me and felt you weren't worthy of me, then I *won't* accept that," she said fiercely. "Because it's bullshit. It's all bullshit. And I will not throw away the best thing in my life because he's decided he's committed an unpardonable sin against someone who has already forgiven him."

"Are you finished?" he demanded.

She nodded.

"Good. Because I fucking love you more than I've ever loved another human being in my *life*. You aren't just the world, Honor Cambridge. You're *my* world. My entire reason for living. Walk away from you because I don't want you or love you? I walked away because you deserve *better* than me. Because you deserve a man who won't fail to protect you and allow you to be nearly raped and then tortured. And I'm not that man," he said in a savage voice.

"Yes," she said calmly. "You are."

Despair crept once more into his eyes.

"You have no idea what kind of life you'd have to live if you were with me. Because of the fact that I've accumulated more enemies over the years than the very monsters I've worked to take down, you would always be a target. You are my greatest weakness, and everyone in the goddamn world would know it and try to hurt me by getting to you. And they would hurt you. They've already hurt you," he said in a tortured voice. "And I couldn't bear it, Honor. I couldn't live with myself if I lost you."

"I'm glad you're such a badass then," she said lightly. "You'll never, never let anyone hurt me."

Guy closed his eyes, his fingers clenching into tight balls.

"Your trust in me staggers me. It humbles me when you have no reason to trust anything I say do or promise. But, Honor, the danger . . . that's only part of. I'm a man who demands and expects complete control. In every aspect. As my woman, I would dominate you. I'd know your every movement. I'd expect you to check in with me anytime you so much as went to the grocery store."

He lifted one hand to run it raggedly over his head.

"I'm demanding sexually. I don't give up control in any aspect of my life, baby," he said in an aching voice, as though he were admitting to murder. "I can't. Control has been ingrained in me my entire life. I've been trained to always be in control of every aspect of every situation. How long do you think it would take before you began to feel smothered? How long would it take for me to kill the thing that sets you so far apart from the rest of the world? Your smile, your sunshine, your kindness and generosity. I would smother you, Honor. And eventually I would destroy you."

She laughed, her smile wide as she took in his utter bewilderment at her reaction to his painful admission.

She held up her fingers, ticking off her points on each digit. "Let's see, first, sexually dominant? I get the shivers thinking about it. I've already had a taste of sex with you, Hancock, and any idiot would know that you're commanding, forceful and dominant as hell. I assure you, I'll enjoy every moment of your dominance."

She pressed another finger. "Second. Your need to know where I am at all times and you going overboard protecting me. Uhm, duh? I'm not an idiot, Guy. I've seen the worst this world has to offer and I've seen into your world. Quite frankly, I'm not going to *want* to go anywhere without you, and furthermore, if you want to hire an entire army to protect us, I'm in."

She held up the last finger. "Now for the smothering, killing, stifling, destroying. I'm not going to give this much of a response because it doesn't deserve it."

She leaned over and touched his face, lightly pressing her lips to his.

"The only way you kill any part of me is if you no longer love and want me. If you walk away from me again. *That* will destroy me. Nothing else."

He kissed her back, forceful, hot, scorching, like he was starved for her. And God, she was starved for him. For the last months she'd lived without the other half of her soul. Never did she want to endure that again.

Then he slipped off the bed, to his knees, reaching for her, pulling her to stand as he knelt before her. He wrapped his arms around her, burying his face between her breasts. Hot tears slithered over her skin, each one hurting her, like tiny daggers to her heart.

"I'm so sorry, Honor," he choked out. "I'm so sorry. I went crazy those days, dying a little more every hour you were in his hands. It was all I could think about. Knowing he was torturing you and knowing that you thought I had betrayed you by giving you to him. I can't sleep at night. Even now. Knowing he's dead. That ANE is gone. That they can't hurt you. I can't sleep, I can't eat. Every second I think about how badly I hurt you and all the times I let you down. Please forgive me," he whispered. "Please give me the chance to prove to you that I will never fail you again. I'll spend my life making sure you don't get so much as a scratch. I want to be a good man. For you. I want to be a man you can be proud of."

"Oh, my love," she whispered. "Don't you understand? I love the man you are. You can't go changing on me. I won't love a man you create thinking it's what I want and need. I need *you*."

She thumbed away the tears on his cheeks, then leaned down to kiss him while her hands framed his face.

"And I've already forgiven you. There's no need to ask it again."

"You gave it without my ever asking," he said quietly. "I should have been on my knees begging your forgiveness and so I gave that to you, because that is what you deserve, regardless that your generous heart had already forgiven me."

When he would have pulled her back to him, she resisted, knowing that at the current angle, he'd have his cheek right over her rounded belly. He glanced up at her, puzzled, a little uncertain.

She smiled and sat back down on the bed, patting the space beside her. "Come. There's one last thing we have to discuss."

He eased down beside her and frowned because she'd suddenly gone tense and she knew he'd picked up on it. He slipped his hand around hers, lifting it to rest on his thigh as he laced their fingers together.

"What is it, Honor?"

"First of all, I wasn't—am not—deceiving you. I'm merely . . . selfish," she said with a grimace.

"You are the least selfish person I know," he growled.

She smiled faintly. "It's just that I had to know . . . I had to know that you wanted *me*. That you loved *me*. I didn't want you to be with me out of obligation. So I didn't tell you right away. But I'm telling you *now*."

His eyes were worried now. Not angry or apprehensive, as though he thought she'd done some horrible thing. He was worried for *her*, and she loved him all the more for it.

"I'm pregnant," she said softly. "I'm having your baby, Guy. I'm almost five months pregnant."

He stared down at her belly in shock and then back up to her face, as if what she was telling him simply didn't compute.

"I don't show unless I wear confining clothing. Hence

the baggy attire I chose for this trip. Not even the others know. Only my parents and siblings. I had lost so much weight and was so starved that when I got back home, I was literally skin and bones, so the weight I've gained with the pregnancy has merely made it appear as though I regained what I'd lost before."

"Show me," he said, his voice cracking. "Let me see our child. Please."

She bunched the hem of her oversized shirt and slowly pulled it upward. Both his hands ever so gently pressed against the mound, his fingers trembling against her skin.

"Are you all right?" he asked anxiously. "You were so hurt and as you said starved. It can't be healthy for you to be having a baby."

She smiled, wanting to reassure him. "My OB has me on a strict vitamin regimen as well as an eating schedule that my mother enforces like an army general."

"Are you happy about it?" he asked, vulnerability creeping into his eyes.

She let him see the full force of her joy as she smiled back. "Oh yes," she breathed. "The question is, are you?"

"Happy?" he asked hoarsely. "I don't think happy can aptly describe my utter amazement right now. Oh God, Honor, I don't deserve you or our child. Do you even *know* how many enemies I have? Do you understand the danger you're putting yourself and our child in by wanting a life with me?"

His hands shook even harder, and she laid her palms softly over where his were branded to the swell of her belly.

"God didn't forget me," he said in awe, tears glittering brightly in his eyes as they lifted to hers. "I'm *not* damned. No man without a soul, a man damned for an eternity, could possibly be given two such precious gifts."

Her heart ached for the pain Guy had suffered for so long. For how so very long he'd been truly alone in the world with no anchor to hold him.

"No, my darling," she said tenderly. "Indeed you are very blessed. We both are. You've now been given a third chance. Tell me. Are you going to take it?"

"Yes," he said fiercely. "*Hell* yes."

He fused his mouth to hers in a hot rush. He was rough, nearly animalistic, his hands roaming possessively up and down her body but instantly gentling when they glided over where their child was nestled in her mother's womb. He drew away, gasping sharply, his eyes glittering like a predator's.

"You've sealed your fate giving yourself to me twice," he said gruffly. "I let you go once. I'll *never* do it again. So be sure, Honor. Be very sure this is what you want and I'm who you want. Because once you commit to me it's going to be for goddamn ever."

"Well thank you, God," she said, feigning huge relief. "I mean, what does a girl have to do these days?"

"Tell me she loves me," he said, his voice cracking. Her heart nearly broke as insecurity flashed in his eyes. And fear.

"I love you," she whispered. "So much. I'll never love someone as much as I love you."

"Thank God," he breathed, crushing her to him, hanging on to her for dear life. Tears burned his eyes and he didn't care. He'd found redemption when he despaired of ever seeing the sun again.

"You're a miracle," he said hoarsely. "My sunshine, Honor."

"Glad you finally recognize that," she said with a grin.

EPILOGUE

HANCOCK carefully balanced the tray he was holding as he made his way from the kitchen into the living room where Honor was feeding Reece, who was now just over eight months old. He'd taken special care with this morning's breakfast, artfully—as creative as he was capable of being—arranged, a single yellow rose in a long fluted vase situated beside the plate and a tall glass of apple juice, his wife's favorite.

Even after all of these months, he paused at the sight of their son nestled lovingly against his mother's chest, one of her hands holding the bottle in place while the other tenderly caressed his downy curls. Her expression so achingly beautiful that it never failed to take his breath away.

She murmured in low tones to Reece, telling him how very much he was loved by his mother and father. And she spoke absolute truth. The sun rose and set at his wife and child's feet. Every single day he awoke, Honor nestled in his arms. Every night he went to bed sated, after making love to his wife, her sleepy, "I love you" or "I need you so much, Guy" brushing over his ears. It undid him every single time and he whispered a prayer of thanks that he'd found redemption and forgiveness, another chance with the woman he loved more than life.

The few times he was away from her, he was besieged by

the need to return to her as quickly as he could. He wasn't sure he would ever get over his fear of losing them, of coming home to find them gone. He, of all people, was all too aware of the evil that walked among ordinary people on this earth, and over the years he'd accumulated too many enemies to count.

It was why they lived as the only inhabitants on this remote island, which was only accessible by boat or heli-copter. He'd made a lot of money during his years as a mer-cenary, fighting the good fight. Money he'd never used. Never had a reason to use. No one to spend it on.

But now? He had a wife and a son to spoil shamelessly, and he did so on a regular basis, much to Honor's chagrin. He had to call back the grin at her exasperation and the statement she always gave him. That she had all she could ever want. She didn't need anything else. But that didn't mean he paid her any attention. If she so much as hinted, in all her innocence, that she liked something, or he saw her expression when something caught her eye, it was hers.

Even now he was gleefully anticipating giving his first anniversary gift to her when Reece was put down for the night and enduring a sound dressing down for going over-board with his present for her. He did so love to indulge her every whim. He loved making her happy. Her smile made everything worthwhile in his life.

Sensing his presence, Honor looked up from where she was speaking in loving, low tones to their son, and she smiled, her eyes so full of love that it instilled a fierce ache in his heart. His soul swelled to near bursting if she so much as looked at him. He'd never grow tired of her love for him sim-mering in her eyes just as he'd always return it in kind.

"Not that I don't love you spoiling me so, but what's this?" she asked in a teasing tone.

He set the tray on the coffee table in front of her and then slid onto the couch next to her, leaning in to kiss her, cra-dling his son's head in his large palm.

"Don't tell me you forgot that today is our one year wed-ding anniversary," he said with mock ferocity.

She grinned mischievously. "Nope. I have my own gift as well, but you'll have to wait a bit. I'm a little busy at the moment."

"You loving me is all the gift I'll ever need," he said with complete sincerity.

"Well, that's easy enough. I do love you, Guy. I'll always love you. That's never going to change and I hope you feel the same. But that gift is given every day. Today? I have something extra special for you."

"You say the dumbest things sometimes, woman," he said, his eyes narrowing, but he knew he didn't look in the least bit annoyed. Honor's eyes were laughing back at his. "As *if* I won't always feel the same," he huffed. "You are my life, Honor. Without you, I have nothing. Without you, I don't *want* to live."

Suddenly she lifted her free hand to his face and caressed his clean-shaven jaw, and he couldn't help himself. Mindful of the precious bundle still feeding, he leaned in and kissed her, tenderly exploring her mouth, absorbing her taste, something he would never grow tired of.

When he finally pulled away, her cheeks were flushed and desire reflected in her half-lidded warm brown eyes.

"How much longer before he finishes with his mother and goes down for his nap so his father can steal her for a while?" Hancock said in a voice thick with arousal.

Other parts of him were just as thick, as heavy, and as aching.

She laughed. "He only just woke up. He has a few hours yet before naptime."

Hancock bit back a curse. If he weren't such a paranoid, overprotective bastard, he would have taken the numerous offers from his and Honor's families to keep Reece for an extended anniversary weekend and he would have had Honor all to himself.

But they rarely left the island. A brief black thought flickered through his mind. Did Honor feel like a prisoner? Never let out and never allowed the freedom to come and go as she pleased? Hancock was a controlling bastard. She never left the island without him. He never left her on the island alone.

Most women would feel stifled and grow to resent such restrictions, but not Honor. That fact still didn't prevent him from worrying that one day . . . He shook off the dark thoughts. He wouldn't go there. Honor had assured him that she loved their life. That she loved *him*.

"Will you burp him and then put him in his bouncer for me?"

Honor's sweetly worded request broke through his dour thoughts, and he sprang into action, gingerly sliding his large, clumsy hands beneath Reece's head and diapered bottom, lifting him up to his shoulder so he could pat Reece's back. A few minutes and several impressive belches later, Hancock laughed and eased the baby into the bouncer that overlooked the sandy beach and sparkling water.

When he turned back, his wife's eyes twinkled with merriment, and he sent her his best ferocious glare. It amused her to no end that even now he was still convinced that he was going to drop the baby or crush his tiny little body with hands that had, until now, been used as weapons. For violence, not tenderness. To inflict pain, not offer comfort.

She patted the space beside her as she repositioned herself on the couch. It was too bad, because her former pose gave him a very good view of her breasts, which were still more rounded. She reached for a plate and handed it to him and then retrieved the other and they sat side by side enjoying the breakfast Hancock had prepared.

She ate while he simply enjoyed watching her. Watching her never got old.

God, he loved this woman.

Honor studied Guy from underneath her eyelashes. Even if she couldn't feel his heated stare, she'd know he was watching her. He always watched her. In the beginning, she gave herself away by blushing and had even asked him why he was forever staring at her.

Very seriously, he'd told her that she was the most beautiful thing in his world and that he still had a hard time believing she belonged to him. And she did belong to him in every possible way.

He'd warned her of his possessiveness. His dominance. His need to control every aspect of his life—their life. And his absolute dedication to keeping her safe at all times. As though that part of his personality would frighten her away.

At times, she could feel his restraint. Could feel him holding back because of his fear of driving her away, but she was having none of that and she let him know it very forcefully. She wanted the real Guy or nothing at all.

It had taken considerable patience on her part, and at times he still needed to be convinced that things he considered faults were things she not only loved but also *reveled* in. She *needed* them. She needed *him*. God, how she needed *and* loved him with every breath in her body.

While he worried about her contentment, she worried about *his* happiness. His life had done a complete 180 in the last year. He no longer lived every day knowing it could be his last, and as crazy as it sounded, she knew he thrived on it. Not because he was an adrenaline junky or *enjoyed* it. But because he truly wanted to make a difference in the world. Protect the innocent, take out the evil. He thought himself to be an evil man when nothing could be further from the truth.

And the very people who had formed Titan, for the greater good, had turned on him and his teammates, branding them outcasts and traitors because Guy and his men were no longer willing to do their dirty work for them.

She hated them for that. For tarnishing Guy's honor and daring to question their motives. Pure motives when they were the very best of men, protecting those who had no one to protect them. Standing up for those without voices and rebelling against those who betrayed their country and the citizens they'd sworn to represent.

She leaned forward to set her empty plate on the coffee table, but Guy intercepted, taking it from her, sliding it onto the wooden surface and then pulling her into his arms, tucking her under his shoulder and against his muscled frame.

A sigh of contentment whispered past her lips as she melted against him.

"You sound happy," he said in a pleased tone.

"Oh I am," she breathed.

She tilted her head up just enough that she could take in his beloved features. The sensual mouth, the warmth in his eyes and his firm jaw and defined cheekbones. She feathered one hand over his chest, coming to rest over his heart, feeling the steady, reassuring beat against her palm.

"Do you remember our wedding?"

He gave her a look that suggested she'd lost her mind. "Like I'd ever forget the day you officially became mine? I remember every single second. I'm not likely to ever forget a moment of it. Or the way you looked. The sound of you saying, 'I do.' The way I forgot that anyone else was there when I tasted the sweetness of your mouth and kissed you forever and didn't want to ever stop. How time stopped and for that single moment in time it was just you and me. Together. Vowing to spend the rest of our lives together. You have no idea what that day meant to me, Honor. I think of it every night after I've made love to you and you drift off to sleep in my arms, and I simply watch you, holding you close and I replay our wedding in my mind."

"Wow," she whispered, heat flooding her cheeks, love filling her heart to near bursting.

"It's a day I'll carry with me every day for the rest of my life," he said with utter seriousness. "Because on that day you gave me something very precious, Honor. You gave me yourself, and I take that—will always take that very seriously. I'll never take it, or you and our child, for granted."

"I love you," she said in an aching voice infused with emotion he couldn't possibly miss.

He kissed her, long and lingering, even as Reece gurgled happily as he kicked and waved his arms in his bouncer. "And I love you, Honor Hancock. Always. Forever."

She settled more fully into his arms, snuggling into his heat and his strength, her fingers caressing a random pattern over his chest.

"Do you miss them? Do you ever regret not remaining with your team? Walking away and never looking back?"

He pulled back, his expression fierce as he stared intently into her eyes. "No! *Never.*" He shifted, turning so he could frame her face in his hands. "For more than a decade, Titan was my entire life. My family. Them and the Sinclairs, though I didn't see them often. But, Honor, *you* are my family now. My entire *world.* You and our son. My sole reasons for living. You give me purpose. A reason for being, a reason to truly *live.*

I never had that before. My missions were just jobs performed by rote. My heart and soul were never in them. I was resigned to the reason for my existence. I never had anything for myself. Didn't want it. Until you. Do I miss *that* life? Hell no. I can't *imagine* my life without you and our child. I don't *want* to imagine it, which is why I will go to any lengths to protect you, to ensure that neither of you ever come to harm. Because without you, I have and am nothing. You are *everything* to me."

Tears flooded her eyes as she stared at her husband in shock. Guy wasn't a wordy man. Nor was he what anyone would call poetic or smooth in his speech. He was brusque, even abrupt at times, though she never took it personally. More often than not, he was just silent. His impassioned statement was so uncharacteristic and sincere that she *felt* each and every word in the deepest recesses of her soul.

She had no reply. What *could* she say in response to the most beautiful, eloquent words she'd ever heard in her life? And they were all for her. He loved *her*.

Tears streamed silently down her cheeks. Even if she had the appropriate words to offer, she'd never be able to speak around the knot in her throat.

"Don't cry," Guy said desperately, his expression one of sheer male panic.

If she weren't so overcome by the moment she would have laughed, because Guy couldn't stand to see her cry. He'd once confided in her that it made him feel utterly helpless, and for a man like Guy to admit to feeling helpless . . . well, that was huge.

Feeling a change in topic was desperately needed, and she still needed a little more time until she unveiled her anniversary present, she grabbed onto the first thing that entered her mind. Guy's upcoming trip to the Middle East.

"Are you still planning to leave in two weeks?" she asked lightly, keeping a tight rein on the emotion swelling her throat.

His lips immediately turned down. He hated leaving Honor and Reece, but the alternative was Honor going herself, and he'd made himself clear, that over his dead body, would she *ever* return there.

Despite the majority of ANE being dismantled and left

powerless, Honor was still a target to many who sympathized with ANE or were simply offended that a mere woman managed to topple an entire terrorist group. Never mind that she hadn't done anything at all. Titan and KGI along with help from a CIA operative had headed up that operation.

Not even in the States was she safe, because the remnants of the ANE group would love nothing better than to assassinate her. And other sympathizers, terrorists, would delight in being the ones to take her out. It would be a badge of honor and they would be heralded as heroes to those who opposed everything Honor stood for. Her courage. Defiance. A woman surviving and coming out the victor when most would have died.

Honor had kept the vow she'd made to herself that ANE would not make her quit her relief efforts. Hancock had been equally insistent that she never set foot in the region ever again, and he'd been fully backed by Titan. Or what used to be Titan. Conrad, Cope, Viper and Henderson. Sadness still gripped her heart over the loss of Mojo. She hated that even one of Guy's men had been killed because of her.

So a compromise had been reached and it had worked surprisingly well for all parties involved. Honor founded a charitable foundation that provided relief efforts to villages desperately in need, places that no one else would venture into. And the former members of Titan found that retirement wasn't all it was cracked up to be, so they recruited new members to replace Mojo and Hancock as well as increasing their numbers, but they didn't take missions. They didn't act as Titan had in the past. Their one and only objective was to provide protection for Honor's relief center and its workers. They even helped train local men and women in the villages so they weren't so vulnerable to attack. It was an arrangement that suited all parties involved.

But Honor knew Guy, and she knew he would never be happy simply doing nothing but staying home with his wife and child twenty-four hours a day, seven days a week, three hundred sixty-five days a year. So he acted as Honor's emissary and made three or four trips to the relief centers a year to ensure that the doctors, nurses and volunteers had all the necessary equipment they needed, though Honor knew he wanted and needed that time to reconnect with the men who'd been brothers to him for over a decade.

Then there were the times he became restless, and Honor always knew when it was time for him to go be a lone wolf for a few days. She never asked and he never volunteered where he went, but he'd lived most of his life alone and isolated, and every so often he needed that again. He still wasn't completely comfortable living a "normal" life and she understood that, accepted it. And he loved her all the more for it.

She benefitted from the arrangement as well because under no circumstances would Guy ever leave his wife and son unprotected, so when Guy took off to oversee operations at the relief center or went off to parts unknown, he always took her to the one person he trusted most apart from Honor. Maren Steele and by extension: Jackson Steele, though no one except his wife ever called him "Jackson," just as no one but Honor and Eden called Hancock "Guy."

As a result, she'd been fully indoctrinated into the Kelly clan and was laughingly told that she was the latest Mama Kelly chick to be adopted. It was also during these times that she got to see her own family. Sam Kelly flew her parents and siblings into the KGI compound, away from the prying eyes of the media or other sources of gossip, and Honor enjoyed the benefits of being able to visit *all* her family.

Eddie, Raid, and Ryker Sinclair came when they could, though now that Reece had been born, Honor imagined Eddie would be in Tennessee anytime his first grandchild was there for a visit.

"That's the plan," Guy said, in answer to Honor's question. "Unless something else pops up. I'll be gone a week at the most. Sam is sending one of the Kelly jets and one of the KGI teams to escort you and Reece to Tennessee."

Honor bit her lip in order not to smile. "Unless something else pops up" was code for the other side ventures Guy was involved in. Though he was careful not to personally involve himself in anything that could kill him, thus leaving his family unprotected, he was a lot of things to a lot of people. He supplied intel to Resnick, a rogue CIA agent who was likely as shadowy as Guy himself had been, any number of government agencies—not just the American government—and even KGI, though he'd probably bite his tongue before ever admitting he was actually helping them.

Guy did a lot of consulting work. He'd worked and lived in the shadows for years. He knew things most law-abiding operatives didn't. He knew how organized crime lords thought and worked. He had vast knowledge of human trafficking and those who spearheaded such operations.

If Honor didn't know the heart of Guy, she'd run screaming in the other direction, because he had "bad news" written all over him. And yet he was honorable. He had a code—a strict code. One he adhered to at all times. He was a law unto himself and yet he didn't abuse that power, his knowledge, skills or contacts.

He was one of the good guys.

"How many children do you want?" she blurted out.

Then she cursed her lack of subtlety. Geesh. Talk about whiplash, going from one topic to another that was in no way relevant.

Guy looked baffled for a tenth of a second and then he scowled. Uh-oh. Maybe she should have waited until tonight when he was sated and mellow after making love to spring this on him.

He rotated around and planted both hands on either side of her hips so he could look at her face-to-face. Guy had been a little—okay, a lot—intense during her first pregnancy. He'd insisted that Maren be the one to deliver his and Honor's child even though she wasn't an obstetrician. She was a general practitioner. But he liked Maren, and Guy didn't like many people, but more than that he trusted Maren, and he definitely didn't trust but a handful of people.

So two weeks before her due date, they'd traveled to Tennessee and Guy had announced they were staying until Honor gave birth and Maren gave her the all clear to travel back home. He just never bothered to tell anyone where "back home" was. That was a highly guarded secret that only Guy and Honor knew, and he'd insisted that not even their families know because they couldn't very well be forced to give information they didn't have.

Honor swallowed because Guy was looming over her, fairly seething, agitation rolling off him in waves at the mere mention of more children.

"I will never put you through that again," he said through tightly clenched teeth as his scowl deepened. Then his entire face softened and love warmed his eyes. "You gave me a son, something I never thought I'd have. You gave me a real family. Something of my own. My blood. You and Reece are enough for me. You'll *always* be enough for me."

She laughed. She couldn't help herself, though he had no liking for her amusement. "Guy, my delivery was as uncomplicated as it gets! It was smooth and went off without a hitch. I was only in labor for six hours."

His face went pale and his eyes were haunted. Her heart twisted as she saw the conflicting emotions so evident in his gaze.

"God, Honor, you were in so much *pain*," he said in a tortured voice. "You've had enough pain and suffering. Pain I caused. Me! And I'll be damned if I cause you any more."

Her entire demeanor went soft and her heart filled with so much love for this man. What would her life ever be without him? She lifted her hand to his face and softly caressed his cheek.

"Honey, pain is normal in childbirth. Since the beginning of time. But the reward . . . Oh, Guy, the reward is worth every bit of pain and suffering because the result is a precious baby boy or girl."

She eased up from the couch, extricating herself from Guy's grasp. She went to where her beautiful son was enjoying the bouncer he'd nearly grown out of, and when he saw her, he rewarded her with a wide grin that sported two partially grown in front teeth on top and bottom. He immediately began kicking and wiggling his entire body, further reminding Honor that the bouncer would have to go soon before he either broke it or launched himself right out of it. She picked him up and cradled him in her arms, gently running her hand over his soft skin. Then she looked up at Guy, all the love she had for both her husband and her son shining like a beacon in her eyes.

"What I hold in my arms is worth any amount of pain. You won't change my mind on that."

Guy shook his head, a stubborn look she was well acquainted with reflecting in his eyes. He crossed his arms over his chest and stared at her, his lips in a thin line.

"Reece will be our only child. I will *not* allow you to go through all that again."

She rolled her eyes and then smiled as she rose up on tiptoe, Reece nestled between their bodies and kissed Guy.

"I love you, but it's too late to deny me another child. You're just going to have to suck it up and accept the inevitable."

He stared at her in complete shock, absolutely stunned. For a long moment he opened and closed his mouth, utterly speechless. He looked as though he'd been hit over the head with a sledgehammer.

"You're pregnant *again*?" he asked hoarsely. "It's too soon, Honor." Panic was fast invading his voice and he began to shake violently from head to toe. "You're not even fully recovered from your first pregnancy!"

He looked terrified, his eyes bleak.

"I can't lose you. You're my *everything*. God, what have I done? What have I done? You were on birth control. This shouldn't have happened. *What have I done?*" he repeated for a third time, desperation unhinging him. "I'll hurt you. I can't put you through this again. Especially not so soon."

He rubbed his hands over his face and then up and over his head, utter despair making his body sag. Never had she seen him this way. Strong. Unbreakable. Always in control. Able to turn it off at will. And yet now, he was falling apart, shattering before her very eyes.

The one thing she couldn't do was to respond in kind. She had to make light of the situation and show him she wasn't in the least afraid.

"I'd say you have some very potent swimmers," she teased. "Birth control has kryptonite and apparently it's you."

He glowered at her attempt at humor.

"How can you joke about something like this? If something happens to you, Reece won't have a mother and I won't have *you*."

Okay so humor was out. She'd pull out the big guns then. She looked at him with big, sad eyes and actually pouted, something she'd never imagined herself doing. But if it worked then hey, she wouldn't spare an ounce of remorse. She couldn't help it because her husband was as dense as fog and insanely overprotective of her.

"Guy, you knew I wanted a large family before we got married," she said in a low, quivering voice that may or may not sound like she was close to tears. "Would you deny me that? Knowing it's something I want with all my heart and soul?"

He scowled and then scrubbed a hand over his head, down the back to clasp his nape. Then he closed his eyes.

"You know damn well I'd give you anything you wanted. I'd give you the world. But damn it, Honor. *I don't want to lose you!*"

She shifted Reece higher on her chest so his head was cradled against the side of her neck and she gazed earnestly at her husband. The man she loved more than she thought it was possible to love another human being.

"Oh, Guy, you aren't going to lose me," she said in a tender voice that conveyed all she felt for this man. "I'm afraid you're stuck with me forever."

He wrapped both arms around his wife and child and rubbed his chin over the top of her head. "Damn right," he muttered. "Never going to give you up, baby. You've already given me something I never allowed myself to even dream of, and now you're giving me *more*."

He tilted his head back enough so he could look her in the eye, so she could see everything that was in his. "I love you," he said, his voice raw and ravaged with emotion. "*Forever*. I know I'm a demanding bastard, and I can be an asshole, but I thank God for you every single day, and just when I think it can't get any better than right then, right there, you smile at me and light up my entire fucking world and it only gets better. Every damn day is better than the last. I don't deserve you, but I'm never letting you go."

So much vulnerability shone in his eyes, and she was shocked to see a sheen of moisture that was gone almost as soon as it appeared, leaving her to wonder if she'd imagined it. She moved Reece to her side so he wouldn't be suffocated between his parents and then she rose up on tiptoe again and kissed Guy long and sweet. And he gave her long and sweet right back, proving he wasn't *always* dominant and demanding.

They reluctantly pulled away when Reece started fussing and Guy took him from Honor's arms.

"I guess we need to go see Maren soon," she said ruefully.

"We'll go next week," he declared, dominance and demand back in force. Then he fixed her with a stern glare. "And you're taking it easy, Honor. With a baby and being pregnant and as sick as you were with your first pregnancy, you're not going to so much as lift a finger and there will be *no* argument.

"And," he said, holding up a finger when she would have opened her mouth to speak, "you're going to give me another son since you're hell-bent on having a house full of children. Our daughter will need big brothers to protect her."

She laughed and hugged the side Reece didn't occupy on Guy. "I live to please you, oh lord and master."

His gaze was full of tenderness as he looked down at her, his son on one side, his wife nestled against his other.

"You *do* please me. Waking up next to you every morning? You going to sleep in my arms every night? You lighting up my entire world when you smile at me and tell me you love me? I'll never ask for another thing in my life. You *are* my life, and there's not a single thing I cherish more."

Seven months later, she pleased her husband once again by having the son he'd asked for.